PRAISE FOR  ...ARIS

"Against the backdrop of bailouts and burnout in America's heartland, Phillip Hurst's *Regent's of Paris* is surprisingly redemptive. The desperate work lives of his cast are undercut by their forlorn faith and ragged courage. Part *Glengarry Glen Ross*, part *Lord of the Flies*, and a pinch of *A Visit From the Goon Squad*, this is a terrific debut novel."

–Brandon Hobson, National Book Award finalist and author of *The Removed*

"In Phillip Hurst's darkly radiant *Regent's of Paris* the machinery of torque and muscle is fast and true. The road of life is peopled by women and men, like us, who wend their way toward a horizon whose vanishing point most often signifies the desperation of unfulfilled dreams. Hurst's novel is made of courage, more than a hint of grace, and the desire, not as uncommon as one would think, for a way home. Who can know the heart of others, who can detect the fundamental mystery of our broken lives? In Hurst's uncanny wisdom: 'Maybe we can only see our biggest mistakes, the mistakes we love, through another's eyes?'"

–Shann Ray, author of *American Masculine, Atomic Theory 7*, and *The Souls of Others*

REGENT'S OF PARIS

Phillip Hurst

Regal House Publishing

Published by
Regal House Publishing, LLC
Raleigh, NC 27587
All rights reserved

ISBN -13 (paperback): 9781646032006
ISBN -13 (epub): 9781646032013
Library of Congress Control Number: 2021943475

Interior layout by Lafayette & Greene
Cover images © by C. B. Royal

Regal House Publishing, LLC
https://regalhousepublishing.com

Printed in the United States of America

For Seed, who loves books

"I thought that what was good for our country was good for General Motors, and vice versa."

— Charlie Wilson, GM President, 1953

"Timid salesmen have skinny kids."

— Zig Ziglar, sales guru

Step One: Meet and Greet

1

The meek shall inherit the wind," Kent Seasons said, and popped another breath mint.

"Sure, I get that. But I feel a little guilty about this one."

"Never realized you were Catholic, pretty boy."

Paul Stenger was a Methodist, actually, though he hadn't attended services in years and admitted as much.

"Sounds like closet atheism to me," Kent said. "How the hell do you expect to sell cars without believing in a higher power?"

Paul sighed and glanced out the rain-streaked window of the sales manager's office. Across Route 150, the Citgo station appeared to have melted and puddled on the wet pavement. Between lay an acre of cement rowed with new and pre-owned sedans, trucks, and SUVs. A sprinkling of raindrops beaded the freshly waxed inventory and dripped from the signage pole—a pole that rose three full stories above the book-flat central Illinois prairie to declaim in yard-high red, white, and blue lettering: REGENT'S AMERICAN DREAM MOTORS.

Between the gloomy May weather and it being a Monday, traffic on the lot was slow—so slow that Paul had killed a full hour reading the *Paris Beacon-Herald* and sipping drip coffee in his little office before heading out to the showroom where he pretended to scan the pre-owned lot while stretching and massaging the tender hamstring he'd tweaked playing pickup hoops the week prior. Finally, bored and listless and half-afraid someone might put him to work Windexing the showroom models, he crawled inside the nearest vehicle—a Pontiac Vibe—and fiddled with the stereo. Then, while drumming the wheel with his fingertips and jamming to the raucous ending of "L.A. Woman" on 92.1 FM, he'd enjoyed an elaborate and steamy fantasy wherein he finally found the nerve to invite the salty blonde who worked his gym's front desk for an after-hours swim in the lap pool.

But all that waiting paid off, as he'd turned a tire-kicking be-backer into a signed-and-delivered buyer. Just ninety minutes from handshake to taillights. The ink was still wet on the paperwork atop Kent Seasons's desk.

"No salesman ever made hay," Kent said, "by feeling bad about closing deals."

"I don't necessarily feel bad about closing, but—"

"Forget it." Kent's voice rose. "Morticia's head is on the chopping block anyhow."

Morticia was Kent's not-so-kind nickname for a fellow salesperson, Jennylee Witt. The name owed to her oft-stated goal of attaining a degree in mortuary science. Or was it a mortician's license? The nomenclature was something of a mystery, as were Jennylee's motivations for wanting to work with the dead.

"You really think I sniped her though? Because *she* definitely thinks that," Paul said.

"Buyer come to the lot?"

"Sure, but—"

"And was Morticia here to sell him that Blazer?"

Paul shook his head. Jennylee had been running late again.

"So we're supposed to tell buyers to kick rocks," Kent said, "to go spend their money somewhere else, because Morticia forgot to set her alarm clock?"

Then Kent railed about how Jennylee had recently bobbled a slam dunk on a school-bus-yellow Chevy Avalanche. This vehicle was the inspiration of the general manager, Billy Jr., who'd deemed the hideous paint job "neat-o" and predicted a quick sale—fifteen or sixteen months back.

"She actually told her customer," Kent said, "that our beloved yellow Avalanche was 'just a soccer-mom SUV with lightning bolts painted on the doors.' Those were her exact words, Paul. I heard them with my own ears. Then she had the gall to act surprised when the guy started lobbing objections like pipe bombs."

While Paul frowned in sympathy with Kent's managerial dilemma, as he knew was expected of him, he actually recognized those words as his own. The Avalanche was a lumbering redneck tank, a Hummer for the white-trash set. It even had a self-draining beer cooler built into the rear wheel well. But when Paul had ridiculed the Avalanche, he'd assumed Jennylee understood he was joking, not suggesting script.

"That trailer park princess closed six deals in March and only four in April," Kent said. "Back in the day, you know what I called four deals?"

"A bad month?"

"Saturday," Kent said.

Kent's carrot-red hair was thinning, but he kept what remained neatly barbered, much as he kept his wingtips spit-shined to a mirror polish. Like most guys his age, he was going soft around the middle, but put a buyer in front of him and Kent Seasons conjured an icy blue stare that commanded the room. Despite being younger and better-looking (and blessed with terrific hair), Paul Stenger had come to suspect a down-home guy like Kent, for whatever mysterious reason, would always wield more charisma.

Not that Paul didn't send his own fair share of rubber down the road. Because he did. While statistics said the hard sell was king ("A. B. C."—Always Be Closing), Paul just wasn't the cutthroat type. But his mellow approach appealed to buyers who hated the negotiation process, and a no-haggle, no-hassle dealership like Regent's of Paris saw a lot of buyers like that. It's why people chose Regent's in the first place: because they were intimidated by the *Lord of the Flies* ethos that ruled the neighboring lots.

"It's tough out there," Paul said. "Everyone's numbers are down."

"Everyone's except yours."

Fair enough. He did have seven deals this month already, which was a promising start. But his improving numbers troubled him too, as the more cars he sold and the more commissions he banked, the easier it became to take someone like Jennylee's Blazer guy, bend him over the desk, and pull his pants down.

"She's out in the showroom right now, blabbing about how I sniped her."

"Look, did you sell the guy some wheels, or not?"

"I test-drove him and bullshitted a little. Bought him a Coke. But I guess he'd talked with Jennylee last week—"

"Wait a minute. Hold up. Who's this *Jennylee?*"

Kent Seasons fancied himself a great bestower of nicknames, and insisted these names be used behind their victims' backs. Besides "Morticia" there was "Jethro," a college dropout named Chadwick who chewed tobacco and wore cowboy boots with his slacks. The assistant sales manager, Brad Howard, was "Sweetness," à la the late Walter Payton of the Chicago Bears, due to Brad's having been a football star back in school. Billy Regent Jr., the general manager, was simply (and dismissively) "Junior," as Kent insisted that Billy and his navy man father, "Nautical Bill," were akin to the former Presidents Bush, with the elder pulling the younger's strings.

Paul Stenger understood, of course, that *he* had surely been nicknamed as well. Although what exactly remained a mystery.

"I probably could've written it up as her deal," he said.

"That's true. You probably could have."

"Just taken an assist, I mean."

"An assist."

"Should I have cut her in—really?"

"Paul, cases such as this fall under an ancient but rarely acknowledged law."

Paul held his tongue. When Kent Seasons took this rhapsodizing tone, you just had to let him finish.

"And unlike most legal matters, the Law of the Junkyard is straightforward and applies equally to everyone in all places and at all times."

"The law of the what?"

Kent leaned back in his chair and kicked his shiny wingtips

atop the desk. "It's a natural law, a reflection of the order man-
ifest in all creation. Like minnows eating flies and bass swallow-
ing minnows and fishermen hooking bass. You've sensed it for
years now, Paul, whether or not you realized the deeper implica-
tions. You been feeling it from the second Mommy and Daddy
patted you on the backside and sent you trundling out into this
cold and lonesome world of ours."

"This is getting pretty heavy for a Monday morning, boss."

"Stop that. Don't play dumb. We both know that *you* know
exactly what I'm talking about."

"Okay, maybe I do. But so what?"

"The Law of the Junkyard," Kent said, "is simple: Big Dog
Eats."

Jennylee Witt had tried not to eavesdrop. Truly she had. But
the door to the sales manager's office was flimsy and Kent Seasons could get mighty loud. His voice had boomed and echoed
throughout the showroom: *Morticia's head is on the chopping block
anyhow...*

"From the sounds of things," she said, "that promotion may
not be coming my way after all."

Chadwick smirked and leaned against the tailgate of a GMC
Sierra, one boot heel tattooing the speckled tiles while he flipped
through the latest issue of *Car and Driver*. "So that sneaky prick
really sniped your deal?"

The sneaky prick sure had. She'd pulled into the lot that
morning, already well on her way to a bad day, only to see Paul
and *her* customer heading out to test-drive the Blazer. This
would've been fine had Paul followed protocol and handed the
guy over, or at least written her in as co-salesperson. But Paul
just closed the deal like Jennylee wasn't even there. Maybe she'd
been running late, but she had her reasons.

"Chast had another doctor visit this morning. The county
clinic's always overbooked, but they said they could squeeze her
in, so—"

"You called Kent?"

"Of course. But you know how he gets about personal stuff."

"Yeah," Chadwick said, "I sure do."

"I should've dragged Derrol out of bed and had him take her. But I wanted to talk to the doctor myself."

Because Jennylee was worried. Chast had been up all night with another tummyache. First the clinic said food allergies or lactose intolerance, maybe gluten. But the special diet and pills hadn't helped a bit. The other day, Chast snacked on an apple and spent the next hour balled up on the couch in tears. Now the doctor suggested they consult some specialist at St. John's Hospital in Springfield.

"I really needed that deal. We still haven't paid off our bills from last time."

"You guys have insurance, right?"

"Not since Derrol got laid off," Jennylee said, feeling the shame of this admission in her own stomach. And Regent's, as Chadwick was well aware, didn't offer health insurance at all.

"Surely they got programs? Payment plans, sliding scales, something."

"Yeah," Jennylee said. "Something."

"Don't let it get you down." He flipped through his magazine. "Stay positive."

But what exactly was there to be positive about—discounted fees on bare-bones public services? Or their family having recently qualified for food stamps? No, at the end of the day, money was all that counted, or at least all that could be counted. Even a guy like Paul Stenger, who seemed friendly, really just wanted to get paid. She'd had a nice talk with the Blazer guy last week. Even called twice to follow up. In Kent Seasons's own words, she'd built a solid *rapport*.

"Whoever talks to an up first has dibs," she said. "That's the unwritten rule."

"Dibs. That's right."

"Never mind who actually closes."

"We're supposed to be a sales *team*."

"And Paul thinks he can just ignore all that."

"You oughta march right into Kent's office and tell him this shit ain't gonna fly."

"You really think I should?"

"Just between us, last week I caught Paul romancing one of *my* customers too. Guy come in for an oil change and there was Paul doing a service lane walk, slapping my loyal customer on the back and talking upgrades."

Jennylee shoved her hands in her back pockets to keep from cracking her knuckles, a nervous habit she meant to break. Chadwick seemed to think she was too dim to realize Kent Seasons didn't give a damn about sniped deals. No, as long as cars got sold, Kent got paid; and as long as Kent got paid, Kent didn't care. Chadwick was full of it though. Like Paul, he'd taken some college, and he talked about it all the time. Courses he'd aced and stunts he'd pulled. How the professors were a bunch of eggheads who couldn't even change a tire. But higher education didn't always seem to pay off, at least not around Regent's.

"Lately our budget's so tight that whenever Derrol mentions selling Bugles—and hardly a day goes by where he doesn't—I can't think of any logical reason to say no."

Raising horses had been her big idea, but Derrol had gone along with it. They'd gotten Bugles as a colt and built a nice stable. Even shelled out for a custom paint job on their hauling trailer ("Witt's End" they'd named their new venture, which earned a snide remark from Kent Seasons). Since the layoff, though, Derrol Witt couldn't be bothered with horsemanship, and Jennylee was the one shoveling manure and forking hay. And this despite Derrol's being home all day long with nothing to occupy his time except the playing of video games and the chugging of Mountain Dew.

"But you love that horse," Chadwick said, while admiring a glossy foldout. "He used to be all you talked about, remember? How you were planning to show him, and how there's good money in studding."

"Sure, but all that's an investment. Our bills are due *now*. Derrol knows of some company that buys horses. Claims they'd pick Bugles up for no charge."

"I'm sure they would," Chadwick said, "but companies don't spend much just to fill dog food cans."

That did it. Jennylee bunched and squeezed her fingers until the knuckles cracked deep and raw. She'd already known what selling Bugles would mean and did not appreciate hearing such ugliness spoken aloud. Chadwick hadn't always been this cold. Selling cars had changed him—changed them all, probably.

In fact, Jennylee had recently noticed something worrisome; her prayers, a lifelong comfort, felt distinctly unheard. She'd been raised a believer—church every Sunday, grace before meals, and devotions before bed, and from her earliest memories she'd sensed God watching over her. But lately that feeling was missing. Then again, maybe the Lord simply didn't enjoy spending His time on a car lot either?

"Looks like you're up," Chadwick said, and pointed out the showroom window.

Sure enough, a tall older gentleman strolled the pre-owned lot, silver hair flaming like steel in the sunshine that'd peeked out after that morning's rain.

"You want him? Mood I'm in, I'll probably just scare him off."

"Go on, girl. Get!" Chadwick rolled up his *Car and Driver* and swatted her bottom. "If Mr. Silver Fox out there has gold balls, he just might save your month."

Chadwick's yeehaw diction echoed out in the showroom, but Kent Seasons didn't seem to notice. The man's wingtips remained propped on his desk and he accordioned his knees open and shut, the result strangely libidinous.

Much as Kent had accused him of closet atheism, Paul sometimes wondered if his boss might be a closeted homosexual. The way he peacocked around the showroom, almost preening. And the hearty way Kent slapped his and Chadwick's butts after a tough close. Sure, that was a sports thing, a locker room thing, but sometimes it almost felt flirtatious. Then again, the butt-slapping was probably just meant to boost his confidence. In fact, everything Kent Seasons had ever said or done—all their lunchtime conversations and every beer pounded after hours—was likely aimed at one thing only—selling more cars.

"Answer me this," Kent said. "When Fatty McScuzzington was regaling you with his hard-luck tale, did you finesse him?"

"I budged ten percent, but I'd already knocked that off his trade."

"That beater had hit everything but the lottery. Skins were bald, motor mounts broken."

"But it was still a grand over wholesale."

"Stop candy-assing around!"

Kent thumped his heel on the desk for emphasis, causing the framed photo of his wife and teenaged daughter to topple over flat. The gesture also seemed to cost him considerable pain. He gritted his teeth and eased his feet down to the floor.

"Listen, Paul, you took that loser to the woodshed. Now rejoice and count your loot." Then he shuffled through the paperwork and frowned. "Thirteen-five? You puked all over the table. What happened to my upside-down pencil at four-teen-eight?"

Kent Seasons had trained himself to write upside down, a trick used to carnival effect while presenting numbers to buyers seated across a desk. He'd stormed into Paul's office to bad-cop the Blazer guy and blasted him with the first pencil. The novelty of writing upside down was a distraction, a ruse, but the Blazer guy still balked at the crummy offer. So Kent, who'd been par-ticularly impatient lately, left Paul to dicker alone.

"That Blazer had seventy-thousand miles on her, Kent."

"You're absolutely right. She was nicely broken in."

"And no extended warranty."

"Who needs a warranty when the first seventy worked all the kinks out?"

"A gust of beer farts wafted up from the seat when the guy climbed in to test-drive. I had to hold my breath."

Kent grinned. "You cranked up the AC, right? Freon is bet-ter than potpourri."

Paul couldn't help but grin right back, as he really had used the air conditioner to mask the stench, a move Kent had taught him way back. "He'd been talking with the guys down at Thompson's. He said—"

"That peckerwood said what they all say." The mention of Thompson's Ford had obviously irritated Kent. He blew the dust from his family photograph and stood it back upright. "Got a better deal waiting down the street, man. You won't believe it, but the oddie on my trade stopped working this very same morning, swear to Jesus."

Kent refreshed his web browser, as online news was his preferred way to kill time. Everyone at the dealership had a time-killing strategy. Chadwick listened to right-wing talk radio until he was feeling righteous enough to steamroll his next up. Brad read the sports section between catnaps in his office. Billy Jr. hid from his father, while Jennylee spent entire days gaz-ing out the showroom glass as if drinking in some strange and oracular vision, her hands jammed in the back pockets of her Wrangler blue jeans.

"Don't ever let some douchebag walk into our house and scrape his boots," Kent said, "then go buy wheels down the street. Especially not to spare Morticia's feelings."

Then Paul mentioned that Jennylee's electricity had recently been shut off again. While he'd known of her financial trou-bles, it'd simply not occurred to him until just now how badly she must've needed the Blazer deal.

"No electricity?" Kent said. "Explains why she comes to work looking like one of those cadavers she's always blabbing about."

Sad but true. Jennylee's hair was prematurely graying and her pale forearms popped with veins and gristle. She and her family lived a few miles east of Paris, in a double-wide ringed in chicken wire alongside Route 150.

"So you don't think I should rewrite the deal—at least give her an assist?"

"You greeted him and did the walkaround. You demoed him, built the deal, talked numbers, and closed." Kent pantomimed shooting a basketball. "He shoots, he scores."

Paul shrugged, figuring he'd quietly rewrite the deal later. Maybe. Sure, he didn't need the commission quite as badly as Jennylee, but what was sales if not a competition? And wasn't competition inherently fair—or at least fair enough that nobody got to complain about losing?

"Paul, can we talk off the record?"

"I thought we already were."

"Confidential, I mean. For no ears beyond this room."

Then Kent launched into a speech about how Paul had what it took to be one of if not *the* best salesman he'd ever seen. "You got the looks, kid," Kent said, "and the smarts and the smooth rap. But none of that ultimately matters, because you don't have the desire. You've got to want it, Paul. That's the key. And I'm not talking about money or prestige—no, you've got to want *control.* Control of the buyer. Control of how much they spend, what they spend it on, even how they feel about having spent it. That's what separates the best from the rest. Like Mr. Miyagi says in *The Karate Kid.* You sell cars yes, or you sell cars no. Either way is fine. But if you sell cars maybe, or I guess so, or gee I suppose I might, then you get squished"—Kent screwed the ball of his thumb into the desk—"just like a grape."

"That's a great movie," Paul said.

Kent pointed at his computer screen. "Check out the latest."

Yahoo! ran the following: "Chapter 11 for General Motors?" Below was a quote from an industry analyst employing the same "too big to fail" rhetoric coined for the megabanks during their recent taxpayer-fleecing bailout, arguing the collapse of General Motors would constitute a blow the slumping U.S. economy simply could not absorb.

"Last year," Kent said, "the CEOs of GM and Chrysler flew to Washington aboard luxury corporate jets, sipping dry martinis the whole way, and then had the *cojones* to look our elected representatives in the eye and ask for twenty-five billion dollars."

"That's brazen."

"No, that's stupid. Somebody oughta test Detroit's drinking water for lead."

Paul mostly ignored the national news, but everyone knew General Motors was upside down. Bush had given them a king's ransom, although it apparently wasn't enough. Now GM wanted more, but Obama was playing hardball. The funds were contingent upon a surrender of controlling stock, with guided restructuring to follow.

"How do you think it'll play out?"

"Who the hell knows?" Kent said. "But I got a real bad feeling."

While management and ownership saw the demise of the American Way written in the Obama administration's mandates, in truth, the thought of GM filing for bankruptcy gave Paul a dark thrill. Unlikely as it seemed, could Capitol Hill skulduggery actually penetrate the cornfields and boredom of Paris, Illinois?

But Paul's heart wasn't really in the car game anyway. No, despite spending fifty or sixty hours a week at Regent's, his true interests lay elsewhere: in musicianship, in songwriting. His heroes were artists like Townes Van Zandt and Emmylou Harris, Lou Reed and Dylan. Always Dylan. In fact, he'd ignored his father's advice and actually majored in music theory back in college.

While he'd sometimes questioned that decision in the decade since, now he finally had a plan. The big Memorial Day sale was coming up that weekend, and after he'd lined his pockets with commissions, Paul Stenger was hitting the road to Nashville, to Music City. Hadn't let the cat out of the bag yet, of course, but he would in due time.

"Government can't even run the post office," Kent muttered, "let alone an automaker." He ground another mint between his molars. "Think you boned Morticia's Blazer guy? Just wait. Eighty-five-fifty-five's gonna bend GM over and skip the lube."

Although long accustomed to Kent's cynical hyperbole, Paul was left momentarily speechless by this. Because 8555, as everybody around the lot knew, was General Motor's code for black paint.

Then a flash of movement out the window caught his eye. Sure enough, Jennylee Witt was stomping across the pre-owned lot, head bobbing and shoulders tensed. In the distance was a tall man with snowy white hair.

"Looks like Jennylee's got a fresh up," Paul said.

"Yeah? Well, you'd best get out there and snipe her again," Kent said, still scrolling the news. "Before she blows it."

2

Back before he'd given up on her, Kent Seasons often advised Jennylee to visualize sales techniques and build her confidence by repeating positive affirmations—*harnessing your chi*, he called it—and so while crossing the lot, she imagined closing a deal with the white-haired gentleman.

First, he'd ask the typical questions about financing, which she'd answer expertly, thereby putting him at ease. Then he'd wonder why his trade-in wasn't appraised higher, as per the Kelley Blue Book, and she'd explain how the Blue Book always ran high and how other dealerships only quoted more for trade because they overcharged on sticker. Finally, she visualized presenting the gentleman with the keys to a beautiful vehicle and waving goodbye as he drove off the lot. Ten yards away now, she steadied herself and affirmed: *I am a successful automotive sales professional. Today I will learn something that will make me an even better automotive sales professional tomorrow.*

"Welcome to Regent's of Paris," Jennylee said, and offered the gentleman her palm. "I'm Jennylee Witt and I will be your sales associate today. How may I help you find the perfect vehicle?"

"Relax, sugar," he said. "I'm just out kicking tires."

Up close, he didn't look quite so old. Tall and trim, dressed in nice jeans and a clean teal polo. A gold chain hung from his suntanned neck and his white hair had a shock of black up front that made the rest seem even whiter.

"Say, how about this one?"

The sedan he meant—a '96 Chevy Caprice—was way overpriced. It was in decent shape, but who wants a thirteen-year-old car? Nobody around Regent's (besides Billy Jr., who'd overpaid for it) believed they'd ever move the thing. Still, a deal for this particular vehicle would go a long way toward getting her back in management's good graces.

"This is a Chevrolet Caprice Classic," Jennylee said. "This pre-owned vehicle has low mileage and comes fully—"

"Ninety-seven-grand considered low mileage these days?"

"Sir, on a vehicle this well-made, I'd say that's pretty darn low."

He balled his fists on his hips. "You're excellent at your job, aren't you, Jennylee?"

Embarrassing as it was, her cheeks flushed. "I try to do my best."

"I'm sure you do," he said.

Like Kent Seasons, the white-haired gentleman had unmistakable charisma. In fact, he was almost like a salesman himself. He knew about strong eye contact and open body language, how you had to sell yourself first and foremost.

"Kent's sly," the man said, almost as if he'd read her thoughts. "He knew your looks would sell the men."

"Wait, you know Kent?"

"I like the style of your jeans, Jennylee. Not many women have the figure for a pair like that."

"Hold on, I'll go see if he's available."

But the white-haired gentleman stopped her with a smile. "Shoot, you think I'd trade *you* for Kent's ugly mug?"

After a little more chitchat, she asked if he'd like to drive the Caprice, to which he agreed—conditional upon her waiting to tell Kent he'd stopped by. "Me and his pop go way back," the gentleman explained, "but you sic Kent Seasons on me and I'm liable to end up leasing the entire fleet."

Back in the showroom, she'd grabbed a magnetic dealer plate and scoured the board for the Caprice's keys.

"Got a nibble?" Chadwick asked.

She hooked a finger in her cheek and tugged, an old joke of theirs. "Sometimes all it takes is one good up to turn your month around," she said, and immediately realized the words weren't hers, but belonged to Kent Seasons.

"Remember," Chadwick said, reclining against the Sierra's

tailgate while pretending to reel in a prize marlin, "the feel of the wheel seals the deal."

As the showroom doors snicked shut behind her once again, she pondered Kent's positive-thinking advice. Sure, it sounded a little hokey, but maybe she really could be proud of being an automotive sales professional. After all, a true professional built deals for the benefit of both her customers and herself. Another affirmation went like this: *Today I will help my customers get exactly what they want, and by helping them I also help myself. Therefore, if I help enough people get the life they want, I can have the life I want too...*

Only then, walking across the pre-owned lot with the keys jangling in her hand, did Jennylee realize she'd bungled the single most important element of the meet-and-greet: she'd forgotten to ask the white-haired gentleman's name.

Mistakes had been piling up lately, as mistakes are wont to do, but not getting a name was a rookie flub. Most people don't get the attention they want—let alone the affection, the love—and so the quickest way to a deal was to use a buyer's name over and over again, to make them feel noticed and important. But asking for the gentleman's name now would be awkward. Worse, it'd mark her as an amateur, and when buyers think salespeople are amateurs they'll dicker and grind for every last dollar.

Just yards shy of the white-haired gentleman now, and Kent Seasons's voice—a voice so familiar she heard it in her dreams—boomed in her head: *Jennylee, how the hell do you expect to sell a vehicle if you don't even know the buyer's goddamn name?*

As Jennylee's latest meet-and-greet unfolded, Kent Seasons sat with his back to the window and his sore left foot propped on his desk beside the photo of his wife and daughter, Linda and Kelsi. Paul Stenger had left the office a few minutes before, but their little chat had left Kent feeling melancholy.

Sure, sniping Morticia was a heartening sign, but Paul still had a bad case of the nice guys, and it was sickening to watch him tread water. And that dusty old "best I've ever seen" speech was mostly just hot air. Great salesmen were blessed with a peculiar ability to see things from outside and above, sort of like near-death experiences on TV, a Zen state of mind that a self-absorbed dude like Paul could never hope to master. Paul could be *pretty* good though. Or at least better. Bottom line, the guy simply wasn't committed to selling cars—and commitment, as Kent's father used to say, was the only weapon a salesman has to pierce the larceny in a buyer's heart.

But a businessman has to face reality, and the reality was that Jerry Seasons had retired from the car game, Paul Stenger was a wuss, and Kent was thirsty.

He listened for footsteps out in the hall and then slid open his bottom right desk drawer. He'd picked up the Jim Beam that same morning. Over the last year this had become habit. A fresh bottle on Monday to carry him through to Saturday, although lately his Monday bottles had only been lasting to midweek.

He took a pull, relished the minty burn, and then put the bottle away again.

The talk with Paul nagged at him. Between that stuff about Obama bending over General Motors and Kent's having referred to the man as 8555 (if only to ruffle Paul's liberal feathers), the whole conversation had been borderline outrageous, even for dealership smack talk. While it remained true that a man couldn't sell cars in downstate Illinois without griping about politics every once in a while, Kent was secretly troubled by the venom spat Obama's way. It wasn't just the smarmy big-city rap either. No, it was the pigmentation. Never mind the guy wasn't even as dark as the goo inside a Caramello bar. Most folks in Paris hadn't exchanged more than a few words with a Black person in their entire life, let alone one who'd smoked 'em at Harvard Law, and yet those same people—Kent's colleagues and customers and neighbors—equated their commander in chief with laziness and welfare and all that other stereotypical bullshit.

Although Kent Seasons was nobody's idea of a Democrat, he *was* a patriot, and patriots had best not go around talking trash about their duly elected president. But he somehow had

to shake Paul Stenger's cozy hammock. Paul wore this perpet-
ually faraway look, like he imagined himself on a beach somewhere with a brew and a babe. The guy was a space cadet, Ziggy
Stardust in a Regent's polo, and he needed to snap out of it.

Way back, not long after hiring him, Kent actually caught
Paul writing a *song* in his office. Three in the afternoon and
instead of working the phones, instead of wooing his be-backs,
there he was scribbling in an artsy little moleskin notebook. The
book even had precious silk ribbons to tie it closed and keep his
deep thoughts secret from the other car salesmen. Paul was into
bodybuilding and he wore too much hair gel, and he was single
and childless despite pushing thirty, so Kent had wondered if
he might be homosexual (didn't give a damn, just wondered)
and he cringed every time Jethro or Nautical Bill cracked a gay
joke in Paul's presence.

He jotted a few notes and gathered his paperwork for the
weekly manager's meeting. There was much he'd like to say
at these meetings—they needed to ban Junior from the closer's desk, for starters, as evidenced by that worn-out Caprice
Classic—but mostly he just dreaded them. Junior pretended to
run the show, but everybody knew his daddy was the one who
banged the gavel and slung the salami. Even when the old man
skipped the meetings (when, as rumor had it, he was enjoying
a happy ending at that new Lotus Parlor massage joint out past
the mall) even then Nautical Bill ran the ship.

It hadn't always been this way though. Jerry Seasons had
co-owned the dealership before Nautical Bill bought him out,
as they'd partnered up and founded the business with money
borrowed from their own fathers back in the late sixties, shortly
after their tours in Vietnam. Jerry had served as a Marine infantryman, while Nautical Bill spent the conflict bobbing harm-
lessly around Southeast Asia and working on his tan. Nonetheless, before Jerry relinquished the family stake, Bill Regent
Sr. promised—"solid as granite, one veteran to another"—that
someday Junior and Kent would be co-general managers. Same
title, same salary, same juice. But it hadn't shaken out that way,
and now every time Kent saw that towering sign along Route

150, saw the impression of his own last name where it'd been lazily painted over, he couldn't help but feel cheated.

Jerry got pushed into retirement by a bum ticker. All the usual mantraps: high blood pressure and cholesterol, cigs and booze and a temper that flushed his face red as a cardinal. For years, Kent's mother had said the lot was killing Jerry and, sure enough, one day he doubled over his putter at Paris Links and nearly walked the 19th hole. Quadruple bypass surgery followed. Angioplasty, blood thinners, a shoots and sprouts diet and no more smoking cigarettes or selling cars, doctor's orders.

Kent knuckled his eyes and resolved to stop dwelling on the past. Then he popped a couple of Tylenol, his second dose of the day. He'd awoken that morning with a mysterious pain in his left big toe, the bedsheet weighing on his foot like lead. Hobbling to the toilet, he'd wondered if he'd somehow managed to break a bone in his sleep.

Having limped to the door now, Kent paused. He visualized the meeting to come in excruciating detail, the stuffy room with its lone window and its framed pictures of '80s Corvettes, the frustrations and backbiting, the glut of wasted time, and he could almost taste the crow that'd be crammed down his throat should he dare speak anything even approaching the truth. Finally, he limped back over to his desk. Then he turned the photograph of Linda and Kelsi to face the wall.

"Pardon me, ladies," he said.

Because amidst all the burdens a man must bear in this life, what could one more sip of bourbon possibly hurt?

Figuring she'd already blown the deal by neglecting to get the white-haired gentleman's name—a mistake that could give Kent Seasons the perfect excuse to fire her—Jennylee resolved to simply buckle down and do her best.

She unlocked the Caprice. "Ready to take her for a spin, sir?"

He snagged the keys and climbed right in, bouncing on the seat like a hyperactive kid. "This bench seating sure is roomy. I like it way better than the new style, don't you?"

Then a simple idea occurred, a harmless fib; she asked to take a quick peek at his driver's license.

"That's not really necessary, is it?"

"Just to make sure you remembered to bring it."

"We're just cruising around the block."

"I'm only looking out for your best interests," Jennylee said, and felt keenly that beat of silence where she should've used his name, "in case we get pulled over."

The gentleman protested that he'd had his license since age sixteen, and hardly a parking ticket in all that time. "Not that sixteen was really all that long ago," he added.

"It's standard procedure, sir."

"Says who?"

"Says my employer," she said, and glanced back at the showroom.

Finally, the man shrugged and flipped open his wallet. Name: Maurice Currant. Address: Country Club Lane, out by Paris Links where all the fat cats lived. Chadwick was right—the white-haired gentleman really might have gold balls.

Relieved, Jennylee slapped the magnetized plate on the Caprice's bumper. Through the back window, she watched Maurice Currant lean across the cab and flip up the passenger door lock. A polite gesture, and a sign he was feeling comfortable. Their eyes met briefly in the rearview and then she was around the side at the door.

She reached for the handle and felt that morning's cool raindrops still clinging to its underside—but then she paused. Vehicles whipped past, racing the stoplights. Across the way at the Citgo, men in Carhartt jackets and John Deere caps sipped coffee while gassing up their rigs. All was normal as could be, so why this hesitation? Figuring it was just residual awkwardness from having forgotten to get Maurice's name straightaway, she reminded herself to focus. Because selling the Caprice could save her month. Get Chastity up to Springfield to see some real doctors. Maybe even convince Derrol not to sell Bugles. She recalled Chadwick's dog food comment and couldn't help but imagine wet, red slop slipping from a tin can.

Maurice cranked down the passenger window. "Forget something, sugar?"

Jennylee forced a smile. Then she said a quick little prayer (*Lord, I know there's folks worse off, but my family really needs this commission. Glory, Praise, Amen*) and climbed into the Caprice.

Maurice dropped the dash-mounted stick into Drive and rolled toward the exit.

"You can make a right and head downtown, Mr. Currant," Jennylee suggested. The preplanned route was all straightaways and easy right-hand turns, which reduced the chances of an accident. But Maurice Currant turned left instead.

"A pretty country lane," he said, accelerating away, "is more my style."

Watching the gas stations and fast-food restaurants give way to farmland, Jennylee thought about how, before they signed the dotted line, the customer was always right—whereas in reality customers were almost always dead wrong. Most were so paranoid they could barely remember what vehicle they'd wanted in the first place. The rest just craved something shiny and jacked up their payments for no practical reason.

If she were honest, though, this bothered her because on her very first day at Regent's she'd purchased a pre-owned Nissan with a snappy gold paint job. After spotting the vehicle, she'd thought if she didn't nab it quick somebody else surely would. So after lunch she walked into Kent's office to inquire. "You mean the pyrite Nissan?" he'd said, but she hadn't quite known what that meant. And as they talked it over, something told her she was making a mistake, like the Nissan was overpriced and she really should've known better. But she'd already opened her mouth, and when Kent (and later Billy Jr.) praised her good eye, she felt a little better. Still, the Cavalier she'd traded had run just fine. Owned it free and clear too. Whereas the Nissan cost four-hundred a month plus full coverage.

Maurice sped deeper into the countryside, talking all the while about nothing whatsoever. Jennylee smiled and laughed at the appropriate spots, but she'd had this same hollow conversation so many times with so many different customers that she found her attention drifting—especially when they passed Higgenbottom's.

The tall white house stood north of the highway on the outskirts of Paris. But it wasn't just any old house. It was a business: Higgenbottom Memorial Chapel and Crematory. The funeral home had fascinated Jennylee even before she'd known of its function. A feeling, almost, that it was meant for her in some way. A few times prior—usually after a particularly bad day at Regent's—she'd turned down the long driveway, coasting under the tunnel of oaks for a closer look. Lots of stately old farmhouses graced Paris, but none quite like this. The roof was steeply peaked, the windows arched, and elegant cornices crowned a lushly shadowed veranda, a place to sip juleps and fan the day's heat from your brow, almost like some relic from the Old South.

But then Maurice Currant mashed the pedal to the floorboard and the low sedan's gas-guzzling engine—the type suitable for high-speed police chases and high school drag races—bucked and roared. Tires bit asphalt, Jennylee was pinned to the seat back, and within moments Higgenbottom's was just a pale dot in the Caprice's rearview mirrors.

3

P er usual, Junior—who dreaded these meetings perhaps even more than Kent—was already seated at the table, fidgeting and digging in his ear with a pen cap. Behind him stood the dry-erase board where they tracked monthly sales. That Junior always sat with his back to this board was surely no coincidence.

While Junior currently had his shirt sleeves buttoned down tight, under those sleeves were mangy bald patches. Those patches were strange indeed. Get the guy nervous enough, which was by no means difficult, and he'd suck on his wrists. The sucking was—as Junior's daddy often pointed out—a disgusting tic. But Nautical Bill didn't fully appreciate the situation: his son, the progeny of his loins, a man whom he'd gifted with the general managership of what was once Kent Seasons's family business, *ate* his own body hair. He indulged this compulsion in front of employees and buyers alike, even, or especially, while trying to close deals. In fact, Junior sucked hair any time the water got choppy, and smooth sailing was rare in the car business.

Kent limped over to the table, doing his best to keep his weight on his heel and off his big toe, but the little muscles in the front of his ankle weren't used to being called upon that way.

"Glad you're here early, Kent," Junior said, paying no attention to his pained gait.

"Wish I could say the same, Billy."

Then Junior asked for Kent's support on a proposal that would see the dealership retain the services of a certain consultant Junior had located (or, more likely, been located *by*) whose particular know-how lay in the selling of new and pre-owned automobiles. "I keep telling Dad we have to spend money to make money," Junior said, "but you know how he pinches pennies."

Kent had already heard tell of this around the watercooler. "Consultant? You mean that oily tomcat out of Dallas?"

Junior wiped the pen cap on his slacks. "His name's Donovan Crews. And believe me, that fella knows how to move steel."

"Met him at an event in Kansas City once—" Kent began.

"His seminar is titled *The Seven Steps to Sales Success*. I think that's just great, don't you? It reminds me of a book from my management coursework, *The Seven Habits of Highly Effective People*."

"The guy was stinking drunk, Billy. Totally blotto. Ready to eat the urinal cakes."

But what Kent remembered best was Donovan Crews bragging how he'd once test-driven a recently divorced and pregnant kindergarten teacher and fingered her in a Kentucky Fried Chicken drive-thru. He'd sported a gold pinkie ring engraved with his own initials. Kent remembered that little detail as well.

"He's an expert," Junior said. "An automotive sales *consultant*."

"Yeah, well, how much does his expertise cost?"

Kent took a deep breath when Junior quoted the fee, which was more than they'd clear in a busy summer week. This boneheadedness wasn't entirely Junior's fault though. He'd grown up flush, as Nautical Bill owned a thousand acres of farmland as well as a local bank (the same bank that held titles as collateral against Regent's inventory), and people like that are often clueless. Because money was the currency of the union as well as the currency of being, and this meant an American's purpose in life turned upon getting all the money he could and then keeping that money away from his fellow Americans by any means necessary. So how were those born swaddled in that milk-warm cradle of holiest green ever supposed to grasp life's true purpose?

While Kent had doffed his cap and gown and gone straight to work, Junior motored up to the University of Illinois. His so-called "academic pursuits" were his father's favorite topic. To listen to the old man, Junior might have been at Harvard unraveling the secrets of the universe, not an hour up the road sleeping past noon. Eventually Junior returned to Paris, the prodigal boner with a degree in economics and an MBA. But higher education hadn't made a man of him. Truth was, Nautical Bill had sent Junior away because he knew his son couldn't handle the real world, couldn't close deals or manage people, and needed some diplomas to disguise the nepotism.

"Bill Sr. gonna show today?" Kent asked.

At the mere mention of his father, Junior cocked his wrist and his purplish lips slicked with saliva. Disgusted, Kent considered saying the old man's name again—saying it real slow, with lots of gravitas—just to watch Junior squirm.

Then Brad Howard sauntered in. Despite his considerable bulk, Brad carried himself with an easy grace that suggested he might tuck the old pigskin and sprint down the sideline any minute, just like back in the day. For some reason, he also sported a seventies-era Burt Reynolds mustache.

"Well, if it isn't sweetness himself," Kent said.

Despite pushing forty, Brad still closed deals due to having been a football star at Paris High—although now he'd barf up a keg's worth of Budweiser if he ran any farther than to the fridge. Kent had always liked Brad though. Long considered him a protégé, in fact. He'd even pushed for Brad's promotion to assistant manager. But now he sensed Brad Howard's sights were on the sales manager's desk—on *his* desk. Hence the subtle jabs, such as nicknaming him after a dead football player.

"Let's get this dog and pony show on the road," Brad said. He cranked his chair around and straddled it. "Billy, where's your daddy?"

Hearing this, Junior paled and tucked his elbows, as if stricken with palsy.

Needling Billy Regent Jr. was a tried-and-true pastime, one Kent and Brad had enjoyed for years, and thinking back on the good times brought a rush of endearment that left him a touch misty eyed. While his calling had allowed him no true friends, these men were the closest thing to it. Watching them, listening to them, he felt weary, but he also felt like giving Junior and Brad each a big hug and shaking their familiar hands—and then kicking their stupid asses straight up into their lying throats.

໖

"I graduated with Kent's old man back in the day," Maurice Currant said. "Considering the mess GM is in, looks like he sold out just in time."

Unsure how best to respond, Jennylee remarked how General Motors had a shortsighted business strategy, which was terminology she'd heard tossed around.

"Shortsighted?" Maurice flashed another grin. "Hell, those auto execs all think they're geniuses, but they're blind as moles."

The horizon beyond the Caprice's windows was familiar as could be, but she was nonetheless struck by its incredible flatness. Fields panned endlessly away, the corn dry and yellow under a relentless sun. The farmland reminded her of seeing the ocean on her and Derrol's honeymoon down in Fort Lauderdale, which, it occurred now, was maybe the last time they'd been truly happy together.

"Tough luck for Kent though," Maurice said. "Get the feeling he doesn't appreciate taking orders from Bill Sr. and that morphodite son of his."

She stifled a laugh, but deep down she actually pitied Billy—if a person can rightly pity the man who signs their paychecks. Billy was just so darn nervous, such a bundle of tics and fidgets, largely due to his father's constant browbeating. But Billy wasn't necessarily a bad person. Selling cars simply contradicted his nature, and the effort of smiling through his misery had worn him down. Although she supposed that could describe everyone at Regent's to some degree—everyone except for Kent Seasons, that is. Kent took to selling cars like a baby takes to a nipple.

As they drove, Maurice prattled on about the bad economy and President Obama being a traitorous Kenyan, but Jennylee was so distracted by her various concerns that the sight of her home whizzing past left her disoriented. It wasn't but ten miles to the Indiana border. At this rate, they'd be in Terre Haute before Maurice even tested the cruise and wipers.

"You could turn around here, Mr. Currant," she said, and pointed out a gravel road—a road which Maurice hurtled right past. "Kent doesn't like us to burn too much gas. Especially since it hit four bucks a gallon."

"Kent won't mind us stretching this old gal's legs a little," Maurice said.

And this was likely true, considering how desperate management was to see the Caprice roll off the lot.

"So, Mr. Currant, are you looking to trade in your current vehicle?"

"Just look at all that corn," he said. "It's dry as sandpaper."

"Were you planning to buy with cash, or would payments suit you better?"

"Afraid that pisser we got this morning was too little too late."

"Have you considered what down payment might best fit your budget?"

"Let's talk numbers later, okay?"

"I have to ask this stuff, Mr. Currant. Kent wants us to gather information—"

She pinched her lips shut. Get her nervous and words spurted out like water from a busted spigot. And nervous she was getting, more so with each passing mile.

"Worry not, my dear. I'll tell Kent you treated me exquisitely."

They soon passed a run of state parkland which featured a popular fishing and boating hole by the name of Paradise Lake. She pointed out another likely turnaround spot, but Maurice just whistled a tune and swung onto an access road.

Overhanging trees cast thick blue shade, but the clammy sweat that slicked Jennylee's ribs owed more to the weird vibes in the Caprice. Her cell phone was in her desk back at Regent's. Kent hated to see salespeople fiddling with their phones, so she made a point not to carry hers during working hours. But she wished she had it now.

Being the only woman around Regent's, she'd naturally imagined what might happen if an up got strange on a test-drive. But
the man she'd pictured hadn't been handsome and well-dressed
like Maurice Currant. Instead, she'd imagined some sketchy
type, all dirty jeans and sunken eyes. Somebody like Derrol's pal
Randy Bauble. Then again, Randy probably only came to mind
because of another time in another car.

"Isn't it pretty out here, Jennylee?"

"Well sure, but we're awfully far from the dealership, don't
you think?"

Trees pressed the road tight as matchsticks and the air conditioner roared. Then Maurice turned onto a dirt path, apparently
having finally decided to flip around and head back. Jennylee felt
her shoulders relax. She'd been imagining the worst. Attributing
bad intentions to an eccentric but harmless older gentleman…

Then Maurice's hand brushed her thigh.

Jennylee went stiff as a post. But a moment later, just as
quickly and just as casually, Maurice's hand drifted down to the
empty stretch of seat between them. It'd been only the briefest
of touches. Hardly a touch at all, really. His expression was se-
rene, studying the road and woods. It'd been an accident, most
likely. Or a fatherly gesture misinterpreted, one which he'd
probably *realized* she'd misinterpreted, thereby embarrassing
himself and throwing a wrench into their already shaky rapport.

"We'd best get back to the lot."

"Is that so?"

"Well, Kent's gonna wonder—"

"Gonna wonder why he never took you for a spin himself,"
Maurice said, and again laid his hand on her.

In the seconds to follow, Jennylee couldn't seem to get a full
breath and her limbs felt numb, as if the blasting AC had frozen
her solid. All along, Maurice kept up his chatter, as if their bod-
ies were in a separate dimension from their words. The hand on
her thigh was tanned and veiny, and it didn't press exactly, didn't
knead or rub, but just sort of lay there, waiting and expectant.
The index and middle fingers had a dusting of wiry dark hairs
in the gaps between the first and second knuckles. In Jennylee's

mind's eye, she knocked that offending hand away, bent the fingers backward, even bit it. But Maurice just tooled along and she did nothing at all, and that hand of his remained planted on her thigh.

The woods thickened and the path narrowed such that weeds tickled the Caprice's doors. The rear wheels slued in loose gravel and the RPMs leaped. After she'd yet again asked Maurice to return to the dealership, he shushed her. "I know just the spot," he said.

"To turn around, you mean?"

"Just a little ways up ahead, past the next bend."

"Please take your hand off me, Mr. Currant."

And he did, just like that. He smiled as if wondering why she hadn't spoken up before. She thought for a moment things might still be all right, that Maurice had finally realized she wasn't inclined to pursue whatever notions he'd taken, but he didn't turn the Caprice around. As they drifted deeper into the woods, Jennylee felt like doing something dramatic—reaching for the ignition, pitching open the door and diving out—although she remained still as a spotlighted deer.

The road ended at a campsite. Axed stumps served as parking blocks and footpaths led off to Paradise Lake. Then "Hotel California" came on the radio. Jennylee had always disliked the song, with its creepy lyrics about pink champagne and mirrors on the ceiling. She tensed her shoulders as the whiny guitar plucked and twanged. Then, after two sharp drum beats, Maurice lunged across the cab. He soon got hold of her wrists and pinned her against the door. Up close, he smelled like citrus cologne, and the pores on his chin looked plugged with tar. When Maurice clamped his mouth atop her own, she pursed her lips against his prodding tongue and coffee breath. He kept right on trying to kiss her though, as if her closed mouth were no real impediment. Finally, he released one of her wrists and began kneading her left breast through her Regent's polo. His touch was odd, almost joking, like how a grown man would squeeze a boy's biceps.

Jennylee slapped her free hand on Maurice's forehead. "Quit

right now," she said, nose to nose with him, "and I won't tell Kent."

"Kent won't give a rat's ass."

"I'm married, Mr. Currant."

"Proletarian concerns."

"You should know that I'm carrying a blade"—she wasn't carrying anything but her business cards—"and I ain't afraid to use it."

"Such tough talk," Maurice said. "But I think you're bluffing."

Then he slid away from her and reclined against the driver's side door. Casually, languidly, he unzipped his fly and pushed his first two fingers and thumb inside. "That's better," he said, as his penis's wrinkled gray foreskin slowly peeled back, like a snake shedding its skin.

Jennylee scratched for the door handle and then tumbled out into the dirt. She found her footing, slammed the door, and fled. Ten yards off, she glanced back just in time to see the passenger window sink into the Caprice's doorframe.

Maurice's snowy head popped out. "Leaving so soon?"

"I'm calling the police, you creep."

"Your word against mine. See any witnesses out here?"

She hurried away on quaking knees.

"Oh, and by the way, *Morticia,* Kent told me all about you…" Double time now, as Maurice shouted after her, "Squeal, and I'll tell everyone how I steadfastly refused to pay you two hundred bucks for a suck job! How you threatened me with lies!"

Jennylee tucked her hair behind her ears and ran until Maurice's voice and the Caprice's throaty rumble were gone. The air beneath the trees was thick and smelled like mud. She feared Maurice might come barreling up the path, but he must've looped around on the park road instead. She kept going, putting one foot in front of the other and telling herself not to cry. They'd passed her trailer a few miles back. A hell of a walk, but what other choice was there? Her legs felt watery, the muscles puddling, and there was a weird fluttery emptiness in the space between her shoulder blades.

Ten minutes later, Jennylee finally cleared the woods. She stood alongside the highway and tried to collect herself. But when she cupped a hand to her brow and looked west down the asphalt in the direction of home, all she could see was the shimmer of heat mirage far in the distance.

There was nary a soul in this world Kent Seasons despised more than Nautical Bill.

The old man was taller and more robust than his son—livelier, balder, louder—which made him both a more effective businessman and a more abusive personality. Having heard the approaching footsteps, Kent dredged up a smile just as Nautical Bill shuffled into the meeting room alongside Tom Partlow, the dealership's head mechanic.

Six-foot-five and stoutly built, Partlow kept his blond hair short as a bristle brush and he still pumped iron at the gym, despite having reached the age where most guys give up on all that and commence drinking beer in earnest. Years ago, Kent had written him off as just another grease monkey turning a wrench for peanuts, but Partlow worked steady, earned his respect, and was the obvious choice for service manager when the position came open.

"You planning to start this meeting, Billy," the old man said, "or need I man the captain's chair myself?"

"Okay, fellas," Junior said, ducking eye contact with his father, "so far this month we're just shy of"—he shuffled a rat's nest of papers—"forty deals."

Brad Howard glanced Kent's way.

"We're really picking up steam," Junior said.

Kent tapped his pencil on the table, waiting for Junior to man up and confess there weren't even thirty deals this month, let alone forty. Instead, Junior danced around the truth like Fred Astaire. At times like these, Kent could almost empathize with Junior's sad childhood. Never quite making the old man proud. Not nearly tough enough for football, too slow for hoops, and deathly scared of the baseball. A chubby prom date who kept her pantyhose on during the morose dry hump in a dealership Camaro.

"We've got twenty-nine closed and delivered, Bill," Kent said.

Junior squirmed and tugged at his sleeves while Kent explained that a few more sales were still pending financing. How unfair all this was though. As sales manager, he put in long hours in the trenches, while Junior took home twice the bread for making boneheaded deals and lying about the numbers. Why had his father ever trusted Nautical Bill's word?

A recent discovery complicated matters. A month back, when Junior was home playing sick and his old man was AWOL, Kent had secretly parsed the ledgers for the years since Jerry Seasons accepted that buyout. Now he had reason to suspect that Junior and his daddy were cooking the books—underreporting revenue and perhaps even embezzling from a shareholder's fund (which included Jerry and Kent's retirement accounts) by not reporting cash and privately financed sales to the bank underwriting the inventory. Floating sales was a serious breach. Normally, any suspicion of floating would have creditors on the lot the very next day, checking the floor plan for missing vehicles—but the bank that financed Regent's, Community Federal, was owned by none other than Bill Sr. himself.

Was there concrete evidence of financial wrongdoing? No. Could he bring it up without risking his job? Definitely not. But Kent had reason to suspect he'd never see that promotion now, as it'd grant him unrestricted access to their deepest financial records.

"What's the dag-blasted trouble, boys?" Nautical Bill asked. "Summer's for making hay. The Crust Fest Blowout Sale starts this Saturday. Y'all forget that?"

As if anyone could. Every Memorial Day weekend Regent's held a sale to coincide with the Paris Crust Fest. Good 'n' Crusty Inc., headquartered in Paris, was one of America's largest pie shell manufacturers. Half the town was coughing up flour dust come five o'clock. But the Blowout Sale was a fiasco. Every year they shot a patriotic commercial and hung streamers, and every year the sale was a letdown, as Parisites mysteriously preferred carnival rides and free country music to car shopping in the heat.

"It's the drought, Bill," Brad Howard said. "Folks are squirreling away their pennies for the next dust bowl."

"Dust bowl my derriere," the old man said. "It sprinkled this morning."

"Gas is four bucks a gallon, Bill," Kent said. "People are cinching their belts."

He and Brad had been cooking up this banter for months. First the weather, then gas prices, then whatever else. Trick was to alter it just enough that Nautical Bill could never quite tell for sure if he was being mocked.

"Arabs are fleecing us," Kent continued.

"We oughta just nuke all them ragheads," Brad said, busily doodling a cartoon rocket on his notepad, "and take their oil."

"Eighty-five-fifty-five," Kent added, "is pussifying America."

Tom Partlow checked his wristwatch, a gesture which itself (unbeknownst to Tom) had become part of the game.

"You're darn right," Nautical Bill said, and patted Kent's hand.

This patronizing nonsense happened every meeting without fail, and yet Nautical Bill remained oblivious. Clogged arteries, arthritis, limp noodle—whatever, bring it on. Going limp in the head though? Not being able to see around the corner anymore? Now that was scary. On the other hand, Nautical Bill had clearly outfoxed Jerry Seasons, and thus, by proxy, Kent himself.

The old man eyeballed Junior. "So how do we get back to being the best little dealership in downstate Illinois?"

Brad mouthed his knuckles, Kent coughed, and Tom Partlow loosed a deep sigh.

"Thompson's is killing us, Dad," Junior said. "They're running financing out to seven years. Buyers just don't understand they're paying out the wazoo in the long run."

Thompson's Ford was a high-pressure dealership across

town. Type of outfit that'd sell a tricked-out Mustang to a twelve-year-old blind drunk on moonshine. According to the grapevine, Junior's analysis wasn't far off. But business strategy was the least of Kent's concerns when it came to Thompson's.

At auction a couple weeks back, he'd met a Ford rep out of Indianapolis who worked the Paris area. The guy mentioned having met Dan Thompson, the dealership's owner. Then he'd grinned and whispered how old Dan was a real poon hound. Despite finding the tone distasteful, Kent laughed for business's sake. But when the rep mentioned that Dan Thompson was shagging the cherry daughter of some loser from a rinky-dink lot down the street, Kent stopped laughing.

Kelsi had been working weekends as Thompson's showroom hostess for the past six months while socking away money for college. There'd been a classified in the *Beacon-Herald*. Reasonable hours, light duties. Kelsi was perfect for the job. Fresh-scrubbed and freckle-faced and sweet in the way of a teenaged girl who hasn't dated much. Goddamned if Kent hadn't suggested she apply. Even sat her down for a mock interview and play-acted the whole process, from handshake to we'll call you in a couple days. But that same day Kent got on the horn with Dan Thompson and called in a favor, one car guy to another. At first he hadn't suspected anything amiss, but in retrospect there were signs. Moodiness. Broken curfews. Hush-hush calls.

"Don't tell me about other dealerships, Billy," Nautical Bill said. "Problem's right here"—he pointed at the sales board—"so you'd best figure out how to con this ship."

Old Bill loved to deride his son with antiquated maritime terms, such as "conning" the Regent's ship. Junior couldn't simply flub a deal, or even fuck up a deal. According to his father, he torpedoed deals, deep-sixed deals, and sank deals down to Davy Jones' Locker.

"Jennylee's dead weight," Kent said. He felt bad about needing to cut her loose, but numbers don't lie. "She comes in late and she's scared of the phones. Just this morning Paul had to close one of her customers."

"Jennylee's a nice girl," Nautical Bill said.

"Didn't say she wasn't nice. I said she's not closing deals."

"Well, isn't it your job—as *sales manager*—to make her better?"

"You can lead a horse to water, Bill, but you can't teach it not to cave for every grinder that slithers through our showroom doors."

"But Jennylee's got a child, Kent. Where's your heart?"

"You'll find that particular item tucked in his wallet," Brad Howard said, now doodling a flock of winged hundred dollar bills, "snug between a crisp pair of Franklins."

The sun torched the groove in Jennylee's scalp and burned the delicate rims of her ears. She'd sweated through her Regent's polo, and her Wranglers clung to her thighs. Eighteen-wheelers roared past, coughing diesel and buffeting her with waves of hot gritty wind, much as Maurice Currant had zoomed by on his way back to town only moments before, sneering and flipping her the bird as he went.

Considering Kent Seasons and Maurice were acquainted, and considering she was in the doghouse, Kent would be inclined to believe whatever lies Maurice fed him. And while she understood full well she'd been victimized, Jennylee had no plans to involve the police. No, as far as she was concerned, the less people knew the better.

Thirty minutes later, the trailer finally came into view, tiny as a beer can in the distance. As usual, Randy Bauble's jacked-up red Toyota pickup sat in the driveway. She didn't appreciate Derrol having Randy over so often, as Randy Bauble's dirt was the kind that rubbed off, but she also understood the manner in which small-town boys stay tight friends largely due to their reminding one another of the time before jobs and wives ruined all their fun. Back in school she'd run around with Randy some too. They didn't have much in common, and probably never would've been friends at all if Paris weren't so little, but Paris was that little.

Her heels were rubbed raw and every step burned. She

considered removing her shoes, but the ditch was littered with broken glass and the asphalt was sun bubbled. Nothing to do but tough it out, and by the time Jennylee finally reached her driveway, both socks were wet with either blisters or blood.

Purely out of habit, she reached down the mailbox's hot black throat. Last week's *Beacon-Herald,* delivered late again. Water bill, past due, with a bright red FINAL NOTICE stamp. Power bill, three times what it should've been after Heartland Electric tacked on an extra deposit, knowing full well the Witt family couldn't even pay what they already owed, let alone any extra. Life was infuriatingly backward in this way. Like how wealthy car buyers always got the lowest interest rates, and how General Motors got a bazillion dollars in taxpayer money as reward for building mediocre vehicles, while working people just got the shaft.

But a parent can't afford to mope, so when the power got shut off the week before, she'd fibbed to Chastity. Heartland Electric made a mistake, honey. That's why the milk was warm in the fridge and that's why they had to brush their teeth by flashlight. She hated lying to her daughter, but a parent has to protect their child's innocence. For some, that meant hiding the truth about the birds and the bees, while for others it meant sugarcoating the fact that everybody has to die someday. Jennylee wanted to protect a different sort of innocence though. She didn't want Chast to have to know about money. Not yet, at least.

There was something else in the mailbox too. A legal-sized envelope stuffed tight, return address: The University of Triumph, Online. She'd been looking forward to receiving this particular correspondence for some weeks now, but after all that'd happened, it took her a moment to recall why she'd sent off for it in the first place.

Feeling the envelope's heft, Jennylee thought of how as a kid she'd allowed other people—trusted people, family and friends and teachers—to convince her it was okay to settle, to be less than she might otherwise be. Misplacing her faith in such people was partly why now, as an adult, she'd begun to ponder studying mortuary science. Aunt Liz had mentioned it during her last visit from Panama City, so the idea wasn't entirely original, and Jennylee drove past Higgenbottom's every day on her way to Regent's, so that surely contributed, but still. With a mortuary science degree she could be her own boss. Plus, morticians never lacked for business, as death was recession-proof. But with their finances sputtering along, how could she possibly afford school?

The machine guns roaring from the trailer raised yet another question: exactly how long had Derrol and Randy been playing Xbox?

Only then did she realize Derrol's truck was gone. This was worrisome, as they'd missed a couple of payments and received some curt letters. And the truck that *was* there—Randy Bauble's Toyota—had an unfamiliar yellow tarp tied across the bed.

Telling herself it was simple curiosity, that Derrol's truck must've broken-down somewhere and Randy was hauling the parts for a repair, Jennylee rose up on her toes and peeked under that tarp.

Three propane tanks lay in the bed, fittings coated in bluish rust. While she had no proof of this, they looked tampered with. Stolen even. Call it a mother's intuition, call it paranoia, but Jennylee did not want those tanks on her property. Randy Bauble clerked at Family Video. What business did he have with propane equipment?

She leaned against the truck and tried to compose herself. The barren landscape—the domed sky and frozen clouds, the drought-stricken fields and simmering asphalt—for one strange moment all seemed to pulse, to contract and expand. Sky breathing, fields cracking and groaning, the sun an unblinking eye staring down at a disheartened young woman with blistered feet who lived in a trailer set too close to the road.

Was the world trying to tell her something—to jar her awake? She closed her eyes and waited, but nothing more came. No revelations, no premonitions. The odd feeling passed and Jennylee opened her eyes. Just Paris again. Fields and sky, same as ever. She dabbed her brow and tucked the educational literature under one damp arm. While climbing the aluminum steps to the screen door, she noticed the windows were curtained in dust—and then a nuclear detonation rattled those same dusty panes.

Inside her home, aliens screamed and died with moist splats.

❧

"Maybe we do need some fresh legs," Nautical Bill said. "What do you think, Billy?"

But Junior was distracted by Tom Partlow, who'd flattened his hands on the table the way he always did before getting up to leave. For reasons Kent had never fully understood, Junior took issue with their head mechanic. All things considered, Partlow should've been his least concern. The man worked hard, was scrupulously honest, and never even made fun of Junior behind his back, which could be said of no other employee in either sales or service.

"Billy, I asked you a question."

"Payroll's sky-high already, Dad."

"Any employee who makes money for the dealership is a bargain. How did you get an MBA without passing Business 101? Kent, can you find us some talent?"

"Done. But we'll need to let someone go to make room—"

"The green pea can share Paul's office. He's last hired, right?"

Kent pointed out that Paul actually made a little money for the dealership, unlike Jennylee, but this logic fell on deaf ears. Then Tom Partlow announced he was headed back to work. Two transmissions and an engine rebuild. Weekly inventory, ordering.

"This is the manager's meeting, Tom," Junior said, "and you're the service manager, aren't you? The garage is just as important as—"

"That's exactly why I'm leaving. Because there's real work to do in my garage." He patted the old man on the shoulder. "Don't take any gruff from these rascals, Bill."

After Tom's footsteps faded down the hallway, Nautical Bill

told his son to stop giving their best mechanic such a hard time. As usual, Junior complained how Tom always left early, how he didn't show enough respect for protocol.

"Then why don't you stand up next time, Billy," Brad Howard said, "and tell him to sit his humongous ass back down?"

The insult took a moment to sink in, but once it did Junior cringed and curled like a pill bug. Pathetic as it was, the sight brought Kent a small but real joy. He considered pulling Brad aside later to hash out their differences. Crack a few beers and clear the air. You want my job, old buddy, but you can't have it, at least not yet. You're a good salesman, but you'd best stop gunning for my desk. Straight talk like that. But confronting Brad Howard frightened him in a way he was hesitant to examine.

Then Junior laid out his case for retaining the consultant. "Donovan Crews," he said, in summation, "is one impressive son of a gun."

After asking a few perfunctory questions and then letting enough time burn that Junior knew unequivocally whose decision it was to make, his daddy okayed the expense, conditional upon Kent's hiring a new salesperson to reap the benefits of the training.

Amidst Junior and Nautical Bill's scheming, Brad Howard had nodded off. Watching his lids flutter, Kent felt both a rush of affection and the urgent need for a drink—but not a drink with Brad. No, he needed a private drink in a quiet room. A chance to elevate his sore foot and parse his thoughts.

"I was out on the used lot yesterday," Nautical Bill said. "You guys have that old Caprice Classic stickered way too high."

The Caprice came in on trade. Kent appraised it nice and low, built a solid floor under the deal, but the buyer (a little old lady with flowers pinned to her bonnet) was a grinder, and the key to closing a grinder—as every decent salesman knows—is to keep your mouth shut. Once you've penciled an offer, to speak is to negotiate against yourself, and once a grinder senses the bottom line isn't *really* the bottom, they'll dicker down to the last cent. Back in the Wild West days, Kent recalled watching his father once make an offer and then sit in polite silence for forty excruciating minutes while a couple whispered and passed notes. They caved eventually, though. *Tough nuts to crack,* Jerry Seasons said, *I damn near fell asleep.*

But Junior was hopeless. He was the anti-closer. An opener. A pants-puller-upper. Rather than let that old lady walk, Junior swooped in and gave the moon—at least two grand more than the sedan was worth. Now their best chance to resell the Caprice lay in its retro value as a lowrider. Mexican buyers, in other words, a demographic that'd grown along with the new turkey processing plant south of town. But nobody would shell out serious cash for what amounted to an engine and a chassis, knowing they'd have to replace damn near everything else, from wheels to stereo. With the notable exception of the yellow Avalanche, the Caprice deal was perhaps Junior's single greatest fuck-up.

Brad Howard snapped awake. "That jalopy's gonna be here come the Rapture."

Junior buckled his nose and showed his small, widely spaced teeth.

"Jesus will have a tough choice," Kent said. "Whether to select for thy chariot a nineties Caprice Classic or a beautiful yellow Avalanche."

"At least the Avalanche's got a beer cooler," Brad pointed out.

"Yeah, but J. C. drinks wine."

"He could lower the Caprice. Maybe even install some hydraulics."

"Put a subwoofer in the trunk."

"With a tricked-out ride like that," Brad said, "he could go drag-racing. Probably even score himself some 'hood rats."

Sniveling noises burbled from Junior's pursed lips, as if a length of rotten plumbing had burst somewhere in his concave chest. Then Nautical Bill asked how much they'd given on trade, which got Junior tugging at his cuffs.

"We went a little high on her, Bill," Kent said—had to back Junior sometimes to keep things rolling—"but we closed the deal."

"It isn't a deal unless it turns a profit," Nautical Bill said. "You think all I look at is the number closed and delivered, Billy, but I do not appreciate you giving cream puff money for a beater. You got to *sell* people cars, son. Not *give* people cars."

Both sleeves were unbuttoned now and Junior's face was a grimace of humiliation. But any potential sympathy was lost when he next told his father it'd been Kent—not him—who'd appraised the Caprice too high. "I had to stop the buyer from walking somehow," he added.

The bourbon boiled along Kent's veins and the pencil snapped across his knuckles. In his anger, he'd unwittingly dug his feet into the floor and a hot jolt of pain blossomed in his toe. He gritted his molars, resisting the urge to come across the table and slap Junior around, to twist his hairless nipples until he shrieked. Clearly realizing he'd gone too far this time, Junior paled and shrank, just like when the old lady played the waiting game on that Caprice Classic.

"Don't you pin that price on me, Billy."

"Now, Kent," Junior said, waving his hands, "let's not get turned around—"

"Admit it. Tell the truth about that deal."

"This is no time for—"

"The truth being that you got bent over and spanked silly by Aunt Bee."

Silence dropped over the room. But then Junior began making odd, high-pitched squeaks, as if attempting echolocation. He eventually managed to get these noises under control, but his body was another matter, as to be called out so nakedly before his father was simply too much for Junior's system to bear. Quietly, as if wanting to be discreet about it—as if he believed those witnessing his plight must surely, in some way, sympathize—he licked his lips and turned away from the table.

"Control yourself, Billy," his father said.

"Deep breaths, Billy," Brad Howard said. "You don't have to do it this time!"

But Junior did have to do it. He desperately needed to do it. And after one last look over his shoulder, Junior's mouth fell slowly open, wet and stringy, and he hunched over to gnaw that well-gnawed wrist. There followed wet snorting noises like a dog chasing fleas. It went on and on, the ugly sounds amplified by the small room.

"We'd best get the consultant on this one," Kent said.

"Billy, you either stop that chewing"—his father rose teetering and steamed—"or I'm gonna bring a muzzle next time, you hear?" Then he faced his other two captives. "Move that Caprice, boys. I'll have no stale bread in my galley."

"Ten-four, Bill," Brad said.

"Aye-aye, Bill," Kent said.

"Afraid I have to leave early today." The old man was already lumbering to the door. "I've got an appointment to get my teeth cleaned."

After he'd gone, with Junior still busy sucking hair, Brad Howard looked at Kent. "That man's got to have just about the brightest smile in Edgar County by now."

Kent chuffed under his breath, as 'teeth cleaning' was Nautical Bill's not-so-secret code for Asian massage, a luxury he'd come to appreciate while on shore leave from those suntan tours in the Gulf of Tonkin—tours that'd occurred while a teenaged Jerry Seasons was humping a rifle through the jungle, tiptoeing around Bouncing Betty and ducking Charlie, but dreaming (or so Kent liked to believe) of staying alive and whole long enough to come home, start a business, and sire a hardworking son to pass it all down to.

4

Sell any cars today, Jen?"

Her husband hadn't even bothered to peel his eyes away from the TV when he spoke, but just kept right on thumbing buttons and chewing his bottom lip. That Derrol Witt asked this exact same question of his wife nearly every single day had somehow apparently escaped him.

A regiment of Coca-Cola cans lined the coffee table beside a jug of Jewel-Osco-brand vodka. Jewel-Osco was just across the parking lot from Family Video, and Randy liked to brag about his deal with the guys in liquor: he'd leave them DVDs behind the trash can, so long as his vodka missed the UPC scanner. A friendly pact, he called it.

The trailer reeked of cigarettes. She'd been asking Derrol to quit for months now, but he was hooked. Kent Seasons had quit smoking not long after she started at Regent's, following his father Jerry's big heart attack. For weeks afterward, Kent paced the showroom, chomping nicotine gum and looking ready to split his gourd. One particularly tense day, he'd pulled her aside. "Smoking kills, Jennylee," he said. "No doubt about it. But right now I'd give Danny DeVito a hand job for one lousy puff off a Marlboro Red."

Derrol still hadn't looked at her. What would it take to get his attention?

"Not only did I not sell any cars," she said, "but I got assaulted by a man with beautiful silver hair. Then I had to walk home all the way from Paradise Lake. My feet are all blistered up and I feel strange, like I might start crying and not be able to stop."

Her husband frowned, blinked. "How's that again?"

Bright orange streaks marred the sofa cushions. She studied those streaks, confused, before finally tracing them to grease on the Xbox controller, then to Derrol's stained fingertips, and finally to a bag of Cheetos crumpled under the coffee table.

"I said I didn't have much luck."

"Yeah, well, it must be something in the air. Because me and Randy been stuck on level four all day."

His eyes were mapped with reddened veins. She believed the part about *all day*.

"You ain't much of a marksman, Derrol," Randy Bauble said. "If space mutants ever really do invade, I believe I'll just fend for myself."

He sat on the floor, a cigarette tucked behind one ear. He wore a flat-billed cap cocked sideways, along with a white T-shirt under a Boston Celtics jersey lettered with an oddly pretty name—BIRD.

Randy also had a Band-Aid beneath his left eye. But there was no injury. It was just an odd fashion statement copied off some MTV rapper from clear back in high school. That Randy *still* wore that Band-Aid, that he actually took the time to apply a sliver of adhesive plastic to his cheek before coming to her trailer to shoot aliens with Derrol, seemed almost apocalyptically strange.

"Considering the complexities of interstellar travel," Derrol said, "I doubt space mutants will bother us much here in Paris."

"They just might," Randy said, "if they're running low on fat chicks."

Jennylee eased out of her shoes and went to the fridge. She ached for something sweet and cold, but the boys had finished all the soft drinks. She couldn't even pour a glass of tap water due to the heap of greasy plates piled in the sink. Meanwhile, Derrol and Randy kept right on bantering like she wasn't just across the counter, like she wasn't one of their wives but both of their mothers.

"You should come apply at Family Video, Derrol," Randy was saying. "Discounts on games and paid lunch after ninety days. Just think, you could be eating Long John Silvers on the company dime."

"You know," Derrol said, "I just might do that."

She'd heard this same conversation a dozen times before though. When they thought she was out of earshot, Family Video's perks extended to include smoking joints in the alley with slutty high school girls.

She leaned over the counter. "Chast will be home soon, Derrol. We need to clean up. Sorry, Randy, but you'll have to visit another time."

Randy Bauble popped up like a jumble of broomsticks. There'd never been much meat on his bones, but lately he made a scarecrow look like a candidate for stomach-stapling surgery. After lighting a menthol, Derrol tailed his friend outside. Jennylee leaned against the doorjamb, grimacing as the cuffs of her jeans rubbed her raw heels.

Down the driveway, Derrol and Randy jabbered and smoked. Eventually, Derrol flipped a butt into the grass. Their yard was full of cigarette butts. She'd complained about it time and again, but Derrol was loath to change his ways. Watching them, Jennylee wondered if their little hush-hush concerned those rusty propane tanks. Derrol even seemed to glance at the yellow tarp a few times, or was that just her imagination? Finally, they performed their complicated palm-smacking, knuckle-bumping, finger-snapping routine, and then Randy climbed into his Toyota and burned rubber.

Moments later, Derrol ambled up the steps and right past her. Since the plumbing company made cutbacks, living with her husband was more like living with some cranky relative twice removed.

"Randy got a new gig?"

Derrol frowned. "Not that I'm aware of. Why?"

"I looked under that tarp."

"What tarp?"

"The one covering those propane tanks."

"What business is it of yours what Randy hauls around in his truck?"

"In his truck?"

"That's what I said."

"So if you didn't know about the tarp, let alone what's *under* the tarp, how did you know those tanks were in the back of Randy's truck?"

Derrol claimed he must've inferred the fact from her tone of voice. When she kept pressing, he shrugged and suggested if she was so curious then she'd best go ask Randy about it herself. "Because," he added, "I have no idea."

Which was truer than he may have known. In the years since their marriage, Jennylee had slowly come to realize she was brighter than Derrol Witt. While he carried strong opinions, he couldn't seem to brain his way through life's problems. Like the time they fell behind on their mortgage. She'd handled the whole thing, despite its feeling like a husband's chore. Met with the officer at Community Federal, discussed variable interest and equity, and read through reams of convoluted legalese. With a little effort, she could probably talk the truth out of him about those propane tanks. Confuse him with questions, wear him out and piss him off and spill his vodka-soaked beans. But it'd be exhausting.

He lit another menthol and claimed he had to go see about some work.

"What sort of work?"

"The paying kind. Now enough with the questions."

"Sorry, but I've got one more—where's *your* truck?"

But he just shrugged and said don't worry about it. Randy was swinging back by in a few. When she asked if the truck had been repossessed, he mumbled something snide and stalked off to the bedroom. Dresser drawers groaned and then water ran in the bathroom. She tracked him down as he was spitting mouthwash into the sink, the cigarette still smoldering between the fingers of his left hand.

"Thought we agreed no more smoking indoors?"

"Last time, I promise."

"This work got anything to do with those tanks?"

He crammed the cigarette into the corner of his mouth and talked around it. "What's with you and them tanks?"

Then he wetted a comb and ran it through his hair. Derrol

Witt had a handsome head of shiny, dark brown hair—hair, Jennylee realized, that one day might silver up just like Maurice Currant's. The comparison turned her stomach, but she forced herself not to flinch when he nuzzled her neck. Feeling his stubbly cheek and smelling the ashy menthol, she realized she would never really tell him about the bad test-drive. Derrol didn't have much of a temper, but he had *some*. Last thing they needed was a fresh set of assault charges. Then his arms circled her waist and he started chewing on her earlobe. She'd missed his touch and the closeness felt nice, but surely he'd noticed she was sweaty and sour from her long walk. Then his hand cupped her ass and she understood: Derrol Witt was angling to smooth things over with a half-hearted mid-afternoon screw.

"Aw hell," he said, looking out the window, "here comes Chast's bus."

She untangled from him and re-buttoned her Wranglers. "So let me see if I've got this straight. Your truck got carted off by our creditors—today, this morning—while you were busy killing aliens with Randy?"

"The games ease my stress, okay?"

"You told me you'd called about the payments last week."

"What was I supposed to do—pull a gun on the repo man?"

Jennylee left the trailer, mindful of her blistered feet. At the exact moment the bus's STOP arm popped out, Derrol hollered from the door: "Why you home so early anyway?"

She swallowed her irritation and reminded herself to focus on their daughter. Today was the second-to-last day of school. Chastity hadn't seemed overly excited about her impending freedom, though, which was probably a good sign. Jennylee had begun dreading school clear back in fourth grade, counting the days until summer break, and this partly explained why she'd never given college a shot. Except as it turns out, college was the only way a person could *keep* enjoying summer breaks. There certainly weren't any vacations from Regent's.

Then Chastity clambered down the steps and came running, one pigtail undone and strands of hair pasted to her damp forehead. The day was plenty hot, but Jennylee worried that the sweat owed to a low-burning fever. Chastity gave her a big hug and squeezed with all her might.

"Why are you home so early, Mommy?"

But coming from her daughter, this question wasn't irritating at all. "I just couldn't wait to see my little pumpkin."

"You always say that, Mommy."

"That's because it's always true."

"Hey, where are your shoes?"

"Just thought it'd be nice to go barefoot for a change."

"Your toes are kinda red."

Jennylee glanced down—her toes were kind of red, and also kind of gnarled and blistered and mannish.

"I like to go barefoot too," Chastity said, and Jennylee couldn't help but look once again at their sun-beaten and cigarette-strewn yard.

Just before they reached the steps, Jennylee asked what the school cafeteria had served for lunch. But her daughter's expression told her that, whatever the food, hardly a bite had been eaten.

"Does your tummy hurt again?"

"A little."

"It's okay. We're gonna get you all fixed up."

Chast looked up at her. "Mommy?"

"Yes, sweetie?"

"You always say that too."

Then Derrol appeared in the doorway holding the phone. "It's Mr. Seasons from the dealership." Derrol covered the receiver with his palm. "He sounds funny. Pissed off or drunk or both."

5

That afternoon, Kent Seasons knocked off early and toured the countryside in his new Silverado while nursing a half-pint of Kentucky's finest.

The Silverado was a quality truck—especially when fully equipped with all the bells and whistles—but the more he drove it, the more it seemed GM was slipping. The Summit White paint job was sharp, and it handled well, but the interior was full of low-end plastics and visible molding lines. Couple of years ago, the Silverado was the undisputed category leader, but this year's model had lost ground to the Ford F-150.

But pondering the shortcomings of General Motors was just a convenient way of putting off thinking about Maurice Currant.

Shortly after the manager's meeting, Maurice had skated into the dealership with a cockamamie tale about Jennylee Witt asking to be dropped off at home midway through a test-drive. He also claimed she'd badmouthed Regent's, and Kent personally. *She called you Junior's little bitch,* was how he put it. *She says he's got your balls in his pocket.*

But Maurice's story was sketchy at best. First, the guy had married into the Good 'n' Crusty pie crust fortune and hadn't driven a used vehicle since he'd ducked the rice and spat out the cake. He operated a photography studio downtown, but that was just a hobby. By all accounts, Maurice Currant was loaded. Second, Jennylee was a lot of things—overly literal, scared of the phones, weird—but she was not a flake. The story only complicated after Kent called her at home.

"He tried to assault me," Jennylee whispered. "Actually, he really did assault me."

"Assault as in—"

"As in assault of the sexual variety."

"The *sexual* variety?"

"He felt me up and exposed his genitals, Kent. Right there in the Caprice."

After getting the rest of the sorry story and making sure Jennylee was more or less okay—"My feet are mighty blistered," she said, "but I'll live"—he'd promised to take care of everything, though what that actually entailed was unclear. That Maurice was a ladies' man was common knowledge among the country-club set, and that his wife, Gloria, remained seemingly unaware of her husband's transgressions in so small a community only went to show she really was as housebound and pill-addled as rumor had it. Still, Maurice may have been a cad and a shameless gold-digger, but a predator?

For a guy like Kent Seasons, who loved his wife dearly, the womanizing impulse was hard to grasp. Was it a desire for anonymous sex, or just plain old misogyny? Actually, most of the womanizers Kent had known—and the car game saw its fair share—hadn't outright despised women. No, those guys didn't seem to understand why they did anything at all. Like petty criminals, they tended to be dim. But Kent suspected Maurice Currant had a firmer grasp of his own motivations, and this was in no way a comfort.

Once sufficiently whiskied, Kent aimed the Silverado toward Country Club Lane.

Maurice answered the door and shook his hand as if they hadn't just spoken. He also shot meaningful glances over his shoulder at Gloria, who'd floated up from the couch on a cloud of Xanax to offer a cup of chamomile tea. But Maurice intervened. "No man in the history of time has ever wanted chamomile tea, sugarplum," he said, and then kissed her on the forehead before hustling Kent downstairs.

This wasn't his first excursion into Maurice's man cave though, as his father had dragged him down here a time or three. Jerry Seasons and Maurice had attended Paris High together, and Jerry still thought well of his classmate—even after Maurice married Gloria and immediately began using her family money to seduce other women. But Jerry liked to see the best in people. He was that sort of optimist. Didn't hurt that Jerry was a big basketball fan, and his old chum coached the junior high squad.

Maurice had spared no expense refinishing his digs. The plush furniture reeked of leather conditioner and above a tournament-quality pool table hung macho prints framed under glass (Chicago skyline at night; 1992's Barcelona Dream Team, hand-autographed by each athlete; dogs dealing poker and chomping cigars). A fridge with a brushed-nickel finish was stocked with nothing but cold Guinness and imported cheese and sausage, quality liquor bottles lined the glass-faced cabinetry, and a sixty-inch flat screen replayed that day's Cubs game. If not for Gloria, no doubt the patriotic NBA players and canine cardsharps would've shared wall space with *Playboy* centerfolds.

Maurice offered Kent a seat, then beer, scotch, pretzels, TV—ESPN? HBO? CNN?—and kept right on offering up acronyms until Kent interrupted.

"Why'd you do it, Maurice?"

"You were looking gimpy on the stairs. Trick knee?"

"Just tell me why."

Maurice smoothed his coiffed hair with his long, spidery fingers. "Pardon?"

"You just thought it'd be fun to screw with Regent's?"

"Kent, I don't—"

"To steam my berries?"

Maurice asked if he was feeling all right. If he'd like an aspirin—Tylenol? Advil? Tequila? Vicodin?

"What I'd like is for you to answer me. Why on earth would you do that?"

"I haven't the foggiest idea what you're referring to, Kent."

While Maurice was busy lying through his capped teeth, Kent ran a finger along the polished oak table between them. Not a speck of dust. Cleaning woman must've come that very morning. Knowing how things worked around Country Club Lane, there was little doubt this woman was undocumented, an individual not unlike the young lot attendant Regent's had recently hired. Somebody Señor Currant could work like a dog and pay like shit.

"I called Jennylee at home. She told me what happened."

"And what, pray tell, might that be?"

"The Caprice? Paradise Lake? What in God's bananas were you thinking?"

"She threw herself at me."

Kent drummed the tabletop.

"Oh, you find that hard to believe?"

"No, I find it totally impossible to believe."

"I'm an upstanding businessman," Maurice said. "As well as a coach with seven straight winning campaigns. My father-in-law founded the Paris area's single largest employer. And that girl, Jennylee, she's a *car salesman.*"

"So am I."

"Yeah, but you're management. That's different."

Then Kent reminded Maurice that those winning campaigns of his, not to mention most of his photography business, involved working with kids. It'd look mighty bad if word of to-day's little fiasco got out. "How many parents would send their daughters to you for senior pictures if they thought you might get a wild hair and pull your johnson out? How many dads want a predator coaching their sons?"

Maurice's eyes glassed over. Being called a predator had caught him off guard, which meant he didn't see himself that way—which in turn suggested he just might be a truly danger-ous individual.

"My kids love playing for me," he said. "Speaking of, have you seen the Meyers boy lately? He does not look like an eighth grader, Kent. He's six-foot-two. Got a dick on him like a Shet-land pony. We might have a shot at state this year if…"

Maurice had spread his hands, as if holding an invisible shoebox. Kent felt a headache coming on. The type that throbs in the tooth sockets.

"Look, you are not to harass my salespeople. In fact, you are not to show your face around my dealership ever again. Got it?"

"You talk like something bad happened, like I hurt the girl."

Kent Seasons prided himself on always having the right words, but what to say to this? Like something *bad* happened?

"Okay, Maurice. I get it. You're the Don Juan of Paris, Illinois. But you're making my life difficult. Capeesh?"

"You said yourself she's no good." Maurice crossed his long legs. "A few months back, right here. 'Horseshit for brains' was how you put it. Can her ass, Kent. Heck, I did you a favor."

Had he really said that about Jennylee? Must've been the booze talking. After a few belts, a truth came out that wasn't really the truth, just a depressed and angry shade of it. "You're suggesting I fire a salesperson because she wouldn't let you fuck her?"

Maurice smirked, as if imagining the Caprice rocking and steamy at the end of Lover's Lane. "Growing up," he said, "me and your dad chased split-tail all over town—"

"Leave Dad out of this. Or I'll tell him what happened."

That mealy grin faded.

"Don't you feel any shame, Maurice? I mean, Jennylee's young enough to—"

"To deep-throat a trailer hitch and swallow the chrome," he said. "Don't give me that crap. I'm not *old*. I liked 'em young when I was in school, liked 'em young when I was your age, and I still like 'em young today. Try and tell me you don't feel the exact same way, you self-righteous sonofabitch."

"I don't, actually," Kent said, which was true. Most days he just felt tired. Chasing young women was way back in the rearview. "I'm married. And I have a daughter to consider, a daughter I try to set a decent example for."

Maurice stroked his chin, as if reminded of a tempting idea, and Kent's hackles rose. He'd only mentioned Kelsi because he'd been thinking about her on the drive over. Surely she wasn't naïve enough to believe a middle-aged man like Dan Thompson could genuinely care for her—and surely Dan wouldn't take advantage of such innocence. Kent didn't know Dan Thompson well, but they'd known *of* each other for years. Done business with the same wholesalers, attended the same events. But as Maurice Currant proved, it could be difficult to see the wolf under the sheep's J. Crew pullover.

"How's Kelsi doing anyway?"

Kent took a breath and reminded himself to stay calm. Across the room beside the liquor cabinet hung a framed Michael Jordan print—again autographed. Jordan soared toward the rim with the basketball cupped like a grapefruit in one huge hand. A lewd pink tongue dangled from his mouth, licking the flashbulb-sprinkled air.

"Don't you sully my daughter's name."

"Christ, you talk like I took Kelsi parking, not that trailer trash princess you got hawking used Chevys."

"You had best know, Maurice, that I would take apart *anybody* who pulled that shit on my little girl."

"Then *you*, Kent, had best brush up on your tae kwon do"—Maurice ninja-chopped the air—"because Kelsi's an awfully pretty girl, but this world ain't always such a pretty place."

Kent closed his eyes and breathed, searching for calm. Strangely, he found himself remembering a fishing trip with his father down in the Keys. They'd caught more of a buzz than fish, but one fish Kent still recalled: a wahoo that'd swallowed the hook. The deckhand yanked and tore at its gullet, trying to save the hardware. The wahoo, dying, squirted a mess of white gunk all down the guy's forearm. "Instinct," the deckhand explained. "Once they sense their time's up, they'll fire that old jizzum anywhere."

A sentiment which could've been engraved on Maurice Currant's tombstone.

Over the phone, Kent had advised Jennylee to keep quiet. Told her he'd take care of Maurice and she should just focus on selling cars. Hard to say if she'd bought it, and harder still to tell if he'd managed to convince Maurice of the wrongness of his actions.

"What am I supposed to do when people catch wind of this?"

"Just lift up the old rug and sweep."

"A good sales manager takes care of his people. How you

think it looks when one of my employees gets molested and I don't do jack shit?"

"Slander me this, slander me that." Maurice glanced at the stairs. "Sure, I charmed the girl, but is that so wrong? Without guys like me, the human race would've died out long ago."

Charmed? Not quite. And without guys like Maurice (and Dan Thompson), guys like Kent Seasons wouldn't have to stay up nights worried sick about their daughters. Instead, they could just relax and have a drink and maybe even enjoy life for one rotten moment before the reaper came to close that last, long deal.

"You really put my nuts in a vise, Maurice. Junior's got this consultant coming. My plan was to get this guy to suggest Jennylee be let go, but now you've gone and made a victim of her."

"I'm surprised Bill Sr. would spring for a consultant," Maurice said, "with GM's pockets turned out and Obama ready to swoop in."

Last time his father dragged him down here, they'd discussed GM's troubles over a few beers. Maurice and Jerry both thought Detroit was the problem: autoworkers stacking up golden parachute UAW pensions despite clocking-in so drunk they bolted the wheels on backwards; blue-blood executives too busy yachting on Lake Michigan to notice shareholders hemorrhaging cash; and a board of directors that scoffed at any connection between seventies-era oil embargoes killing the gas-guzzler and the current oil wars, skyrocketing gas prices, and SUVs sitting unsold at dealerships all across the country. The Big Three were no more because American automakers got outsmarted by the Japanese and let unions protect the rights of lazy dickheads, all while insisting the bloody writing on the wall was actually General Motor's classic Torch Red paint.

But Kent believed GM's troubles—and thus America's troubles—ran deeper than that. People nowadays would spend fifty grand on some panzerwagen or some bento box glued together with sticky rice, not because foreign vehicles were any better, but simply because they *weren't* American. Progressivism had led to some good things, sure, but modern liberals wanted to

sodomize traditional values. And how better than by national-
izing General Motors? By collaring and neutering the company
that helped America and her allies win World War II, put fins
on a Cadillac, built the first moon rover, and gave the Beach
Boys something worth singing about.

"If the feds get controlling stock," Kent said, "Old Bill
swears he'll close the dealership. Says Obama ain't gonna tell
him how to sell Chevrolets."

"Think he's serious?"

"Serious? Him and Junior truly believe the nineties are coming back any day now and gasoline will be cheaper than bottled
water again. But they're not optimists, they're ostriches."

Maurice nodded encouragingly, as if hanging on his every
word, and Kent realized he'd been baited. "We gotta straighten
this thing out, Maurice. It's a real problem."

"If anyone can understand the automotive industry, it's
you—"

"I meant the thing with Jennylee."

"Oh."

"Oh?"

"I have to be honest," Maurice said, again smoothing his
snowy hair.

"Yeah, let's try that for once."

"I think she was into me."

In the moments to follow, Kent seriously considered flipping over the table. It was a heavy table and he was hobbled,
but he could probably do it. Instead, he heel-walked over to
the liquor cabinet and popped the cork off a fresh bottle of
Woodford Reserve. He took a deep swig of the sweet corn and
rye. Heat bloomed in his chest.

"Young women appreciate distinguished looks," Maurice
said. "My philosophy: just leave her better than you found her."

Another swig, more heat. "Ever consider you might be a bad
person, Maurice?"

"Now that right there is the difference between us." Maurice
lifted his chamois-soft palms heavenward. "Why you sell cars

with a bunch of inbreds and live a life of monogamous misery, while I embrace the finer things."

"Because I don't assault women?"

"No, because you truly believe there's a big scoreboard somewhere up in the clouds. Your dad knows better. That's why he sold out to a sneaky dog like Bill Regent, despite suspecting you'd get the shaft."

"It was his health," Kent said, "his heart…"

"Blood's thicker than water, but not as thick as dough."

Kent held up the Woodford bottle like a talisman. Maurice's devilish face swirled amber through the depths. Kent licked his dry lips. "I need to go home now."

"What you really need to do is to snatch a little happiness before what's left of that red hair washes down the shower drain."

The bottle grew heavy in his hand and sank. He stared at Maurice while pondering his life: his marriage was limping on three cylinders (he'd forgotten their anniversary recently, and Linda kindly ignored his birthday) and his daughter had been compromised by a man Kent himself had handed her over to; and every morning that he walked into Regent's and flicked on the lights marked a colossal struggle not to dive headfirst straight down to bottle's bottom. On his worst days, he felt already dead.

"I'm taking this bottle, Maurice."

"Hey now. That's primo stuff."

"Double-dog dare you to try and stop me."

After gimping back upstairs, Kent climbed into the Silverado and pressed the Woodford to his lips. His heartbeat pulsed in his thumb and his thumb was pressed to the bottle's neck: potent reverberations traveling from the very core of him into the darkly rippling liquid—but then came a feisty knocking at the window.

Maurice again, standing there grinning. Kent reluctantly lowered the bottle and even more reluctantly lowered the glass. "Told you I'm keeping this bourbon."

Maurice looked the Silverado over. "Whatever possessed

you to buy a white truck with white trim? Every bit of dirt will show."

"Some of us get into less dirt than others."

"You asked me—kept asking me—why I did it."

"Because you kept lying."

"Would you really like to know?"

Now Kent wasn't so sure, actually.

"Imagine this," Maurice said, having rested his elbows on the door and leaned his face into the cab. "I wake up in the morning—not to an alarm, mind you, but of my body's own accord—and after an hour of calisthenics and yoga, I fix myself a perfect three-egg omelette and a bowl of steel-cut oats. Then, as I'm enjoying this nutritious breakfast, it dawns on me that it might be fun to test-drive some little two-cent gash of poontang. And so I head down to my friendly local auto dealership, where it seems a man might take his desires for a quick spin."

"Step away from my truck, you degenerate."

"In short," Maurice said, "I pluck the nectarine and suckle the juice."

"Something wrong with your ears? I said step away from my truck."

Instead, Maurice Currant extended a pinkie and finessed a remnant of dinner from his canines. After studying this particle, he rolled it into a ball and flicked it on the Silverado's dashboard. "That, my not-so-young friend, is *why.*"

6

Goodnight, Billy," Paul called down the hallway. Like always, though, Billy was too busy web-surfing and drinking chocolate milk to answer. The guy was weird like that, childish in his habits.

Paul would've said goodnight to Kent as well, but he'd left early. Just limped out the door without a word and fired up that big white Silverado. In the past, Paul had made a point of popping his head into the sales manager's office come quitting time, but no longer—not since he'd caught Kent taking a slug of Jim Beam. Whiskey explained the constant breath mints, and also foretold what awaited the man who spent his life selling cars.

Out in the parking lot, he keyed open his Toyota Camry. Early on at Regent's, ownership had balked at his driving a foreign car, but they lost interest after realizing he couldn't be shamed into a trade. Heat plumed from the cab, stale from the basketball sneakers unlaced and breathing on the passenger seat. His guitar was in the back as well, draped in old gym clothes. The Camry was a gift from his parents for college graduation. The sedan hadn't seen a washing or waxing in months though. In fact, his mother had recently commented on its neglected appearance. Irritated, Paul had pointed out that graduation was a long time ago, which stopped the conversation cold.

His mother just couldn't understand the patience that musicianship entailed. Music was a calling, and callings demand a raw surrender of time. Hanging around other talented musicians at Millikin University, Paul had quickly realized he was no instrumentalist or composer, but he'd also discovered he could write lyrics. In fact, he'd known he could write a great song before he'd even written a passably decent one. And in this way, he began thinking of himself as a songwriter.

He'd pondered moving after college—Los Angeles, New

York, Austin. It was the usual fantasy. Living hand-to-mouth. Penning lyrics on street corners and playing open mics at coffeehouses. He pictured a gaunter, longer-haired version of himself onstage—dusty boards creaking underfoot, a glass of burgundy on a wobbly pub table—performing originals for an audience of strangers, when one of them (usually an exotic woman with a gauzy scarf twined around her throat, but sometimes an older man, all salt-and-pepper mensch) pulled him aside to say he'd been discovered.

Throughout his mid-twenties, he'd traveled the country working seasonally, including a stint in Zion National Park where he waited tables, covered Top 40 around the campfire, and fell for a trail-running waitress from coastal Maine with a butt firm as a coconut. He played some of his originals for her and she'd liked one in particular—"Endless Blue"—which was about the ocean and sadness. It being a summer romance, however, their plans to move to Kennebunkport together at season's end fizzled.

For years he'd indulged this bohemian lifestyle. Periodically, he'd sock away cash for his big move, but then the Camry would need repairs, or he'd sicken of waiting tables and float on his savings. All the while, one after another, friends and roommates became claims adjusters or financial advisors or died some other slow death, and yet Paul clung to his dreams: he kept his guitar tuned, kept the water glasses topped and the bread baskets filled. But waiting tables had never really bothered him, or at least not enough to necessitate a change, because it'd been a literal waiting: a prelude to his real life.

Now Paul was squirreling away money once again. His thirtieth birthday was coming up and he had no intention of passing that milestone in Paris. While he'd never actually been to Nashville and didn't know anyone there, let alone anyone in the music industry, if he wanted to be a real songwriter—a *known* one—it was now or never.

He cranked the Camry's air-conditioner, which reminded him of using the Blazer's A/C to disguise its stench, which in turn reminded him of the situation with Jennylee Witt. Her car, a gaudy gold Nissan she'd purchased her very first day at Regent's, still sat in the employee row. Rumor had it she'd gotten bent over the finance desk by Kent Seasons and Billy Regent Jr. A sad tale, but her latest up must've been promising to stay this late. Maybe she'd accompanied the buyer to his local credit union?

The workday was done, though, which meant he no longer had to worry about ups or test-drives or sniped deals. No, now it was time to hoop, as the local YMCA ran a 3-on-3 league composed largely of Paris area dealerships. Paul looked forward to playing, so much so that lately he'd even been practicing solo. Bank shots and threes from the wing. Baseline turnarounds and dribbling drills.

Then he put on *The Late Great Townes Van Zandt* and reversed from the parking stall, only to see one of his teammates—Lloyd Rivera, the new lot attendant—locking and blocking the exits. Upon spying the Camry, Lloyd grabbed a tall orange parking cone and started ramming it with his pelvis in a pornographic frenzy. His tongue flicked the warm evening air and he cranked his right arm in an outrageous rodeo circle.

But Lloyd came by this vulgarity honestly. In fact, he'd learned it from Chadwick and Paul himself, as the truth of closing car deals was oftentimes difficult to convey without at least some simulation of sexual intercourse.

"See you at the Y, *pendejo!*" Paul shouted out the window.

"*Pinche* Paulino!" Lloyd said, and spanked the cone's rubber ass.

Laughing, Paul flipped his blinker and pulled out. But as he navigated the river of brake lights, his mood turned ruminative. After Zion, he'd found himself back in Illinois, first couch-surfing around Chicago and then in his old college town (a brief and humiliating detour), before he finally swallowed his pride and returned to Paris. The plan was to live at home for a few months and bolster his savings. His parents seemed happy to have him, and he soon picked up shifts at a local steakhouse. The money wasn't great, as Parisites didn't appreciate the fine art of tipping any more than songwriting, but he wasn't paying rent. Smooth enough sailing, until the night he served a table of businessmen, one of whom suggested he just might make a fine car salesman.

"Thanks," Paul had said, laughing, "but I'll stick to selling steaks and wine."

The man gave him a cold blue stare that seemed to drain the clatter and hubbub from the dining room. "I'm dead serious, Paul."

Funny, but he couldn't recall having given his name. That wasn't something he typically did. He hadn't been wearing a nametag either. Later, he found a business card tucked in the checkbook.

Kent Seasons: Sales Manager
Regent's American Dream Motors
New and Pre-owned Vehicles at No-Haggle, No-Hassle Prices

Selling cars? He'd scoffed, but he'd also felt flattered—appreciated, recruited—and in the weeks to come each time a table stiffed him or some recidivist cook cussed him out, he remembered that business card. The day he finally visited Regent's, Kent draped an arm around his shoulders and steered him straight back into the sales manager's office. Filling out his W-9, Paul promised himself he'd sell cars for only a few months, just long enough to build a nest egg...

But that was almost three years ago.

It'd be pushing 6:30 by the time he reached the gym, leaving an hour to lift and warm up. Their squad consisted of him and Chadwick, Lloyd, and sometimes Tom Partlow. All in all, they weren't bad. Chadwick and Tom were rugged defenders, and Lloyd Rivera was quick-footed and full of machismo, having grown up playing fútbol in the dust of Matamoros. Humility aside, though, Paul was their ace. He'd been a solid player at Paris High (second-team all-area senior year), a streaky shooter and deft passer with a slick rocker-step move. He'd even toyed with walking-on at Millikin, but the long practices would've interfered with his music.

Townes was finishing "Pancho and Lefty" just as Paul

reached the YMCA's parking lot. Humming along with that last sad refrain, he fished around in the cooler he kept in the back seat and then wolfed down an orange and a Ziploc of hard-boiled egg whites. Had to watch the diet these days. A year prior, he'd glimpsed himself nude in a full-length mirror only to see a shaven monkey with puffy nipples and a protuberant gut. Thereafter, he'd added weights to his routine and began smoking marijuana in lieu of drinking quite so much beer. This new lifestyle required discipline, but his motivation sat feisty and blonde behind the Y's check-in desk.

Motivation's nametag read: Annie Turner.

Then Paul took a black moleskin journal from the console and recorded the calories and protein grams he'd just consumed. The book contained a detailed dietary history, as well as his bench-press, squat, and pull-ups numbers. It hadn't started out that way though. The journal was originally for songwriting, for lyrics and chord progressions. But it was nearly full now. For the umpteenth time, he reminded himself that he'd have to buy another one.

Gym clothes and journal in hand, Paul entered the YMCA. As always, the building reeked of chlorine, which reminded him of that morning's daydream in the Pontiac Vibe: Annie's long blonde hair in a lovely swirl atop the chemical blue water.

"What's up, buttercup?" he said.

Months before, he'd mentioned Annie's resemblance to that wholesome-but-sexy actress from *The Princess Bride*, which had caused her to blush deeply. Paul had never been a particularly successful flirt. He didn't have any sisters, so girls scared him a little. While Annie logged in his membership number, he recalled a Kent Seasons-ism: *If you can pick up a date in a bar, you can sell a car.* The same principles applied—establishing rapport and overcoming objections, building desire and obligation, and of course the trickiest part: closing.

"So are you still playing the Buck on Thursday?" Annie asked. "My cousin says you haven't been returning his calls."

"He called me? My phone must be screwed up again."

"Well, get your phone fixed. He needs to know one way or the other."

Upon first meeting Annie, he'd casually mentioned his music. He hadn't thought she was paying attention, but last month she surprised him by saying a cousin who managed a local honky-tonk called The Gunning Buck wanted to bring on a musician. Paul was lukewarm about the idea, and his Nashville plans had been percolating even then, but nevertheless he'd found himself telling Annie sure, great, he'd love to play the Buck. Now her cousin kept leaving annoying voicemails. The acoustic show was scheduled for that coming Thursday night.

"Tell your cousin I'm looking forward to it."

"Why don't you call him back and tell him yourself?"

"You're coming, right? I've been trying to work on some originals."

Trying being the key word. But he'd need some fresh material for Nashville. That, and it'd be nice to impress Annie Turner.

"Eh, the Buck's not really my scene."

That objection stung, but he had the presence of mind to smile right through it. "Got the 3-on-3 schedule back there?"

She glanced at the schedule and said the Honda guys had canceled.

"They canceled? So we're not playing?"

"Don't start crying yet," Annie said. "Sanders Toyota canceled too. They were supposed to play Thompson's."

"Wait, you mean we're playing Thompson's Ford—tonight?"

Thompson's had nipped them by a bucket in last year's championship game, a fundraiser held during the Paris Crust Fest, which—like the Blowout Sale—took place over Memorial Day weekend. This season, Team Regent's and Team Thompson's again had the best records in the round-robin, so a rematch loomed. Playing Thompson's tonight would be more than just a tune-up though. It would set the tone.

"Oh my goodness," Annie said. "Everybody hold their breath. The middle-aged car salesmen are playing bush-league basketball again…"

Her sarcasm was nothing new, but that one word echoed: *middle-aged?*

The year before, Annie had been engaged to a salesman from Thompson's named Seth who fake-bake tanned and wore his hair slicked back like Pat Riley. But they'd apparently been happy together—right up until Annie's pee started to burn. According to Chadwick, who'd graduated with the guy from nearby Marshall High School, Seth had always been a dog. To make matters worse, he'd hit the winning jumper in the previous year's championship. In fact, Seth had looked Paul dead in the eye and shouted *"Game over!"* right before he launched that final shot.

Lloyd and Chadwick ambled in while Paul was ruminating. Lloyd was still dressed in his garage blues. Fierce as a mongoose on the court, he was the heart and soul of Team Regent's—but only about five-foot-six in his Nikes. Chadwick towered over him, although that was partly due to his penchant for cowboy boots.

"It's too bad you can't hoop in those shit-kickers," Paul said. "Tom's out tonight and we could use some extra height."

Thompson's Ford fielded a six-foot-seven and disturbingly humorless ringer who'd played second-string power forward at Eastern Illinois University. Rumor had it Dan Thompson hired the bruiser solely for his mean elbows.

"We'd have plenty of height if you didn't spend so much time pussyfooting around the three-point line," Chadwick said.

"Yeah, well, you'd best get ready, because we're playing Thompson's."

"You're shitting me?"

"Nope."

"Man, I knew I should've skipped the pizza at lunch."

"You should've skipped the pizza your last three hundred lunches," Paul said, and poked a finger into the soft belly lapping over Chadwick's western-style belt.

"Whatever." Now Chadwick pointed at Paul's journal. "Not all of us can spend our time writing poetic odes to tofu and bean sprouts."

"Those Thompson's *jotos* think they rock stars," Lloyd Rivera said, "but we gonna bend them over."

Hearing this, Annie Turner scowled at Paul as if to say, *That's your fault, buddy.*

But Paul secretly loved how Lloyd joined in the dealership banter—and despite halting English, he'd quickly mastered the finer nuances. In fairness to Annie, though, car lot repartee was something of an acquired taste. When he'd first started at Regent's, the constant and lowbrow badinage had seemed crude, unnecessary, and wholly tasteless. But it actually wasn't, not entirely. After all, a salesman had to depersonalize buyers somehow. Otherwise, he'll pity them and take his foot off their neck.

Paul slapped Lloyd on the back and said he was exactly right; Team Thompson's was about to get bent over and spanked. "Talk to you later, Annie," he added.

While they headed for the lockers, Lloyd pointed out that Annie hadn't said anything back.

"She must not have heard me."

"Oh no, Paulino. She hear you. She hear you real good."

Having changed into his shorts and sneakers, Paul hit the weight room. He plugged earbuds into his iPod and clipped the device to his shorts. A friend had mentioned a new artist, some Rust Belt hotshot all the reviewers were calling the next Woody Guthrie. But Paul didn't even make it through the second track. Too much soapbox politics, too little storytelling. This guy was no Woody Guthrie. He wasn't deep because he'd happened to notice the steel mills closed, and having slept in his truck a few times did not make him Tom Joad. He must've known the right people, had an in.

After cranking up The Misfits and loading up the bench with a buck-eighty-five, Paul hammered out a good, slow set, feeling his shoulders and triceps swell. After powering through one last rep, he racked the bar and sat up. Feeling strong and ready, he licked the tip of his pencil and recorded his latest reps and poundage in the journal. Then he snuck a peek into the lobby.

No luck though. Buttercup had her back turned, folding towels.

7

Home finally, Kent Seasons limped through the front door only to find his wife tidying up in the kitchen. Aiming for casual, he thumbed through the mail on the hall table. Bills, more bills, a coupon flyer (for where else but the Lotus Parlor), and a quarterly breakdown of Kelsi's college savings account.

Linda approached him with a smile. "Stop at the Buck on your way home?"

"Something like that."

She'd let her hair grow out recently, and was that a hint of perfume? The house looked great too. Carpets vacuumed. Countertop sparkling beneath a bouquet of blood-orange marigolds. Linda had been busy tidying up while Kent was stuck down in Maurice's sleazy basement, arguing about Jenny-lee Witt. What different nights they'd had. What different lives they were living. What a shame he hadn't come straight home.

"Did you finally have that talk with Brad? You said it might take a few beers."

He'd confessed his concerns to Linda, but even while joking about it ("Brad's itching for my desk, babe, but I'm still the man") he'd felt old, had seen in his wife's eyes that he *was* getting old. But Brad Howard was the least of his concerns.

"Why isn't Kelsi home? It's..." Kent glanced at his watch and realized his first drink had come nearly eleven hours ago. "I don't like not knowing who she's with."

This all sounded like reasonable dad talk, didn't it? Not too domineering or bossy. Around Regent's, his role was clear: he was the closer, the bad cop, the last pencil. But lately it'd been harder to check those instincts at the door, almost as if the more things spun out of control on the lot, the greater his need to control his home.

"You look exhausted," Linda said.

"Kelsi may act grown up, but she's still just a kid."

"How long were you at the Buck anyway?"

"And kids really oughta be home before midnight. Is that too much to ask?"

He slumped in a kitchen chair and rubbed his temples. After leaving Country Club Lane, he'd driven around collecting his thoughts and sipping from Maurice's bottle. This meant he'd recorded, conservatively, at least three solid hours of drinking and driving—and it was only Monday. But most guys Kent knew drank beer in their trucks. Hell, the local cops didn't even seem to mind, so long as you kept the cans out of sight. Bourbon wasn't Bud Light though. He needed to be careful, but how could a man sober up with the likes of Maurice Currant in his life? He considered telling Linda what the creep had pulled on Jennylee, then thought better of it.

"Kent, are you okay?"

"Manager's meeting this afternoon. You know how those go."

His act was wearing thin. He could feel it. A few drinks took the edge off work—made the day feel like it was on rails, as if a judicious regimen of whiskey might carry him through work and dinner and deliver him peacefully unto bed—but those same drinks also took the edge off *him*. Linda kneaded his shoulders and the day's tension broke and leaked down his back.

Her lips brushed his ear. "Are you having an affair?"

He snorted. What sort of affair would involve getting this sozzled? No, if anything illicit was going on around the Seasons household, Kent was not the culprit.

"Seriously, where is our daughter?"

"That's your answer?" Her thumbs laddered up into his hairline.

"She never answers her phone anymore, and that gizmo is sewn into the palm of her hand."

"You better get used to this. She's off to college in three months."

If only their daughter were at the University of Illinois already, meeting kids her own age and taking classes. Not being sucked down into a world any decent father would've shielded her from. God forgive him, though, he'd actually *helped* Kelsi get hired at Thompson's. Figured a little dose of reality might do her some good, but he'd forgotten—perhaps willfully—how teenaged girls were often seen as the juiciest commissions of all.

"I'm just worried about her. She won't talk to me."

"Did something happen?"

"It's like I'm a pariah around here."

His wife pulled out a chair and faced him. Any fool could see that Linda Seasons would be a beautiful older woman. Ten years down the road, she'd look like some well-preserved aunt of Kelsi's, while Kent himself would be bald as a troll and whiskey fat. For years after marrying, he'd wondered if he'd low-balled his own value on the dating market. After all, in negotiations neither party should ever accept the first offer—not even if it's an attractive one—because they'll just end up wondering if they could've held out for better. Linda Sue Handley had been a Paris High cheerleader, the cutie who worked the Dairy Queen drive-thru, the chick a few lockers down. They'd dated some, but never exclusively. After graduation, though, a seriousness crept in, a sense of being pushed together by time and circumstance.

But now Kent had no reservations. In fact, his wife was almost certainly too good for him—or at least too good for Kent 2.0, the bourbon-slugging, Certs-chomping sales manager of the goofiest dealership this side of Pyongyang Motors.

"Does she date anybody, Linda?"

"There was the radiologist's son. Remember him?"

"Haven't seen that kid around here in months."

"Kelsi says he isn't cool, and we both know a girl's boyfriend has to be *cool.*" Linda took his hand. "Why do you think I picked you, stud?"

"You probably thought I'd be rich someday. Own my own dealership, like Dad."

"Is that what this is about? Kent, you *are* a success. We own a home, our debt's paid down. And we raised a daughter who knows right from wrong—"

Kent gently freed his hand and stood, again hiding the pain in his foot. His head throbbed too, although he was used to that. Out of respect for Linda, he'd left Maurice's bourbon in the truck. What excuse could he possibly make to go back outside now?

He'd quit smoking for solidarity's sake after his father's coronary. Growing up around the lot, all the salesmen enjoyed cigarettes. Rain or shine, they stood outside the showroom and lit smokes and cracked jokes and all of it had felt just right. But as Linda was fond of reminding him, a person had to be suicidal to smoke nowadays. That wasn't entirely true though. After all, Jerry Seasons had his chest cracked open like a Maine lobster, and yet he never said one ill word about cigarettes, as he understood that a smoke afforded a man time and space to gather his thoughts—a rare and private luxury.

Besides Team Regent's and Team Thompson's—and one elderly woman walking the elevated track, her fists pumping high above her heart—the gym was empty. Paul Stenger stretched his sore hamstring, knotted his laces, and scoped out the competition.

Seth was doing his usual thing, spinning the basketball on his finger and cracking jokes on everybody. The legs that poked from his gym shorts were slender—especially compared with his bulky chest and shoulders—and also weirdly smooth, as if he shaved them. Then Seth passed the ball to Dan Thompson, who promptly bricked a jumper. Dan was a terrible player, but spry for his age. Thick gray hair contrasted with a jet-black goatee and, despite a spare tire, he was solidly built. A guy who clearly still enjoyed working out, but enjoyed his evening beers just as much.

"Dan's looking sharp tonight," Paul said in the huddle. "I'd better start on him." Then he asked Chadwick if he could handle the buzz cut and violent-looking six-foot-seven ringer.

Chadwick just shook his head. "You are one chickenshit sonofabitch, Paul."

Lloyd strutted over to the bleachers, kissed the crucifix he wore, and stripped off his garage blues. Soccer shorts hung below his knees, the shiny fabric dyed the guacamole colors of the Mexican flag. Lloyd's pregame routine was like a boxer sluffing off his robe. Just needed some mariachi music to pipe through the speakers.

After Thompson's won the shootout, Seth checked the ball to Lloyd, who immediately unleashed an incendiary string of Spanglish trash-talk. But Dan Thompson was more low key. He clapped Paul's shoulder. "Good seeing you again, Paul."

Paul returned the greeting, but then wondered why he felt so pleased by this man's remembering his name. And why was he considering letting Dan drive the lane once or twice, early on when it didn't matter so much?

"How's business, Dan?"

"We're keeping our headlights above water. Sorry to say it, but the bad press y'all are getting from this bailout deal has boosted our sales. Customers tell me how much they appreciate Ford hauling herself up by the bootstraps."

The ball swung their way and, after dribbling around aimlessly and squeaking his shoes, Dan threw a sloppy bounce pass meant for the ringer which Lloyd Rivera promptly swiped. Paul sprinted to the elbow and caught the rock. He pivoted and faced Dan Thompson in textbook triple-threat position— shoot, pass, or dribble—a fundamental which separated good players from the mediocre, similar to how understanding all facets of a buyer's budget was key to building a deal. Because a salesman can't sell a car the bank won't finance, the trick was to get buyers excited not about the vehicle they wanted, but the one they deserved.

"How's Kent lately?" Dan was already huffing and puffing. "His little girl works for me now, you know?"

Paul jab-stepped and a rubbery screech echoed around the gym. "Surprised Kent lets her work for the enemy."

"Me too. But Kelsi's one sharp young lady"—Dan pawed at the ball, slow as a bear—"good with customers, friendly. And cute as a button."

Paul could've easily gotten a clean jumper, but he passed to Chadwick instead. Unfortunately, Chadwick telegraphed his every move. Worse, the guy guarding him was seven inches taller and loved nothing more than to humiliate other men. Chadwick let out a little whoop of victory when the ball left his fingertips, but he was just dreaming; the ringer's eyes widened as he leaped and swatted away the layup.

At some point, Annie had materialized beside the bleachers.

"Switch!" Paul yelled, and faced off with Seth.

But Seth recognized Thompson's advantage. He made eye contact with the ringer and then raised his free hand and twirled one finger at the ceiling.

Chadwick realized a bit too late that he'd been singled out on the play, and when the ringer simultaneously spun toward the basket and yelled "Oop!" Chadwick dutifully gave chase and tried to hold his ground. But his pizza belly wasn't enough leverage to make up for the difference in height and athleticism, and the bigger man leaped over and through him. As Chadwick groaned and toppled to the floor, the ringer caught the ally-oop pass from Seth and mashed down a two-handed dunk that rattled the cables securing backboard to wall.

Annie tooted a whistle and walked onto the court. She scooped up the ball, tucked it against her bluejeaned hip, and declared the basket didn't count.

"What's up with the chick ref?" the ringer said.

"Can't you read?" She pointed up at the big sticker atop the backboard: NO DUNKING! NO HANGING ON THE RIM!

"Take it easy," Seth said, and reached for the ball.

She stepped backward and out of reach. "These rims aren't breakaway. Hanging on them is dangerous." Now she raised and twirled her own finger. "Oop! *Oop!* You guys and your stupid *oops* are gonna break our equipment and ruin it for everyone. You know that, Seth. And Dunkenstein"—now she pointed at the ringer—"knows it too."

"We're just playing a hard, clean game," Seth said.

"Yeah, well, your hard, clean game is going to get you disqualified."

Dan Thompson slid between them, palms up, and assured her they all understood the rules. "Crystal clear, young lady," he said. "And thank you for the clarification."

She dropped the ball and walked away, her hips swinging back and forth much as a cat's tail betrays its irritation. Watching her go, Paul tried to conjure up a quick lyric that might do the sight justice. In fact, his lingering distraction gifted Seth with a bunny layup on the very next possession.

Twenty sweaty minutes later, though, the score was 12-9, Regent's. One more basket and they'd beat Thompson's Ford. Sure, the championship game wasn't until Saturday, but when Paul faced Seth for the game winner he wanted to prove a point, to make clear that things had changed since last season. Annie had come and gone, but now she was back, sitting on the bleachers and sipping bottled water.

"That Annie's really something, isn't she?" Seth whispered.

Paul faked a jumper—really sold the move: eyes on the rim, feet and elbow in perfect shooting form. But Seth didn't bite. He had more to say, apparently.

"You can forget about her. Chicks like Annie don't go for Mr. Nice Guy types."

Paul dribbled between his legs, once, twice, then feinted left. Seth didn't budge. Suddenly Paul began to feel a little clumsy, a little unsure, but he kept his dribble.

"Oh, I see you mooning over her." Now Seth hand-checked him off balance. "Most guys figure this shit out by your age. What are you, thirty?"

He passed to Lloyd and drifted toward the baseline. "Twenty-eight," he said.

The lie just slipped out, like air from an old basketball.

Then Seth suggested that if Paul really wanted to date Annie, he should treat her like a waitress, pinch her ass, let her know who was boss. In response, Paul jabbed an elbow into Seth's sternum and once again called for the ball. "Yeah, I heard you two shared something really special," he said, and dug the elbow in deeper. "But I don't actually *have* gonorrhea."

Seth's voice lowered. "That's just a rumor."

"Is it?"

"And you'd best not go around repeating it."

"Or what?"

"Just remember I warned you," Seth said.

Across the court, Lloyd dribbled rapid-fire, leather pounding the hardwood, while down in the paint Dunkenstein had Chadwick in a brutal headlock, as if they'd ceased playing basketball and commenced to professionally wrestle. Chadwick clung to the giant man's waist, eyes rolling in his skull and his forehead popping with veins.

"You're awfully sensitive," Paul said. "Suspiciously sensitive, I'd say."

"Dating a girl is like devaluing a trade-in," Seth said. "First step's to point out a flaw or two."

After catching the pass, Paul pivoted and dragged the leather through Seth's wheelhouse, tempting him to go for a steal. Normally, you wanted to keep the ball low and out of reach, whisking it across an opponent's shoelaces, but Paul's intention here was different. He meant to draw Seth in closer, as he was timing a move he'd so far kept in his back pocket. He'd actually been saving this move for the championship game—for game point, in fact, if the basketball gods saw fit—but oh well.

"Gotta bring her down to earth," Seth whispered, "or she'll walk all over you."

"If you're so smart, how come you lost her?"

"At least I had her, asshole—"

Then Paul snapped the basketball up into Seth's nose. From a distance, it could've been mistaken for a shot fake. The idea was to just graze the opponent's face and get him blinking long enough to go around him, but Paul had grazed a little too hard. Seth cussed and backpedaled, hands covering his nose and mouth.

Path to the basket suddenly clear, Paul took two hard dribbles and leaped. As he floated toward the hoop, he sensed Annie watching, seeing each and every detail of how he'd bested her ex mano-a-mano—but then Dunkenstein rumbled across the lane and trucked him.

His trajectory broken, gravity reasserting itself, Paul tumbled and struck the court with a meaty slap. The impact knocked the breath from his lungs and the basketball squirted off toward the bleachers. Sprawled there with his eyes closed and his teeth clenched, the tip of his nose dripping sweat on the hardwood, he could think of nothing except how much it hurt—a bone-deep aching. He'd taken spills on the court before, but nothing like this. A cracked rib? Ruptured spleen? After much groaning and cursing, he finally managed to roll onto his back, whereupon he opened his eyes to find Chadwick and Lloyd silhouetted like angels against the gymnasium's pearly lights. Far above, paused on her circuit around the track, was the elderly power-walker. She looked spooked. Paul touched his chin and then dabbed his tongue, tasting pennies.

"*Dios mio*, Paulino," Lloyd said, fists tugging on the hem of his soccer shorts.

"If I was you, Paul," Chadwick said, "I'd get up and slug that big, mean prick right in the kisser. Hell, I'd do it myself, but the wife's too young for widowhood."

Dan Thompson knelt and patted Paul's belly. "You okay, son? Gosh, that was a hard fall. Your head didn't smack the court, did it?"

"I think I'm okay," Paul said.

With Lloyd's help, he limped over to the bleachers. The game was called. On the bright side, Seth seemed fairly certain his bloody nose was no accident. He stared hard, as if about to start something, but Paul just ignored him and sat down beside Annie.

"Shake it off, Paul," she said, and then stood and walked away.

"You worry about broken backboards, but not broken bones?"

She paused just long enough to remind him he'd signed an injury waiver, which included a clause about big boys not crying when they fell down and scraped their knee.

"Talk nice to this man, Annie," Lloyd Rivera said. He yanked his shirt down to expose his breast. "He play *con corazón.*"

"No, *you* played *con corazón,* Lloyd." And, as she pushed through the gym's swinging doors, "All Paul did was embarrass himself."

"Why would she say that?" Paul dabbed at his chin once more. "I didn't *embarrass* myself."

"Poor Paulino," Lloyd said, and patted his leg. "De world is no his friend."

After they'd all toweled off and headed for the parking lot, Chadwick fired up his big truck. He leaned out the window and shouted over the rumbling engine. "Hey, Paul—karma's a bitch, ain't it?"

"What?"

"Cosmic justice for sniping deals, amigo!"

Laughing, Chadwick thundered off, all eight cylinders blatting in the muggy Paris night. Leaning on Lloyd's shoulder, Paul headed for the Camry. He carried his gym bag and journal. He'd forgotten to tie the ribbons closed while playing ball and wondered if Annie might've snuck a peek.

Then, out of the blue, Lloyd asked if Paul would sell him a car. He needed a car, and Paulino sold cars, so maybe his friend could help him out?

The question caught Paul off guard. Lloyd lived with family, so rent was shared, but he still couldn't have much saved on minimum wage. And hadn't Tom Partlow mentioned something about Lloyd sending money home—a sick mother in Mexico?

"Cars don't burn gas, Lloyd. They burn cash. And you'd have to carry full-coverage insurance, which is almost as expensive as the payments themselves."

"But I *need* a car."

"You'll end up working more just to pay to drive to work."

Lloyd pulled the rubber band from his ponytail and his hair curtained around his cheekbones. He looked startlingly young.

Then he explained that his primo and his hermanos had recently gotten hired at the new turkey-processing plant across town. "Killing turkeys pay good," he said, "but they got to get there."

"Then why don't they buy their own car?"

"Six people live in my home," Lloyd said. "My wife, she threaten to leave."

"You're married, Lloyd? You never told me that."

"You never ask, Paulino."

This left a strangeness in the air where Paul felt he should've said something personal, but instead he found himself promising to keep an eye on the trade-ins.

Lloyd thanked him and said he was a fine man for a gringo. "And la senorita blondie," Lloyd added, jogging backward into the darkness, "she like you very much."

They'd never spoken of Annie though. In fact, with the inglorious exception of Seth, he'd never spoken of her to anyone. Maybe his crush really was obvious? Bad news if so, as the surest way to lose a girl's interest was to show your own. Before Lloyd was out of earshot, Paul asked why he was so certain Annie liked him.

Lloyd passed under a streetlamp, the yellow cone boiling with insects. The night swallowed him and his disembodied voice piped down the street: "Never believe a woman's mean talk, Paulino. Words no mean nothing…"

Kent claimed he'd left some paperwork out in the Silverado.

As always, he'd parked at driveway's end. No conscious decision in this, but he realized—as he once again uncorked Maurice's Woodford—that he'd begun parking this way only after Kelsi got her license. The morning of her sixteenth birthday, he'd purchased her a vehicle, a Chevy Impala (she called it a "grandpa car," but safety over style), and he always parked in a manner that blocked her in. A protective gesture, wasn't it? Shielding his little girl from all the dangers lurking down the road.

Amidst his sipping, Kent thought of his own childhood

around the dealership. Joking with the clever salesmen and be-ing teased by the pretty secretaries. And then those early days in business with his father, teaming up six days a week to bring home the bacon. He'd loved the work. Loved the beautiful ve-hicles, the contagious energy, how a big close got the entire sales floor hooting and hollering.

He remembered a time he'd struggled to close a woman on a used Bonneville. The Bonny had a flawless candy-apple paint job, but it also had red guts, which wasn't to her taste. Worse, she'd brought along a brother-in-law to coach third base. After going back and forth with offers and counteroffers all after-noon, Kent's father (who desked all the deals) finally got fed up and dragged him outside.

"A closer's got to *believe*," Jerry Seasons said, and lit a smoke, "that every pencil he gets from the desk is the last pencil. That's sales, Kent. Conveying sincere belief in our product, building a deal, and then shutting the door politely and professionally. Any monkey can run back and forth begging for a lower pencil, son. You're better than that."

"But they're so stubborn. They object to everything I say."

"That's because you don't honestly believe in this deal yet. You don't believe, you don't earn a commitment, and without commitment you'll never close. It's like Jesus said: Find ye faith, fill thy wallet."

Just then, the woman and her brother-in-law approached the showroom exit. They had their jackets on and she'd gathered her purse.

"Quick," Jerry Seasons said, dropping his cigarette, "give me their keys."

Confused, Kent passed his father the keys to the woman's vehicle, which they'd appraised for trade-in earlier. Jerry stepped around the corner out of sight, reared back, and pitched the keys atop the roof. He wore a wild and joyous look when he did it.

A moment later, the woman stepped outside and said she was tired of all the haggling and was ready to go. Kent looked to Jerry for help, but his father ignored him. Just stood there with his hands in his pockets. Then, feeling *this* close to panic, something extraordinary happened: a calm confidence washed over Kent unlike anything he'd experienced before, a sense of knowing what would happen next so clearly and precisely that it was almost eerie.

"My keys?" the woman said, and then Kent's jaw fell open and a string of words rolled out butter smooth. In no time at all, he'd persuaded them to head back inside and listen to a last-ditch offer.

Later that evening, the Bonneville sold and delivered, Kent and his dad split a bottle of Wild Turkey. They rapped about sales, the St. Louis Cardinals, future business opportunities— everything that awaited them down the road. It was a limitless night, a harmonious night, and one of finest nights of Kent's life, right up there with Kelsi's birth.

A knock on the window broke his reminiscence. But unlike when Maurice Currant had knocked earlier, Kent didn't hesitate to lower the glass.

"This a private party?" Linda asked.

He swallowed the bourbon resting on his tongue and opened the door.

Having snuggled up in his lap, Linda unbuttoned his shirt and slid her hand inside. Kent buried his nose in her hair and closed his eyes. Her weight made the knocking of his heart curiously palpable, made the organ's machine-like nature at once wondrous and appalling. Without any real fear, he imagined the coronary he'd someday suffer. The jolt of pain, stolen breath, a tingle down one arm. Collapsing to his knees to make absurd noises before barfing up lunch. And those last helpless moments with his face flush to the carpet, shouting and footsteps all around, while he savored the grim satisfaction of dying that most patriotic and midwestern of deaths.

"You ever regret marrying a car salesman, Linda Sue?"

She undid another button. "I'd rather have my husband drunk in the house than in the driveway."

"I used to love my job," Kent said, staring at the cab's roof as another man might've stared at the Milky Way. "Loved knowing I was in control. Loved the art of persuasion. After Dad got out, though, it all changed…"

Headlights flashed through the cab and then Kelsi's Impala swung around them. The sedan nosed up to the garage door, brake lights stuttering.

"Shush," Linda said. "Let's hide out for a minute."

Kent gave her butt an appreciative squeeze, remembering how they used to dodge her father while necking in the driveway after dates. Linda laughed and pinched him. But he grew distracted the longer Kelsi remained in her car. The toxic green radiance of her cell phone filled the Impala's cab.

He sat up, blinking. "Linda, look at her license plate."

Linda peeked through the gap between dash and wheel. "Oh, that? It's harmless."

After purchasing the Impala, Kent had walked outside with fresh plates and a frame, squatted on his haunches, and personally secured them. That license frame sported the dealership's classic red, white, and blue color scheme, and had REGENT'S OF PARIS printed along the top and THANKS YOU FOR YOUR BUSINESS! along the bottom. Drive around Central Illinois and you'd see a lot of those frames. Not so many as before the economy tanked and gas prices skyrocketed, but still a lot. Yet Kelsi's license plate frame was different now. An ugly red and silver.

THOMPSON'S FORD, it read.

"Is that supposed to be a joke? What company does she think paid for that vehicle? Hell, for the bed she sleeps in and the roof over her head?"

Linda rubbed his chest more firmly now. "Relax."

"Some nerve. Driving around insulting the dealership her grandfather founded."

"It's her first job. She's proud of herself."

"Damn it, Linda, we made *her* in a Chevy."

"Kent, don't—"

"No daughter of mine is gonna whore herself out to Thompson's Ford!"

Linda bolted upright. "Kent Seasons, listen to yourself."

He reached for the door handle, but she pinned him down. Her hair tickled his face and her knee was in his groin. A dull nausea crept up into his belly.

"Do you really want to fight over a dollar's worth of plastic?"

"Definitely," Kent said. "Absolutely."

Linda frowned, as if seeing not her husband but some exotically ugly zoo creature, like a Brazilian tree slug or a Peruvian sloth. "Fathers only get so many righteous moments. Better make sure yours count."

Then the Impala's door sprang open and Kelsi hopped out. Her jeans rode down and showed the top of her butt.

"I hate those damn jeans of hers."

"It's the new cleavage," Linda said. "All the girls are wearing them."

"They're too risqué."

"Oh, go eat your prunes, Grandpa."

Kent tipped the bottle again and watched their daughter slam the door of the car he'd selected and purchased for her—selected because of its five-star safety rating and purchased because buying a solid car for his daughter is what a solid dad does. She stomped up the walk, heels clomping pavers.

She was weeping. Kent's body clenched like a fist.

"Stay put," Linda said, aiming a finger at his nose (which Kent crossed his eyes to see), and then said she'd go find out what the waterworks were all about. But before leaving, Linda snatched the bottle and dumped it in the yard. She shook out every last drop. Seeing this, Kent lurched down from the Silverado, but—off balance due to his bum toe and a whole lot of whiskey—he staggered and nearly fell. By way of salvaging his dignity, he commenced hollering about senseless waste and conspiracies to kill his lawn. From the porch his wife studied him.

"Linda," he finally said, "I'm not."

"Sober?"

"Come on."

"Reasonable?"

"Earlier you asked if I was having an affair—I'm not."

"You're not?"

"I swear."

"Well, thank god for whiskey dick," Linda said, and went back inside the house.

8

It was a fifteen-minute drive from the YMCA: fifteen minutes of headlights burning through the cornfields, of dry wind roaring through the windows, of Springsteen's *Nebraska* album—and by the time Paul Stenger got home, he felt thoroughly defeated. Dignity plundered by the drama with Jennylee. Faith in indie music undercut by wannabe Woody Guthrie. Manhood enfeebled by Dunkenstein's flying elbows and confidence plagued by puerile images: Seth with Annie, his greasy hair slicked back, slapping her rump while congratulating himself on having closed the deal.

He gathered his gym clothes along with his guitar and dumped the melted ice from the cooler into his father's lovingly tended flower beds. His parents were older and semi-retired. More like grandparents, really. Paul avoided his father of late—even though Alvin Stenger was easygoing and kind—because his father always made a point of asking, in all apparent sincerity, if he'd had a nice day at the dealership. (*Sure did, Dad. I bent 'em over and lubed 'em up.*) Strange as it sounded, it might've actually been better had his father been more like Kent Seasons—a guy who'd spit in your eye and call you a moron, or at least say it behind your back loud enough you'd inevitably catch wind.

Inside, the house smelled floral and musty. He propped the guitar near the coat rack as their elderly spaniel, Balderdash, trotted up to greet him. Drool swung from the dog's mottled lips and his breath was like old newspaper, but still it was nice to come home to an old friend. Paul wiped away the drool with his gym shirt and Balderdash, tasting the salt, latched on. "Careful you don't lose a tooth, fella," he said.

Then his mother called his name from the living room, called it like a question, as if it could possibly be anyone else. While his father gardened, his mother's hobby was chairing various small-potatoes committees around Paris. Her leadership style consisted of Socratic questioning—a rhetorical technique she also used with her son: How many other salesmen have degrees from private universities, Paul? Does it bother you that Regent's doesn't offer insurance or benefits? But he let it all slide. He was leaving soon, on his way to bigger and brighter. She'd have to nag him over the phone.

"It's me, Mom. I'm gonna grab a quick bite and hit the sack."

Moments later, he was rifling through the fridge when his father approached. "Dash's ruining your shirt, son."

Alvin Stenger stepped near and Paul leaned back into the still-open fridge. Cold tendrils tickled his shoulder blades. Then his father's hand rose and plucked a dab of toilet paper from Paul's chin. He'd forgotten about using it to staunch the bleeding.

"Ouch. That may leave a scar."

"So what'd I miss around here today?"

His father squinted at the wound. "You got hurt playing basketball?"

"It gets pretty competitive."

"You always did go awfully deep into things," Alvin Stenger said.

When Paul asked what that was supposed to mean exactly, his father smiled. "Just that when you were a boy you were sort of…almost temperamentally incapable of taking it easy."

"I still don't know what you mean."

"Heck, I probably don't either. Maybe I'm talking about prioritizing."

Paul waited for his father to go on, to finally speak his mind.

"Can I offer some advice, Paul? I know you probably don't want to hear it from an old guy like me, but I think this just might be important."

Quite the contrary, Paul realized he'd been waiting for his father to speak like this for years. Maybe it even helped explain his return to Paris? His father waffled, though, picking his words or perhaps simply not finding any. If this kept up, Paul would have to make some compensatory gesture. Say it was okay or pat the old man's shoulder. Something awkward and embarrassing like that.

"Ever hear that old expression, 'Don't lose sight of the forest for the trees'?"

"You think that's my problem?"

"I'm not only talking about basketball, you know…"

"I know, Dad."

"It's just that with your birthday coming up, your mother and I were wondering if you'd made any plans—not that we're pushing you to, of course."

"But you're worried I've lost sight of the big picture?"

"Well, what do you think?"

"I think crafting songs takes time. It's something that has to grow organically out of the writer. You can't rush the process. You just can't. I know it seems like I'm treading water, but I really don't feel like it's time to give up. Not yet."

In the silence to follow, something in the air of the room flattened out. Then Alvin Stenger glanced back at the guitar propped by the coatrack. Finally, he produced a square of paper from his trouser pocket and carefully unfolded it: a classified ad clipped from the *Beacon-Herald*. Paul cocked his head to read the cramped and smudgy print.

"Pharmaceutical sales?"

"Automobiles aren't the only option, son."

Later, after a long shower wherein he debated how exactly he'd explain Nashville to his parents, Paul locked the door of his childhood bedroom and loaded a pipe with marijuana. A friend from high school sold killer homegrown. He tamped the bowl and lit it. Holding in a big lungful, he stared up at the ceiling's opaque light fixture, a plate of insects cooked under X-ray glass. Then he thought again of hipster Woody Guthrie and his phony songs. What if most guys lived the way they did— nine-to-fives, golf, beer belly—because they sensed, rightly, that there simply wasn't anything else?

He exhaled out the window, pressing his lips to the mesh

screen until the last wisp of smoke trailed out into the night. The bedroom reeked anyway, of course. But he waited until his parents were asleep to smoke, just like he waited to practice his music.

Priority-wise, he really needed to write some new songs. Couldn't just show up in Nashville without fresh material. That, and he needed to rough out at least one new song for his Thursday-night gig at the Buck, and thereby make the experience somewhat worthwhile. But Paul was tired from his long day and inspiration has a way of evading the tired. So instead of his journal, he picked up his guitar. After tuning it, he strummed the opening of Cat Stevens's "Father and Son." The strings bit his fingertips, as his calluses had gone soft. Nevertheless, he sang the opening verse in the voice of the father, but then stopped and squeezed the guitar's neck to quell the sound.

Father and Son—really?

What could be more maudlin than playing that particular song after an awkward moment with his own father? Wouldn't a real artist make something original of that? Focus on how he'd misunderstood, even dreaded, his father's touch. How he'd put so much weight on the old man's advice, only to realize they were on entirely different wavelengths. But instead of writing authentically, he got stoned and ripped off some old hippie's overplayed angst. What if once he got to Nashville they all just laughed at him?

Paul closed his eyes and heard (in Cat Stevens's plaintive voice) a truer version of that opening verse:

Son, it's time to make a change
Get your shit together, be a man
You sell cars, that's your fault
There's so much more you could have done
Found a girl, a real career, made some cash and grown some balls...

Smoking pot had seemed revelatory at first. The substance hadn't made him stupid and reckless like alcohol, but instead granted moments of clarity and insight. Once, for example, he'd glanced down at his jeans while thoroughly baked and realized they were at once a simple object—just a practical covering for his legs—and yet also imbued with tremendous complexity: gendered symbols, status indicators, the denim washed with pumice stone torn from the crumbling hearts of volcanic mountains, garments woven of cotton once harvested by American slaves but now sewn in Asian sweatshops by modern slaves who cut and stitched fabric that would be packaged and sold in faraway lands for ten times their weekly pay. It'd struck him that an awakened soul would reject this, would wear whatever was inexpensive and locally made, would take pains to reduce in some small way the world's injustice. But if a person were to actually do that—to purchase and wear the *wrong* jeans—what social repercussions would they face from the flock who wore the *right* jeans? Could a lousy bolt of denim seal your very fate?

The resulting song—"501 Blues"—had a simple chord structure but deceptively complex lyrics. He'd experimented with hooks and intros for weeks, and retooled the pacing again and again, before scrapping it all and starting anew. But slowly, eventually, from that lone moment of introspection he'd crafted a fresh lyrical narrative.

At the steakhouse the night he'd finished "501 Blues," Paul floated around his tables, smiling and writing down drink orders, dropping off salads and firing entrees, and it seemed all his life might be so peaceful. But the feeling faded after no other songs materialized. While he'd finally written something authentic, it hadn't come easy.

Often he imagined old college friends gossiping about him—*Whatever became of Paul Stenger? You won't believe it, but I heard he's a car salesman. Seriously? That can't be right. No, it's true. He still lives at home with his parents*—and imagining the weight of the coming years bowed Paul's spine over the guitar. No wife, not even a steady girlfriend, just the occasional beer-numb rut with a Marlboro-perfumed barfly from some shithole like The Gunning Buck. Certainly no children, no evidence of Paul Stenger's having walked this earth at all. He stared down at the weird object in his lap. Totemic wood, a heraldic shape hearkening back to lyres and ballads sung around long-lost Mediterranean fire pits. The sound hole yawned at him like an open grave.

He laid the guitar aside and hung his head between his knees.

Up through his early forties he would continue to date and people would say, *That Paul Stenger's a good catch. Why doesn't he marry a nice girl?* But as the years piled up, it'd become obvious: a case of arrested development; a grown man who claimed to write songs. And not just to entertain his buddies at halftime— no, Paul Stenger considered himself an *artiste,* the poet laureate of the pre-owned lot. And yet his real life consisted of selling Chevys, shooting baskets at the YMCA, and then going home (to his *parents'* home), and getting stoned and strumming a few chords before passing out.

A songwriter? Sure thing, pal. Send some tickets when you hit the big time.

Wind buffeted the curtains. Elms creaked in the yard. He glanced at the door and imagined the darkened house and his parents asleep in their bed. The Stenger name would end with him, wouldn't it? His father surely realized that too. Paul squeezed his eyes shut until veins of light burst and sizzled. Twenty years from now the wreckage would be obvious. When he still lusted after girls like Annie, as if he could have back all the time he'd wasted. When all the pitying looks he'd ever received made sudden, crushing sense. When his senile parents could no longer quite recall who that loser with the guitar even was. But he'd keep the old instrument tuned no matter what, wouldn't he? Pull it out like a skin rag every so often and strum a little ditty—

A soft rapping at the door. "Paul?"

He bolted upright, spots dancing before his eyes.

"Your chin okay, son?"

Wondering how long his father had been out there, Paul cleared his throat and said he was fine—but his voice sounded hollow and alien.

"You sure it doesn't need stitches?"

Paul insisted he was fine, and after a moment his father said goodnight. Then footsteps, a familiar creaking of boards, and silence. Overhead, a moth zapped itself on the hot bulb and dropped to the fixture to bake and curl.

A sleepless hour later, Balderdash whined at the door. Despite Dash's notorious shedding and night-barking, Paul was glad for the company, and as he finally drifted off his fingertips pressed languid chords into the feathery down behind the old dog's ears.

Step Two: Building Rapport

9

Thank you, JENNYLEE WITT, for your interest in The University of Triumph, Online®.

The University of Triumph, Online® combines EXTRAORDINARY OPPORTUNITY WITH EXCEPTIONAL VALUE© and is the TOP FLIGHT CHOICE© for students who demand more: *more from their instructors, more from their university, more for their futures. A career in MORTUARY SCIENCE requires an Associate's Degree,* and Triumph, Online® is here to help you achieve your dreams...*

Tuesdays being Jennylee's day off, she'd risen early and taken the opportunity to peruse the educational literature over her morning coffee. With Derrol's truck being repossessed, she'd have to cab it down to Regent's to fetch her Nissan, but that could wait. Because it felt nice to have the kitchen all to herself, and the more she read, the more it seemed becoming a mortician wasn't just pie-in-the-sky stuff after all. Maybe, like her father had always said, she really could do anything she put her mind to—or like her mother used to say (but *stopped* saying after she married Derrol Witt) she could accomplish all things with the grace of the Lord. Mostly, though, Jennylee wanted an education for her daughter's sake, because a respectable career would mean the doctors and medicines would always be there.

Then she followed that little asterisk down the page, where in fine print were listed other requirements for becoming a licensed mortician, one of which was an internship. Although a potential hurdle, this made sense, as just taking some classes wouldn't do. Over the next hour, she read through the literature twice more, reminding herself she could handle anything so long as she remained patient and kept her faith. That's what her father would've said, anyway, as those virtues were the bedrocks of Davis Sykes's philosophy, and he preached it to his daughter right up until the cancer took him away. As a widow, however, Evelyn Sykes had scrubbed patience from the equation and doubled down on the faith. That Evelyn had become yet another Paris Holy Roller didn't particularly surprise Jennylee, but the more righteous her mother talked and the more she dragged Chastity to those namby-pamby church events, the more Jennylee dreaded attending church herself. Her mother blamed Regent's for this—"Spending all day with car salesmen would test anyone's convictions," Evelyn claimed. But Jennylee needed Regent's, sinful snake pit or otherwise. Besides, Triumph's courses were expensive enough that her educational journey would have to start outside the online classroom, at least until she figured how to swing tuition.

A person has to start somewhere, though, and in this spirit Jennylee considered that tall white funeral home on the outskirts of town, the one she drove past every morning on her way to work. Emboldened by the bright sunshine and the caffeine buzzing along her veins, she dug out the Yellow Pages and studied the listings.

Back when business was good, it'd been perfectly acceptable for the Regent's crew to brag about money, to gloat over a thousand-dollar pounder or crow and laugh after ripping a buyer's head off to the tune of two grand—but to complain about the recent *lack* of profit was taboo. The national press felt no such qualms, however, and the auto industry's troubles were debated daily on the TV. Policy wonks alternately praised President Obama's withholding taxpayer billions, or—with a click of the channel—different pundits argued that the government's requesting compensatory shares and a guided bankruptcy constituted a radical leftist hijacking of Detroit steel.

But Paul Stenger thought about money in more practical terms, as the upcoming Memorial Day sale was his chance to squirrel away some cash before hitting the road to Nashville. Besides swearing off marijuana and Cat Stevens, the upside of the previous night's anxiety attack was renewed focus. He'd awoken clearheaded and calm, and he arrived at the dealership with his shoes spit-shined à la Kent Seasons—as it was Kent's philosophy that confidence, more than any other factor, dictated success.

"True confidence," Paul said to Chadwick, "is rare as 800 credit."

It was just the two of them in the showroom. Chadwick slouched against a fireball red Corvette, a bait car for the mid-life-crisis types with 401Ks burning holes in their retirement portfolios. Just to stir the pot, Paul then suggested that Barack Obama (whom Chadwick despised) was a prime example of a supremely confident man. "He's got that swagger, that strut. I mean, think about it—a Black man needs an awfully big pair to run for president in this racist, peckerwood country, wouldn't you say?"

Chadwick shook his head. "Looks like a cushy gig to me."

"And the Constitution," Paul said, "which Mr. Obama has taken a solemn oath to uphold, originally counted him as only three-fifths of a person."

"Yeah, but just for voting purposes."

"Meanwhile, the NRA defends the right of white supremacist psychopaths to own high-powered rifles."

"Sounds like somebody's been watching too much CNN."

"Admit it—if the Republicans were proposing this bailout, you'd be all for it."

"Whatever. It's liberals like you who want to regulate everyone right out of business."

"Liberals like me? Man, I spend all my time trying to *sell* these shitty cars."

Chadwick folded his arms across his chest. "Bailout my ass. Obama's just itching to get his mitts on Cadillac."

"You know what you really need, Chadwick?"

"No, but I bet you're gonna tell me."

"You need to start listening to Bob Dylan."

"Oh boy, here we go."

"Now I realize a Toby Keith fan such as yourself has a hard

time recognizing authenticity, but Dylan is a prophet. He could always tell the good people from the bad, the workers from the takers. Listening to his songs can—"

"Can what?"

"Can make you a better person."

Chadwick raised an invisible joint to his lips and toked. Beyond the showroom windows, a few million dollars' worth of inventory sparkled under the summer sun. Cobalts and Impalas faced off like chessmen before regiments of broad-shouldered Silverados, while a row of Suburbans gave off an eye-watering glare, waxed hoods bright as flame.

For Paul, Chevrolet's gas-guzzling Suburban exemplified everything wrong with General Motors: an insistence upon bigger and brawnier in an age when foreign automakers embraced sleeker and smarter, buoyed by a misguided faith in every American's inalienable right to seating for nine. Seeing these big, dumb, beautiful vehicles, he couldn't help but wonder what Bob Dylan would've made of selling cars. Knowing the Bard, he'd have gotten a song or two out of the experience, but he wouldn't have lingered long. A track like "Workingman's Blues," but no album titled *Pushin' Steel.*

Over by the service bay, Bill Sr. and Junior were shooting their annual Crust Fest Blowout Sale commercial spot, which would run locally through Monday evening. Bill Sr. was dressed like a cross between Wyatt Earp and Lee Iacocca, doing a chicken walk while chomping a cigar and tipping his Stetson. They'd hired the same production crew as last year—a pair of high school dropouts with a camera and a van.

Finished mugging, Junior made his way into the showroom. He shivered as the AC washed over him. "Man the turrets, fellas," he said, and fired off a salute.

"Looking sharp out there, Billy," Chadwick said. After their boss turned the corner, he said, "What a turd. Kent's the one oughta be running this place."

"Nepotism trumps talent," Paul said.

"Yeah, Junior's got it made in the shade."

"You think? He takes some serious crap from his old man."

But Chadwick had a point. Junior got pushed around, sure, but he also owned a nice home and drove new vehicles. Had cash in the bank and his name on the door. What did he and Chadwick have—complimentary polo shirts? Business cards with some former salesman's name blacked out with a Sharpie?

"The wife's on my case about finishing school again," Chadwick said. Then a press-stud on his cowboy belt scratched the Corvette's paint job; he glanced back to admire the damage. "But when I ask who's gonna pay the bills in the meantime, she just shrugs."

"Your wife's probably just sick of hearing you talk about it."

"Yeah, well, I'll finish my degree when you move to LA or Nashville, or wherever wannabe musicians go to starve."

Irritated, Paul very nearly dropped the bomb and announced that he *was* headed to Nashville and *would* be pursuing his dream—but then a Dodge Ram pulled onto the lot. It was towing a trailer. A potbellied man and his presumptive wife climbed out.

"Folks don't usually bring their camper trailer to the lot," Chadwick said.

"Not unless they're far from home," Paul said, "and something's wrong."

"You'd best let me take this one. Hate for Kent to see you blow a slam-dunk."

"Actually, *you* were the one who got dunked on last night, remember?"

"Fine, I'll just stand here and watch you choke. Just like in last year's championship game."

Paul made for the door. "Watch and learn, Jethro."

Crossing the lot, however, he wondered why Chadwick put up with being called Jethro—more specifically, why Chadwick never fired back with whatever Kent had nicknamed *him*. Hard to imagine it was all that mean. Had to do with music, most likely. James Taylor or Harry Chapin. Elton John. Someone corny.

Then again, maybe Kent hadn't nicknamed him at all?

Because Paul Stenger had a certain edge on his coworkers—smarts, looks, moxie—and Kent Seasons was no fool. He knew talent when he saw it.

Prior to making such an important call, Jennylee took a cue from Regent's and dressed for telephone success, which meant church clothes and a dab of makeup.

She'd caught flak at the dealership for having telephone terror and not cold-calling or following up on her be-backs. And while she really did hate bugging people, she'd learned a few things. First, you speak how you feel. Therefore, making a good impression over the phone requires a salesperson to smile so big the person on the other end can actually *hear* it. Second, you sound as professional as you dress. Pride in one's appearance meant pride in one's work. By the third ring, however, she nearly hung up. Why had she ever listened to Aunt Liz? The woman smoked dope and rode a Harley, for heaven's sake. But Jennylee didn't hang up. Not on the fourth ring, not on the fifth, not even after someone at Higgenbottom's picked up. Because while she had no real evidence that she'd excel in the funeral business, Paul Stenger and Kent Seasons—and most of all, Maurice Currant—had made it clear she wasn't cut out for selling cars either.

Only the machine had answered though. A hushed message, a somber beep. She stared out the window at the horse stall, phone to her ear, daydreaming. Mrs. Jennylee Witt, Funeral Director. Mrs. J. L. Witt, Licensed Mortician. But while she'd gotten into a professional enough frame of mind, she hadn't actually planned a script. On second thought, maybe she'd best visit Higgenbottom's in person? Convince the man who ran the place that she was serious about becoming a mortician, not with words over the phone, but with bold and confident actions.

Then Chastity's footsteps pattered down the hallway. Her daughter was dressed in her favorite sleepies—Derrol's old Pearl Jam shirt and gym socks stretched up past her knees. An ensemble wardrobe Jennylee found ridiculously cute.

"Want some cereal, sweetpea?"

But Chastity claimed she wasn't hungry. Never was lately.

"If you don't eat, you won't grow up big and strong like your daddy."

Her daughter really was too thin. Last year she'd been about average, but now she was the smallest, boniest girl in her grade. The change in her school pictures was startling. Then Derrol ambled in, kissed their daughter atop her head, and went straight to the fridge. No lost appetite there. In fact, Derrol didn't speak a word until he'd poured and milked a huge bowl of cereal. As was his habit, he used a tablespoon to eat it.

"What's up with the church clothes?" he asked, cheeks bulging.

"I was reading. And I needed to make a phone call."

That this answer was really no answer at all somehow escaped Derrol Witt. Then he noticed the newspaper. "Anything in the classifieds?"

But that was pure baloney. Only one studying the classifieds lately was her.

"I was actually looking over that school literature I told you about."

He dropped the tablespoon into the sink, raised the bowl, and slurped the sugary milk. "Not that fly-by-night mortician college again?"

"Maybe try not shooting down my dreams first thing in the morning?"

He crossed his eyes at Chastity and pushed his nose up flat. She giggled as he snorted, oink-oink, and buried his snout in the bowl. Then he asked the inevitable follow-up: "Okay, so what's this program cost?"

"They charge by the credit hour. I'll have to do some calculations."

"Then they promise you a job—that how it works?"

Chast watched them, her neck swimming in the big shirt. Lately she'd been picking up on their frictions. Cooped up in the trailer like they were, how could she not?

"This sounds just like bartender college," Derrol said. "Mixology 101? Garnishing basics? Five-hundred bucks right down the drain. If only—"

"If only someone had warned you," Jennylee said, as she'd heard this one a time or two before. Having finished his so-called mixology degree, Derrol laminated his diploma and visited every bar within forty miles. But the managers kept saying the school he'd paid for didn't count for much, that an applicant needed hands-on experience. Derrol never got over the disappointment. He also refused to consider another possibility: that he simply didn't *look* like a bartender. No, her husband looked like a guy who unplugged toilets and dug hairballs out of shower drains—and Jennylee loved that guy.

"Don't shoot the messenger, Jen, but this mortician thing sounds like a big load of—" He glanced at Chast. "Well, I'm just not sure it's a smart investment."

Despite his troubles, Derrol was considerate of their daughter, which was a good sign. Still, Jennylee sometimes caught herself imagining life without him. Things she could do, places she might go. Even leaving Paris for good. But then she'd see Derrol and Chast reading a book together or just palling around, and she'd recall how lost she'd felt after her father's death—that sense of abandonment which never quite faded. She couldn't put Chast through that. Losing a father so young (although divorce wasn't the same as pancreatic cancer) was a forever wound. Love may guarantee little in this world besides heartbreak, but that lesson could wait.

Besides, of all the boys she'd grown up with, Derrol had been the kindest. Back in school, guys liked to joke how Jennylee Sykes was a carpenter's dream—*flat on both sides and never been nailed,* was how they liked to put it. High school boys were scared shitless of girls, of course, and oftentimes used cruelty to mask it, but Derrol had never been that way.

"If school was for you," he said, "don't you think you'd have done it already?"

"Don't you speak to me that way."

"It's time you stop pretending you're some bigshot—"

"Daddy," Chastity said, "quit being mean!"

Jennylee smoothed their daughter's bangs and said it was okay. Mommy and Daddy were just having a grown-up talk. She'd gotten *so* thin though. With her huge eyes and pale skin, she resembled those aliens Derrol and Randy Bauble spent their days shooting on the Xbox. Connections a mother hesitated to ponder. Wasted time and a little girl wasting away. Mindlessly punching buttons and thoughtlessly bringing a child into this world. Stuck on level four all day. Game over. What was to become of them?

"I'm just making sure nobody fools Mommy," Derrol said. "There's lots of people out there who'd like to fool you, Chast. They want to trick you into giving them the money you worked hard for, so they don't have to work hard themselves."

Jennylee could only shake her head. A hard-work speech from Derrol Witt?

Ten minutes later, she emerged from the bedroom, having touched up her makeup and said her affirmations. Sure enough, Derrol had commandeered the TV. He'd plugged in headphones, at least. Jennylee drew the line at Chast growing up to the sounds of interstellar decapitations. While getting ready, she'd realized—or maybe acknowledged, accepted—that her family's well-being was solely up to her. She'd thought through the people in her life, starting with her mother and relations, from Aunt Liz in Panama City to some cousins in Stillwater she hadn't seen in years, clear down to her coworkers at Regent's, asking who might be counted on to help in a pinch.

The answer?

The ones who would couldn't, and the ones who could wouldn't.

10

Welcome to Regent's," Paul said, and introduced himself to the couple. He'd stopped a few yards shy and opened his stance, hands up, as if proving himself unarmed.

"That Tahoe come with a tow package?" the potbellied husband asked.

From the corner of his eye, Paul noticed smoke leaking from under their Ram's hood. Hot days like this, hoses and head gaskets popped in big trucks like that. Best of all…Missouri plates.

"Sure does. It'll pull stronger than your Dodge."

"Our truck's not pulling anything," the wife said. She pointed at it like a dog that'd messed the rug. "Transmission's slipping. Not to mention all that smoke—"

"Cathy," her husband said. He faced Paul again. "Had I my druthers, our truck would be up on the rack and we'd be checking into a motel, but"—he glanced at his better half—"we're headed to Cincinnati."

"For my baby sister's wedding," Cathy explained.

"Her *third* wedding," the husband added.

"What's that supposed to mean?"

While they bickered, Paul pretended to listen, as listening indebted buyers. That rare, sweet feeling of truly being noticed transferred nicely into obligation, then guilt, then a deal. Paul nodded and frowned when appropriate. He cooed sympathy and purred understanding and struggled not to grin. Just wait until Kent Seasons caught wind of this fiasco. Broken down interstate travelers, a hitched trailer, and a hitching in Ohio.

"Cathy," Paul said, "would you like to take this beautiful new Tahoe for a spin?"

Her face beamed, but her husband spat on the cement—greenish yolk like a chunk of diseased lung. Paul smiled and asked his name. He had to ask again before getting an answer: Harlan. Harlan and Cathy Hovarth of Joplin, Missouri.

Back in the showroom, Paul grabbed a dealer plate and told Chadwick about the wedding in Cincinnati, the slipping transmission and smoking engine, the marital strife.

"Bow and ribbon," Chadwick said, "you lucky prick."

As Paul again crossed that acre of baking hot cement (leisurely now, admiring the mountainous flat-bottomed clouds) he pondered how a salesman's good luck so often depended upon his customers' ill fortunes. Selling cars was never win-win, but always and only win-lose. The guy who cashes the check and the chump who writes it. There was little poetic about it, but seen in a certain light, selling cars was refreshingly honest. After all, win-lose was life's dark secret: the pie is finite, and you'd best sink your fingers in deep before somebody else licks the plate.

He unlocked the Tahoe and handed Harlan Hovarth the keys. Then, ever chivalrous, he held the passenger door for Cathy. As she climbed into the cab, he glimpsed himself in the side mirror. He licked his fingertips, smoothed his eyebrows, and hopped in the back.

Cathy caught his eye in the rearview. "Don't you just love that smell?"

"There's nothing better, Cathy."

New-car smell was a combination of things—sealants, glue, leather treatments, flame retardant—some of which were almost certainly carcinogenic. But new-car smell was also the smell of money. Hence, everyone loved it. Hence, it so quickly vanished.

Throughout the test-drive, Harlan wasn't concerned with the Tahoe's performance and handling so much as Cathy's prickly mood. Hauling that bulky trailer was obviously his idea, probably hoping to save on hotels. Now look. Broken down in Paris, Illinois. By the time they circled back to the lot, Paul had a sense of both their down payment (three grand) and their Ram's real value (also only about three grand, considering mileage and mechanical problems). Harlan wouldn't like that appraisal one bit though. His truck was barely five years old.

Here was the problem with no-haggle sales: because the dealership didn't jack up the sticker, there wasn't much wiggle room. High-pressure outfits like Thompson's Ford stickered vehicles far higher, thereby making it profitable to "give" buyers more for their crappy trade-ins.

After they'd parked, Paul asked Harlan what he thought— was she the one?

Harlan gave Cathy a look. "Depends on what she costs."

For a moment Paul pitied the man. Because unless Harlan Hovarth raped his checkbook they'd miss the wedding and he'd go to his grave maligned as a cheapskate. And he was clearly on a workingman's budget…but that was his problem. Cathy's moodiness was his problem too. And the Dodge that'd died with four thousand pounds of trailer hitched to the bumper— guess whose problem that was.

"Let's talk turkey," Paul said, and led them through the icy showroom, thinking all the while of Lloyd Rivera's relatives feeding doomed birds down the kill-chute.

Once in his office, Cathy smiled and nested down, her pale thighs spilling over the plastic chair. Paul could tell she liked him. Hell, she probably *wanted* him. He'd charmed her and bathed her in his pearliest grins, even resisted the urge to recoil when she'd surreptitiously rubbed her dumpy ass against his crotch as he held open the showroom door. Cathy had married a man she no longer believed in, and now she needed Paul to convince that man to sign a bad deal. A chilling tale indeed. But until he finally got to Nashville, Paul Stenger was all about taking pounders and stacking Franklins.

At the end of the long driveway sat an engraved stone: HIGGENBOTTOM MEMORIAL CHAPEL AND CREMA-TORY.

Jennylee parked beside it. At Regent's she'd had the cabbie pull up right next to her Nissan, and then she'd hopped out of the one vehicle and into the other so quickly that if anybody in the showroom noticed her, they didn't have time to flag her down. Then she was headed back east, in the direction of what she quietly hoped was her future.

The Nissan's engine had sounded a touch balky, though, as if spending the night on the lot had sickened it. Just one more thing to worry about, and she already had enough worries. She took a moment to fetch up her courage and remind herself she could do this. That she owned the moment. That Jennylee Witt was in charge of her future, was in touch with her chi, was in control of her life…and yet each step across the lawn brought more anxiety. As she neared the funeral home's looming double doors, she questioned whether she'd even gone about searching for an internship in the proper way. Because all she really knew about mortician work she'd learned that same morning, perusing the literature from Triumph, Online. But again, she reminded herself that a mortician had to start somewhere—a *person* had to start somewhere.

So she climbed the front steps and tried the doors, which were unlocked. But it felt like trespassing to just let herself in, as Higgenbottom's closely resembled a private dwelling. Of course, it was actually a business open to the public, much like a car dealership, which suggested no appointment was necessary. Then again, *she* wasn't here to retain the business's services. No, she meant to ask for something. She considered the rough treatment Kent Seasons gave sales callers who dared trespass at Regent's (even that sweet old man who peddled silk ties and jewelry to all the local dealerships). Absent intent to buy, Kent had little use for people. Maybe she really should've made an appointment, or at least tried calling back later?

Then the doors swung inward—the handles pried briskly from her fingers—and Jennylee let out a surprised hoot.

A smartly dressed woman stood in the entryway. She was all of five feet-tall and had an odd hairdo, like Prince Valiant from that old comic strip. When this woman asked how she might be of assistance, Jennylee realized she must've been spotted. After all, the Nissan was the only car in sight and she'd been standing on the porch second-guessing herself for quite some time now.

Not the best first impression. Certainly not how Kent Seasons would've handled things. Had he wanted an internship, Kent would've marched straight into Higgenbottom's and asked where the goddamn rib-saw was.

"Hello, ma'am," Jennylee said. "I'm here today because I'm wondering if you guys"—she took a breath and cursed her nerves—"Higgenbottom's, I mean. If y'all might need some help?"

Y'all? For months now she'd been working to scour that particular word from her vocabulary. It was one thing to talk hick with other hicks, but the funeral director was a professional business owner.

"Help doing what, precisely?"

Her manner of speech was elegant, almost European, not the typical Paris drawl.

"I received some literature in the mail, from a school with a mortuary science program. It claims I need an internship."

The dwarfish woman studied her, a dignified but practical assessment, and Jennylee found herself copying that look. She even clasped her hands at her waist, just like the director clasped hers. Such aping was inappropriate, of course, but she couldn't help herself. It reminded her of a time she'd test-driven a visiting professor from Eastern Illinois University. Irish literature was the man's specialty, and she'd fallen right into his cozy brogue. Probably feeling mocked, that professor took his business elsewhere.

"Did you perchance phone here this morning?"

Embarrassed, Jennylee considered lying, but she wasn't a very good liar, which was also why she wasn't very good at selling cars, which was why she was standing here on the veranda of this funeral home. The director asked if she was feeling all right and Jennylee nodded. Dark green boards creaked under her shoes.

"There was a curious message on the machine. The caller breathed into the phone for a long time, only to hang up without a word."

"I'm Jennylee Witt," she said, and stuck out her palm.

"And I'm Alice Higgenbottom."

"Pleased to meet you, Alice," Jennylee said, and squeezed the small woman's surprisingly large hand, relieved to have gotten a name right off the bat this time.

Then Alice led her inside. They passed through rooms with vaulted ceilings and old-fashioned wooden furniture with carved trim. Speakers were mounted in the high corners, but the funeral home was every bit as silent as its outward appearance suggested. Alice finally showed her into an office with an ornate desk holding a bouquet of roses and a crystal paperweight that caught sunlight from the window. Prismatic rays sprayed across Jennylee's pale blue pantyhose. Not the ideal color for an interview maybe, but at least they matched her church clothes.

"Thank you for your time, Alice," Jennylee said—but she could've kicked herself. Upon first starting at Regent's, she'd habitually used the phrase during her fishing calls, until the day Kent Seasons jumped down her throat about it. *That's some weak script*, he'd said, and punched the switch, ending her call. *That's what a salesperson who expects to hear no would say...*

"You're quite welcome," Alice Higgenbottom said.

"Do you live here—in the funeral home, I mean?" She imagined the strangeness of sleeping in a house of the dead.

"It often feels as if I do, and I did grow up in this house. But we moved after my father converted it for business purposes. Now I own a condo catty-corner to the mall. I detest cutting grass. Plus, a girl must shop."

The crystal paperweight burned with colors. As a girl Jennylee had seen one just like it in a fortune teller's booth at the Crust Fest. But could that fortune teller have predicted she'd end up here, a young mother looking to go from selling cars to coffins?

Then Alice asked her about herself, about her background and motivations. Funny, but she'd never really thought of herself in this way. She'd always assumed she wanted the same as everyone: a healthy family, enough money, love. But *motivations* implied a more formal plan—a plan, she realized, that until just recently she hadn't had. Maybe getting specific was the key? After all, everybody wanted love and happiness, but precious few seemed to have it.

"I've heard mortician work pays real well," Jennylee said, but immediately clamped her lips. That wasn't what she'd meant to say either. Not even close.

"One should certainly consider earnings when choosing a career"—silhouetted against the window, Alice's hair could've been a cast-iron mold—"but let's set financial considerations aside for now and talk of aspects less conspicuous."

Jennylee had been nervously rubbing her knees and a callus snagged her hose and left an ugly run. By sheer will, she stilled her hands in her lap and met Alice Higgenbottom's gaze. She determined to stop trying to think like a salesperson, to stop worrying whether she sounded clever, and simply be honest.

"I sell cars for a living, ma'am."

"You're a...saleswoman?"

"That's right. Just down the road at Regent's."

"Ah, yes. Regent's *American Dream* Motors."

"Yeah, but nobody actually calls it that."

"Capitalism often indulges in hyperbole. It's endemic to a system predicated upon mass appeal and the lowest common denominator."

"If you ever happen to stop in, watch out for a salesman named Paul Stenger. He's handsome and seems like a real nice guy, but it's all for show."

"Jennylee, I'm afraid I remain a bit confused. Am I correct in understanding that you're here today in hopes not of selling me a vehicle, but of finding work in the funeral industry?"

"I strive to keep things professional and help my customers. Truly I do. I'm as honest as a person can possibly be without getting fired, and I try to live by the philosophy my sales manager preaches, even though it's not always easy."

"So you're considering a career change?"

"I bite my tongue daily and remind myself to keep humble—remind myself that when things seem their absolute worst is usually when there's something valuable to learn. But at the end of the day, I question whether all my prayers and affirmations aren't for nothing. Whether all of it, every rotten second, isn't just a complete waste of time."

"Now we're getting somewhere," Alice said.

"Not to put too fine a point on it, but I've come to realize I hate selling cars. I hate every single thing about it, from the steps we're trained to follow, to the sales calls we have to make, even the cars themselves."

"Well, I can appreciate how one might feel that way"—Alice's expression softened around the eyes—"yet I fail to see how discontent with automobile sales has led you here today, to me."

Jennylee was about to start blabbing about Aunt Liz and how she just knew she'd be good at comforting the bereaved and all that, but when she finally spoke something else popped out. "My daughter's been awful sick," she said, "and the doctors can't figure out what's wrong. She can barely eat a popsicle without throwing up. That, and I'm afraid I just may have married a deadbeat."

"Goodness!" Alice Higgenbottom said.

"I figure it's high time I made some changes, ma'am."

"How about I get you a couple of ice-cold sodas, folks?"

Buying refreshments was an easy way to build obligation, and it was amazing how often a one-dollar investment returned a five-hundred-dollar commission. Little things matter to little people, and nobody wants to feel indebted. Best of all, the nicer and more humble the buyer, the better this sneaky shit worked.

"It'd be my pleasure," Paul said. "Honest."

Harlan Hovarth raised an eyebrow.

"I'm a car salesman," Paul said, borrowing one of Kent's cheekiest lines, "would I lie?"

Harlan smirked and asked how much they'd give him for his Dodge.

"My sales manager is appraising your vehicle as we speak."

Earlier, Paul spied Kent outside looking over their truck. He was shaking his head, surely having noticed the high mileage. He'd also stood on one leg, like a flamingo.

"I still owe some on her," Harlan said.

"Who doesn't nowadays?" Paul smiled like it was no impediment whatsoever. "How much are we talking about, exactly?"

"About thirteen."

"Thirteen hundred is nothing. We can fold that right back into your payments—"

"Well, no. I meant thirteen *thousand.*"

Paul somehow managed not to blink. Thirteen grand? Kent would appraise the Dodge around three, maybe four tops. The mechanical problems were bad, but not fatal, as repairs were done in-house and built back into the sale price, but the 125,000 on the odometer was a killer.

"That's all?" he said. "How did you pay it down so fast?"

Cathy patted Harlan's thigh. "See?"

"You really don't think it's a problem?"

Paul recited some asinine script about Regent's not believing in problems, only opportunities, then suggested they relax while he talked it over with his manager. Down the hall, he found Kent studying Thompson's Ford's website. Researching their pricing scheme, maybe.

"Those knuckleheads are at least twelve grand in the hole," Kent said. He tapped the printout. "What are they putting down?"

"He's hoping three."

"Three *times* three, maybe. Otherwise this one's sunk, buckaroo."

But Paul asked for a first pencil anyway. "I better get back in there," he said. "The wife's got him by the short hairs, but he knows they're better off fixing the Dodge."

He was almost out the door when Kent stopped him. "You play hoops with Dan Thompson, right? What's your take?"

"Dan's got some game."

"Game?"

"For an older guy, I mean."

Kent sucked his teeth and drummed the mouse pad. For a moment, he seemed less like a boss and more like a real person—a worried, nervous human being. But as with every sale, time was the enemy. Paul imagined Harlan Hovarth finally managing to talk sense to Cathy, explaining how you can't shop for a vehicle behind the eight ball, how her sister would divorce again in six months anyway, and so they'd best get the hell out of this dealership before they got taken to the cleaners.

"Dan ever say anything weird?" Kent popped a mint in his jaws. "Anything that made you think…"

"Think what?"

"Hell, never mind. I just like to know my enemy."

"Something wrong with your leg, Kent? Saw you limping outside."

"Believe it or not, I broke my foot while asleep in bed."

"Were you dreaming about kicking ass?"

"Don't get old, kid."

"You're not old, boss."

"Who you think you're kidding? Back when this great nation of ours was founded, most guys were dead by my age."

After hitting the break room, Paul hustled back to his office. He cracked open the sodas and slid them across the desk. "My sales manager," he said, "will be joining us any minute." In the meantime, he distracted them with pointless questions about Joplin. Ever seen a Missouri twister? Scary, huh? You folks build a shelter on your property? How's the barbecue down your way?

Then Kent bowled in, smiling and pumping everybody's hands and showing no sign of that nasty limp. Harlan and Cathy's eyes instantly glued on to him. Charisma was a truly mysterious commodity. From the look on her face, Cathy Hovarth could've been meeting George Clooney, not some balding and whiskey-bloated car salesman.

"Pardon me, folks," Kent said, "but I need to borrow Paul for a minute."

Out in the hallway, Kent tossed hand signals like an infantryman. Paul followed him out of earshot. "This one's a dud,"

Kent said. He winced and leaned against the wall. "They're so far upside down the banks won't bite unless they sign clear out to eighty-four months at an ungodly rate. Interest alone would pay for a European vacation. Berets, canal rides, the whole works."

"But it's approved at eighty-four?"

"Nobody's that stupid. Cut them loose and get a fresh up."

Paul explained the situation—the wedding in Cincinnati, how the Hovarths couldn't wait the day or two needed for ordering parts and making repairs.

"Then tell them to rent a truck. This is the worst contract I have ever seen, and I been selling cars since the Bee Gees were selling records."

"They really want to get something done today."

"Look, I'm just offering some sage advice." Kent pointed back down the hallway. "Explain to those numbskulls how much interest they're looking at. Talk sense."

Letting buyers off the hook? A bout of conscience? Kent Seasons was clearly going soft. Must've been all that bourbon he'd been pouring over his Wheaties.

Back in his office, Paul smiled at Harlan and Cathy. "Excellent news, folks. Your loan's approved and I've got the numbers right here." He flattened the offer sheet upside down on the desk (upside down just like their debt-to-credit ratio) so they could read it. "Special long-term financing is a great way to keep your payments affordable…"

"Your forthrightness is refreshing," Alice Higgenbottom said, "yet I still have some concerns. Being a mortician calls for tact. For a carriage befitting the most solemn of occasions. Do you consider yourself a woman possessed of such qualities?"

"Yes, ma'am, I do," Jennylee said.

After all, she'd learned her tact at Paris High, growing up with farm boys who played grab-ass in the hallways, and her dignified and ladylike carriage won the heart of Mr. Derrol Leonard Witt, whose gallant ways included passing gas in the bathroom while she tried to brush her teeth. The roses on Alice's desk were lovely though. So red and plush and delicate. Jennylee closed her eyes for a moment and imagined the pleasure of working in a quiet space adorned with freshly cut flowers.

"A mortician's duties are emotionally taxing. Are you prepared to work closely with clients experiencing the worst moments of their lives? Widows facing decades alone. People who've watched a parent slowly fade and are counting on you—on *you*, Jennylee—to comport yourself in a manner which honors the gravity of their loss. Are you prepared for such responsibility?"

While thinking of mortician work did sometimes recall painful memories of her father's funeral, most of what Alice said didn't worry her too much. Jennylee actually *preferred* the idea of working with dead people. It'd be calm and predictable, for one thing. And the dead wouldn't try make her feel stupid, or bully and disrespect her simply because she was female. Plus, dead guys didn't get handsy and expose themselves on country lanes, like the living ones were prone to do.

"I'll intern for free. I'll do anything you need done."

Alice's expression reminded her of that girl from the Addam's Family who never smiles, which in turn reminded her of Kent nicknaming her Morticia. Never should've run her mouth about funeral directing around the lot. Earnestness only provided ammo for people to hurt your feelings. Of course, she had the goods on her coworkers too. Chadwick always bragged how he'd finish college someday, but chances are he never would. And Paul claimed he wrote songs, when all he really did was play basketball and snipe deals. And Kent Seasons pretended he was in charge, even though he never would be, not really. Everyone wanted something. That couldn't be helped. But sincerity made you a mark, and there was nothing the Regent's crew enjoyed more than heckling one another's hopes and dreams.

"I'd like to get a sense of how you handle difficult situations," Alice said. "Could you describe a time you've faced stress in the workplace?"

Naturally, Jennylee recounted that bad test-drive of the day before. Halfway through the telling, though, she realized it probably wasn't the best of examples. So she skipped the part about Maurice flashing her, instead focusing on how she'd kept calm, kept her composure, and handled his advances as best she could.

"This man who accosted you, his name is Maurice?"

"Maurice Currant, that's right."

"Jennylee, I know exactly who you encountered. Off-color rumors have swirled around his character for years. He runs a photography studio just off the town square. A studio purchased and supported with his wife's money, I might add. Maurice's father-in-law founded the Good 'n' Crusty Pie Crust Company. Unfortunately, the businessman's daughter—Gloria is her name, I believe—married injudiciously. Now Good 'n' Crusty Inc. funds Maurice's shutterbuggery."

"I never did care for those pie crusts," Jennylee said.

"Rather doughy, aren't they?"

"Like goop. No matter how long they cook for."

"He also coaches the middle-school cagers," Alice said.

"Cagers, ma'am?"

"Hoopers."

"Hoopers?"

"Ballers." Jennylee nodded, as if this explanation explained anything at all. "I've always loved the sport," Alice continued, "but the thought of Maurice Currant wielding authority over impressionable boys is chilling."

It sure was. Jennylee felt uncomfortable just thinking about Maurice with a camera in his hand, let alone around kids.

"There's a reason," Alice said, "that people snicker and call him *Photo Mo*."

"Now that really is the perfect name for him," Jennylee said. "Not even my boss, Kent Seasons, could've dreamed up a better one."

"This boss of yours likes to nickname people?"

"He sure does."

"Well, if you don't mind my asking, what did he nickname you?"

Jennylee hesitated a moment and then just blurted it out.

Alice pursed her lips. "That, I fear, is rather unkind."

"You don't know the half of it, ma'am."

After warning her to steer clear of Maurice, Alice provided a slew of helpful advice, including the skinny on licensing requirements and which mortuary science programs were reputable. "I've not heard of Triumph, Online," she said, "but distance learning seems a sound investment, assuming it's supplemented with practical training."

Unfortunately, Alice wasn't so certain Higgenbottom's actually needed an intern, as she already had a part-timer to help with the driving and cleaning and heavy lifting. Sure enough, mentioning Maurice Currant had blown her chances. Made Alice Higgenbottom think she was just some fool who'd gotten taken advantage of by the local playboy. Earlier, while speaking her mind so freely, she'd felt an upwelling of hope. But now she felt worse for having worn it.

"Don't look so glum, dear. Give me a few days to ponder how you might be of use. If the stars align, perhaps I can even pay a modest wage."

"No shit?" Jennylee said, then clapped a hand over her mouth.

"No shit, indeed. However, I will need to sleep on it."

With this, Alice led her out and they said their goodbyes. Walking to the Nissan, Jennylee felt that regardless of what Alice ultimately decided, she was glad to have made her acquaintance, glad to have finally gotten a peek inside that pretty old farmhouse, and glad to know the individual who ran Higgenbottom's was so very interesting. Who would've ever guessed a woman like Alice lived in Paris, Illinois?

"Be bold in your aspirations but humble in their pursuit, Jennylee," Alice had said as they parted ways, and Jennylee would return to these words in times of doubt. "If this work teaches us anything, it's that we live but once and thus had best live well."

Paul Stenger waved goodbye as the Tahoe left the lot, the trailer caboosing along behind. He'd broken a sweat in the wash bay, as he and Lloyd vacuumed and Windexed the Tahoe, laid down paper mats printed with the Regent's logo, and cracked all the usual jokes about the pounding Paul had given Harlan and Cathy Hovarth. So the context was off—jarringly so—when Lloyd asked if any vehicles had come in that might be good for him. But while Paul had promised to keep an eye out, he'd forgotten all about it.

Now, still holding the electric screwdriver he'd used to transfer plates, he found Kent Seasons leaning against the showroom door, studying him. "Making it in car sales," Kent said, "is about understanding that people don't really buy cars."

"Not around here they don't. Paris is truck country."

"Teenagers buy manhood, whereas guys like me buy back their youth. Young women buy freedom and self-confidence, and mothers buy safe children and jealous neighbors. Once you understand all that, you'll see selling cars is about embracing your own inner asshole."

"Excuse me?"

"Like the Buddhists say, about seeing with your third eye."

Paul aimed the screwdriver toward the heavens and squeezed the trigger—*whirr!* "I'm a god-fearing member of the Church of Mucho Dinero."

But despite this quip being right down Kent's alley, the man barely cracked a smile. "A good salesman goes for the pounder," he said, "no doubt about it. But there's a line, kid. Care to sleep at night, you'd best determine where yours lies."

Paul lowered the screwdriver. "You're saying I went too far?"

"That's not for me to judge. Truth is, if you hadn't stomped those roaches, somebody else would've. They'll come out of the ether soon enough though. Realize they're paying for two trucks but only driving one. And every month for the next seven years they'll curse your smiling, friendly soul straight to hell."

"That's a rather unflattering interpretation of my hard day's work," Paul said.

"Although who's to say if such qualms should bother you?"

Exactly. Who was Kent Seasons, the Kingsnake himself, to preach ethics? If Kent wanted to sneak drinks and play car-lot Jesus, that was his prerogative, but Paul was playing hardball.

"A job like this," Kent said, "can make a man do things he knows are wrong."

"Now you're saying I did something wrong—by closing a deal?"

"Lately I've been afraid, Paul. Afraid of a truth I never wanted to believe was really true, if you catch my drift."

Paul didn't, actually.

"Sometimes it seems like to reach the top of this profession—the very pinnacle, I mean—requires a moral flexibility that no decent man could live with."

"All those jokes have to come from somewhere, right?"

"What I'm talking about goes beyond selling cars."

"I thought selling cars was all that mattered? Remember that *Karate Kid* speech you gave me—how I need to stop testing the water and just go for it?"

"I guess what I'm really suggesting," Kent said, "is that deep down, where the soul supposedly resides, a salesman can't afford to believe in jack shit."

"Like you said before, Kent—they chose to sign the deal."

"A deal?" Kent laughed. "With who? What I really wonder, though, if you want to know the truth, is what being around a dealership does to people meant for better..."

Paul should've felt flattered, he supposed. Pleased his boss considered him too good for auto sales (not that he didn't know this about himself already), but he wasn't in the mood. He wanted to enjoy a victory lap, to slap fives and drink beers. Screw introspection. Besides, this entire conversation was ludicrous. Regent's had been dolling out raw deals for years, and Kent Seasons's signature was dashed across most of them.

"Thanks to me," Paul said, "Mrs. Hovarth will make it to Cincinnati to see her lovely sister get married."

"For the third time."

"For the third and final time."

"Rock on, superstar," Kent said, and gave Paul's butt a hearty slap as they reentered the showroom.

11

Thankfully, Randy Bauble's truck wasn't parked in the driveway when Jennylee finally got home. She'd picked up a sack of burgers, even though she preferred not to feed her family fast food. Chast loved burgers, though—or at least she had before the tummyaches—and it was just a once-in-a-while thing.

She visited the stable before heading inside. Bugles cantered up, hung his big head over the fence, and blew a hay-scented breath through his velvet muzzle. Jennylee rubbed his ears and told him he was the sweetest horse in all of Edgar County, and that the wide strip on his nose and his high white socks were just as handsome as could be. The horse blinked his soft brown eyes, as if in modest agreement. But then a semi veered onto the soft shoulder and a wave of grit buffeted the trailer. Bugles clomped backward, whinnying and agitated.

Once inside, she was pleased to find Chast and Derrol quietly reading a book together. He gave her a funny look, though, and laid the book aside. "Sit tight, Chast," he said, and then led Jennylee down the hall past the washer and dryer. He spoke quietly: "Some doctor called. I could barely understand the lady. Pakistani or Indian some other variety of dot head."

"Knock it off," Jennylee said.

"Well, I'm just saying," Derrol said.

A couple months back, Derrol had a nasty ingrown thumbnail, bright red with infection and pus. Jennylee suspected the problem owed to too many hours playing Xbox, but she'd kept that theory to herself. For weeks, Derrol experimented with home remedies—trimming the afflicted edge, shoving cotton balls under it, Epsom salts—before he finally made an appointment at the county clinic. He came home all bandaged up and cursing the entire country of India, as the doctor had treated

his ingrown thumbnail by squirting it with a dribble of Novo-
cain and then ripping the entire business out by the roots. None
of that excused his ugly words though.

"That's Dr. Patel," Jennylee said. "Chast really likes her. And
she's from Sri Lanka, by the way."

He fished out a menthol. "Done with your geography lesson?"

"If you're done being rude."

"That latest batch of tests came back, Jen."

Jennylee laid the sack of burgers atop the dryer. "And?" Her
husband seemed to recall his promise not to smoke inside and
tucked the menthol behind his ear. "Derrol?"

"It don't look good."

"What do you mean—?"

But before he could explain, Evelyn Sykes's arrival was her-
alded by the cannonading backfires of her old Buick. The car
sounded like a tank crunching through the yard—which was
exactly where Jennylee's mother insisted on parking: in the
front yard beneath the elm tree. Derrol groaned and cussed
under his breath.

"The better you behave"—Jennylee headed for the door—
"the quicker she'll go back home."

Her mother had gained seventy or eighty pounds in the
years since her widowhood, and the trailer's aluminum steps
gave her trouble. Evelyn pressed her hands into the flesh above
her knees with each achy stride.

"Mother," Jennylee said, "you really need to start watching
your weight."

"And you, honey," Evelyn said, "need to remind that husband of yours that cleanliness is next to godliness. Your lawn is
filthy with cigarette butts."

Jennylee glanced back to see Derrol in the hallway entrance,
shaking his head. Evelyn kept on about how disgusting all those
cigarettes were as she made her way into the trailer. If Derrol's
mother-in-law noticed him standing there scowling, she paid no
mind. Figuring she might change the subject with a little gossip,

Jennylee offered Evelyn a seat in the kitchen, but her mother was on a mission. "There's my baby doll," she said.

Chastity yawned and stretched and said hi to her grandmother, who immediately launched into the usual litany: How's that little tummy feeling? Was that mean old stomachache all gone? Had she been eating enough? Was she hungry?

Then Chastity glanced at Jennylee—only the briefest of gestures—before she looked her grandmother flush in the face and lied. "My tummy's okay, Grandma."

So far as Jennylee could recall, this marked the first lie she and Chastity had ever shared. It didn't feel like a behavior in need of correction, though, but inevitable and even tender. Chast must've overheard her and Derrol talking about how unwelcome Evelyn's constant questions were, and from there deduced that *she* was causing worry among the grown-ups—and so she'd told a fib to spare her mother grief.

"Oh, that's so good!" Evelyn was saying. Jennylee tried to distract her mother with some coffee or iced tea, but Evelyn was a bulldog. "Now, Chastity," she said, "just because you're feeling better doesn't mean we can forget who healed you."

"You mean God?"

"I certainly do mean God. Now scooch that little fanny over." Evelyn eased her bulk down onto the couch. Then she laid a palm on Chast's forehead and frowned. "I do believe this child's running a fever."

"It comes and goes," Jennylee said.

"Evelyn," Derrol said, "we were in the middle of something. Would you mind coming back tomorrow?"

"You get over here too, Derrol Witt," Evelyn said.

Derrol sulked over to his mother-in-law's side.

"Now everyone come together and join hands," Evelyn said.

Where these shows of righteousness were concerned, it was easier just to play along, so Jennylee took hold of Derrol's and Chast's free hands.

"Dear Lord Our Savior," Evelyn began, "please accept our thanks for all your blessings. And bless this child. It's Chastity Witt, Father, and she needs…"

Jennylee tuned out the rest. She'd heard some version of these prayers all her life, and suspected most were plagiarized from her own grandmother. What bugged Jennylee was her mother's insistence upon *naming* Chast so specifically. As if the Lord—who was everywhere and all-knowing—still might need a cue every so often. Beyond that, the prayer was a reminder that God already knew of any illnesses visited upon anyone, including children. And because He was both aware and all-loving, He either had His reasons for not fixing the problem (and also, she supposed, for creating it in the first place), such as needing the individual to grow stronger or to live as a lesson unto others, or He simply *couldn't* fix it. This suggested God was like the foreman of a GM assembly line: while most of His vehicles ran A-okay, some had bugs or even fatal flaws.

"In Jesus's name, Amen," Evelyn said.

"In Jesus's name, Amen," Chastity parroted, just like she'd been taught.

"Thanks a bunch, Jesus," Derrol said.

"Derrol Witt!" Evelyn hollered, and released his hand just long enough to whack him on the shoulder. Then she gave Jennylee a curt nod, meaning for her to finish the prayer and set a good example. But Jennylee didn't appreciate seeing religion used as a cudgel. Evelyn Witt browbeat people this way because she was certain she understood exactly what the Creator of the Universe wanted and also, more practically, because people got intimidated by God talk and tended to just let her have her way. This was a common enough human foible, though, and it didn't necessarily mean Evelyn's heart was in the wrong place. Nor did it cheapen Jennylee's own relationship with the unseen—or so she kept telling herself.

"In Jesus's name…" Jennylee said, and then closed her eyes.

In the silence to follow, she struggled to honestly feel that divine presence. It was still there, somewhere in the dark, but like a wave receding. Was this the inevitable pull of tides and moon, or had the empty beach in her mind's eye been there all along?

A considerable amount of time passed, at least insofar as Jennylee's prayers were usually practical and straight to the point. Finally, her mother gently spoke her name. But Jennylee paid no mind to Evelyn. She wasn't searching any longer, wasn't even praying. In fact, she was just slowly counting backwards from ten in her head.

"Jen?" Derrol said.

"Mommy?" Chastity said.

Finally, Jennylee opened her eyes and gave her daughter a look that almost perfectly matched the one Chast had given her grandmother earlier. "Amen," she said.

12

After wrapping up the Tahoe deal and calling all his be-backs in what he sincerely hoped was the middle of dinner, Paul Stenger arrived at the YMCA, feeling in tune with the cold and vacuous nature of the universe—with the knowledge that we are all solo agents on a doomed mission, and thus our ethical concerns boil down to so much pissing in the wind.

On his way past the front desk, Annie Turner tossed him a towel which looked unusually fresh, handpicked even. He set a new personal best on bench press (205 for five reps) and swished his first three jumpers.

In fact, Paul was still shooting in the otherwise empty gym when Annie came to rack the loose basketballs. Clearly, tonight was the night to ask her out—although it was bittersweet how the momentum only swung his way once he'd decided to leave town. Then again, Nashville wasn't too far away. Annie might jump at the chance to escape Paris for a long weekend. Paul had been on top of his game all day—on the lot, in the weight room, on the court—and if closing the Tahoe deal had taught him anything (other than that Kent Seasons was losing his edge) it was that the Big Dog truly does eat.

"Come here a second, Annie."

She glanced up from the gym mats she'd been folding. He hadn't asked, *Do you have a second?* Not, *Hey, can I ask you something?* Instead, he'd given her a command. And sure enough, after locking the alley doors, Annie joined him at the free-throw line. The gym lights sparkled in her pale blue eyes. Why hadn't he been this bold months ago?

"Tuning up for the championship this weekend?"

He said he thought they had a good chance, so long as that alley-ooping Neanderthal from Thompson's didn't cheapshot him again—but then he paused. Had *tuning up* actually been a subtle dig at his musicianship?

"How's that cut healing?"

He raised his chin so she could see it. "Girls dig scars, right?"

But she glanced away and Paul heard his lame line echoing between them. *Girls dig scars?* He'd gotten sloppy. Being aggressive wasn't enough, not with a firecracker like Annie. No, he had to be cool too (whatever that ephemeral notion actually entailed), or at least he needed to seem cool until she decided she liked him.

"So, you're not dating anyone?"

Annie admitted she wasn't, not at the moment, but her expression was unreadable.

"Then let's go out sometime. For dinner, or drinks." He summoned his brightest Regent's grin. "Or both."

Eyes on the hardwood, Annie crossed one running shoe atop the other and brushed a strand of hair from her cheek. With each passing moment the day's confidence ebbed away. This wasn't remotely like closing on the Tahoe. If he'd lost that sale, his disappointment would've lasted all of twenty minutes. But he'd been pondering asking out Annie Turner for nearly a year now.

"That's sweet, Paul. Really. I'll have to think it over though."

And with that she walked away, shapely hips mocking him from beneath her satiny track shorts. "Gym closes in five minutes," she called over her shoulder.

After bricking one last free-throw, Paul headed for the showers.

The locker room reeked of disinfectant, socks, and sweat. Despite being alone, Paul made a point of acting as if nothing of consequence had occurred. He met the mirror with bored eyes before digging a shampoo bottle from his bag and warming the shower. He untied his sneakers and stripped off his damp clothes in his usual unhurried way. After draping the towel over the door, he stepped into the blue-tiled stall and let the spray pound his neck, hot water streaming down his back as he mulled over what'd just happened. Of course Annie Turner didn't want to date him. He was an almost-thirty-year-old guy who sold cars—the snakiest job on the planet short of politics. Tasting iron from the old pipes, he asked himself a simple, direct, and long-overdue question: if he were Annie Turner, would he want to date Paul Stenger?

The answer was a resounding possibly not. Even in a town like Paris, there had to be other options for a girl like her. Or maybe it wasn't necessarily all about him?

Consider the last time Annie dated a salesman. Seth had broken her heart. That much was obvious. But Seth also possessed something that Paul clearly lacked—charisma, manliness, vigor. Something. Paul lathered his hair and the shampoo streamed down his flanks. The tiles underfoot were slick as river rocks, moldy and lime-scaled. Suddenly, Seth's passing a bug to Annie seemed fundamentally connected to the probability of his picking up a foot fungus from this ill-maintained public facility, as all the available evidence suggested that Paul Stenger was the sort of guy who forgot to wear shower sandals and caught plantar warts, whereas Seth was the sort of guy who forgot to wear a rubber and caught something else entirely.

I'll have to think it over...

Did Annie even realize how shitty that was?

I'll have to think it over. I'll have to think *you* over.

The last of the day's rainmaker mojo drained away, much like the suds rinsed down the drain between his pale feet. He imagined Annie at the front desk waiting for him to hurry up and go. Hell, she probably worried he was in here cutting his wrists, that she'd find him curled in the fetal position and bleeding estrogen down the drain.

He'd just grasped the faucet handle, rinsing the last dregs of soap from his face and wondering if he could somehow sneak out through the gym exits, when the stall door creaked open. A plume of steam wafted out and a cool draft slipped in. Annie Turner was topless, silky blonde hair loose to her collar bones, the skin of her arms pebbled with gooseflesh. Paul had covered himself in his surprise, but this became something of a moot point when she skimmed off those satiny track shorts and let the fabric fall to her ankles. He gave a most unnecessary nod as she stepped into the stall. Annie hugged his neck and curled her fingers into his wet hair. She was so long legged that their belly buttons aligned perfectly and winked with a soft little pop under the falling water.

"Well," she said, "I guess this means I thought it over."

Step Three: The Walkaround

13

That Wednesday, Jennylee called Regent's at nine a.m. sharp, after Chast was already deep into her testing at St. John's Hospital in Springfield. "Kent," she'd said, watching her daughter from the doorway of the exam room, "just wanted to let you know I'll be using one of my vacation days today. My daughter's seeing a specialist for her tummy."

For a moment, Kent Seasons was silent. "Vacation days?"

"I've never used a single one, so I figure I'm due."

"You're due all right," Kent said, and just before he hung up, "Hope she's okay."

Regent's didn't provide vacation days, of course. And while it might've been prudent to have played sick herself as opposed to telling the truth, it didn't really matter. She hadn't been closing very many deals lately, and if a salesperson didn't close deals, excuses weren't worth the breath it took to make them.

But it was afternoon now and they were on their way home. Derrol drove while Jennylee sat in back with Chast. They'd tried to color at first, but the bumpy road left green and red marks outside Ariel's tail and hair—that, and Chast had lost interest in coloring books recently. She was getting savvy, piecing together the adult world. How much of the doctors' talk had she understood? Jennylee couldn't be sure, but the way her little girl stared out the window, too still and pensive for a child trapped indoors all day, suggested she'd at least understood this wouldn't be her last hospital visit, or the last time some stranger gave her a phony look and said, *Don't worry, this won't hurt a bit...*

Like the day before, the Nissan was struggling too, its engine sloppy and hiccupping. A car repair simply wasn't possible right now though. How disheartening it was that when every bit of her focus should've rightly been on Chast, she had to worry about a dumb, money-sucking object, about being unable to afford the selfsame necessity she spent her life peddling to strangers. Jennylee glanced at the drought-stricken fields and assured herself the car trouble was just a figment of her over-stressed imagination—but there'd been no mistaking what the bowel specialist said: Crohn's disease.

Apparently, Chast's bowels were flaring up and possibly even infected. That's why she was prone to diarrhea and bloody stools. And Crohn's explained why she wasn't growing. Her tummy hurt, so she didn't eat, so she lacked nutrition, so she didn't grow. There was no cure for Crohn's and nobody even really knew what caused it. And while the specialist was quick to say the disease was treatable so long as they followed strict orders, those orders were awfully expensive. When asked about their insurance, Jennylee admitted they didn't have any and the man's face had blanched.

Afterward, she and Derrol found out why. They'd both stared at the billing receptionist with their mouths hanging open. Chast had had a series of blood tests performed, a stool sample taken, and a tube with a camera on run down her throat. A few hours that mostly involved waiting around empty exam rooms and trying to ignore those creepy posters of people with their skin peeled off. But today's treatment alone—just the first of a series—had cost many thousands of dollars. "And to be clear," the specialist had said, "leaving Crohn's disease untreated can have catastrophic consequences." He'd spoken of blockages or even *holes* in Chastity's intestines.

Later, back at home, Jennylee and Derrol squared off across the kitchen table.

"Maybe we could hold a benefit?" Derrol said.

Jennylee pictured a coffee canister with Chast's picture taped on it at a Paris High football game, a slit cut in the lid for spare change and ones. But she hadn't actually seen a canister like that in a long time. "Benefits are online nowadays," she said. "Assuming folks are still decent enough to donate at all."

"You're always thinking the worst of people, Jen."

"I'm just being realistic."

"Been that way ever since you started selling cars."

"Well, you might start seeing the world differently too, if you got up and went to work every morning."

But then Jennylee found herself distracted not by Derrol's reddening face and ever-louder words, but by his shirt—an old Metallica concert tee. Shit Hits the Sheds Tour, 1994, with a musclebound demon thrashing an electric guitar. She'd been so consumed with her worries that she'd failed to notice that Derrol had chosen to wear this particular shirt, threadbare and with a hole near one armpit, the neck crinkled, lettering gone patchy. The demon had glowing green eyes and pointy red horns and long sharp teeth. There was even the suggestion of a monstrous prick beneath his ripped trousers.

What had the doctors made of this? Shit Hits the Sheds? To wear a garment espousing the wisdom of Metallica to a hospital, to a place of science, of life and death—it was almost aggressively stupid, like decorating your vehicle with a Confederate flag. She and Derrol must've seemed like white-trash idiots, the type of no-account parents who'd sickened their own child through neglect. But no, Crohn's wasn't like that. The disease just happened. That's what the specialist said. More act of God than bad parenting. And so Jennylee planned to pray before bed tonight. To ask the Lord for help with this trial, although perhaps she'd be better off praying for simpler blessings—like a husband who knew better than to wear such a crude garment.

"We've hardly got money for aspirin," she said, "but Chast has to have her treatments. Now I know you're having a hard time finding work, but—"

"But what? You want me to go bale hay like some teenager? To beg?"

"Derrol, you at least have to try."

Hearing that, he reared back and royally bit her head off. Accused her of blaming him for their money troubles, their lack of insurance, even for Chastity's illness. "Times are hard out there," he said. "There aren't any jobs that pay a decent wage and that ain't my fault no more than them holes in our daughter's belly are *your* fault."

"There are not"—she stilled her hands on the table—"any holes in her belly."

"Not yet."

"Stop."

But he kept ranting, spilling his worries and anxieties, cussing about Barack Obama and the Chinese government, about bankruptcy laws and Hollywood liberals, raising his voice and slapping the table and not making a lick of sense. At first, Jennylee regretted getting him so irate—she hated how his mouth shrank and his brow beetled up—but as he hollered and repeated himself, she grew angry. Derrol vented his frustrations on her too much. As a new wife, she'd thought that was just part of the gig, like laundry and cooking and getting pawed at come dark. But being a doormat wasn't her job anymore. Maybe she'd gotten laid off from that job, like Derrol got laid off from his, or maybe she'd just finally worked up the nerve to quit.

"Wearing that crappy old shirt to St. John's," she said, pointing at his chest, "was a stupid thing to do."

Stunned, he followed her finger as if tracking a laser beam. Then he crossed his arms over his chest. "Think we could we ask your mother for help?"

"My mother hasn't got a pot to piss in."

"She loves Chast—"

"I know she does, Derrol. But love don't spend."

"You say that like you got all the answers, like you're just waiting to see if I'm man enough to step up."

"That's not true," she said, although maybe in some sense it was.

As for Jennylee's in-laws, forget about it. Derrol's mother was a mouse and his father, Richard Witt, was an iceberg. The first time Jennylee met the man, clear back in high school, he'd given her a once over and then totally ignored her. Even after she'd married his son, Richard Witt was more interested in whatever hunting and fishing magazine happened to be in his lap. After seeing the score around the Witt household, Jennylee's love for Derrol only deepened—a mothering instinct that kicked in before Chast was even a glimmer.

As if sensing her thoughts, Derrol reached across the table and took her hand. He rubbed with his thumb, dragging her skin over the bones. "Me and Randy been drumming up a business plan," he said.

She took a breath and told herself this was a good thing, but in her mind's eye rose the image of those rusty propane tanks. "Nothing dangerous or illegal, I hope."

"Jen, really? That's what you think?"

"Nothing to do with them tanks."

Derrol's rubbing was irritating, borderline painful.

"What are you even talking about?"

"Because I cannot handle you getting hurt or arrested, Derrol."

"Well, what's your plan—to go to work tomorrow and *not* sell any cars again?"

"Damn it, that rubbing hurts."

He looked down at her reddened hand as if surprised by its very aliveness. Then he excused himself and went outside. A glance out the window revealed him firing up a menthol and fiddling with his phone. No doubt texting Randy Bauble, as this mysterious business plan of theirs seemed to require lots of privacy. Or maybe Derrol just needed a few beers with his friend. Hard to blame him, really, considering the day they'd had.

Then she noticed a message waiting on her own phone. Must've been left while they were at St. John's. The number was local and vaguely familiar.

Probably just another creditor though. So instead of listening to the voicemail, Jennylee scanned that day's *Beacon-Herald*, which only proved that bad days can always get worse. Because there in the classifieds, coldly staring back at her in black and white, was a help wanted ad for a professional automotive salesperson at Regent's of Paris. The ad listed the hours when applicants were encouraged to come by and speak with management. This advertisement was for her replacement. Of that she had little doubt.

§o

"We'll call you, don't call us," Kent Seasons said, and shook another derelict's hand before Brad Howard walked the guy out of the meeting room.

The classified had run just that morning, but they'd already received a flurry of walk-ins. Kent dreaded parsing the applications: a steaming pile of exaggerations and outright lies, of misspellings and childish penmanship. A number of these applicants seemed to believe slinging hamburgers in a drive-thru window constituted sales experience, while the rest apparently considered "professional attire" to include shorts and flip-flops. Of course, half these losers were just creating a paper trail for the unemployment office, but still.

As managers, he and Brad Howard were responsible for the hiring, but they hadn't been working very well as a team. Tension reigned, primarily due to Kent's suspicion that Brad was talking to Junior and Nautical Bill behind his back, pointing out the dipping numbers and lean returns on advertising. When times got tough, heads rolled, and impossible as this would've seemed back when his father was around, Kent could almost imagine his own head on the block—scarred wood under his cheek, the scent of freshly notched pine, the whistle of the falling ax.

The last applicant had been telemarketing since quitting school. He'd had a decent rap (and enough sense to wear slacks and loafers) but he also sported a ponytail.

"I hear you, Kent," Brad said, once he got back. "The guy could use a haircut." He flipped through the applications. "But he was better than the rest of these bozos."

"Say we hire pony boy," Kent said. "He'll see what, fifty ups a month?"

"That's optimistic, but okay."

"And let's say one out of twenty-five buyers would rather do business with someone who doesn't look like an extra from *Miami Vice*. That's two lost sales a month. Now this dealership averages around five-thousand dollars per deal, figuring in sales and incentives, maintenance, accessories, and bird-dog referrals. So that fucking ponytail costs us a hundred twenty grand a year."

"That right there was some fuzzy math."

"If pony boy sticks around long enough, we lose a fortune."

"I'll drive him over to Supercuts," Brad said. "Get him faded up high and tight."

"Gonna take more than an eight-dollar haircut to turn this place around, amigo."

"Nautical Bill's breathing down my neck. Says he wants somebody hired in time for Junior's consultant." Brad mimicked the old man's bellowing drawl: "Brad, you and Kent need to quit playing slap-ass and find us a topflight salesman..."

"I do not trust a man with long hair," Kent said. "I got enough knives in my back already. In fact, I wouldn't hire that goober even if he was slick enough to sell Junior's yellow Avalanche."

But he shouldn't have said this. Knives in his back? Hell, Brad Howard was filing the shiv. Then Brad leaned in real close, like he had a secret to tell. His nostrils flared, chocolate brown mustache wiggling, but his eyes went stone-cold still. "You sneak out for lunch when I wasn't looking, Kent?"

Kent recoiled and spoke out the side of his mouth. "Was just getting ready to pick up Kelsi for a quick bite, actually."

He hadn't planned to take his daughter to lunch at all. The words just popped out. This instinct had served him well over the years, as dead air leads to questions and questions lead to problems. A late lunch with Kelsi was a fine idea, though—not to mention an excuse to drop into Thompson's Ford unannounced.

"Could have fooled me," Brad said. "I'd have sworn I smelled booze. Figured you might've popped down to the Buck. Today's the hot-wings special, right?"

"Your sniffer's off," Kent said. "And we can do better than pony boy."

Brad bowled toward the door, shoes groaning under his

bulk. "Worst-case scenario, the guy doesn't sell very many cars. That'd just lump him in with the rest of our crew."

"Wrong." Kent flipped the light, casting the room in darkness. "Worst-case scenario—for you—is he sells lots of cars. So many that Nautical Bill decides Regent's might be better off if our assistant sales manager sported a nice long ponytail."

With that, Kent headed for his office, doing his best not to limp. His toe was worse. Pain now radiated clear to the ball of his foot. If it reached his heel, he'd need crutches, and if he was on crutches he wouldn't be closing deals, and—considering the state of the union—if Kent didn't close deals there might not *be* a Regent's much longer. So much for not tipping his hand though. That morning's drinks had eased his pain some, but also thinned the filter between brain and tongue.

Brad Howard's voice trailed him down the hall. "You really think that dude had his sights set on management?"

As Kent's fingers closed around the doorknob, the bourbon in his desk called to him. He could almost feel the charred sting on his lips. "I think everybody eventually figures out that the easiest way up the ladder is to step on the guy in front of you."

"That's a downright pessimistic philosophy," Brad said.

"Wrong, buddy. That's wisdom."

He'd kept a quote-of-the-day calendar for a while there. Was it Mark Twain who said the only thing more pathetic than a young cynic was an old optimist? Had Twain ever broken *his* foot in his goddamn sleep? While positive thinking could work for a young buck like Paul Stenger, in the long run it made for a Mickey Mouse world view. With no wife or kids to worry about, with a head full of hair and a hard-on that cut diamonds, any doofus could see the bright side. But the years teach a man something different: that his life is drudgery, his neighbors venal and cruel, the truth ugly and dispiriting—and truth, Kent Seasons had come to believe, was no mere philosophical concept. Like morality, truth was as real and tangible as a Chevy Silverado.

❧

Having considered your proposition and crunched some numbers, Alice Higgenbottom said in the voicemail, *I believe an internship is feasible, after all…*

So it actually hadn't been a bill collector. Jennylee listened to the message in its entirety three more times, savoring Alice's every pert syllable. The pay wasn't much, but it was more than she'd expected, as she'd expected to work for experience alone. Alice also said she could set her own hours and intern around family and work obligations. This was better than she'd dared imagine, and a surprise too, as it was rare in Jennylee's experience to ask for something and receive it without having to grovel or fight.

But reality soon stomped back into the picture. Considering Chast's illness and their empty bank account, she had about as much business interning as Evelyn Sykes did applying to ballet school. The cloud of forced optimism, the buzz from her daily affirmations, the slim comfort she still managed to wring from her prayers—all deflated.

She blinked and looked around the kitchen. The counter paneling was cracked and the drop ceiling yellow from Derrol's cigarettes. Hard little chairs with wobbly peg and glue joints surrounded a table most folks would've hesitated to use for patio furniture. She yanked open the microwave's door—the appliance was so cheap and lightweight it nearly slid off the counter before the latch gave. Popcorn grease was nuked to its insides, orange slime that filled their home with a nauseating stench. She'd asked Derrol to clean the microwave weeks ago, as he was the popcorn lover. Three separate times he'd promised to do it, yet the mess remained.

Becoming a mortician? Running her own business? No, Derrol was probably right. If higher education was in the cards, she'd have done it already. She dribbled a sponge with dish soap and scrubbed the microwave, having to cock her wrist at painful angles. Part of her wished she'd never gone to Higgenbottom's at all. Never made herself out to be some go-getter when she was really just like everybody else around Paris. As for Chast, who was napping in the next room, she would always love her parents no matter what—Jennylee was sure of that—but how long before Chast came to see their home for the dump it was? Before classmates started poking fun at her hand-me-downs?

She tossed the sponge in the sink and raised the blinds. Down the driveway, Derrol was still busy texting. Drivers whizzing past must've noticed her husband standing there: a squirrely guy in need of a haircut who, like a lot of men around Paris, sported an overly ambitious goatee. They probably noticed the horse stall too, which was really just a cheap fence with one skinny and surely miserable animal trapped inside. Nothing but a waste of money and time. A naïve girl's corny dream.

How embarrassing it was, how hurtful, to realize your dreams were stupid—although wasn't this the very lesson Regent's had been teaching all along?

Exhausted, she went to check on Chastity again, pressing her wrist to that warm, damp forehead. Chast had toughed out a real hard day, a day no kid should ever have to endure—although even as Jennylee had carried her daughter in her womb, she'd known of this possibility: known she might be gestating her own heartbreak. This was the nature of the world, though, and there was no use pretending it was otherwise. But while she couldn't banish pain and worry, she could at least do something practical—she could go thank Alice Higgenbottom for her generous offer.

"Derrol," she said, after grabbing her purse and heading for the Nissan once again, "Randy Bauble better not be here when I get back."

In his surprise, Derrol Witt looked remarkably like the teenager she'd fallen for. His brown eyes big and wet, posture loose and lanky. His figure quickly shrank to nothing in the rearview, but as she puttered back toward town she was on edge, awaiting some clank or pop from under the hood that spelled doom. The Nissan did okay, though, and she assured herself Billy Jr. and Kent Seasons weren't quite crooked enough to dump a lemon on their own employee. Assuming Alice was still at work,

Jennylee intended to thank her and also apologize for having wasted her time. To explain Chastity's diagnosis and how she couldn't afford Triumph, Online's tuition. Admitting all this would hurt, would feel an awful lot like giving up, but a bruised ego was no excuse for bad manners.

Besides, selling cars had taught her the value of a polite follow-up. Even when you thought the deal was dead, what was the harm in keeping the door open?

14

Within seconds of pulling into Thompson's Ford, a mob of salesmen bum-rushed the Silverado, hemming her in and cutting off escape routes. Some lurked and circled while pretending they were merely out for a smoke, while others provided helpful hand signals, smiling and pointing out empty parking stalls.

Jaw clenched tight, Kent Seasons squeezed the wheel and let that 5.3-liter V-8 rumble as he parted the jackals with his bumper. Finally, he neared the building itself and eased the big front tires up and over a parking block. He rolled closer still, until the grill's golden Chevrolet bow tie idled just a hair's breadth from seventy-thousand dollars' worth of pristine showroom glass. Inside, a salesman rose from his desk and slowly backed away.

Kent remained in the cab as the pack slunk up on his tailgate, wary now, as he'd departed from the usual script: he hadn't climbed out and nervously returned their smiles, hadn't surrendered his name and number, hadn't offered up a pound of flesh. In the rearview, their rapacious eyes glowed with all-too-familiar thoughts: *This guy's driving a brand-new rig—see that Regent's license frame? Looks like a case of buyer's remorse. Probably wishes he'd bought an F-150 instead. Six grand upside down the second he rolled off the lot. But hey, if he was stupid last week...*

Finally, Kent popped the door. "Hey, maybe one of you friendly dudes can help me out. I blew my down payment on this here Silverado, see, but today I got laid-off so now I'm looking to get out of my lease."

They scattered as if he'd hosed them down with roach spray.

Kent dry-swallowed another dose of Tylenol before easing his tender foot down to the cement. He'd read that painkillers like Tylenol damaged either your liver or your kidneys, but he couldn't recall which, and at the moment didn't really give a damn.

He locked his truck and then heel-walked into Thompson's cavernous, oxblood-tiled showroom—but his daughter wasn't at the greeter's stand.

The place reeked of tire rubber and a musky cologne of testosterone and commerce. Much as Kent hated to admit it, Thompson's Ford looked and felt how a dealership was supposed to look and feel. Take, for example, the enclosed glass box in the very center of the showroom: the kill-box. At a high-pressure rodeo like Thompson's, salespeople romanced their ups, test-drove them, and dickered over the inflated numbers, all while pretending to be oh-so-upset with how "management" or "the desk" wouldn't budge and give their good buddy the customer a square deal. This malarkey could go on for hours. In fact, that was exactly the point. Wear them out and soften them up. Some dealerships even required salesmen to slow-cook their chickens for a set time, forty-five minutes or an hour, as the more of a buyer's day they managed to waste, the more desperate that buyer was to be finished car shopping. But when the foreplay was finally over and the exhausted buyer was lured into the kill-box—often under the auspices of meeting another manager with a better offer—that's when the closer (Dan Thompson himself?) entered with the cuffs and hatchet.

Being a friendly no-haggle, no-hassle dealership, Regent's had nothing so pleasantly demented as a kill-box, and no designated closer other than Kent himself—who was also the desk, trade appraiser, and F & I man, as well as resident counselor, bouncer, and therapist. But their modus-o wasn't all that different lately, now that everyone had five-hundred credit scores and counted their bankruptcies on their fingers. The salespeople closed lay-downs and roll-overs, but tough deals brought out the heavy artillery.

Kent wasn't here to compare sales philosophies, however. On the drive he'd mulled over the evidence. Foremost was the Ford man's slip at auction—joking about the honcho at

Thompson's cavorting with some other car guy's daughter. That didn't mean it was necessarily *his* daughter, of course. The Paris area featured a handful of dealerships. But Kelsi's being at Thompson's made the story more than suspicious. Especially considering those midnight tears in the driveway. After speaking to her, Linda had said only, "Boy trouble," the implication being Kent was too old-school to *get* a teenage girl's love life. It didn't look like boy trouble though. More like full-grown man trouble.

Then an alarm blared over the PA and a hearty voice announced: "CONGRATS, MR. DAVID RUFF! YOU JUST PURCHASED A BRAND-NEW CAR!"

A regiment of salesmen in white shirts and colorful ties stood and clapped, watches flashing and bracelets jangling. In the kill-box, a startled guy raised his palms like a mime fending off a mugger. The shout-out was a classic move. The gist was to announce the sale publicly as soon as the buyer verbally agreed—or better yet, as soon as he'd *almost* agreed—and thereby obligate him and quash any second thoughts.

Kent paced the showroom, brooding, until another salesman spotted him. The guy made gluey eye contact as he weaved around the featured vehicles. Eye contact established who was alpha. In a street fight, a man never breaks eye contact, and neither should a salesman. But just before this salesman could reach him (hand already assuming the shake), a different salesman skated right between them, skidding on his heels. This guy sported slicked-back hair, an orange tan, and what appeared to be a recently broken nose. Kent wouldn't have purchased a three-speed blender from this wannabe Corleone.

"I'm Seth," he said, and stuck out his hand. "Beautiful day to car shop, isn't it?"

Looking at those proffered digits, Kent imagined the pudgy index finger twirling a key ring and greenbacks peeled from a money clip. What the industry needed were clean-cut professionals, not bottom-feeders slithering around tasting the air with their tongues. He slipped his own hand safely into his pocket.

"Saw you pull up in that Silverado." Seth smiled. "Thought for a second you were about to park her *inside* the showroom."

"I gave it serious consideration."

The guy didn't even blink. "What sort of vehicle are you in the market for?"

"I'm not. I'm looking for Kelsi Seasons."

Seth glanced at the empty greeter stand. "Oh, well, she's…"

"I'm her father."

The toadying melted away instantly. "Oh, yeah. It's Kent, right? From Regent's?" Again he tried for a handshake, the appendage dangling there, pleading. Kent finally surrendered his palm, squeezing and mashing their skins together, all the while wishing for a tube of hand sanitizer. He asked if Kelsi had already taken her lunch, but Seth claimed not to know. Kent wouldn't have wanted his daughter around this guy either. Not for a second. Why had he ever helped her get work here? Christ, he may as well have shoved bloody hamburger in her pockets and tossed her in the Atlantic.

"I'll go find her," Seth said. "She might be back in Mr. Thompson's office—"

"Hold up"—Kent snatched his elbow—"let me surprise her."

He left the showroom, passed by a dishearteningly busy call center, and soon found himself outside Dan Thompson's office door—his *closed* office door. Kent stood there for some time, eyes on the waxed red tile between his wingtips, blood thumping in his ears. He imagined whispered voices, imagined worse. He raised a fist to knock, lowered it, and then considered simply turning around and leaving. But these thoughts were overwhelmed by a desire to kick that door off its oily fucking hinges.

What sort of businessman invites a teenage girl into his office and shuts the goddamn door? Didn't Dan Thompson even care about appearances, or was everyone in on it? He imagined the salesmen sipping coffee and firing up smokes and laughing about what a hound dog their old boss was, still putting the wood to the teenyboppers.

Kent balled one fist and wrapped the other around the door handle. He gritted his teeth, gave a hard two-beat knock, and lunged inside—

"Dad!" Kelsi shouted.

She was clothed, thank god, and across the desk from Dan Thompson. The man himself was cocked back in an espresso leather chair with his fingers laced behind his head. He sported a red power tie complete with a silver tie-tack and matching cufflinks. With his robust salt-and-pepper hair he looked more like a GOP congressman than a small-town car salesman. But Kelsi was clearly upset. They'd been talking personal. The office stank of secrets like a Motel 6 stinks of Camels and pussy.

"Dan," Kent announced, "I'm here to take my daughter to lunch."

The dealer's confusion melted into a polished smile. He rose and said of course, great, sure thing. "By the look on your face, Kent, I was afraid there was a problem."

"Who says there isn't?"

"Pardon?"

Kent kept his eyes on his daughter, who looked about ready to scream and run.

"We were just discussing Kelsi's future plans," Dan said. "I like to get to know my employees."

"Is that so?"

Now it was Dan's turn to ignore a question. "I'm sure you already know this, Kent, but your daughter's a terrific worker. She's great with our customers. A real people pleaser. I know she's off to college soon, to bigger and better, but if she ever wants to come home, there will always be a job waiting right here at Thompson's Ford."

On the wall hung a photo of Dan's family, wife and sons grinning like loons on some far-flung beach, turquoise sea white-tipped in the background. Another at a football game— Soldier Field—the boys handsome and ruddy-cheeked. Kent felt rash and foolish. Barging into Dan Thompson's office had been an 80-proof decision. Dan, eager to smooth over the awkwardness, made small talk as they headed back through the showroom.

"Tough times are upon us," he said. "Some are saying the end is nigh."

"Business is down," Kent said.

Between them Kelsi stomped along, fists balled and spine stiff.

"Down all over town, as they say."

"Actually," Kent said, "it doesn't look so down over here."

"Ford and GM are competitors," Dan said, "but we're all a brotherhood. You, me, every dealer in downstate Illinois—hell, every dealer in the country. We've got to stick together and weather this storm. Ford understands the tough spot you're in. And believe-you-me, it's a damn shame what Obama's got up his sleeve for General Motors."

"Government Motors," Kent said.

"What's become of the America we grew up in, Kent? What happened to her?"

"Moral decay," Kent said. "A decline in family values."

Then he planted a hand on his daughter's waist and steered her along. Seth called out a hearty see y'all later, but Kent was already pushing through the door. Once safely alone in the Silverado, Kelsi burned him with her snottiest look.

"That was *so* embarrassing."

"Tell me about it," Kent said.

"What's wrong with you?"

"Better question is what's wrong with you?"

"Dad!"

"Kelsi?"

"*Dad!*"

"You sound hungry, sweetheart. How about we go and grab a bite?"

15

Needing time alone to temper her disappointment before speaking with Alice Higgenbottom, Jennylee decided to do some grocery shopping first. She'd always loved the cleanliness and order of a nicely kept market, the produce section most of all. Fresh greens spritzed with mist. Neatly arranged bunches of bananas and cartons of ripe strawberries stacked in rows. Something heavenly about all that.

On the outskirts of town, however, she spied Kent Seasons's unmistakable gleaming white Silverado in the oncoming lane. It'd look mighty bad to be spotted out and about after calling in. But just before their vehicles would've passed, an aquamarine Hyundai cut Kent off. Sunk down low in the Nissan's seat, Jennylee watched Kent palm his horn and swerve across the divider. His big truck sent the little Hyundai's elderly driver careening onto the shoulder, her grandmotherly face gawping in terror.

Apparently, Jennylee had chosen the right day to miss work.

At the IGA, she picked up only the barest of essentials: eggs and bread, gummy bear multivitamins for Chast (the pill kind made her throw up) and, of course, more milk and cereal for Derrol. But after loading the Nissan and heading back east through downtown, she found herself distracted by yet another vehicle.

Despite her dissatisfaction with selling cars, as a professional Jennylee couldn't help but notice them—and also make inferences about their owners. For example, if some dude pulled up in a three-quarter-ton pickup, you knew he was either legitimately blue-collar or a Marlboro Man wannabe, but not a doctor (SUV, leather, all the trimmings) or a lawyer (foreign sports car, leather, all the trimmings) or a teacher (stock sedan, cloth, no trimmings). A person simply couldn't sell cars six days a week and *not* learn these basic truths. So when Jennylee spied that cute little lime-green Mazda coup parked a block off the square—and right outside Currant Family Photography—her attention was piqued. In fact, she parked beside the coup for a better look.

It was newish but dinged up and scratched like a starter car. Furthermore, *Class of '09!* was scribbled on the rear window in faded white shoe polish. The rainbow dice dangling from the rearview didn't tell her much, but the wallet-sized photos of young men lining the dashboard spoke of popularity, of cheerleading and pep rallies, bonfires and dates. A girl around the same age as Kent Seasons's daughter, most likely.

Perhaps that morning's stress—St. John's, Crohn's disease, Metallica—explained the impulsive behaviors to follow? That's all Jennylee could think of later by way of explaining it. Or maybe she just wanted to put off declining her internship for as long as possible. Or perhaps it was the still-fresh memory of Maurice Currant's penis catching a ray of buttery sunshine as the Eagles crooned and bass jumped in Paradise Lake, and the suspicion he was likely up to something similar with the little Mazda's owner. Whatever the case, Jennylee forgot all about driving to Higgenbottom's.

Downtown Paris was quiet in the afternoon, as the new Walmart Supercenter north of town had killed most of the small businesses. Still, as she creeped alongside the building, her head was on a swivel. Feeling vaguely criminal, she got up on her tiptoes and peeked through a window, but Maurice's studio was empty. Just a vanilla backdrop and some fancy camera equipment. But then she heard a high-pitched giggle followed by a deeper voice—pleasant, but also pushy—almost like a salesman's voice.

A tall wood fence ran down to the alley. Jennylee imagined what lay on the other side: manicured grass and flower beds, a whitewashed gazebo, the perfect spot for engagement photos and toddler pictures. She pressed an ear to the splintery boards; the voices rose and fell, seesawing, and one of those voices

definitely belonged to Maurice Currant. Hearing it now took
her back to those awful moments in the Caprice. But she also
felt emboldened—almost as if, by invading Maurice's privacy,
she might take back a modicum of the self-respect he'd stolen
from her. Careful to keep quiet, she climbed atop a nearby trash
bin and balanced on her knees, breathing through her mouth
to avoid the bin's ripe funk. Then she grabbed the top of the
fence and peeked over.

Oh boy, she thought.

She knew some folks were into this fetishism kink-type stuff
(she'd even found an example on Derrol's laptop once, to her
dismay), but she'd assumed it was just fantasy, the sort of thing
people watched movies about but didn't actually do. Apparently, she was more naïve than she'd realized.

The brunette was tall and slender, her face painted up like
a geisha, all catty eyes and ghostly cheeks and wine-dark lips.
She wore a bone-white vintage wedding dress and heels, but
her groom was nowhere to be found. Instead, there was old
Maurice with his long black camera, snap, snap, snapping away.
The brunette was bent over against a tree on the far side of the
enclosure, that beautiful ivory dress hiked up to reveal a yard of
athletic-looking leg—

Wait. The girl was *handcuffed* to that tree.

Bondage made sense, actually. A helpless victim was right
down Maurice Currant's alley. The girl didn't seem scared
though. In fact, as Maurice circled her, shooting his roll, she
made pouty faces and tickled her teeth with a wormy pink
tongue. For his part, Maurice sighed and cooed ("Good little
doll...Just like that, you naughty thang!") and the sights and
sounds made Jennylee regret her curiosity. Maurice was too
much. He was a sick person and she and this handcuffed girl
had suffered the misfortune of crossing his sick path. Still, there
was something fascinating about someone so utterly shameless.
Absent the criminality, there was even a strange liberation in it.

Camera tight to his sweaty eyeball, Maurice dropped into
a crouch—*click*—scuttled in for a close-up—*click*—and then

circled the girl, snapping one smutty photograph after another. Having apparently gotten his fill, and after running his hands up her dress and nuzzling her neck, he finally unhooked her wrists. For her part, the girl seemed quite spirited about the whole enterprise. Free to move about now, she lifted her hair and pranced around the grassy enclosure, rangy as a colt. And Maurice Currant could hardly have looked any more pleased. Alice Higgenbottom had said that certain people around Paris called Maurice "Photo Mo." That nickname sure did fit.

Hey, Photo Mo, take any good pictures lately? Click, click, you old rascal!

This lunchtime friskiness made more sense after Jennylee spotted the wine coolers. A half-dozen bottles glistened under the checkered awning. Still, Maurice must've worked on this naïve girl for a long time—flirted in a thousand harmless ways, made her feel noticed and special—before she agreed to be porno-handcuffed by an AARP member.

Humanity may well be noble, a claim Jennylee had heard made, but individual human beings tended more toward disgusting. This (well, not *exactly* this) was why selling cars was so difficult. You had to court people, even people like Maurice Currant. No matter your personal feelings, you had to speak to such people, to touch their hands and look them in their creepy eyes and pretend to like them. Maybe the secret to happiness lay in figuring out how to make a living without having to deal with the public. After all, everyone claimed it was such a wonderful asset to be a people person—to be *good with people*—but most days Jennylee wished she could stay as far away from people as humanly possible.

After watching Maurice unzip the wedding gown, Jennylee was ready to sneak off and spare herself the inevitable—but then the young girl did something truly unexpected: she pulled off her long brunette hair and tossed it to Maurice like a Frisbee.

The girl's unusual appearance suddenly clicked, just like Maurice's camera. The broad shoulders and narrow hips. The stenciled abdominals above a pair of polka-dot boxer shorts. Grinning like a satyr, Maurice fitted the wig atop his own head. Then he fired up a hand-rolled cigarette from his shirt pocket. After a long toke, he passed it to his youthful companion.

"Son of a gun," Jennylee whispered, catching a pungent whiff of marijuana—and right then Maurice's head swung her way.

She ducked, heart jack-hammering, and only dumb luck kept her from tumbling ass-over-teakettle into the alley. Frozen on her haunches, she counted her shallow breaths as her knees and hips screamed for mercy. She imagined being called into Kent's office tomorrow and having to explain why she'd been caught peeping on Maurice Currant. What excuse could she possibly give? *Well, Kent, I suppose I got a little curious about the old goat after he sexually assaulted me, disrespected and humiliated me, and thereby spoiled whatever faith in humanity that selling cars hadn't already done in...*

Finally, the banter across the fence resumed. Awash with relief, Jennylee was yet again about to quietly slip away, when another thought occurred.

Careful to keep quiet, she worked her phone loose from the pocket of her Wranglers. She pondered her actions for a moment, just holding that phone in the palm of her hand and projecting her mind into the future, imagining potential scenarios, and considering all the likelihoods and pitfalls—and then she thumbed on the camera feature.

Slowly, silently, this phone of hers rose above the crest of the fence, not unlike a periscope.

Meanwhile, in the courtyard of Currant Family Photography, Maurice and his racy young friend took turns blowing marijuana smoke into each other's mouths. Hands found their way inside waistbands and zippers toothed slowly apart. Other things happened as well, some of the expected variety, others quite surprising. By making liberal use of her camera's zoom feature, Jennylee captured all of these happenings, the summer sun beating down hot and bright, every last detail illuminated in high-pixilation digital splendor. Her phone shot video as well, and so she recorded the young man's impromptu booty-shake dance, his polka-dotted behind jiggling to Maurice's preening applause. That the young man seemed to find the combination of Maurice's witchy brunette wig, red thong underwear, and shrunken buttocks *attractive* was and would remain one of the more mysterious things Jennylee Witt ever had the misfortune to witness. And amidst all these goings-on, glittering faintly in the checkered shade under the latticework awning, those six sugary wine coolers filled with small dead flies.

16

O nce they were comfortably seated at The Gunning Buck, Kent Seasons began methodically munching peanuts from a tin bucket. The floor around their table was littered with empty shells. The Buck provided these roasted nuts complimentary, but of course they weren't really free—no more so than the tank of gasoline buyers got "courtesy of Regent's of Paris" after parting with forty grand.

Kent cracked yet another nut and pondered what'd just gone down. Sure, Dan Thompson's trousers were fastened, but that line about wanting to get to know his employees was weak sauce. What dealer chats one-on-one with the showroom hostess? Especially the czar of a slaughterhouse like Thompson's Ford...

"You could've run that old lady into a ditch and killed her," Kelsi said, her voice exaggeratedly calm. "You need to take a chill pill or something."

Or something was right. He'd let his anger get behind the wheel. And sideswiping a senior citizen would've been some real bad karma.

"Dan must think I'm such an idiot," Kelsi said.

"Dan?"

"You could've at least knocked."

"I did knock."

"No, you burst in like a drug bust on *Cops!*"

He tucked his sore foot behind the other one, irrationally afraid his daughter might stomp it under the table. The odor of fried food wafted from the kitchen to complement the spilt beer and old cigarette smell that seeped from the flooring and booths.

"Why not take the summer off? Before you get busy with school."

She fixed her eyes on the glowing *Dukes of Hazard* pinball machine across the room. "I like my job."

Kent sipped his Diet Coke and wondered exactly which aspects were so appealing. Repeating *Welcome to Thompson's Ford* fifty times a day, or something else?

"Dealerships are rough places. You're too good to spend your time on the lot."

"Then why do you spend all *your* time on one?"

Seeing her close to tears, Kent felt something tender shred in his chest, like wet paper. His daughter was tall and pretty, healthy and confident, but she still had that same daffy expression she'd worn at age ten. She hadn't quite let go of childhood yet, or perhaps childhood hadn't quite let go of her.

"You're the one who helped me get hired in the first place, remember?"

Oh, he remembered all right. Looking back, he should've realized Kelsi would attract the lot lizards. Most salesmen were male, after all. Usually young, always competitive, and some even had a cockiness that passed for charisma. But he hadn't wanted to think about his little girl that way, so he simply hadn't. Now, though, he pictured it all too clearly. *Fresh meat at the greeter stand.* One of them straightens his tie, while another polishes his watch. *Man, I'd love to take that little honey for a test-drive—*

"Why are you doing this to me? Do you want to ruin my life?"

"Your mother and I worked hard to keep you innocent, sweetheart. So maybe this is partly our fault—"

Kelsi's eyes shrank to dark buttons and she said, "Oh my *God*, Dad, and what are you even *talking* about, Dad, and stop treating me like some dumb kid"—but her dad was lost in thought.

"Used to consider myself above the fray," Kent said. "Thought I was keeping my shoes clean. But I wasn't, not really. Surround yourself with sketchy people doing sketchy things, and it's bound to take a toll. There's just no way around it."

"Did someone from the dealership call—did Dan?"

A call from Dan Thompson? Jesus, she really was naïve. He cracked yet another peanut, tossed the shell, and imagined this hypothetical call: *Kent? Dan Thompson here. Just wanted to let you know your daughter's doing a bang-up job. She's polite with the customers, punctual, efficient. And she's one fine piece of ass, to boot.*

Then he remembered the salesman who'd greeted him. Seth. The guy was closer to Kelsi's age, after all... But surely not. Dan Thompson was her boss—suave, rich, and locally famous from endless TV spots. Understandable how he might lure an impressionable girl, how a mentor relationship might morph into something else.

"Nobody called. Should they have?"

Then their bowling ball of a waitress rolled up to the table and slammed down their plates. A dozen hot wings, nuclear orange, lay piled beside a ramekin of blue cheese dip and a stalk of limp celery. Steam rose from the wings, pungent with vinegar.

"Just so you know," Kelsi said, "there's no way I'm quitting my job."

"Okay, but will you answer me one thing?"

She seemed to actively debate just how deeply to sneer. "What?"

"How come you don't trust your old man's judgment anymore?"

That mellowed her out some, although she was too smart to risk an answer. The key here was to remain calm. Had to stay loose, feint and jab. An outright confrontation with Dan Thompson would go no better than this confrontation with his daughter. If he was mistaken, he'd humiliate himself abominably. But even if he was right, which he was, Dan would simply deny it. And Kelsi would most likely protect the sonofabitch— as if they were star-crossed lovers, like Romeo and Juliet, only with Regent's and Thompson's as the warring families and Romeo with gray fur on his nuts.

"I spent my morning interviewing potential salesmen," Kent said, in a bid to change the subject, "and do you know what?"

"Seriously?"

"Come on, Kelsi. Meet me halfway."

"Fine. What?"

"Finding a good salesman in Paris is like finding hay in a needle stack."

His daughter merely stared at him, and so Kent felt obliged to explain how hay was slang for money, which was valuable, just like a good salesman, and needles were painful, and so having to dig through a big stack of them would be terrible. He rattled on like this, defending his play on words even as he realized it wasn't all that clever.

"Can't we just eat this shitty food," she said, "and not talk?"

But Kent was in no mood for silence, and so while eating his shitty food he recounted the morning's interviews, one by one and in as much detail as he could muster. After making clear (via eye rolls and ever louder sighs) that she couldn't have cared less, Kelsi mentioned that a salesman had recently left Thompson's. She'd noticed the guy's name was always at the top of the sales board.

"The top of the board, you say?"

"He was our assistant manager. Or something like that."

Kent dropped a scorching hot wing, cursed, and dabbed his fingers with a paper napkin. That collusive *our* reminded him of that damned Thompson's Ford license frame on Kelsi's Impala. (The morning after she came home crying, he'd politely asked her to remove it, which only started her crying again.) But she'd also said *assistant manager*. The guy had probably left for greener grass, but maybe he just needed a change of scenery—or per-haps harbored reservations about working for a cradle-robbing scumbag.

This could play out nicely on a number of levels: first, snip-ing a manager from a rival dealership was considered a slap in the face, as former employees tended to take their customers with them; they also tended to blab about their former em-ployer, and Kent could already imagine just how easy it'd be to get the inside scoop on Dan Thompson; and finally, hiring somebody with Brad Howard's exact same credentials would put his pampered cheeks square on the burner.

"Tell me about this guy," Kent said.

"Who?"

"The guy who just quit."

"Oh. His name was Erik."

"Erik what?"

"Sharkey."

She sipped her cola; Kent arched an eyebrow.

"What? Stop looking at me like that. I can't help it if he has a weird name."

He prodded a little more. Turned out Kelsi didn't know the guy very well and didn't have a clue why he'd moved on. She was just the showroom greeter, remember? And why was he suddenly so interested in the people at Thompson's? But by the time their waitress dropped the check, Kent had decided to look up Mr. Erik Sharkey on Thompson's Ford's website, assuming they hadn't scrubbed his presence already, and see if he might like to drop by Regent's and talk over an opportunity. He could even sell Sharkey on Junior's consultant, Donovan Crews, who was coming all the way from Dallas to prep the team for a record-setting 2009 Crust Fest Blowout Sale.

Feeling a little better, Kent dunked a wing in blue cheese dressing and sucked the fatty meat from the bones. Across the table, his daughter's scowl only deepened.

17

"One more deal by Friday," Paul said, "and I'll hit my bonus."

Lloyd Rivera was Windexing a new Equinox Paul had sold that morning, polishing the glass while Paul buffed the Chevrolet emblem with his shirttail. But he was too distracted by thoughts of his personal life to enjoy the usual post-close buzz.

Following the surprise shower duet, he and Annie had gone straight to her apartment. Between the wine and conversation and sex (lots and lots of sex), he'd barely slept. A wonderful night by any definition, and yet he'd awoken with a whole new set of worries. How could he date Annie Turner if he was skipping town after the Blowout Sale? They'd talked a little about his songwriting, but when the moment came for total honesty, he couldn't quite pull the trigger. He had no illusions though. This was his last chance—but his last chance for what, exactly?

"How much this bonus you get, *mijo*?"

Power tools shrieked in the garage behind them.

"Two hundred bucks," Paul said. "Chump change."

Actually, the bonus was seven hundred dollars, but he couldn't very well say that to a friend making minimum wage.

"You know how many hours I got to work in this hot-ass garage to make two hundred dollars?"

Paul pretended he hadn't heard this and climbed into the cab to preset the radio to the buyer's favorite stations, which he'd inquired about while test-driving. Small details like presetting the radio (and promising a referral fee) were what turned buyers into bird dogs—although, of course, Paul wouldn't be around to sell whatever friends and family the Equinox guy eventually dragged into the dealership.

Then Lloyd began talking about basketball at the Y later,

but Paul told him he'd have to skip it tonight. Something had come up.

"You no play? But Paulino love basketball…" Lloyd smiled and nodded his head. "Oh, I see. I see, Paulino. Es blondie, no?"

Paul couldn't help but grin.

"I told you she like you, remember? She *really* like you, no?"

"Apparently so."

"Apparently so, he say. Apparently so!"

"I should've asked your advice sooner, Lloyd."

"Yes, you listen to your friend Lloyd and you soon be married."

The word rang strangely in his ears: *married?* But unless Annie Turner was down for an impromptu move, that particular future wasn't in the cards. Not that he couldn't see a life with Annie down in Music City. But that was just daydreaming. Hell, she'd probably laugh in his face. Nashville? As in the state of Tennessee?

Then Lloyd said he had an idea for them both. "You one car away from dis bonus, see"—he polished the side mirror—"and I still need car. Why not we help each other?"

He'd been hoping Lloyd would let this one drop. Nothing promising had come in on trade, and with his price range Lloyd was better off hunting the classifieds. Paul tried to explain all this, but the garage was too loud. That, and he suspected Lloyd's heart was set on something shiny. The dealership did that to people. Being around mint vehicles all day, breathing in that new car smell, the taut feel of leather seats—it was seductive. Look at Jennylee Witt, for example. She'd driven home from her very first day on the job in that mechanically suspect gold Nissan.

Then, as if to confirm his suspicions, Lloyd asked about the Caprice Classic.

"The Caprice is old," Paul said, "and Junior paid way too much for it."

"Mi brothers y mi primo, they drive my wife loco," Lloyd

shouted over the racket. "Dey stay up all night drinking cervezas and watching movies of war."

Paul suggested he ask them to turn the TV volume down, but Lloyd kept on saying how he needed them gone, *ahora*, *hoy*, how they needed to get to the turkey plant and out of his home and away from his angry wife.

The garage's clatter hit a crescendo and Paul cupped his hands to his mouth: "Sorry, but I think you'd better keep looking."

"My credit," Lloyd shouted, "is how you say? *Purísimo.*"

"Perfectamente?"

"*Pinche* spotless. Like this car you sell and make shitload of dollars."

He had, in fact, made a shitload of dollars. Between this deal, the Hovarth's Tahoe, and Jennylee's Blazer guy, he was doing great. It was undeniably liberating to finally bury his snout in the trough. You want something? Take it. No pussyfooting around. Why, though, had it taken so long to see the obvious? Consider Annie. For an entire year she'd been right there, single and pretty, and yet he'd done nothing. She'd admitted to having almost given up on him. At first she'd thought he was just shy. Later she wondered if he wasn't attracted to her. (She'd even admitted wondering if he was gay—"All the bodybuilding," she said, "so much hair gel.") In a roundabout way, these thoughts led back to his bonus. One more sale before Friday and he could spring for a surprise getaway. California? Hell, Maui. But selling the Caprice was shady. While Kent Seasons said all along that a Mexican buyer was their only shot, this was *Lloyd.*

"Forget the Caprice," he shouted, "and keep checking the classifieds—"

"Paul!" a shrill voice barked in his ear.

Wincing, he turned, only to find Junior standing right behind him.

ço

"And Sharkey is your real name?" Kent asked their latest interviewee.

"Not some sorta alias?" Brad Howard said.

Kent popped a breath mint. "Like a secret identity?"

Erik Sharkey's stalagmite hair had ash-blond tips and the skin on his jaws and cheeks was rough-looking, almost like sandpaper. Sharkey hadn't filled out any paperwork yet, so Kent didn't know his exact age. Late twenties, most likely, although his face had a blank quality that made it difficult to read. Earlier, under the guise of clarifying the dates on his résumé, Kent had casually mentioned Sharkey's having recently held Brad Howard's exact same job title at Thompson's Ford. But Brad was a talented salesman himself and the surprise hadn't shown for long.

"My father's name is Jim Allen Sharkey." He stared at Brad. "You wanna see my birth certificate?"

"Not as much as I wanna see Obama's," Brad replied.

From handshake on, Sharkey had been trying to intimidate Brad Howard. Staring him down. Ignoring his questions. This alone told Kent all he needed to know. One, Sharkey was cocky, and cocky salespeople sold more cars than humble ones (as for who would inherit the earth, Kent Seasons did not presume to know, but smart money was on the closers). Two, Sharkey was alpha, and alphas sold more cars than betas. Finally, Erik Sharkey was a total asshole, which helped explain the split from Thompson's Ford.

"What's Obama's birth certificate got to do with selling vehicles?" Sharkey asked.

Total assholes didn't watch the news, apparently.

"You're right, Erik," Kent said. "We practice the art of sales here, not politics. Although the bailout proposal has naturally been on all of our minds lately."

"Guys down at Thompson's been talking about it too."

"Speaking of," Brad said, "how about telling us why you left Thompson's."

"Me and Dan were just too much alike"—Sharkey gave Brad an awesomely fuck-you look—"both of us hardheaded and stubborn, both set on winning. I got nothing but respect for him and his dealership, but it was time to move on."

"Rumor has it your name was always at the top of the board," Kent said. "Must've irked Dan to watch a strong salesman walk."

He hadn't told Sharkey that Kelsi had mentioned him, as it would've looked bad for her if word got around. Instead, he'd let Sharkey think the grapevine was abuzz with tell of his killer rep. An easy fib for an egomaniac to swallow.

"Turn me loose on your lot and I will jam cars down buyers' throats."

Having observed him for a few minutes now, Kent had little doubt this was true.

"You'd best understand how we operate here," Brad said. "Regent's is a no-haggle dealership, see? Ripping heads off may fly at Thompson's Ford, but we aim for repeat business and friendly word of mouth. High pressure just ain't our style."

With bittersweet nostalgia, Kent recalled giving Brad this same speech back when he'd been a green pea. The no-haggle, no-hassle model was Nautical Bill's preference—not because of sales ethics, but because he imagined it'd be the no-work, no-sweat way to sell cars. But all that talk about respecting the customer was horseshit. Regent's may not have gone for the testes quite as ruthlessly (or at least not quite as obviously) as other dealerships, but they were still car salesmen.

"I know sales," Sharkey said, seeming to pick up on Kent's vibe, "and whatever a dealership calls itself, salesmen either close deals or the lights go off."

"But look, Erik—"

"He's got a point," Kent said.

He'd hired gunners like this before. Sharkey would be petulant and rude. Play mind-games, swoop ups, snipe deals. But he'd also wear down buyers, especially the timid ones. Kent didn't even particularly care if Erik Sharkey was a great salesman or not, so long as he got deep in Brad Howard's craw. More importantly, he needed Sharkey's insight on Dan Thompson. Dealerships were gossipy. If there was dirt, Sharkey would know.

"I'd still like to hear more," Brad said, and glanced at Kent—

"we'd like to hear more, about why you're no longer slinging Mustangs down at Thompson's."

"Pasture only has room for one bull."

"What in the world is that supposed to mean?"

"I think you know exactly what it means."

"Actually, I'm gonna need you to spell it out for me," Brad Howard said.

"In my experience, gentlemen"—Kent ran his tongue slowly across his teeth—"there's only one way to really gauge a salesman, and that's to watch him perform. The rest is just pissing in the wind."

Sharkey's upper lip curled back and his eyelids disappeared. "You're saying you want me to take an up, Mr. Seasons?"

"You're goddamn right I do!" Kent said, and pounded his fist on the desk. Then he pointed out the window at the lot, where a fresh couple had just pulled up in a ten-year-old Ford Escort. "Oil your six-shooters, kid. It's showtime."

Because the wash bay was so terribly loud, Paul hadn't heard his boss creep up behind him. How long had Junior been eavesdropping?

"Follow me," Junior said, and snapped his fingers.

They headed for the square of light beyond the bay doors. Paul squinted against the sun. "The Equinox is ready for delivery. I topped off the gas and—"

"Paul, what do you think your job is here?"

Apparently, Junior was PMSing already. Caught in that prickly mania which overtook him each month when Bill Sr. blamed him for not turning Regent's into a high-volume cash cow. The guy looked stressed to breaking, like a cold stick of taffy.

"My business card says I'm an automotive sales associate," Paul said. "See?" He pulled out one of the cheaply printed cards and wagged it under Junior's nose.

It felt good to stomp his feet around the dealership once in a while, and he'd always gotten away with it in the past, but Junior didn't suck his wrist this time. He didn't yank out any stray nostril hairs either. "Your job is to sell vehicles and provide customer service," Junior said. "That's *all* your job entails."

So arose the ghosts of stern teachers, of that time his father spanked him for crossing the road in pursuit of a neighbor dog, the countless piddling humiliations of adolescence that snowballed over time, through manhood, into either depression or rage.

"Do you understand your job description?"

An oddly childish liniment wafted from Junior's rash-stricken neck. Baby-fine hairs floated about his scalp and his lips were thin worms. He looked, more than anything, like a man who might dress his penis in Barbie doll clothes.

"Paul?"

Finally, Paul nodded.

"Okay, then why did I just hear you talk someone out of buying a vehicle?"

"Lloyd's not *someone,* Billy. And he can't afford a monthly payment."

"You're a car salesman, not a financial advisor."

Now the situation was coming clear, and it was worse than he'd imagined. The Caprice was Junior's baby—his two-headed Thalidomide baby—and Bill Sr. had been carping about stale inventory for months. From Junior's perspective, there was little worse a salesman could do than sink a deal to move it. Paul fumbled for words, arguing Lloyd could end up defaulting on his loan, that he'd resent the sale, maybe even quit.

"I think it's nifty," Junior said, "that Lloyd wants to keep his money in the family."

"Nifty?"

"If only all my employees were so loyal. Look at you, Paul. You drive to this dealership every single day in a *Toyota.*"

He'd forgotten Junior could get this way.

"Frankly," Junior said, "I'm shocked. Good thing our consultant's coming. You need corrective training as badly as the rest."

How quickly a day could turn. From waking with Annie Turner, to being condescended to by a daddy's-boy car salesman. From making love in clean warm bedsheets, to having another man's spittle dapple his cheek. Looking into his boss's sniveling face, Paul had never felt further from musicianship, from being an artist.

"Come back inside," Junior said, his tone softening, "and let's fix up our friend Lloyd with a nice set of wheels."

༄

Kent limped to the showroom, trailing after Brad Howard and Sharkey. Out in the pre-owned lot, the Escort couple were kicking tires.

"Sic 'em, Erik," Kent said.

"I think you're confusing your animals," Brad said.

"My pleasure, Mr. Seasons," Sharkey said, and shot through the doors.

After the requisite hellos and handshakes, Sharkey talked his way around an '08 Grand Prix program car. It wasn't a bad ride overall, with less than 4,000 gentle dealer-driven miles and everything still comfortably under warranty, but it was definitely overpriced. Sharkey performed a classic walkaround: beginning at the hood, pointing out the external features, but steering the couple away from actually sitting in the driver's seat (which got them itching to do just that), before wrapping it up beside the open passenger door, leaving them with a whiff of new-car smell and a view of all that smooth leather and shiny electronics.

Most importantly, Sharkey planted himself squarely between them and their Ford.

"Notice that move?"

Brad nodded, but he hadn't noticed a damn thing. These days Brad Howard lived off flips from ownership. Whole weeks passed where he didn't take a fresh up.

"Watch. He won't budge."

"We'll see about that," Brad said.

"He's got them right where he wants them."

"He's got a bad attitude is what he's got."

Sure enough, though, Sharkey held his ground for ten solid

minutes. Once, when the man made a move toward their Escort, Sharkey blocked his path and opened his stance like a nightclub bouncer. But it worked. The guy hesitated, lost his will. Finally, the couple cracked and agreed to test-drive, shoulders slumping in unison.

"Good work, kid," Kent said, as Sharkey grabbed the keys and a dealer plate.

"Thank you, Mr. Seasons."

"Don't burn too much gas," Brad said, but Sharkey was already out the door again.

Half an hour later, Sharkey planted the couple in Jennylee's office (she'd called in a "vacation day" that morning), while Kent and Brad introduced themselves as managers, offered their assistance in any way that might be helpful, and sat down to observe.

First, Sharkey asked a series of leading questions about the Grand Prix. He smiled and said "absolutely" every time they said anything remotely positive, and he silently yes-nodded their various objections, as if they were in fact praising the vehicle. But the real fun started when the young woman, Sabrina Mercer, interrupted Sharkey's extolling the virtues of the Bose Premium Sound System to make it crystal clear—"Let's get something straight"—that under no circumstances would they buy today. They were just out gathering information. "And give us a business card," she said, "in case any questions pop up later."

From the corner of his eye, Kent noted Brad Howard's smirk.

Sharkey raised his palms as if a revolver were leveled at his heart. "Sabrina," he said, "tell me what I can do to earn your business."

This was just standard script, but when Sabrina Mercer said sorry, but they were still comparing prices, Sharkey dug in. "Hold on," he said. "You took the time to test-drive the Grand Prix, and you obviously enjoy its looks and performance. It's the exact vehicle you want. So be honest. How can I earn your business today?"

"Like I've already told you," she said, "we're not ready to

buy, but go ahead and quote us a price." The boyfriend nodded. "And write down your best number on a sheet we can take home. Otherwise"—she'd clearly rehearsed all this—"don't even bother."

Letting grinders walk with a written offer was verboten, as once the next dealership got hold of it (which they inevitably would either while snooping during the trade-in appraisal, or straight from the buyer's backstabbing hands) sniping the deal was easy as badmouthing the competition and going a couple hundred bucks lower.

"If I quote a price," Sharkey said, "it stands. Inside these doors and out."

After sending Sharkey and Brad to go write-up some numbers, Kent took the opportunity to quiz Sabrina Mercer and her boyfriend on their shopping experience at Regent's of Paris. Were they satisfied with their customer service? Had their salesman been friendly and helpful?

"Frankly," Sabrina said, "I prefer a salesman who listens more and talks less. Not that there are many like *that* around."

Kent smiled in sympathy and kept right on smiling until Sharkey and Brad returned. While Brad looked disgusted, Sharkey was in fine form. He presented the numbers in a blur, repeatedly flattening his hand atop the offer sheet, as if pinning the good deal to the desk (while conveniently covering up the high interest rate). The boyfriend had succumbed to the energy and seemed about ready to roll over, but Sabrina reminded Sharkey yet again that they weren't buying anything, not today.

"I'm confused here, Sabrina," he said. "You two are out shopping for a vehicle this afternoon, test-driving and asking all the right questions and getting to know salespeople such as myself, but you *don't* actually intend to buy a car?"

He shook his head sadly, as if just having realized his customer was a touch slow.

"You," she said, "do not tell me how much to pay. That's *my* choice, not yours."

Her words reeked of some consumer website. Tips for

outfoxing the foxes down at the local dealership. That sort of thing. Bottom line, though, Sharkey was baking her brownies. You could smell it in the air.

"We both know I make my living on commissions," Sharkey said. "That's no secret. But I just made you a great offer on an excellent vehicle, and I would hate to lose your business after we've invested so much time together."

Now Kent truly was impressed. Obligating the buyer, making them feel guilty for not spending a year's pay on short notice, was the sort of move that took a salesman straight to the top. No wonder Sharkey had sold so many Fords. Meanwhile, Sabrina flushed with the realization that no matter what she said, and no matter how many times she said it, Sharkey would always have a comeback. That Sharkey had been drilled sixty hours a week in the fine art of always getting the last word. That, in fact, there *was* no last word—absent signing on the dotted line.

Then she lurched from her chair and dragged her startled boyfriend from the office. Sharkey clocked their heels, with Kent and Brad hurrying along behind, Kent cussing under his breath as his toe flared with each burning stride. But the pain was worth it, because all the way down the hall and into the showroom, Sharkey's mouth never stopped running. Come on now, Sabrina, let's talk. You don't want to miss out on a great deal, do you, Sabrina? He repeated three or four variations of this in the eight or nine seconds it took to reach the showroom doors. Then, just before Sabrina Mercer and her boyfriend might've escaped, Sharkey passed on the inside, slick as Richard Petty. His shoes actually squeaked as he whipped around, arms out like a traffic cop: HALT!

"Get out of my way," Sabrina said. "Jesus, how do you people sleep at—"

"We understand you want to sell us the car," the boyfriend said, his voice cracking, "but this has gone just about far enough, don't you think?" He tried rubbing Sabrina's shoulder, but she batted his hand away. He looked to Brad for help, then to Kent. Nothing going there either.

"Thing is, Sabrina," Sharkey said, "you still haven't seen my best number yet."

"No, no, no," she said, wagging a finger in his face. "You told us there was no haggling, remember? You guys aren't like all those *other* dealerships."

"No haggling. You're absolutely right. There truly is only one price."

"And we've already heard all about it, so—"

"I'll eat my commission," Sharkey said. "Knock it right off the bottom line. All you have to do is take delivery—today, right now—of a beautiful and well-equipped vehicle you already know you'll enjoy."

Kent glanced outside and noticed Paul Stenger pacing the lot, looking troubled. Too bad he hadn't witnessed this little fiasco. Sharkey's antics would've blown his mind.

"Forfeit your commission? Get real. Exactly how stupid do you think we are?"

The answer to that one, of course, was very stupid. Awfully stupid. *Plenty* stupid.

And then Sharkey dropped all pretense of friendliness. He held his tongue and held his ground, simply staring at the woman from beneath his heavy brows, bottom jaw open just enough to show teeth. It was oddly reminiscent of that look Jack Nicholson gives Shelley Duvall in *The Shining* right before he chases her with an ax.

"Hell's bells," Brad whispered, "put a bullet in this one, Kent."

Intrigued, Kent shushed him. Ten more awkward and excruciating seconds passed, as the staring contest escalated to palpable absurdity. Sure, this was getting out of hand, but they'd come this far, so what the heck? Worst case scenario, the couple walked, and that's exactly what would've happened if anybody else had taken the up.

Outside, the Caprice Classic made a left back onto the lot. Kent hadn't even realized the jalopy was being test-driven, so taken was he with Sharkey's impromptu cabaret show. Strangely, a child appeared to be driving. Stranger still, Junior was riding shotgun. But if Junior wanted to take ups with little kids that was his business.

"We could at least listen, Sabrina," the boyfriend said. "I mean, what's the harm?"

۹۰

After chewing Paul's ass, Junior had marched straight back into the garage and had taken Lloyd Rivera for a personal test-drive. Now Paul stood outside with Chadwick in the shade of the building, watching Lloyd and Junior cross the lot together. Lloyd glanced up into his boss's sardonic grin, as Junior patted him on the back.

"Seriously?" Chadwick said. "You're gonna take a pounder off Lloyd?"

"This is Junior's deal, not mine. I told you that already."

"You sure Lloyd knows that?"

"Well, what would you do?"

Chadwick scuffed the asphalt with one boot heel and said that if he were in the same position, this would likely constitute his last day at Regent's of Paris.

"You'd just quit? With nothing lined up?"

"Hell, most days I think about quitting for no good reason at all."

Which Paul did as well. And yet he found himself holding open the door as Junior reentered the showroom. Lloyd trailed along behind, looking unsure of what he'd gotten himself into. As he walked through the door, Lloyd looked Paul square in the face, his dark eyes searching, asking, *Dis all good, Paulino?*

Before Paul followed them inside, Chadwick had one last thing to say. "So apparently that good advice of yours is a one-way street, huh?"

"Excuse me?"

"Yesterday. All that pompous shit about Bob Dylan."

Paul was too distracted to recall what exactly he meant.

"You said Dylan would make me a better person. That those old songs would show me how I been living life the wrong way.

But if that's the case, I'd say *you're* the one who needs to take a good hard listen."

Back in his office, still at a loss for words, Paul played second fiddle to Junior. Considering Lloyd struggled a bit with English, Junior seemed to believe he'd finally found a buyer he could dazzle. "Now, Lloyd," he said, "I think the Caprice is the perfect vehicle, don't you? It's spacious enough for your growing family, and—"

"Like I say before, Mr. Regent, I no have any children—"

"It's luxurious too, Lloyd. They just don't make 'em like that anymore. Those nice, wide bench seats and that deep, rich stereo. It rides low too. Did you notice that?" Then Junior winked. God help them, he actually winked. "Heck, I'm half-tempted to grab that Caprice for myself. But for you, Lloyd, I'll make a sacrifice."

"Sacrifice, Mr. Regent?"

"Why, you ask? Because it makes me happy to know my employees drive only the best. All of us, Lloyd, every single one of us in the car business, should be proud of America. And that means driving Detroit steel. Nothing else will do. Think about it—how does it look to come to this great country of ours only to purchase an *Asian* vehicle?" Now Junior smirked at Paul. "That's not right and you know it, Lloyd."

"Yes, but—"

"And gosh darn it, that's important. That's called patriotism. Regardless of how you and your family got here"—Junior's face briefly and weirdly froze—"regardless of all that paperwork nonsense, I mean, I'm *proud* of you."

Lloyd stared at Paul.

"We're family here, Lloyd," Junior said. "And family comes first. Just ask Paul—wouldn't you say Regent's is more than just a job?"

Paul couldn't find his words. He looked from Lloyd to Junior and back to Lloyd.

"Paul?"

"What?"

"Wouldn't you say"—Junior's rheumy eyeballs widened—"that we're one big family here at Regent's?"

"A family," Paul said. "Sure."

Junior kept talking and Lloyd tried to follow along, asking questions about the loan and contract, although it wasn't clear if he actually understood the answers. But while Junior humored Lloyd, he didn't budge on the sale price, only coming down a hundred bucks for a so-called "employee discount." Worse, when Lloyd studied the confusing numbers, he placed his faith in Paul. There came a moment when Lloyd ignored Junior's insipid banter and looked directly at him, a moment when Lloyd was clearly asking—asking his teammate, his friend—whether the deal really was as good as their boss made it seem.

Feeling Junior's greedy thoughts pulsing into his skull, his mouth stuffed with cobwebs and his ears ringing, Paul finally nodded. He even showed Lloyd where to sign, where to initial.

"Now, Lloyd," Junior said, grinning like a coyote, "just because you bought a nice vehicle today doesn't mean we're giving you the afternoon off."

After dispatching Lloyd to go wash the car he'd just purchased, Junior turned on Paul. "What was all that grumbling about? I thought we got our priorities straight."

"Billy, I feel rotten about this."

Sick. He felt sick.

"You just made a lot of money. What's to feel bad about?"

While Junior had done the talking, Paul's name was on the write-up. He studied the paperwork and realized Chadwick had called it: a pounder. Between commission and bonus, he'd earn over seventeen-hundred dollars. "I'm giving the commission to Lloyd," he said. "To pay him back for helping me hit my bonus—"

"The heck you are. How would that look to the other grease monkeys? You will shake Lloyd's hand and put that money in your billfold, or we have a problem."

An hour later, amidst fantasies of simply jumping in his Camry and driving away forever, Paul's self-loathing was interrupted by Tom Partlow. The big mechanic stormed through the showroom and straight into the general manager's office. Paul ducked behind a featured vehicle, but Tom didn't pay him any attention. Nor had he bothered knocking on Junior's door—although he did slam that same door hard enough to crack the frame.

Tom's shouting ripped through the showroom like he was on the loudspeaker.

"Big Tom sounds mad enough to piss hornets," Chadwick said. "If I was you, I'd steer clear."

Paul closed his eyes and listened to the awful commotion. Why hadn't he just told Junior to shove it? He was quitting anyway, wasn't he? He'd felt the wrongness of it all, felt Junior bending over his conscience and lubing up his ethics, and yet he'd done nothing, absolutely nothing, to stop it.

"It was Junior's deal," Paul said. "I—"

"You what?"

"This whole thing is Junior's fault."

Chadwick whistled a few familiar bars of "Blowing in the Wind."

Then Kent Seasons poked his head from the sales manager's office and waved Paul inside. "Heard what you ruthless fuckers did to Lloyd Rivera," he said, after he'd shut the door behind them.

"It was Junior, not me."

"That ain't the rumor down by the tracks."

Paul began to defend himself once more, but Kent interrupted. "If we're lucky, Tom will rip Junior's balls off and shoot 'em like marbles."

"I'm worried he might do the same to me."

Kent flopped into his chair. "Remember what I said yesterday, about crossing the line?"

"Billy was going to fire me, Kent."

"Tell yourself whatever fluffs your pillow, but you could've walked away from that deal." Kent studied the write-up. "From all seventeen hundred cold, hard smackers."

Five agonizing minutes later, upon hearing Junior's office

door slam once again, Paul did his best Jennylee impression and froze like a potted plant. But it didn't work. Tom Partlow burst into the sales manager's office, pointed at Paul, seared Kent with a look, and told them both they should be ashamed of themselves. "From now on," he said, "anybody from the garage needs a vehicle, it goes through me. Got it?"

"It was Junior's deal, Tom," Kent said. "I didn't know a thing about it."

"You expect me to believe that?"

"Me and Brad were busy hiring a new salesman. And boy, is he a doozy."

"That's just what this place needs"—Tom glared at Paul—"another snake in the grass."

Paul might've tried to conjure up some further excuse, but the heated confrontation had left him feeling paradoxically cold. Months ago, he'd sold a woman a pre-owned sedan with a broken defroster, which she didn't discover until after signing. They'd had a good rapport. She'd liked him, trusted him. But when she came back to point out the defect, Paul had to break the bad news: the sale was as is. Dealership policy. Of course, had she discovered the broken defroster *before* signing, it would've been repaired pronto. Yes, ma'am, right away. Instead, she got hoodwinked. Paul considered paying for the repair out of his own pocket, but it would've cost at least five hundred bucks, and the look he gave the woman that day—the same look he gave Tom now—said sorry, but business was business.

"I expected better of you," Tom said. "Lloyd thinks you're his friend, Paul. He hasn't worked here long enough to realize you guys are all alike. I should've warned him. If it walks like a duck and quacks like a duck…"

Disgusted, Tom Partlow turned and left.

Kent Seasons kicked back in his chair, a big snarky grin on his face. "And if it bends people over like a duck," he said, cheeks flushed as red as his neatly barbered hair, "and lies its feathery ass off like a duck"—he tucked his fists into his armpits and flapped his elbows—"and goes balls-deep for the pounder like a duck…"

❧

Not twenty minutes later, Brad Howard ambled into the sales manager's office. "Well, today sure was interesting," he said, and helped himself to a seat.

Caught off guard, Kent had to snap the desk drawer shut. He cringed as the bourbon spilled, a faint glug-glug wetting the old contracts. Brad normally whistled as he walked the halls. Was today's silence intentional? After all, Brad had accused him of smelling boozy earlier, and his tone suggested the secret wouldn't necessarily keep.

"Paul's gone rogue on us," Kent said. "Him and Junior just tag-teamed Lloyd Rivera on that old Caprice Classic."

"That's not what I meant."

"Bending over a lot attendant who barely speaks English? I've seen some cold shit in my day, but that was downright frosty."

"Come on, Kent. I'm talking about Sharkey's interview." Brad's mustache twitched. "Or whatever you wanna call that boondoggle."

"Memorable, wasn't it?"

"That desperado crap won't fly around here." Brad lassoed the air, rodeo-style. "He may as well have hogtied those people."

"Once they walk out that door, we won't see their ass no more."

"For God's sake, Kent. He water-boarded those suckers like terrorists at Guantanamo Bay."

Kent fluttered the paperwork. "Hard to criticize the means, when the ends are right here, signed and sealed for the next sixty months. That slick sonofabitch built a grand of profit into the back end without even knowing where we keep our F & I forms."

"He's a monster."

"Maybe so, but when's the last time you laid one away like that, old buddy?"

It truly had been a breathtaking display of salesmanship. Sharkey had methodically sapped the couple's faith in their trade-in, circling the Escort while frowning and silently fingering every ding and paint chip, scribbling meaningless notes as he went—all the while knowing his appraisal was just for show. Nevertheless, he tsk-tsked a brownish stain on the upholstery, pinched a shred of foam from a tiny split in the roof liner, and asked what breed of dog they owned while caressing a rough patch on the emergency brake. Finally, while recording the mileage, he chided them for "getting every ounce of value out of their car." From there, he'd scared them into an extended warranty and a gap insurance policy to go along with a full-metal-jacket, rust-proofing job. The cherry on top was a two-hundred-dollar anti-theft kit they could've picked up at AutoZone for the price of a warm case of Budweiser.

Bottom line: Sharkey grinded down the grinders. He pushed them to that elusive tipping point where spending thirty grand felt like a bargain compared to spending even one more second on the lot. Had they cooled their jets, they'd have realized that despite their salesman's forfeited commission, they still didn't get a particularly good deal.

"He's one hell of a car salesman," Kent said.

"Ted Bundy probably would've made a good car salesman too."

"Except for the lack of repeat business."

"Thing I've always liked about no haggle," Brad said, "is that we don't have to put up with bullies—"

"Besides Nautical Bill, you mean."

"Sharkey's gonna give me high blood pressure, Kent."

"Pot getting too hot for you?"

"Look me in the eye and tell me you really wanna work with a guy like that."

"Ownership's gonna keep flipping you deals. Don't worry, you'll eat."

"Don't do it, Kent. Don't hire Sharkey."

"Too late, hombre. He starts tomorrow morning."

"Normally your appraisals are spot on," Brad Howard said, shaking his head as he rose from the chair, "but this time your radar's off."

18

Hard as this was to admit, Maurice Currant was winning.

He was rich but didn't work a real job. He indulged his outlandish and criminal fantasies, all while enjoying a family man's reputation. Mayhem was his nature, and he gave no consideration to others, and yet he was respected around Paris in a way Jennylee and her family could only dream of. Maurice was sneaky and two-faced, of course—nobody really knew what lurked behind that handsome mask—and he'd married well, and money was often confused with virtue, but there was more to it. Maurice simply ignored the rules. He ran his own life.

Strange as it sounded, a woman could learn a thing or two from a guy like Maurice, just as she could learn a thing or two from selling cars. And so, resolved to finally start running her own life, Jennylee had decided to accept the internship at Higgenbottom's after all. She'd boldly pursue her aspirations, just as Alice had advised.

She turned down the funeral home's long driveway. Nearing the whitewashed mortuary, she tapped the brakes and cringed when the Nissan sputtered, the idle hiccupping. Before climbing out, she checked her phone for any word from Chast's doctor or from Derrol. No new messages, but she did call up those images of Maurice Currant and his boyfriend. Scrolling, Maurice's hands were on the kid's shoulders, then resting on his slim hips. Maurice's grinning face was tossed back in hilarious laughter one moment, then swooping in for a peck on the lips the next.

A shot of Maurice and his friend drinking wine coolers recalled a song from her wedding: "Strawberry Wine." It'd been the big slow song during the reception's first dance, when it was just her and Derrol all alone on that American Legion ballroom floor, friends and relatives smiling and watching them twirl and—Jennylee now understood—taking bets on how long until they'd be at each other's throats. But none of those wedding guests could've known that "Strawberry Wine" had been playing on the boom box in Derrol's parents' basement their very first night, their very first time.

Soon enough, though, Jennylee found herself once again face-to-face with Alice Higgenbottom. "In the future," Alice said, holding the door, "feel free to let yourself in."

The chapel smelled of pine wax and was utterly spotless. Even the intricately carved whorls and divots footing the pews showed not a speck of dust, as if Alice had gone over every inch with a Q-tip wetted in oil soap.

"I was beginning to think you'd had a change of heart, my dear."

"I still want to intern, Alice, but…"

Her feelings got in the way of her words and she just stood there with her eyes glued to the swatch of carpet between them. Finally, Alice asked if anything was wrong.

"Not to burden you none, but remember how my little girl's been sick? Well, we finally got her diagnosed. Ever hear of Crohn's disease?"

Faint lines grooved Alice's brow and Jennylee wished she'd never mentioned her personal troubles. Nobody wants to hear that stuff. But then Alice spoke: "Indeed, I suffer from inflammatory bowel disease myself. Not the exact same etiology, but similar."

After the surprise wore off, Jennylee asked if this was why Alice was so small. This was rude as all get out, of course, but she was too discombobulated to mind her manners. She imagined Chastity growing up (or *not* growing up) to be like Alice. The teasing in school would be awful. On the bright side, though, the disease hadn't stopped Alice Higgenbottom from achieving.

"Slightness of stature runs in my lineage," Alice said.

"I apologize, ma'am. I didn't mean anything by it."

Alice squeezed Jennylee's elbow. "Even had I been born perfectly healthy, I doubt I'd have seen much playing time for the Chicago Bulls."

Jennylee asked more questions then: about the disease's progression, the symptoms, how Alice coped; as she rambled on, sympathy lit that apple-shaped face. Tending to the dead hadn't made Alice coldhearted. Not at all. Jennylee had trusted this woman straightaway, and that'd been right. She wasn't as good at judging her coworkers around Regent's, but maybe mortician work wouldn't require so much guile?

As Alice led them deeper into the cavernous rooms, she explained how the business had been bequeathed by her father, who'd been a farmer originally, which explained why the funeral home was out in the countryside, and how back in his day there'd been no standardized education such as Triumph, Online provided. Back then, a mortician learned the trade just like a farmer learned theirs: by watching and doing.

It certainly would be simpler if things were still that way, although the educational requirements did set mortician work apart. After all, if anybody could buy an embalming studio and call themselves a mortician, just like anybody could buy some vehicles and call themselves a dealer, greedy types like Bill Sr. would end up running funerals. Screwing people over on casket prices and reusing flowers and turning what should've been solemn and dignified work into just another lap in the rat race.

They entered a viewing room, chatting like old friends now, and Jennylee relaxed enough to confide about Derrol. In fact, she told more than was likely proper: her husband's unemployment and bumming around the trailer, his depression and drinking and how being married was harder—more work, more stress—than she ever could've imagined. But Alice seemed content to listen, and so Jennylee prattled on. Maybe she'd needed a female friend? After all, with the exception of Chastity, she spent almost all her time in the company of men, and men (or at least the men around Paris) were afraid to admit they even *had* inner lives, let alone talk about them.

"What about you, Alice? Are you married?"

"Always a bridesmaid, my dear."

"Did you never meet anyone special?"

"Oh, there have been special men. But aren't there always?"

Then Jennylee asked if a mortician's hours were too long, if Alice was simply too busy to date.

"Men fear death," Alice said, "so much so that nesting with one is nearly impossible. Because they cannot bear children themselves, most feel deep in their hearts that *they* are eternal children, and thus needn't bear much, if any, responsibility."

Jennylee thought of Derrol and his video games.

"Note the prevalence of second marriages late in life," Alice said. "The near-universal inability to age gracefully. The obsessive capital accumulation."

"I actually wouldn't mind if Derrol tried to accumulate a little capital."

"Men remain boys, Jennylee, right up until the day we plant them in the earth."

"Still, you must get lonely."

"Loneliness is only ever relative to the quality of one's company, is it not?"

Come to think of it, that made sense. Sometimes, living with Derrol was worse than being alone. Because he was there, but he sort of wasn't there too.

"My profession taps into something most men simply cannot abide," Alice said. "I'm a walking, talking, embalming reminder of mortality. Their neuroticism would be tragic if only it weren't so pathetic, so pitiable."

Alice's tone suggested she wasn't the least embarrassed over not having a man, like most any other woman around Paris would've been. Most unusual of all, Alice seemed to have consciously decided this. Then Alice led her past the low dais and down a hallway to a closed door. "May I also share something personal, Jennylee?"

She said sure, please do, but what Alice shared rocked her on her dime store flats.

"When I was a little girl, my older brother, Oliver, fell ill. Like small stature, inflammatory bowel disease runs in our family"—Alice's voice was as delicate as her grip on Jennylee's elbow—"and Oliver wasn't properly diagnosed until he'd already developed severe complications."

"Oh no," Jennylee said.

"There was a surgery, infection, and more surgeries. It all happened very quickly. I was too young to understand, you see? I kept asking when he was coming home."

After finding her voice, Jennylee told Alice how sorry she was, how her father died when she was little, and she'd not fully understood that either.

"My brother's death is why I'm a funeral director today. My father had envisioned Oliver running the farm one day, and if that had happened—if he'd lived—then my father never would've sold the acreage, never would've become a mortician, and never would've converted our home into the business you see here today."

"Sometimes it almost seems like death hovers over children," Jennylee said.

"It follows them around like a specter," Alice said.

The big empty house seemed to draw in a deep breath.

"I don't share my story for sympathy," Alice said, "much less to frighten you, but simply to acknowledge a fact: this world lacks a sense of fair play. If life doesn't teach a funeral director this lesson first, the work most certainly will."

Strangely enough, speaking with Alice Higgenbottom about death left Jennylee pondering an occurrence from her own youthful past, although later it would seem the subjects had more in common than a person might initially think.

Clear back in sophomore year, the phone rang one evening just after dinner, and Jennylee was surprised to hear Randy Bauble's voice inviting her to go for a cruise and talk. She and Randy said hey in the hallways, and Randy was never mean like some guys (*Hey, Jennylee, are those boobs or mosquito bites?*), but it wasn't like they were best friends. A cruise wasn't the best of ideas either, as she had an essay due on the War of 1812 come the following morning. But history was a snooze and when

Randy pulled up in his old T-Bird not ten minutes later, she was grateful for the distraction.

Inside the coupe, Jennylee noticed a bottle wrapped in a brown paper bag between Randy's skinny thighs. "This here's Mad Dog 20/20," he said. "Go ahead, have a tug."

Not wanting to be a killjoy, she tried some, but it was a sticky and grape-flavored dose of awful. As for music, Randy had brought only two cassettes: Dr. Dre's *The Chronic* and a single of Hank Williams Jr.'s "A Country Boy Can Survive."

After a half hour of cruising the dirt lanes around Paris, Jennylee had heard just about all the gangsta rap she could stomach. "That Dr. Dre sure does like to brag about his hos and his pistols, doesn't he?"

Randy gave her a disbelieving look.

"Maybe we could just listen to the radio for a while?"

Instead, he played the Hank single, letting it flip sides over and over, trading the pistols for shotguns and the gangbanging for buck skinning. Randy was funny like that though. He wore clothes like a rapper—NBA jerseys over baggy tees, fake gold chains, and always that little Band-Aid under one eye—but being a Paris boy, he'd still blast a little country in his ride. Other kids accepted his peculiar ways. Randy was popular with the jocks, the stoners, the hicks. In fact, Randy was so popular it made her wonder why he'd wanted to hang out in the first place. Because she wasn't popular, not really.

"So what was it you wanted to talk about, Randy?"

He waved the bottle under her nose. "Sure you don't want some more?"

A syrupy, industrial odor rose from the bottle's neck. "Pretty sure."

"Come on. Have a toot."

She pushed the Mad Dog away. "Toot yourself."

Randy mumbled something that may not have been entirely kind, and then lit a smoke. Meanwhile, Hank Jr. sang (again) about his childhood friend who'd gotten tragically knifed over forty-three dollars in New York City. Jennylee rolled down her window and breathed in the musk of the nighttime country.

Her hair stirred around her face and the T-Bird's motor rumbled up through the seat. It felt nice. She thought of that old
song by the Beach Boys, "Fun, Fun, Fun" about a girl who
bebop's around in her daddy's T-Bird. She'd always preferred
Chevys, though. Her father had driven Chevrolets and was
fond of saying how pretty he found that word, *Chevrolet*.

"Here's my favorite part," Randy said, and sang along with
the verse about spitting Beech-Nut in some dude's eye and
shooting him with an old .45. Peach fuzz ran wild on Randy's
upper lip, glowing a weird downy green in the dashboard light.

"So how come you ain't got a boyfriend, Jennylee?"

They rattled across a bridge. The woods and fields lay dark
and quiet.

"Guess I haven't found much use for one. Why do you ask?"

"Just wondering why a pretty girl like you doesn't have a
man, that's all."

Pretty? That was no Randy Bauble word. She decided to play
it casual, and asked Randy why he didn't have a girlfriend himself, but while he waxed philosophical on the pros and cons of
relationships, her thoughts drifted to Derrol Witt. For a time
in second grade, she and Derrol were study buddies, their little
desks snuggled up close. She recalled how one day her shoes
splashed in a mysterious puddle on the floor. She'd looked
down at that water, thoroughly puzzled. Derrol sat beside her,
his round face fixed on the chalkboard. "Mrs. Beatrice," she'd
said, kicking in the puddle, "there's water under me and Derrol's desks." Mrs. Beatrice seemed surprised, but when Jennylee
came back from lunch the puddle was gone. So was Derrol
Witt.

"The way I see it," Randy was saying, "I'm better off looking
for a girl-next-door type, you know? I mean, cheerleaders are
great and all, but…"

Derrol had come back later, during story time, and only
then did it click. Unlike the other kids, Jennylee didn't laugh
at Derrol though. Because she understood how he must've
been feeling, how it hurt to have gotten scared and made an
embarrassing mistake. "Good thing you changed your britches,

Derrol," she'd said, and smiled to let him know it was okay. But he just put his head down on the desk and cried.

All through school she'd felt an inexplicable connection with Derrol Witt. Like at the eighth grade Sadie Hawkins when he'd put his arms around her and swayed to Whitney Houston, their church shoes scuffing up the fearsome green hawk on the gym floor. Or their walks home from school, just talking and kicking rocks. Once, not long after her father passed, Derrol gave her an unprovoked hug—a hug Jennylee would remember all her life, the way he'd flung his arms around her, their hearts beating so close together.

For a long time, she'd told herself Derrol just wanted to be friends, but intuition said otherwise. Sure, peeing under her desk was an odd route to a girl's heart, but really she thought (as moonlit cornfields rolled past and Randy Bauble lit another smoke) the memory was kind of sweet—although it did make her wonder about Derrol's home life. Because maybe he'd just gotten nervous and had an accident, or maybe there was more to it. Maybe Derrol Witt was growing up in a home that made him feel ashamed of even his most basic needs, a home run by adults who intimidated a little boy into soiling himself.

"I just remembered a story," she said, "about me and Derrol Witt."

Randy had pulled over alongside the dirt lane. Weeds swayed in the burning headlamps and a rooster tail of dust bathed the hood and windshield. The tape clicked sides yet again. Then Randy reached across Jennylee's lap and popped the glove box. The little door dropped down right between her knees.

"Did you have Mrs. Beatrice for second grade?" she asked. Randy's torso pressed her thigh while he rooted through the papers and junk. "Or were you in the other class?"

Then Randy pulled out a funny little red and blue blown-glass pipe, like a miniature piece of genuine artwork. He flashed her one of those famous Randy Bauble grins. "How about me and you smoke a little chronic, Jennylee—"

❧

But when Alice Higgenbottom pulled back the crisp white sheet covering the embalming table, thoughts of sophomore year vanished, like smoke.

"Jennylee, meet Mr. Norvis Bell."

Her stomach penny-dropped straight down to the tiles. Norvis Bell was pale and fat and nude, his mouth frozen in a moan, eyes a pair of hard-boiled eggs. For one awful moment, the dead man's face reminded her of Derrol's face when they made love after he'd been drinking his vodka.

"The eyelids will be glued shut," Alice said, having followed Jennylee's stunned gaze, "after the insertion of caps which maintain the proper shape."

Hearing this, Jennylee couldn't help but imagine how those eyes would look if they were in *improper* shape.

"Setting the eyes is crucial for a successful viewing. Windows to the soul and all that sentimental hokum."

"What about his mouth?"

"We'll bolt the jaw shut and then build Mr. Bell a pleasing smile."

Alice had put on a pale green nonabsorbent smock, sort of like the butcher wore at the meat counter, and she offered Jennylee a matching one. She draped it over her neck and studied the dead man's body. Dark veins mapped his lower legs and one knee was crisscrossed with ghastly scars. His toenails were long and yellow.

"Should I be seeing this, Alice? I'm not sure his family would approve."

"You're my assistant now"—Alice pressed two fingers into Norvis Bell's gut and the dent slowly pushed back out, like that memory foam mattress out at the mall—"and this is the reality of our profession."

Our profession? Jennylee was thrilled by the sound of that, but still the corpse was unnerving. Norvis's body seemed somehow fake. Hard to believe it was ever really alive—to picture that fishy slab up and about, smacking golf balls and eating cantaloupe.

She looked away and took a breath. It wouldn't do to get spooked or weird.

The embalming lab itself was tidy, the walls off-white, the floor freshly mopped. Everything spoke of purposeful arrangement. The surgical table was the centerpiece of the room, seven feet of gleaming stainless steel, complete with gutters and drains and a flushing device hooked to a waterline beneath the sink. A bank of fluorescent lights emitted a sickly buzz. Across the room sat an imposing machine which at first struck Jennylee as a piece of high-end restaurant equipment, like the big oven at her and Derrol's favorite pizza joint. Of course, that wasn't what it was.

"That thing looks awfully expensive," Jennylee said.

"My father installed her just prior to his retirement," Alice said. "The Power-Tech 3K Smokeless cremator. And, yes, she's one pricey cooker. I fear I'll be making the payments until I'm ready for her myself."

"She's sort of pretty, if that's not too strange to say."

"Not at all. In fact, she's a total *hottie*." Jennylee smiled at this, and Alice seemed pleased. "She can reach two thousand degrees Fahrenheit when time is of the essence."

Now Alice returned to the task at hand. "Mr. Bell's viewing is scheduled for tomorrow evening. Besides sanitation and disease prevention, viewing is the primary reason we embalm. It's up to us to provide Mr. Bell's loved ones a dignified final memory image, which is the only afterlife we can be certain he'll enjoy, I'm afraid."

Thinking this over, Jennylee wanted to ask whether Alice believed in God. But that wasn't the right question for now—maybe not ever—and so instead she asked about the possibility of helping with Norvis Bell's services.

"That would be fine." Alice snapped on a pair of rubber gloves. "Except won't you be tired from your long day of selling automobiles?"

"Sure, but I've decided to rearrange my priorities."

Alice smiled, as if this were the very thing she'd been hoping to hear. "Our first step," she said, "after Mr. Bell's bath, is to rub the kinks out."

Then Alice scrubbed the corpse with a lime-scented soap. After toweling the limbs dry, she grabbed one arm and started rubbing, kneading the muscles, flexing the elbow—basically giving the dead man a massage.

"We have to loosen up the rigor mortis," she said. "Because once embalming fluid is injected, the muscles set and that's that."

"You mean, I should touch him—now?"

"Grab some gloves and start with his other arm."

Despite her desire to learn, Jennylee took her sweet time pulling on those gloves. She recalled her father, who'd advised her to jump right into new tasks, saying she'd only ever regret what she was too scared to try. While dispensing advice, Davis Sykes had conveyed a simple faith in doing right. Maybe that, and not her memories of his funeral, were the real final memory image? Her father may not have been the smartest man in Paris (at least according to Evelyn), but he'd said what he meant and meant what he said, and Jennylee desperately needed that compass now.

Nonetheless, she circled the table and continued to stall.

"Go on," Alice said.

"Alice, I don't know—"

"Take his arm in your hands, Jennylee."

"But—"

"Stop hesitating. There's absolutely nothing to fear."

And so she began. The arm was surprisingly hard and heavy, but not quite like she'd imagined. It wasn't repulsive and sad because it'd once been alive—not like touching a dead pet—but more just strange, almost like a waxwork. She took a steadying breath and began rubbing the cool, stiff flesh, copying Alice's every move. She wiggled Norvis's frozen wrist, hearing it creak and groan, working his hand to and fro until it got some slack. But when she tried to bend the elbow, it was stiff as a log.

"Put some muscle into it," Alice said.

So Jennylee adjusted her grip, one hand holding the wrist

and the other braced inside the joint, and torqued downward. She was strong from her horse chores and maybe she used too much of that strength, because then she heard—and worse, *felt*—the hardened tissue tear apart.

She dropped the now crooked arm to the table with a bang. She stepped back and covered her mouth with her gloved hands. Finally, she looked at Alice Higgenbottom. "Sorry, ma'am, but I feel like I'm hurting him."

Alice laid Norvis's other arm down. "Rigor mortised tissue can feel as if it's breaking or shredding, but it isn't. And even if it were, Mr. Bell is far beyond pain. More importantly, I appreciate the care you've shown. It takes a special woman to empathize with the dead, Jennylee. You just may have found your calling."

What Jennylee wouldn't have given to embalm and preserve this moment. Her eyes even teared up a little and she had to blink them dry. She'd missed being praised. With her father gone, her mother had done so little praising that she'd almost forgotten how nice it felt. Was that why she'd always tried so hard to earn Kent Seasons's respect—because Kent was the only one around with the authority to say good job?

Then Alice went to work on Norvis's face, rubbing and stretching the jaw until it hung naturally. "One particularly harsh flu season," she said, "my father was so overwhelmed that he neglected to properly seal a client's jaw."

"Ought oh," Jennylee said.

"Ought oh, indeed. The mouth fell open mid-eulogy. You can imagine the scene—people gasping, the grandchildren shouting and crying and bemoaning this cruel trick that'd been played upon them."

"Those poor kids."

"They were just sure their grandpa was merely playing possum," Alice said. "That the funeral was all some hideous ruse put on by macabre adults."

"Childhood really is confusing, isn't it? Now that I have my daughter, I see through her reactions just how strange growing up really was."

"I'd like to meet your daughter, Jennylee."

Jennylee promised to bring Chast by the funeral home some-day soon, as she wanted her daughter to meet Alice Higgenbot-tom too. Alice was a good influence, someone a girl could look up to, maybe even model herself after.

Next, Alice demonstrated the embalming process. First, she shaved the corpse's neck and face with a disposable ra-zor—"Otherwise, the cosmetics won't look quite right"—be-fore she mixed the preservative chemicals—"Norvis is rather portly, isn't he? We'd best prepare a little extra. And I like to add a touch of dye for that lifelike bloom"—and finally she made a pair of incisions, one in an artery near the groin and another in a vein. Except for a syrupy trickle, these incisions didn't bleed, and Jennylee understood that this was because the corpse had no blood pressure. While hardly a revelation, the insight pleased her nonetheless.

Then Alice unspooled a rubber catheter and explained how they'd flush the body with the preservative, pumping it in the one incision and pushing the stilled blood out the other—"One can literally see the vascular system engorge"—and there was more, so much more, and Jennylee found herself wholly ab-sorbed in learning for the first time since…well, since she'd been a sophomore and her schooling was at constant risk of interruption by the likes of Randy Bauble.

"Hate to break the news, Randy"—Jennylee shifted her hips under him—"but I do believe you've got a flopper."

They'd been kissing in the T-Bird's cramped back seat, which had been fine, but then things got progressively heavier. She'd not really wanted her first time to be with Randy Bauble, but after they'd gotten going she'd not exactly *not* wanted to either. The romance was fading fast though.

"A flopper?"

"I've heard it happens sometimes. To lots of guys."

"A *flopper*?"

"It's nothing to worry yourself over—"

Randy cursed and swore, demanding she stop saying such weird things and trying to distract him. He said all this while straddling her and licking his palm, doing his best to crank himself up. She recalled a pit stop earlier—the door hanging open while Randy pissed in the weeds—and here he was now, desperately licking that same dirty hand.

As her head cleared, Jennylee realized it was the chronic that'd gotten her into this mess. After the initial coughing jag, she'd felt plunged deep down inside her own head. Smooching Randy Bauble became more interesting, the smacking lips and twirling tongues. She'd kissed boys before, but never really ventured beyond the edges of her own shyness—not like tonight. Time slowed and the stereo thumped in her belly. Curiosity, more than anything, had gotten her Wranglers off.

But then Randy had climbed atop her and started chewing her earlobe and sex had become a real possibility. She'd always imagined her first time happening on her wedding night in some swank hotel in St. Louis, but apparently not. No flowers, no clean sheets, and no soft music. Just Randy Bauble and his peach-fuzz mustache, a Band-Aid on his cheek and his pecker in his hand. She had to stop thinking like this though. The muscles around her mouth trembled, aching to laugh. She turned her face aside and bit her cheek. Because if that laugh escaped, it would destroy Randy's feelings—especially considering the difficulties he was having.

For his part, Randy wrangled himself ruthlessly, as if his penis were no more sensitive than the pommel of a rodeo saddle. The cassette clicked sides for the thirtieth time, and while it'd been beaten into her skull that a country boy could survive, that he wouldn't be run off his land and could hunt and fish for his dinner, it wasn't at all clear *this* country boy could achieve a firm erection.

"Sorry, bud," she said, "but I think you'd best be getting me home."

Randy ignored this in favor of continuing his ministrations. By his expression, he might've been having a toe amputated.

"Get off, Randy," she said.

"I'm trying, girl."

"I mean let me up."

"Stop rushing me, damn it. I'm almost—"

Jennylee bucked her hips and flung him down to the floor-board. Under all his gangsta clothes, Randy was just skin and bones. He cussed and covered himself and looked close to tears. While she fished for her clothes amidst the empty Coca-Cola bottles and abandoned schoolbooks littering the back seat, Randy said a number of hurtful things. This was all her fault. She wasn't pretty enough, was too flat-chested, and wasn't worth his time or his chronic. Other girls had loved it, he claimed, while hauling up his baggy shorts. Other girls had downright *begged* for it.

"But you just laid there like a corpse," Randy Bauble said.

"It's been fun," she said, wiggling back into her jeans, "but I've got an essay due on the War of 1812 for Mr. Crawford's class tomorrow."

"You better not say nothing to nobody about this, Jennylee. I'm serious."

Then she'd looked at Randy Bauble, at this goofy kid she'd grown up with, and in the gentlest way possible pointed out that, frankly, there wasn't a whole lot *to* say…

She was remembering all this long-ago stuff on her drive home from Higgenbottom's. Strange how the spectacle of Mr. Norvis Bell had turned her mind to sex. Or maybe it wasn't so strange? A sort of yin and yang. And wasn't there a certain sensuality to the way Alice carried herself? Not a lesbian vibe, but a sense that Alice wasn't as buttoned up as most folks. Like she'd learned to truly value having a warm and living body. Still, Jennylee would've preferred not to think about Randy Bauble at all, and certainly not in an intimate way. On the bright side, he'd been so embarrassed that he never breathed a word of that night to anyone, so Derrol never caught wind of it.

Once home, Jennylee found Chastity in front of the TV, eating Goldfish crackers. Not the healthiest of snacks, but at least she had an appetite. Maybe those expensive medications were helping already?

"Where did Daddy go, babe?"

Chastity yawned and stretched. "Daddy's friend Randy came over."

"You don't say? And when was that exactly?"

"A little while ago."

Leaving Chast home alone was just one more thing to squabble over, but she'd worry about that later. She'd been thinking about her little girl all day, and while she still hadn't worked out exactly how they'd afford the Crohn's treatments, she would not stand idly by and watch her daughter be sick. Neither would she allow Chast to grow up with a mommy who hated her job—a mommy who slowly grew bitter because she couldn't control anything of importance in her life. No, things were changing around the Witt household, and interning at Higgenbottom's was concrete proof.

"Wanna help me feed Bugles, hon?"

Chastity tugged on her shoes, eager as always, but Jennylee dreaded the day Chast went to the stable only to find that friend of hers gone. Despite the promise she'd made to herself, the day would come when the expense simply could not be borne any longer, and Bugles would be sold to pay off a doctor or the mechanic or even GMAC, whom they still owed a boatload for that unreliable Nissan. Worst of all were the lies she'd have to tell. Lies that stank like dog food, like glue. *Bugles went to live with another family, Chast. He needed more space to run...*

Outside, Jennylee put her daughter in charge of filling the water trough, while she hefted the feed bag. Bugles was the color of the dust he'd been clopping around in and his ribs showed. One way or another, she'd been failing everybody: horse, daughter, husband, even Kent Seasons and her customers on the lot.

Chastity turned the hose on Bugles and splashed him withers to rump. The horse grunted softly, appreciatively.

"Not too much now," Jennylee said. "That's drinking water, not playing water."

"Bugles says he's hot." She sprayed him some more.

"Oh, is that what he says?"

"Yep. That's what he says."

Chast was a sweet kid. Despite their bickering, she and Derrol were raising a good little girl. A girl who loved animals and helping her mother with chores. But also a girl who couldn't understand why her tummy always hurt and why she vomited so often—let alone why the doctors looked at her and her parents in such a troubling way.

After emptying the feed bag, Jennylee got Chastity started on her bedtime routine. Teeth, Tush, Talk: brush the teeth, use the potty, and tuck in for a goodnight talk. While Jennylee enjoyed telling bedtime stories, she wasn't particularly good at dreaming up tales of time-traveling turtles or police ducks or whatnot. Derrol, who'd been an avid reader as a boy, was an excellent storyteller, but he wasn't home (again) and while Chast was busy discussing the likelihood of Bugles growing wings and a pretty horn like the magical horse from TV, Jennylee found herself thinking of the man Derrol had abandoned them for tonight. Maybe she hadn't remembered her little fling with Randy simply because he could so often be found playing Xbox in her living room? No, there were undeniable similarities between that night in Randy Bauble's T-Bird and this past Monday with Maurice Currant in the Caprice. Worked up and let down in the back seat at sixteen, ambushed and sexually assaulted in the front seat at twenty-seven. From a kid who couldn't get it up, to a geezer who couldn't keep it in his pants.

Such was life, apparently.

"I'm not sure Bugles wants to fly, Chast. He might be scared of heights."

"Not if I flew with him he wouldn't be."

"Yeah, he'd probably do just fine, so long as you kept him company."

They talked some more, until Chast finally drifted off. Jennylee watched her daughter's little chest rise and fall under the quilt and realized that, pathetic as it'd been, that night with Randy had brought her closer to Derrol Witt. Sure, their dates to Burger King and the movies almost couldn't help but charm when compared to Mad Dog 20/20 and Dr. Dre on a dark country lane—but it was more than that. She clicked off the light and gave silent thanks to Randy Bauble, because it was that long-ago night in his T-Bird which had ultimately awakened her to the kindness and decency of her husband.

But then she thought: Derrol, where did you go?

19

After grabbing a twelver at the Citgo, Kent drove to a ball diamond south of town and parked in the darkness beyond the right field fence. He and Erik Sharkey sat on the tailgate, tipping suds and watching Little Leaguers hit, field, and pitch. The diamond was carved from the surrounding bean fields, the outfield grass thick and green, the chain-link dugouts strewn with bats and mitts and bright orange coolers of Gatorade.

Kent Seasons enjoyed few things more than watching kids play ball on a well-lit field. He'd enjoyed the sport himself as a youngster and was secretly miserable after Kelsi—a careless fielder and nearsighted hitter—quit softball in the ninth grade.

"Remind me to steer clear of Thompson's," Kent said, and wrenched the cap off a fresh bottle. "Way you boys do business, a person would come in for a set of wiper blades and end up buying the whole candy store."

"There's nothing I love better than taking a stroker for a long, bumpy ride," Sharkey said. He drank up praise even more greedily than he drank beer, and he was on his third beer already. Further proof that he was a real salesman, were any further proof needed.

"Want another brew, kid?"

Sharkey nodded absently. Across the fence, the team in white pounded their mitts and raised a communal chant: *Hey, batta-batta-batta-batta...*

"Dan Thompson teach you to beat down a trade-in like that? Because that was just about the meanest silent walk-around I've ever seen. By the end, those people were embarrassed they'd even driven to the lot. You had them wishing they'd called a cab."

"Gotta bring buyers back to reality somehow."

"A trade-in's like a child," Kent said. "You see it every day, so you don't notice the gradual imperfections. Chipped windshield one year, spot of rust the next, then a faint rattle under the hood that you keep telling yourself is just your imagination. Buyers see their own cars with rosy-colored glasses. See them how they used to be, or ought to be."

Sharkey lowered the beer bottle. "No doubt."

Since Kelsi was on his mind anyway, it seemed opportune to ask about the culture down at Thompson's Ford. Kent took his time, sipped his beer, and parsed out a few innocuous-seeming questions.

"The culture at Thompson's," Sharkey said, "is kill, fuck, eat."

Sharkey's jouncing legs vibrated the tailgate. He was fidgety, his shoes scissoring the weeds. Was he a cokehead? That wasn't so unusual in the car game, after all.

"Salesmen ever go out for drinks?"

"Only every other night."

"You gotta chew the fat, compare notes."

"Better part of business happens after hours," Sharkey said.

"And boys need to shoot a few racks of pool and chase a few women."

Sharkey glanced his way.

"To blow off a little steam, I mean."

"Right."

"So, how about management? Did old Dan Thompson ever join you—?"

But just then a heavyset lefty really got hold of one. The right fielder chased it, but if you play right field in Little League, it's for a reason. The kid tripped and skidded on his face, losing his cap and grass-staining his uniform. The ball dribbled up against the fence while half the boys cheered, and the other half groaned and kicked the dirt.

"Dan isn't one to hobnob with the help," Sharkey said.

Kent nearly spit up his beer. "Oh no?"

The fallen boy hopped to his feet and trotted to the fence,

grabbed the ball, and flung it somewhere in the general vicinity of second base. Kent cupped his hands and hollered, "Good arm, right field!" The boy turned and glared before retrieving his lost cap. A minute later, after needlessly tearing up the field with his cleats, the boy tossed his mitt aside, sat down, and began pinching the heads off dandelions.

"Dan Thompson runs a tight ship," Sharkey said. "He yells jump and everybody in that place looks like Kobe Bryant. Silk ties get caught in the ceiling fans."

"That why you left?"

Sharkey tipped the bottle and foam sluiced down his chin. He wiped his mouth with the back of his wrist. "Better question is why did you call me?"

"Figured I'd get the benefit of Thompson's training program."

"Speaking of, what's this I hear about a consultant? That guy with the mustache and the beer gut, the one who sat in on my interview, he mentioned it."

"His name's Brad Howard," Kent said, "and he's your manager—your boss."

Despite having hired Sharkey partly to throw Brad off his own tail, Kent now felt oddly protective of his old protégé. This was similar to how he'd been searching for cause to fire Jennylee Witt, only to have Maurice assault her, which stirred up a bunch of unhelpful paternal feelings. Of course, most of that was probably just displaced anxiety concerning his own daughter.

"You may have been a salami slinger at Thompson's," Kent said, "but you're the green pea at Regent's. Got it?"

"Got it," Sharkey said.

"Consultant's out of Dallas. He's about what you'd expect—wears a pinkie ring engraved with his own fucking initials."

"Sounds like this dude must've sold his fair share of vehicles," Sharkey said.

Unsure how best to respond to so depressing a comment, Kent suggested they finish their beers and head on home. No need to press for more info tonight. They'd have plenty of hours to burn around the lot. He polished off his longneck, hopped down from the tailgate, and then yelped in pain.

"You okay, Mr. Seasons?"

"Do I sound okay?"

Distracted by the brews and his own machinations, Kent had stupidly dropped all his weight onto his left foot, and a burning rip of god-awful pain seized the tightly swollen joint. If not for the impressionable kids within earshot, he would've cussed Jesus up one side and his Father down the other. He needed to see a doctor, but that'd have to wait until after the Blowout Sale. Otherwise, Nautical Bill would claim his priorities were out of whack. But how to explain the fractured foot? Could he have early-onset osteoporosis? Had all the bourbon leached the calcium from his bones?

"Sharkey," he said, "you ever hear of somebody breaking a bone without even knowing how it happened?"

"Sure. Happened to me back in school."

"No kidding?"

"Tried to pop a wheelie on a ten-speed one night and woke up the next day with my wrist all purple and swollen. Was in a cast for six weeks."

"Thought you said you didn't know how it happened?"

"I didn't."

"Well, it sounds like you fell off a bicycle."

"Yeah, but I forgot all about that until I sobered up and called my buddy."

Kent rotated his ankle clockwise in slow circles. He and Sharkey both studied the wingtip's waxy blue gleam. "My foot is absolutely killing me. I can barely sleep at night, let alone chase buyers and salespeople around the lot."

"You want a little something for the pain?"

Kent cocked an eyebrow, but Sharkey shook his head and said it wasn't like that. Just happened to have some medication left over from a root canal. He dug a Tic Tac bottle from his pocket and tapped three little white tablets onto his palm. The tablets were scored crossways and printed with faded numerals.

"Root canal, huh?"

"Can't say I'd recommend the experience, but these really did help."

"What are they?"

"All I know is they work."

"How old are they?"

"I don't think these expire like a quart of milk, Mr. Seasons."

"Desperate times," Kent said, and plucked the pills from Sharkey's hand. He put them in his pocket and made a mental note of having done so. Wouldn't serve for Linda to find mystery pills bouncing around the washing machine. "And don't say anything about this around the dealership, okay? People jump to conclusions."

"Of course."

"How much I owe you?"

Sharkey shook his head. "I sell cars, not pills. Besides, it's me who owes you."

While gathering up their spent bottles, Sharkey quizzed him about the GM bailout proposal. Would politicians be designing cars from now on? Could they really force everybody to drive hybrids? But the kid didn't seem to know much about the reality of the issues, likely because all he'd heard was the gloating down at Thompson's Ford.

"It's complicated," Kent said. "You just focus on moving our inventory."

"Right, but I'd still like to get your take on what Barack *Hussein* Obama's got planned for GM. I'd hate to find myself working for the bloodsucking Democrats."

Kent patted Sharkey on his oddly hard back—not hard like he was an athlete, but hard like he was wound too tight—and told him not to worry about that rascal Obama. Washington would do what it always did, string up red tape and waste money, while the real movers and shakers took care of the auto industry. "But it's good you think that way, kid," he said. "Your opinion squares with ownership."

He suspected Erik Sharkey didn't actually give a damn about politics though. Didn't care about much of anything in this world except the thrill of the hunt, locking horns, the close. No, the guy was simply engaged in a little tactical brown-nosing. Sure enough, he'd fit right in around Regent's.

Before they left, Kent hollered at the Little Leaguer who was still busy killing dandelions. "Look alive, right field! Never know when one's gonna come your way."

Step Four: Test-drives and Write-ups

20

That Thursday morning, Paul Stenger sat in the meeting room, struggling to listen through the misery of a red wine hangover as Donovan Crews made a production of introducing himself. The man spoke ostentatiously, theatrically, loudly, and he sported oversized gold cuff links and a matching and equally outsized pinkie ring. Paul vaguely recalled something Kent (who sat beside him, looking equally hangdog) had mentioned earlier in the week: the consultant's gaudy ring had his own initials engraved on it.

"I'm gonna break you down and teach you how to walk again," the consultant said, "how to talk, how to *move*. Because if you doubt car sales is showmanship"—a dramatic polish of his watch face—"you're just kidding yourself."

"Yes, sir," Chadwick said.

All through the intro, Chadwick had been busy sucking up. He'd even raised his hand to parrot the importance of demo qualifying. While Paul was too queasy to sweat first impressions, Chadwick's behavior got him wondering if he really should pay better attention to this seminar—because what a guy *does* fifty hours a week is pretty much what he *is*. Thus, for all intents and purposes, selling cars was his real life; as despite his plans for Nashville, he wasn't writing any new songs. He'd read somewhere, maybe in a Dylan bio, that artists create when the pain of not creating outweighs the pain inherent in creation. If enduring *The Seven Steps to Sales Success* wasn't painful enough to get him writing again, what was?

Across the room, Bill Sr. was dressed in a teal and orange aloha shirt and cream slacks, like a castaway from a senior citizen's cruise. "Donovan," he said, "I'm glad I had the foresight to bring you here"—Junior cringed, Gollum-like—"because the way Washington's headed, little dealerships like ours are gonna need an edge."

The consultant nodded gravely. His tie tack, also gold, flashed in the light streaming through the dusty blinds. Why were car salesmen, along with gangsters and circus people, the last bastion of jewelry-festooned men?

"If y'all take this training to heart," he said, "and implement my tried and true techniques, we'll have done our part to keep America free. Don't laugh now. I'm dead serious. Only thing that's gonna stop the cancer of the welfare state is our hard work."

"Who'd have ever guessed," Kent whispered, "that Dick Cheney's stepson sold cars?"

Then Jennylee piped up. "I did some reading on this bailout deal," she said, "and if GM doesn't get it, they say the whole kit-and-caboodle could go under. That Detroit will be a ghost town. But if the government gives them all that taxpayer money, shouldn't they at least have some say in how GM spends it? Isn't that just common sense?"

This constituted—by a country mile—the boldest and most logical words Jennylee Witt had ever strung together at work. Especially considering she had to know ownership opposed the bailout. What'd gotten into her lately?

"Common sense?" Bill Sr. craned around. "Jennylee, that devil Obama just wants to nationalize private business. He's a Marxist Commie. Besides, we're talking about *General Motors* here, not Studebaker. The General will have a plan for Detroit. GM filing for bankruptcy is about as likely as…as…"

"As a soul brother grooving in the White House?" Kent whispered.

"I feel your frustration, Bill," Donovan Crews said. "People just don't understand this so-called bailout. Even our own people don't get it"—he burned Jennylee with a look—"so maybe we'd best clear the air, considering those rascals on Capitol Hill mean to screw with our livelihood."

Chadwick raised his hand, fingers splayed and wiggling.

"Permission to speak freely, sergeant," Donovan Crews said.

"It's just like with the Second Amendment," Chadwick said. Hearing this, Kent Seasons buried his head in his hands and groaned. He reeked of mouthwash, and suspiciously heavy aftershave wafted from his neck. Paul imagined him up late on the couch, a tumbler rising to his lips as the baseball highlights blurred on ESPN, the anchors' grinning bonhomie seeming less clownish and more sinister with each passing sip.

"They're taking away our freedoms," Chadwick said, and cast a nervous glance Kent's way. "Before long, a man won't even be able own a firearm to protect his family."

Everyone had heard Chadwick's GOP slippery slope rants concerning the Second Amendment, abortion, immigration, and so on. Talk-radio rhetoric fit the dealership's intellectual tenor. Tax increases? Government's out of control. Next they'll take our guns. Long line at the DMV? Government's run amok. Which article of the Constitution says they can make us stand in line all day just to drive on God's highways? Somebody pass the lube, Lady Liberty's got her skirts up.

"On second thought," Donovan Crews said, "let's not talk politics. That Obama sours my coffee." He took a timely swig. "Now how about we try a mock sale?"

Then Crews put Chadwick through the paces of selling an imaginary vehicle parked beside the monthly sales board (where Paul was now tied with Brad Howard for the lead), but Paul was distracted by the sight of Junior struggling to contain his tics, which rekindled his ill feelings about Lloyd and the Caprice. This goony pansy, this pencil-dicked nose-picker—*Junior*—had forced him to screw over a friend. He'd confessed it all to Annie the night before, carefully explaining his no-win position, but she wasn't particularly sympathetic. ("Apologize to Lloyd," she'd said. "Find a new job.") Apologizing wasn't so simple, though, as Lloyd apparently still believed his friend Paul Stenger had helped him negotiate a fair deal.

"What if the salesman," Paul said, interrupting the mock sale, "was a close acquaintance of the customer? Like a relative or a friend. A coworker, even."

Kent nudged him. "Tread lightly."

Everyone present, except for Donovan Crews, understood the subtext, and Paul waited out the awkward silence that fell over the room, and the crazy eyes Junior shot his way. Then the new guy spoke up.

"There's no such thing as *friends* at a dealership," Erik Sharkey said. "This is a place of business. Friends are for the bar come Friday night."

If Sharkey's cocksureness was off-putting before, now Paul outright despised him. Never had a job gotten to him like this. Certainly not the restaurants. He'd been a moonlighter, not a career man. But if Regent's was just another pit stop, if he was on his way to Nashville after the Blowout Sale, why such bitterness?

"Relatives need cars too, Paul," Brad Howard said.

Kent Seasons spoke through splayed fingers. "Friends and family make the best bird dogs."

"Believe me," Jennylee said, her expression oddly masklike, "Regent's takes care of its own."

"Amen," Bill Sr. said, nodding his big bald head. "Now that's the spirit, team."

As the training session droned on, Paul's mind drifted back to the night before. Annie's bedroom was as small and cramped as a dorm room. Combined with the need for quiet (Annie had a roommate), it reminded him of all the girls he'd known as an undergrad.

For Paul Stenger, college had been four glorious years of good books, culturally sanctioned unemployment, and casual sex with brainy young women beneath prints of Millais's floating Ophelia and that swirling blue starriest of nights. Then graduation came, and unemployment was suddenly frowned upon and sex lost much of its mystery. But Annie wasn't like those other girls. She was down-to-earth, paid her own bills, and scoffed at light beer. With Annie, Paul felt closer to whatever instinct had initially piqued his songwriting—but how could he be with her and still pursue his music?

Regardless, it'd been more than troubling when, in the middle of making love, Annie hung her head off the mattress and met his eyes in the closet mirror and asked, "What's with the show, hotshot?"

Sure, he'd been admiring his reflection a little. He looked good, strong and lean, virile. Annie's body shone palely beneath his own, both of them glowing in the blue wash of an unwatched movie. Paul had been feeling like he'd used to while playing a gig—imminently watchable, a star—until Annie had to go and ruin it.

"Where are you right now, Paul? Because you're not here with me."

He flopped onto his back and tucked his hands behind his head. Then he sat up and chugged most of a bottle of cheap merlot. His angst beat in tune with the ceiling fan's dust-furred blades. Annie asked if he was okay, and when he didn't answer she tweaked his nipple. He brushed her hand away. He hated that.

"Were you...not going to?"

"Really? That's what you think I'm worried about?"

Thoughts of Seth moldered in his imagination. He'd never been troubled by an ex before, but Seth was different. His gangster hair and overdeveloped pecs. His fake tan. Maybe it was the basketball rivalry, or the dick-measuring that came along with selling cars, but he couldn't help wondering if Annie compared him to Seth.

"You tell me," he said.

And she did. Told him more than he'd bargained for, in fact. Considering he was a musician, Annie had imagined him having a more artistic and dreamful side. Was he making it all up? Was musicianship just a line to get girls into bed? And, yes, she was nervous to date another salesman. Of course she was, considering Seth had brought his shady work habits home with him. But she still believed that he, Paul, was different, and that their night in the YMCA locker room was more than just a steamy mistake.

"So, yes," she said, "it does bother me when you stare at yourself in the mirror while we're having sex."

A riff of dust broke from the fan blade and floated down to the carpet. Paul denied having been staring at himself.

"Then why didn't you notice I had my eyes crossed? Too busy flexing your muscles?"

"You did not have your eyes crossed."

"Sure I did. I even stuck my tongue out."

On the TV a helicopter crashed into a horde of zombies. Paul thought of ups shambling around the lot, just waiting for a salesman to come along and put bullets in their brains. Then the helicopter fell off a skyscraper and exploded like an A-bomb.

"That's absurd," he said, and reached his toe for the TV's off button. But it was too far away. Annie turned her back to him as a zombie with sensational abs performed a stylized ju-jitsu routine and blood splashed the camera lens. Paul Stenger was certain then, feeling the world's chronic idiocy sink into his bones, that soon he really would be in Nashville. This was his shot, and he'd never forgive himself if he didn't take it. He lay there and sipped more wine (spilling some in the hollow of his throat), but then another thought occurred: what if, when he asked Annie to come along, she actually said *yes*?

He looked at her hip mounded under the bedsheet. Annie was young, but someday she'd want babies. They all wanted babies.

"Sometimes I wonder," he said, "if music is…"

"Is what?"

Paul swung his legs off the bed. Beside his left foot lay that chunk of ashen dust. The last slice of bread in the hamper at Pompeii. "I wonder if it's ruining my life."

"Don't be so dramatic."

"Dramatic? Annie, look—"

"No, you look." She pointed at the closet mirrors, and there they were, au naturel. The stubborn roll of chub below his belly button appeared a bit thicker than he'd imagined, and was that a hint of cellulite on Annie's hip? No, her mirrors must've been off somehow—like a funhouse mirror that made you appear slim and attractive one minute, then like a thirty-ish car sales-man the next.

"That's us," Annie said. "That's you and me."

He easily could've taken this olive branch. Could've met her eyes and pretended he'd learned some deep lesson before pulling her back down into the sheets. Instead, he studied the little thrift-store bedroom, the faded blue linens and tube television, a candle melted on the nightstand. A sketch of a pony that looked like a cow with bat's ears.

He opened another bottle of wine. "I knew I wanted to make music," he said, "after seeing this songwriter in Louisville when I was a kid. I'd tagged along on one of my dad's business trips. The songwriter was headed to Nashville, just bouncing around playing gigs for beer money."

Annie asked what songs the man had played. In the mirror, her throat corded beautifully.

"Covers mostly. Radio stuff. But he played some originals too."

Her fingernails carved loops down his back.

"I remember Dad kept saying, 'Isn't he great?' and 'Wouldn't it be something to play guitar like that?'"

Annie asked the singer's name, asked if he'd ever made it big—the question people always asked of artists, which actually means: *Did he ever make any money?*

"Dad enjoyed the show," Paul said. "He got a real kick out of it."

But Paul had gotten more from it than that.

The singer was tall and sinewy, dressed in threadbare jeans and a rust-colored cowboy shirt with pearl buttons. His road-weary Stetson might've once been white and his guitar case was covered in stickers from juke joints all across the country. Somewhere out in the parking lot, Paul sensed, was a truck with a bug-spattered windshield. The musician spent nights in this truck with nothing but his coat and a bottle for warmth. He sipped black coffee in dawn truck stops amidst the rifle shot glances of hard-living men. He knew about motels and ice clinking in glasses and all the mysteries of women.

Paul had never tagged along with his father before, as Alvin Stenger's business rarely required travel. He'd never seen his father drink so much beer either. Five or six bottles already, starting with one beside the hotel pool while Paul took a swim, two with dinner, and more here in the candlelit lounge.

Then the cowboy singer said good evening to the crowd, the mic a gray snow cone in his hand. "My name's Travis Bryson," he said, "and I'm gonna play a few songs. Y'all kick back and relax now."

Throughout the opening set Paul's father kept bugging him and making him agree that Travis Bryson could really play, that the lounge was neat, the hotel classy, the soda pop top-notch. "What a shame," he said at one point. "All that talent and nobody knows him from Adam." But Paul wished his dad would just be quiet and listen.

Up on the stage, Travis Bryson swigged beer and turned the pegs on his guitar. He strummed a bit and adjusted the pegs some more. "Next one's a sentimental favorite," he said, his voice rolling around the lounge like an apple in a wooden barrel. "Have to confess I wrote it for my ex, but I refuse to let that woman kill my inspirations."

His father laughed at this, but Paul didn't quite get the joke. The hotel, Louisville, his father—nothing was like normal.

"Song's called 'Bubbly Champagne,'" Travis Bryson said.

He strummed fast and hard, his grip snapping up and down the guitar's neck, and Alvin Stenger began tapping his foot to the rhythm. His tie had come loose, and his face was not the face he wore around home, but a younger and more joyous one.

Travis Bryson played until it seemed he couldn't possibly pick any faster, until sweat dripped from his brow and his boot heels tattooed the stage, until the speakers poured out one long riff that rolled and swelled but never quite broke. Then he ducked toward the microphone and sang the opening verse. It was about a man and his girlfriend taking a bath while eating a bucket of chicken. There were lyrics about sparkling wine and bubble bath, about steam and shampoo, some confusing talk between the man and his woman that made Alvin snicker. Then came the chorus: "Bubbly champagne and deep-fried chicken...baby, your toes are finger-lickin'...good!"

"Fantastic," his father said, after the song was done. "Wasn't that just great, Paul?" He clapped and clapped, but in the near-empty lounge's dim red light, the clapping sounded weirdly hollow, almost like they were underwater—

႙

"Paul? Earth to Paul?"

Paul blinked and glanced around the suspiciously quiet meeting room. Had someone been speaking to him?

Kent Seasons elbowed him. "Ground control to Major Tom. You'd best tune in."

"Care to step up here and help us out, Paul?" Donovan Crews asked.

More role-playing, apparently, as Paul realized he'd been invited to perform a meet-and-greet. While he wanted to say this was all a waste of time and they'd be better off renting *Glengarry Glen Ross* from Family Video, he swallowed his irritation, stepped forward, introduced himself, and shook the consultant's hand.

"No, no," Donovan Crews said. "Weren't you paying attention? Start over."

So Paul shook the guy's hand again, more firmly this time, but he'd clearly missed something while daydreaming.

"Look," the consultant said, and seized Paul's hand yet again. "Pump, pump, break," he said, jiggling his arm. "Pump, pump, break. Got it?"

Up close, Donovan Crews smelled like Aqua Velva and burnt coffee.

"I think I know how to shake someone's hand," Paul said.

"Actually, you don't. Your handshake's a dead fish. Come on now, Paul."

He reminded himself he was being observed and played along. Two hard pumps and then release, as if the handshake were not a greeting, but a challenge.

"Moving on," the consultant said. "Paul here has given me a handshake that establishes who's the boss. So what's next?"

The man smiled encouragingly.

"Welcome to Regent's of Paris," Paul said. "My name is—"

"Whoa, whoa, whoa." Donovan Crews rocked back on his heels, palms raised. "Hold there, pal. I'm just looking…"

I'm just looking was an up's favorite line. Paul really should have seen this one coming, but he'd been distracted imagining how pathetic he'd look if Annie could see him, how she might wonder if Seth would perform better in a sales situation—if Seth might perform better in other areas too. All eyes were upon him now and yet only Jennylee's held any trace of sympathy. He felt a renewed lump of guilt over that Blazer deal back on Monday.

"Anybody notice how Paul froze up?" Donovan Crews asked.

"He sure did freeze up," Jennylee said, her tone one of dawning mirth.

Apparently, he'd misinterpreted that look of hers.

"Great, Jennylee," Donovan Crews said. "Now describe what you saw."

"Well, if Paul was a deer," she said, still wearing that Mona Lisa smile, "he'd be either run over or shot, depending on the buyer's proclivities."

Donovan Crews got a hell of a laugh out of that one. The whole room did, in fact.

"That's exactly right, Jennylee. Because Paul let the up control the meet-and-greet." The man repeated the ominous phrase—*I'm just looking.* "Bottom line, folks, they're *all* just looking. Until one of you decides who's the boss. Remember: buyers are liars." Crews raised his voice. "Say it with me now: Buyers. Are. Liars."

Everyone mumbled under their breath.

"You selling cars to mice? Louder! Buyers—Are—Liars!"

Paul's lips moved, but soundlessly. It wasn't that he'd stumbled through the training, and he wasn't afraid his poor performance would alter the pecking order. It wasn't even having been publicly heckled by Jennylee Witt. No, this was worse: somehow, just weeks before turning thirty, he'd ended up being scrutinized, nitpicked, and criticized—judged—by a Texas car salesman wearing a pinkie ring.

"Let's take it from the top," Crews said, and stuck out his hand yet again.

Manicured nails and not a callus in sight. Earlier in the week, Kent had shared an ugly story about the consultant and a pregnant kindergarten teacher in a KFC drive-thru. Again recalling Travis Bryson's original song in that long-ago Louisville hotel, Paul now imagined that same deep-fried chicken clenched in Donovan Crews's grubby digits. He also imagined a woman bewildered by the prospect of car shopping since her husband abandoned her, a woman who hadn't been touched intimately in months, who hadn't felt desirable or even fully human in far longer. Someone desperate for any respite from the creeping empty, from the knowledge that even motherhood couldn't fill the vacuum, that she would stumble on alone and lost until she awoke one day wrinkled and leaking on her deathbed, surrounded by grandchildren with utterly bored faces—and yet some memories are simply too stubborn to fade, and as that woman, this teacher and mother, closed her eyes for the final time, she would meet death with the remembrance of Donovan Crews's engraved pinkie ring, slimy with chicken grease, slipping inside of her.

Paul seized the consultant's hand and squeezed hard—squeezed until Donovan Crews squeaked and they'd definitely established who was the boss. Then Paul lowered his mouth to the man's ear and whispered, "Better wear shorts, you greasy finger-fucker. Because the place you're headed is even hotter than Texas."

21

"A bsolutely not," Kent said.

"But, Dad—"

"That is not happening. No way."

He'd just limped through the door, Linda having texted that Kelsi was coming home for lunch too. But he'd hardly gotten his leftover pizza into the microwave before their peaceful meal went all to hell.

"You're not listening to me," Kelsi said.

"Oh, I'm listening all right. Now look, you're gonna love college. Trust me."

"And how exactly would *you* know that?"

Kent sucked his teeth and tried to keep his expression neutral. His education was real world only, and he was fine with that, but his daughter's belittling him hurt—sorely hurt. "Once you get off track," he said, "it's hard to get back on."

She just stared at him.

"Time snowballs, kiddo. Trust me on that too."

Moments before, Kelsi had pushed her turkey sandwich aside and announced her decision to take a year off to "think things over" before committing to the expensive coursework at the U of I—as if she would be paying a dime herself. She'd also dyed her hair again, sort of purplish this time. Kelsi's hairstyles never quite worked out because of the ginger coloration she'd inherited from him. Did she secretly blame him for that too? Kent wanted to tell her to stop worrying, to realize how beautiful and unique she already was, but that would've only made her more self-conscious.

"Just because I'd do anything for you," Kent said, "doesn't mean you shouldn't trust my judgment."

"You never listen to me."

"That's not true."

"She's right, Kent," Linda said. "You're not listening."

His wife had spoken while staring at the beer in his left hand. He wasn't even thirsty, really. Just cracked the damn thing out of habit. She'd been on his case about drinking ever since she'd poured out Maurice's bottle, and while she hadn't used the word *alcoholic*, it was there, cocked and ready. It'd been a rough morning at the dealership, though—the sales seminar was pure torture—and he'd hoped to unwind and recharge over a nice lunch, not get ambushed by a self-destructive daughter and a judgmental wife.

Probably shouldn't have had that last slug of bourbon before leaving the office though. And he wouldn't have, if not for his blasted foot. The toe was no longer the worst of it. As of this morning, the flat was just as painful. Rising from bed was sheer agony, needles and fire. All day he'd fought the urge to pop one of Sharkey's pills. Just codeine, most likely. Hardly stronger than the Tylenol he was already using.

"Okay, so taking some personal time isn't necessarily a bad idea, but you got to have a plan."

"I have a job, Dad."

When exactly had she become so snotty?

"And just this morning, Dan was saying we need someone full-time in F & I—"

"F & I?" Kent thumped the table with his beer-free fist. Plates and forks jumped. "Jesus, Kelsi, you sound like a lifer."

For the next five minutes, he pleaded with her that deferring college was a mistake, that time was the most precious commodity of all, that higher education was a necessity and the timeline for procuring it brooked little delay. He went on like this, repeating himself and groping for the right words. "No daughter of mine," he said in conclusion, "is gonna waste her time pushing Ford Credit loans for ten bucks an hour."

"You can't tell me what to do anymore. And besides, it's *my* time to waste."

"Honey," Linda said, "don't talk that way."

Her time to waste? Kent took a breath and looked around.

The kitchen was tidy and the appliances higher-end; the house itself stood in a cul-de-sac on the better side of town. New vehicles sat in the driveway and always would. The lawn was trimmed and edged and his daughter's hurtful words flowed past teeth made beautiful via five thousand dollars of orthodontia. Kent had paid for all of this, for every stitch of clothing and every stick of furniture, and he was fine with that. Proud, even. Except he'd paid in hours, in days and months and years. That was the price nobody talked about. He would exit this world one day relatively soon and these things—these walls and vehicles and college funds—were his only evidence of having lived a meaningful life. This was the bargain he'd struck with manhood, with America, and it'd seemed a fair one right up until Kelsi announced she was no longer interested in honoring her end of the deal.

"You wanna end up like me," he said, "and spend sixty hours a week glad-handing people you wouldn't piss on if they caught fire? Wanna watch your dipshit coworkers get promoted because they got a diploma, and you don't? Wanna look back on this moment and see the future you could've had wither on the vine?"

"Kent," Linda said, "you need to calm down."

"What's wrong with working at a dealership?" Kelsi said. "You do it. Grandpa did it."

And here was that most adult of paradoxes—that just because the people you love do something does not necessarily mean that thing is good. Clearly he'd done too convincing a job playing Ward Cleaver. Should've punched some holes in the walls. Shot the TV and cursed out the dog, or maybe vice-versa.

"How about you tell me what—or *who*—this change of heart is really about."

For a moment, Kelsi's spiteful veneer cracked, but the truth didn't quite seep out. Here was the difficulty in arguing with a teenage girl: she wasn't smarter than you; she was just so self involved that the idea you might actually be right was unthinkable. Then she fixed him with a curious look, one he didn't care for. "Dad, are you sure that's the only beer you've had today—"

"Cut the bullshit!"

The kitchen fell silent as Kent lurched to his feet. The pain this cost him only fueled his anger. "We both know what you've been doing"—Kent's hand closed seemingly of its own accord, crushing the beer can and wetting the table—"and God help me that is gonna stop. And so is this cockamamie talk of skipping college and flaunting your ass around Thompson's Ford!"

A strange moment passed in the wake of this outburst, one divorced from the regular flow of time and being. Had he just now been shouting in his daughter's tear-streaked face? But then his father entered the kitchen, just popped into existence like some potbellied phantom. He must've let himself in through the patio.

"Bad time?" Jerry Seasons asked.

Kent dropped the crushed can into the wastebasket. "I gotta get back to the lot. We've got this consultant in from Dallas—"

"Kent," Jerry said, his paunch taut against a Paris Junior High basketball T-shirt, "maybe we'd best go smack a few golf balls first."

"I can't, Dad. Not today."

"Sure you can. I'll call old Bill myself if need be. He doesn't own my son."

22

Maurice Currant gawped. "*Excuse* me?"

"You heard right, Mr. Currant," Jennylee said, although the most important communication hadn't actually been spoken aloud. Instead, it was penciled on a Regent's offer sheet, which she'd slid across Maurice's desk during this impromptu meeting. After all, buyers were less likely to balk at a big number if you wrote it down. Made the number seem formal, more businesslike, and—most importantly—less negotiable.

"You've made a serious mistake by coming here, Jennylee."

A thin gold chain sparkled around Maurice's country-club-tan neck. Its shade, she realized, was the exact same as her Nissan.

"Now, I understand numbers can be confusing, but it's all broken down for you right here. At the end of the day, it's just a series of small, easy-to-manage payments."

He laughed at her. Laughed long and loud, right in her face. "What's confusing me," he finally said, "is just exactly what sort of drugs you're on."

The night before, her family's troubles left Jennylee sleepless, but as the sun rose, she found herself thinking back on Monday's test-drive out by Paradise Lake. At first, she'd tried to bury the memory, but maybe that wasn't the right move? Instead, she'd forced herself to replay the events in her head, to parse through exactly what'd happened. And in doing so she'd recalled Maurice's words: *Squeal, and I'll tell everyone how I steadfastly refused to pay you for a suck job! How you threatened me with lies!*

Funny how an idea just sinks roots. Like becoming a mortician. Aunt Liz planted the idea, but Jennylee's own hopes had watered the notion until it'd sprouted into a real possibility, which led her to take steps (such as requesting educational literature and meeting with Alice Higgenbottom) to see that possibility flower into something real. Lots of folks around Paris believed that ideas didn't actually matter, that we can't control what happens to us. But blackmail—which, she understood, was exactly her intent—was just another idea. In fact, blackmail wasn't much different from a threat, and a threat was just a stone's throw from a demand, which was really just a bolder way of *asking*.

Earlier that morning, it'd seemed Donovan Crews had come all the way from Dallas just for her. While no man who wore a pinkie ring could be trusted, by the time the consultant was done schooling Paul Stenger on how to shake hands, Jennylee was determined to implement his advice: to show who was the boss and not let the up—in this case, sickness and poverty—dictate the deal. So she'd hustled out over lunch hour and driven, in that weird window of clarity that occasionally graces the deliriously tired, to Currant Family Photography.

Standing on the stoop, she'd gathered her courage and quietly whispered, "A. B. C."—*Anything (to) Beat Crohn's*—and then marched inside and caught Maurice unawares. He'd been in the middle of a shoot, hoochie-cooing some unsuspecting family's preschool-aged daughter. Upon noticing her, however, Maurice hustled those clients right out the door.

"So what do you think of these numbers?"

He laughed at her again. "I think you're off your fucking rocker."

"If payments seem like a hassle, you could always just pay a lump sum. Cash only though. No offense, Mr. Currant, but I don't feel comfortable accepting your personal check."

"I wouldn't give you crabs," Maurice said, "let alone *cash*."

"I figure crabs would be the least of a girl's worries so far as you're concerned."

"Now lookie here. This has been an interesting little diversion, but it's time you head back to Regent's where you belong." He pushed the offer sheet back across the desk. "Who knows, maybe you'll get to go for another test-drive in that old Caprice?"

At this point, just as planned, Jennylee took out her phone and pulled up the slideshow she'd created: a sort of highlight reel of images and video of Maurice and his young boyfriend. She'd edited it carefully, emphasizing the best shots. She held the phone up, maxed the volume, and hit play. Wine coolers and handcuffs, dancing and kissing, marijuana smoking and dappled sunshine, and lots and lots of fellatio.

Maurice didn't blink once.

"It's human nature to fear commitment," Jennylee said. "I understand that. But if we can't reach a deal, you'll come to regret it."

"How dare you? You stupid little—"

"I'd think twice," she said, "about cussing me any more than you've already done."

Maurice's work covered the studio walls. Senior pictures. Engagement and wedding photos. Children's birthday parties. All air-brushed and glowing. A series of team photos of junior high basketball squads hung behind Maurice's desk, some of the boys already tall and strong, others baby-faced and swimming in their jerseys.

Jennylee pointed out the photos. "Exactly how old was that boy you were with, anyway? Nineteen? *Eighteen?*"

"Wouldn't you like to know—"

"And was he by any chance one of your former players? You know, someone you kept in contact with over the years, a player you had a special relationship with? A boy you sort of *groomed?*"

"This is a joke, right?" He grinned. "A little payback—"

"It won't be so funny when the local parents discover a bondage artist is coaching their sons. The school board would almost have to share info like that, don't you think?" And here came the kicker, the line she'd rehearsed beforehand while visualizing this negotiation from A to Z. "I don't suppose you shower in the same locker room as those boys, do you, Mr. Currant?"

The skin twitched below Maurice's left eye.

"And I suspect your wife—Gloria is her name, right?—well, I can't picture her being too pleased either."

"Take this"—Maurice stabbed a finger at the offer sheet—"and get out."

"Now I suppose Gloria might not get too cross over your having a boyfriend. For all I know, you two are swingers. But I doubt she'll appreciate hearing about our trip to Paradise Lake. How you exposed yourself and left me to walk home like a stray dog. Women, wives especially, tend to frown upon that sort of thing."

"Your word against mine," Maurice said.

But this was an easy objection to overcome. "Not if Gloria gets the skinny from Kent Seasons himself. And I have to say, Kent's been in a real honest mood lately."

"Your bluff needs work."

"If I were to decide to press charges—if you leave me no choice, I mean—how do you think Gloria will enjoy reading about her husband's peccadilloes in the *Beacon-Herald*?"

Watching Maurice sweat was satisfying, but it's what a salesman *doesn't* say that counts most. Buyers might be afraid to ask for a better deal, but they aren't afraid to listen to one—and so, having made her offer, Jennylee sat back and zipped her lip. But in the escalating silence, she realized she'd neglected to tell anyone where she was going. While Maurice didn't strike her as the murderous type, and the studio was full of cameras and tripods, not guns and knives, it was still nerve-wracking.

"I'm a part-time photographer and a volunteer coach," Maurice said. He fluttered his hands at the offer sheet. "What makes you think I have that kind of bankroll?"

There'd been a few pleasurable moments here—not the least of which was seeing Maurice realize he'd been video recorded dancing around in a thong and a wig—but none compared with having anticipated these words of his. Because before ever stepping foot inside Currant Family Photography, Jennylee had known Maurice would claim he couldn't pay. She'd known it this morning while listening to Donovan Crews lecture on how best to counter common objections ("I'm just looking!"), and she'd been rehearsing this exact scenario in her head ever since.

Was this what Kent Seasons meant by seeing around the corner?

"Good 'n' Crusty? Gloria's father? I know all about that, Maurice. And seeing how you and Gloria are married, that means you've got money too. Believe me, I know how *that* goes. My husband swipes our credit card every chance he gets."

"You bitch."

"Crust Fest is this weekend. Mighty bad timing if all this came to light while Paris was busy celebrating the family business."

"I should've drowned you in the lake that day."

"Guess you'll just have to decide whether you'd rather fork over the money and say it was for a fancy new camera—well, a dozen cameras—or whether you'd prefer a very public trip to divorce court."

Maurice squinted and chewed his cheek. Finally, he opened his desk drawer and stared at whatever was inside. The longer this continued, the closer Jennylee came to sprinting for the door. But then Maurice lurched into motion, tossing knickknacks aside and muttering darkly. Finally, he produced a bottle of talcum powder. He removed his loafers and peeled off his socks. He twisted the bottle's cap, sprinkled a pile onto his palm, and rubbed the thick yellowish powder into his feet, paying special attention to the grooves between his toes. His eyes looked doped and far away. Was he in shock?

But then Jennylee remembered Donovan Crews's mantra: Buyers Are Liars.

"Perk up, Maurice," she said, and gently slid the offer sheet once more across the desk. "As you can see, most of your payment is for my daughter's health care. I've figured in the bills we already received and estimated some coming down the pipe. The rest is for my education. Got the figures off Triumph University's website. Look them up yourself if you don't trust my math."

Maurice rose to his freshly powdered feet. "Leave. I need to use the bathroom."

On her way out, Jennylee handed Maurice a Regent's business card. "My offer stands for twenty-four hours. I'll be expecting a call at this same time tomorrow. If I don't hear from you, I'll have to assume there's no deal."

But Maurice would call. Like Kent Seasons said: if a buyer takes a potty break during negotiations, they're rolling over. *Once they give up all hope, the sphincter unclenches. May as well write them up while they're still on the can.*

Out on the stoop once again, Jennylee looked up into Maurice's bloodless face, and then seized his limp hand and shook hard: pump, pump, break.

23

The driving range at Paris Links was a narrow strip in the cornfields across the road from the par-three course. Downrange, a string of hay bales was spray-painted with yardage numbers and bull's-eyes. If Kent hadn't felt so guilty for blowing up at Kelsi, he never would've agreed to come here—especially considering he could barely walk—but his father had been adamant. Besides, Bill Sr. had ordered him to show Donovan Crews the town later that night, so he deserved a long lunch.

"Feeling okay, son?" Jerry stood back, critiquing his swing. "You look wobbly."

"I'm fine, except for my foot."

"What'd you do to your foot?"

"I woke up on Monday morning."

He crushed out the cigarillo his father had shared with him. Jerry Seasons claimed a man had to pick his battles when it came to the zipper-club lifestyle. Twenty Camels and a case of Coors? You're asking for it. But one little cigar on the range followed by a tall club soda with lime was cardiac copacetic. Such hedging was probably a necessity past a certain age. Kent teed a fresh ball and recalled how, growing up, his father had often taken him golfing with salesmen from the area dealerships, overcoming his objections that golf was boring by declaring it a business necessity. It really wasn't though. Kent hadn't golfed in years and had suffered no appreciable career damage—or maybe he had? After all, Dan Thompson probably golfed his ass off. Swung a nine iron both on and off Paris Links…

Feeling overwarm and exhausted, Kent squared up with his weight on his back foot, then laid his thumbs on the leather grip and reminded himself not to choke the club. Beyond the farthest bales, dry cornstalks stood still as sentinels. Then he wound up and blew out his cheeks, and, in a moment slow with liquor, he visualized Donovan Crews's and then Maurice Currant's and finally—inevitably—Dan Thompson's smug faces grinning up at him from the surface of that little white ball. He grunted like an ox, squeezed the club hard enough to wring sweat from it, and took a savage cut: whiff!

His momentum spun him off the tee box, and only planting the club in the grass like a cane prevented a humiliating tumble.

Jerry frowned and squared up to his own tee. "You always did swing too hard, son," he said, and then rocked smoothly into his backswing, shifted his weight from rear foot to front, and smacked the ball downrange in a pretty little rainbow. He'd lost weight and given up eggs and beef, and it'd helped his stroke. Small compensation for choking down a dozen pills a day and eating nothing but salads and broiled cod, though.

"I'd give anything to be your age again," Jerry said, "bum wheel or not."

"You haven't tried rolling on my wheels, Dad."

"Have a business to run, some steel to push."

"In case you haven't heard, now's not the best time to be selling Chevrolets."

"Ignore the doomsayers. People will always need cars."

"This one feels different," Kent said.

But his father reminded him how the so-called experts made the same dire predictions back in '69, when Ralph Nader convinced America the Corvair was a death trap, and again in the seventies, when the draft-dodging hippies got tired of smoking pot and killed the muscle car with the Clean Air Act. After they'd founded Regent's, the talk was about how the UAW was too powerful, how the Jobs Bank made sure nobody worked but everybody got paid, and how the Japanese invasion was Pearl Harbor all over again.

"Sky's been falling for decades now, Chicken Little," Jerry said.

Listening to all this, Kent felt like jumping his father's ass, and not only for trumpeting the same denials that'd gotten GM into the red, but for having surrendered their family business to an arch sonofabitch like Bill Regent Sr., for wimping out and folding his cards after one lousy quadruple bypass. Instead, he mentioned Kelsi's threats to skip college. He left out all suspicions about her personal life but admitted as to how his own choices might've steered Jerry's granddaughter toward a bad decision.

"Ever notice booze makes it harder to deal with women?" his father said.

"I find just the opposite to be true."

Jerry looked at him. "Sure about that?"

While no stranger to the bottle as a younger man, Jerry Seasons had never gotten violent or chased skirts, but there was a stretch where Kent's parents rarely spoke, when his dad retired to the couch after dinner each night with a tumbler and his thoughts.

Ultimately, the heart attack stopped Jerry's hard living, and—according to Kent's mother—saved their marriage. In the years since, Kent couldn't help but imagine life without his dad. Once he'd even caught himself thinking how it might feel to slip a set of car keys into a cold, stiff hand—a goodbye token to speed Jerry along to the afterlife, like the ancient Egyptians stocked the pharaohs' tombs for their long night's journey. Kent and his father both had gasoline pumping through their veins, and nobody except another car guy really knows how that feels.

"You were slurring," Jerry said, "and shouting at Kelsi."

"Yeah, well, her and Linda treat me like I'm just some machine they can wind up and send off to work. Like I couldn't possibly have anything to say worth hearing."

"Maybe they're treating you that way for a reason."

"And what might that be?"

"You sounded like a mean drunk, son. It's barely past noon."

"I had one lousy beer."

"Didn't look like one beer. You'd best lay off the sauce."

As if possessed, Kent's good foot kicked over the bucket. Range balls spilled past his father's shoes. In Jerry's disappointed expression, Kent briefly saw himself: a red-faced guy without much salad left on top and a twenty-pound donut wrapped around his waist. Not the apple of anybody's eye anymore, not even his old man's. But Kent wasn't in the market for cathartic father-son talks. That ship had sailed long ago, for the both of them. He pointed at the Paris Junior High hoops logo stenciled on Jerry's shirt.

"You shouldn't get so cozy with Maurice Currant."

"Why's that?"

"Because he's a smug, womanizing, gold-digging reprobate."

"You two have a run-in?"

"Let's just say Maurice had best steer clear of my dealership." A moment passed. "What should've been my dealership, that is."

His father lit another cigarillo. "Kent, I know you aren't happy with how things played out, but you gotta let it go. I had no choice."

"That's not what this is about."

"Funny, but it seems like that's always what it's about."

Kent ached to tell his father how Nautical Bill and Junior were floating sales and cooking the books. The words bubbled in his throat, words that would make Jerry finally admit Junior's MBA was a sham, mere justification for a gift-wrapped general managership—how his father must've seen this coming and should've warned him. Kent wanted to tell Jerry he'd gone soft and gotten bent over by Nautical Bill. To watch the truth sink in, to watch it hurt. But considering Jerry's Himalayan blood pressure, the thought of his old partner scheming behind his back might've been just infuriating enough to kill him. Plus, Kent had no concrete proof. Sure, the numbers didn't quite add up, and Nautical Bill was sly enough to pirate another dog's biscuits, but by the time they hired a lawyer and filed complaints, any paper trail would be shredded. Sketchy bank accounts closed, and stories gotten straight.

"Would you do it all again the same way?"

"Paris ain't the place for a midlife crisis, son." Jerry teed fresh balls for them both. "Trust me, you're better off not worrying about shit like that."

"I feel like I'm cracking up."

"Keep your head down this time. Grip her and rip her."

"Ever wonder if we drink in order to hit bottom sooner—so there's still time left?"

"I was a Marine and car dealer," Jerry Seasons said, lining up his drive. "I don't do philosophy."

"You don't think about your own life, Dad?"

"Just make contact. Let the club do the work."

"For a while there, I thought about college. Remember?"

"You could've been anything you wanted, Kent. You know that."

But Kent felt like saying that he *had* become what he'd wanted, exactly what he'd wanted, at least until the last couple of years when it all went south. Jerry wasn't really listening anyway, though. Lost to routine: lock the pinkie around the index finger, head down, square the shoulders and let her rip. The ball leaped in a great spray of dirt and sailed high and far, sailed until both men—hands to brows, stomachs protruding, balding heads slick with perspiration—lost sight of its arc in the blinding May sky.

24

When it comes to selling cars," Donovan Crews said, "honesty is crucial. But be careful, because if you're *too* honest you'll scare buyers off and lose the chance to show just how honest you can really be…"

Listening, it occurred to Paul that anyone who got paid for saying such a thing clearly had life by the short hairs. The consultant hadn't much appreciated being told he would burn in hell though. There'd been genuine shock in his eyes. Paul felt bad about it in retrospect. After all, Crews was only trying to help them all make money. He'd debated apologizing over lunch, but then thought better of it. Ownership would hear about the comment regardless.

He'd also been distracted by Jennylee Witt, who'd hit the door running only to return an hour later with an air of total serenity, as if she'd solved the riddle of existence over a ham sandwich. Paul considered asking her how things were at home, as a way of thawing the ice from that Blazer deal, but the prospect of three more hours of car sales training was so disheartening that he'd thought better of that too.

Now, having reconvened, Chadwick was playing the buyer and Donovan Crews the salesman. Everyone's eyes were on them—everyone's except for Paul, as he'd slipped his vibrating phone from his pocket. A text from Annie: *Call me!* ☺

"I want my payment at three hundred a month." Chadwick crossed his arms and scowled. "That's my budget."

"Great," Crews said. "Three hundred…up to?"

Up to? was a budget stretcher. Trick was to let the buyer speak the numbers and make the commitments. Used properly, it could build thousands onto the sale price, at forty or fifty bucks multiplied over the lifetime of a loan, plus additional interest.

"Up to…maybe three-fifty?" Chadwick said.

"Excellent," the consultant said, and pumped Chadwick's hand. "We have ourselves a deal."

Then he faced his captive audience and adopted a power stance, fists balled on hips, elbows flared. "Up to," he said, "is the single most valuable question you can ask. If you'll just remember that one simple question—and how to lay the groundwork for asking it—I guarantee you'll earn ten grand more every year. That's your retirement account right there, folks. It's that easy."

As the minutes ticked by, Paul considered his reaction to the consultant, and realized he was probably just misplacing his hurt feelings from the previous night. Sure, he'd opened up to Annie about that singer-songwriter from Louisville, and how that might've impacted his life more than he'd realized, but he hadn't found a way to talk to her about his writer's block, let alone his plans for Nashville.

"For our next exercise," Donovan Crews said, "let's have everybody stand up." The sales team did as told. "Now imagine I come strolling along and you're preparing to meet and greet, when…"

Paul's cell vibrated again. Had to be Annie. Combined with last night's spat, her mystery news was distracting. He eased the phone from his pocket.

Can't w8 to see u play the Buck 2nite! <3, Me.

The Buck? The gig had totally slipped his mind. When he'd agreed to play, he'd imagined it'd give him motivation to rough out a few tunes. But he hadn't written a single verse, let alone a new set. He was rusty on the strings too, his fingers soft and clumsy. Besides that ill-fated night with Cat Stevens, he'd hadn't played more than a few lousy chords all month…

Then Donovan Crews lunged at his face: "Pay attention!"

Badly startled, Paul dropped his phone and it clattered away under the metal folding chairs. In the long seconds to follow, Kent Seasons pinched the bridge of his nose; Jennylee cocked her head; Chadwick covered his grinning mouth; and the new guy, Sharkey, curled his upper lip in leering, sneering schadenfreude.

"What in tarnation is going on?" Bill Sr. wanted to know.

Junior's eyes bugged. "Everybody needs to get serious!"

"Sorry to get loud with you, Paul." The consultant breathed on his pinkie ring and polished it on his cuff. "But Bill Sr. has trusted me to whip this team into shape, and I take that responsibility seriously."

Paul's hands wouldn't stop shaking. Today's humiliation was apparently bottomless. He tried to collect himself as Donovan Crews imparted one last message: they would embrace competition, because competition was the American way.

"Kent told me about that yellow Avalanche," he said. "She's been on the lot a long time, huh?"

"It hasn't been that long," Junior said, and shot Kent a hateful look.

For his part, Kent had rolled in late from lunch, sweaty and flushed. And the way he'd been limping lately suggested the sweat owed to booze, not exercise. "Donovan has a great idea," Kent said. "A little contest for motivation."

"Fifty dollars per test-drive on the Avalanche," the consultant said. "A Franklin if they sit for numbers."

"How much if we sell it?" Sharkey asked.

"Tell them, Kent," Donovan Crews said.

All eyes fixed upon Kent Seasons then. He wore a sly smile, as if the subtle dig he'd gotten on Junior had brightened his mood. "Two grand," he said, "plus commission."

The room quieted. Then Brad Howard whistled, and Chadwick repeated the number as a question. But it was Erik Sharkey who set the tone. He struck a pose to make Arnold Schwarzenegger proud: arms flexed and trembling, tendons straining from his neck and trapezius bouldered up to his earlobes. Then Sharkey threw back his head, closed his beady eyes, and loosed a loud and throaty war cry.

25

There's fresh-squeezed grapefruit juice and chicken apple salad in the fridge, dear."

"That sounds wonderful. I'm starving."

Alice Higgenbottom glanced up from her work. "Did you skip lunch?"

"You might say that."

Jennylee had arrived at Higgenbottom's twenty minutes after the sales seminar wrapped up for the day. And what a day it'd been. Just before she left for her meeting with Maurice, Paul whispered something that got the consultant royally flustered. Nothing but bad vibes and dark energy from there on. Later, though, when the consultant shouted at Paul, Jennylee hadn't felt good about it. Deep down she still wanted to think well of him—although Chadwick had mentioned a deal Paul had swung with Junior to sell that overpriced Caprice (a vehicle she'd had her fill of, frankly) to Lloyd Rivera, the new lot attendant. Lloyd seemed like a real sweet kid. If that deal went down the way Jennylee suspected, Paul Stenger just might have sold his soul to Regent's.

After parking the Nissan, she'd let herself in through the back door with the key Alice had given her, feeling a little burp of pride when the teeth fit the tumblers. Nice to be trusted like that and given the benefit of the doubt for once. She'd found Alice in the lab, hard at work on Mr. Norvis Bell, whose service was scheduled for that same evening. Alice wore paint-spattered jeans and fuzzy slippers. That such a competent woman worked in her comfy clothes was truly inspiring.

Jennylee peeled plastic wrap off the chicken salad and slathered a dollop onto a slice of bread. Chewing, she covered her mouth with her hand. "Alice, I suspect most folks might hesitate to eat food that's kept right next to embalming fluids."

"But *you* aren't like most folks, are you, Jennylee?"

"I guess not," she said, thinking that neither was Alice Higgenbottom.

"The man of the hour is looking sharp, wouldn't you agree?"

He really was. His suit was stylish, at least by Paris standards, and his face was looking much better than the first time Jennylee had seen him.

"His makeup looks great, Alice. Very tasteful."

"Yes, well, we'd hate for Norvis to remind his loved ones of those old photographs of the dead from the Wild West—you know the ones, those sepia ghouls with their cheeks daubed red."

"Heck, he's probably more handsome now than he was, well, you know."

"You'd be surprised how often clients—new widows, in particular—express that very sentiment."

Together, they spent the next hour finishing the preparations. While running an oiled comb through the dead man's hair, Jennylee pondered the similarity of mortician work to car sales. "Strange as it may sound, readying the deceased for a viewing isn't so different from fluff-and-buffing some old beater."

"Do tell," Alice said, and squared the knot on Norvis's tie.

"Well, once you vacuum out the guts, shine the dash, and air the skins, you're pretty much good to go."

"Fair enough. Although your metaphor has limits."

Jennylee trimmed the nested hair from Norvis's nostrils with an electric razor. "There's not much market for pre-owned Norvis Bells, you mean?"

"Right. Because no matter how competently we rebuild Mr. Bell's smile, it won't ever shine again in quite the same way."

"I didn't mean to sound flip, Alice."

"Quite the contrary. Gallows humor is necessary to balance the gravity of—how best to put it?—our *reality-intensive* line of work."

"That reminds me of this sales consultant who's hanging

around the dealership this week. The guy makes everything sound like life or death, but none of his advice really matters—at least not until you apply it to more important things than selling cars."

"This great nation is floated on men's hot air, Jennylee. Two and a quarter centuries of smoke and bullshit."

Smoke and bullshit. That could've been printed on her business cards. But Jennylee was done thinking about Regent's for the day. Come seven o'clock, Alice explained, friends and family would file into the chapel. Jennylee was to greet each mourner at the door and offer condolences before seating them along the pews. Imagining these tasks, she thought of her church and suffered a stab of guilt. The old, deep feelings had been fading for some time, though, and a person can't fake their faith.

"Should anyone inquire as to your presence," Alice said, "explain that you are assisting me in a professional capacity."

"In a professional capacity," Jennylee repeated.

"You are my understudy," Alice said. "My official protégé."

She recalled Kent Seasons using that same word—protégé—although never once in reference to her. But Alice was different. Alice judged her performance and character based solely on what she did and said, not on what she didn't have dangling between her legs. But her eyes kept returning to the gussied-up dead man, and she remembered Alice's brother. Irrational or not, that doomed little boy made her think of Chast. Maybe a funeral home wasn't the ideal work environment for the mother of a sick child? The prognosis wasn't all grim though. So long as Chast got her treatments, Crohn's was manageable. Yes, they were staring down enough medical bills to wallpaper the Chrysler Building. And, no, they couldn't get insurance now—*preexisting condition* was the phrase she kept running into—but at least there were treatments available, unlike for Alice's poor brother.

"I want to say thanks again, Alice. This opportunity means the world to me and my family."

"Please don't take this as a criticism, Jennylee, but to listen to you talk, one might think you've never been shown any kindness at all."

Alice Higgenbottom had a way of saying things that made her cry. She had to turn away and wipe her eyes, which Alice was good enough to ignore.

A bit later, after they'd finished with "makeup and wardrobe" (as Alice put it), she helped transfer Norvis to his casket—a solid pecan wood outfit with a champagne velvet interior and hand-rubbed satin finishes. Consummately businesslike, Alice quoted these specs even quicker than Jennylee could rattle off horsepower and gas mileage.

"There," Alice Higgenbottom said, "now he's finally ready."

26

Mardi Gras beads and old cobwebs hung from the antlers of the taxidermy deer mounted beside the Buck's front door, their startled glass eyes watching the heavyset factory workers elbow to elbow along the bar, like a string of beer-chugging angels cut from thick paper. The air was oily with burgers and popcorn, roasted peanut shells littered the floorboards, and every so often a dart thumped cork or some wannabe hustler broke a rack of nine ball. As he listened to Garth Brooks lament on the jukebox, Kent Seasons nursed a sweaty longneck and pondered just how quickly time passed.

How could the Blowout Sale be upon them already—where had the days gone? His foot was killing him too, which necessitated an uptick in the longnecks. That morning he'd slipped Sharkey's pain pills into his wallet, just in case, but thankfully their waitress returned with some holistic medicine: double bourbons for himself and Donovan Crews. She set the drinks on paper napkins while Crews leaned back and scoped her out. Before he could spit his inevitable game (*A. B. C. Always Bring Condoms*) Kent spoke up: "Looks like folks are getting a head start on Memorial Day."

"We got live music tonight." She pointed at the stage where a chalkboard he'd failed to notice read, PAUL STENGER! ACOUSTIC GUITAR! 8:30–CLOSE!

Kent showed Donovan Crews the board and mentioned that Paul had studied music theory back in his college days.

"Community college, you mean—like continuing education classes?"

"No, college as in a four-year university."

Crews frowned. "That guy actually paid tuition to study *musical theory?*"

"I believe so."

"He smoke pole?"

"What's it to you—feeling lonely?"

The consultant was obviously down on Paul, but Kent hadn't bothered to inquire why. Paul was all right. Not the world's greatest salesman, and maybe not the world's greatest guy, but all right. Whereas Donovan Crews was a total douchebag.

"If that punk's so smart," Crews said, "so goddamn sophisticated, then why's he selling cars just like the rest of us? That's what I'd like to know."

"Ask him yourself. He'll be here any minute."

The consultant shook his head and shot his bourbon.

"Back when I first heard he wrote songs, I nicknamed him Carly Simon. Never stuck though. Nobody remembers her these days, I guess. So I gave him another nickname, one that really fits, but it's even more obscure."

"Carly Simon was a sexy lady," Crews said. "Gotta love those big, fat lips."

Used wisely, bourbon could make the unbearable bearable. Thankfully, Nautical Bill had given him the company credit card. "Bill Sr. sure does admire your training methods," Kent said, hoping to steer the conversation to less nauseating waters.

"Old Bill's a trip. He sent me to this place out past the mall this afternoon for a truly professional full-body massage…"

The Lotus Parlor? Unbelievable. It was bad enough that Nautical Bill sauntered onto the lot reeking of baby oil and General Tso's, but now Regent's was paying for this greaseball's shiatsu too?

"Hope you tipped your masseuse," Kent said.

The consultant grinned around his beer bottle. "There's a secret code. When the girl offers hot tea, you ask for cream and honey."

But Kent was in no mood for such talk, especially after whatever Kelsi had gotten herself into at Thompson's. Until recently, he'd thought little of Nautical Bill's sailorish habits or the lewd proclivities of other men. He was glad to be married, but everyone wasn't so blessed. No, for some men, sex fell into

the realm not of love, but sport, much as sales was a sport.
The game changed, though, when the woman was no woman
at all, but a girl—and despite what the law may have said, Kelsi
Seasons *was* still a girl.

Donovan Crews produced a file from his pocket and buffed
his nails. Then he blew on his precious fingertips before
launching unbidden into a diatribe about the bailout proposal
and Government Motors and creeping socialism. But Kent was
sick of hearing about it. Sick of people's partisan opinions. Sick
of TV pundits who spent all day decrying the evil, disastrous,
un-American bailout, instead of asking why GM continued to
build gas-guzzlers that dealerships could hardly give away. The
stupidity of it all was enough to make a man start believing in
Saudi Arabian–Bush family conspiracies and sympathizing with
pantywaist liberals like Paul Stenger—

"First, Washington nationalizes General Motors," Crews
said. "Next thing you know, Fords are being glued together by
the yellow man in Beijing. Maybe you oughta think about getting in bed with Toyota."

"Beijing isn't in Japan. You know that, right?"

The consultant pointed over Kent's shoulder. "Sooie and
sweet Jesus. Check out that honey pie."

A tall blonde stood beside a table behind them, idly texting.
Her blouse rode up and twin dimples winked just above her
hip bones. She was heartbreakingly pretty, the type who makes
a man lament his lost youth, but her jeans were the same low-
cut style Kelsi wore. Kent averted his eyes, sickened to imagine
men like Donovan Crews leering at his daughter. No shame, no
class. Just creeps wondering if tight jeans meant loose morals.
The blonde was alone and seemed to be waiting for the music
to start. Watching Crews watch her, seeing the dip and bob
of the consultant's jowly throat and knowing the low tenor of
his thoughts, Kent forced himself to raise his glass yet again
and swallow both a gulp of bourbon and the words boiling in
his throat. He considered his and Linda's retirement plans (the
Southwest, not Florida), and reminded himself not to risk all

that for the short-lived pleasure of bitch-slapping some goa-
teed Texas tulip.

"Finish that drink." Kent checked his watch. "I'll order us
another round before Paul starts singing."

But the consultant was distracted. "She ain't got but a handful up top, but that booty's so round you could rest your beer
on it."

"She's pretty, all right."

"I'd take my time with that one, by god."

"Yeah, I heard it takes a while for that Viagra stuff to kick
in."

"Man alive, I would lick her from the back of the knee all
the way up—"

Kent jammed his fingers in his ears and hummed deep in
his throat. He kept humming until his companion's lips finally
stopped moving. Why was he cursed with lecherous men? He'd
been good himself. All his life he had. Perhaps the Donovan
Crewses and Maurice Currants of this world feared another
man's virtuousness might blow their cover, and thus felt compelled to drag him down alongside them?

The blonde hitched up her jeans, as if sensing the consultant's gaze. Kent flagged down their waitress. More longnecks,
more bourbon. Stat.

"Maybe you two should slow it down a little," the waitress
said.

"You don't understand the gravity of my situation."

"Yeah? Well, do you understand that I can get blamed if you
leave here and plow into somebody?"

"I intend to harm no one except myself," Kent said. He
looked at the consultant, who was still busy leering. "And possibly this guy."

"Last round," the waitress said, "then you two are cut off."

Kent was still pleading with her when what he'd feared the
day before while having lunch with Kelsi actually came to pass:
Donovan Crews, apparently having decided the blonde's rear
had shifted into an angle of repose that simply could not be

missed, kicked Kent's foot under the table. It caught his sore toe right on the button.

Kent shrieked and cussed, spraying beer and chewed peanuts all over the tabletop.

"You really need to lighten up, partner," the consultant said.

"Getting cut off ain't *that* big a deal, honey," the waitress added.

꙳

Later that evening, after the mourners had all gone home, Jennylee helped Alice transfer Norvis Bell from his rented casket to a bare fiberglass box.

"The family was wise to rent," Alice said. "Why incinerate funds which might otherwise benefit the living?"

One side of the casket was lowered via clever little hinges, which allowed them to slide Norvis down into the box, which now sat on the Power-Tech 3K's motorized lift.

"Good point," Jennylee said.

"As a funeral director, I believe deeply in ritual, but I do not believe in symbolic gestures. Wasting money is a sentimental indulgence."

That made sense too. Directing funerals really was the most practical of careers.

"It's funny, Alice. The guys at Regent's like to brag how the car business will be around forever, how no matter what happens in Detroit or Washington or the Middle East, folks will always need vehicles—and absent a damned thorough bus route, that's likely true. But all that doesn't hold a candle to the funeral business, does it?"

Alice cranked open the Power-Tech's door and activated the lift. A motorized drone and Mr. Bell slowly rose toward the chamber's entrance. "People have been driving automobiles for a century," she said, "but they've been dying since they lived in caves."

Together, they slid the box inside along the rollers. Then Alice explained how to operate the oven. All was computerized, of course. Buttons and switches and readouts.

"Fifteen hundred degrees should do the trick," Alice said.

A deep whoosh issued from the belly of the chamber, like a match put to a massive pilot light.

Moments later, Jennylee was studying the door's little window when Alice touched her shoulder. "I can't recommend looking through that particular shade of glass, dear. Flame and heat will incinerate everything but mineral and hard metals, such as those orthopedic implants in Mr. Bell's knee."

"Pardon my asking, Alice, but have you ever looked?"

The woman paused before admitting she had indeed risked a look. "But I wished I hadn't," she said, and then took Jennylee by the elbow and led her away.

As the cremation chamber heated, they chatted over a pot of tea about family, about Edgar County's best restaurants, and even some celebrity gossip. They passed the hours as any two women might, in a laundromat, a waiting room.

After the oven cooled, Alice demonstrated the second part of the process, which involved using a long, magnetized tool to remove the metal before running the remains through a grinder and then raking and grinding again. "To ensure a uniform powder suitable for urning," Alice explained, sifting through the ash with the rake. "Amazing, isn't it? How little of us is of any lasting substance."

"What's left wouldn't hardly fill a coffee can," Jennylee said.

"Personally, I find it reassuring."

"That there isn't much to us?"

"That we're but stardust and water," Alice said. "That whatever makes us uniquely human is liberated by fire."

Cremation was an eerie and fascinating spectacle, and having witnessed it firsthand, Jennylee felt something inside herself bloom. She knew—or at least hoped so hard it felt like knowing—that she wouldn't have to sell cars forever. A woman like Alice Higgenbottom could show her the path to a better life. If she took all the right steps, if she stopped making mistakes and stopped wasting time, she just might have what it took.

"Guess he doesn't take music any more serious than selling cars," Donovan Crews said.

Kent glanced at his watch: Paul had been due onstage thirty minutes ago.

Under the table, his left foot still quivered. After the consultant kicked him, he'd decided the hour was nigh and chewed two of Sharkey's pain pills. Gritty and acidic, they tasted bad enough to work, but they hadn't worked yet. The ache felt permanent, as if pain's tender ghost meant to haunt him all the rest of his days.

As the minutes passed, the pretty blonde (whose body parts Crews systematically rated and catalogued, like headlamps and brake calipers) had grown visibly agitated. She kept checking her phone and sending texts. She'd also come nearer the stage, which brought her nearer their table.

"Excuse me, miss," Kent said, intending to exchange some harmless small talk before Donovan Crews could voice whatever ogling innuendo he was obviously cooking up. That way, at least the blonde would know they weren't tandem creepers. She lowered her phone and faced him. "If you're waiting on Paul Stenger," he said, "don't hold your breath. Guy works for me selling cars, and he isn't committed to that either."

She again glanced at the stage and then told Kent in less-than-delicate terms that his commentary was unappreciated, and that he could shove his opinions of Paul Stenger up a certain famously dark crevice. "And you," she said to Donovan Crews, "need to keep your middle-aged eyeballs to yourself."

With that, she walked away, heels crunching spent peanut shells. She paused to ask something of the bartender, checked her phone one last time, and then pushed through the door. In her wake, the guillotined deer looked heartbroken.

"Let's roll," the consultant said, "before you sweet-talk any more babes."

"Yeah, I'd best be getting home."

Donovan Crews stood and loosed a sonorous belch. "Still got Bill Sr.'s plastic?"

"Want some eats to go?"

"I wanna make tonight worth my time."

"It's late."

"Now I realize Paris is no Dallas, but it ain't late. Not yet."

Twenty minutes later, Kent turned onto Paradise Lake Road while his copilot dug into a fresh twelver of Heineken.

"This stuff tastes skunked," Donovan Crews said, and tongued the lip of his bottle. "Like Eurotrash pussy."

The road was curvy and tree-lined and dark. Kent swigged from his own bottle and wiped his mouth. He wasn't seeing double yet, but he'd listed to starboard a few times and then overcorrected. Probably find weeds in the bumper come morning, and the mud would show against the white paint job. Just one more thing to explain to Linda. The cab felt awfully warm too. He cracked his window and risked a glance at his companion. Eurotrash pussy? Who was this joker—Maurice Currant's long-lost brother?

But Maurice had been on Kent's mind, as he'd phoned that same afternoon, not long after the seminar ended. And an interesting call it was. Maurice had been irate and blubbering, and at first Kent hadn't followed much of what he said, except for one particular line—"No redneck twat of a *car salesman* is gonna blackmail me."

Kent asked him to repeat his story and, sure enough, it appeared Jennylee Witt was craftier than her Wrangler blue jeans might otherwise suggest. When he finally stopped laughing and told Maurice it sounded like Jennylee had him bent over the desk, Maurice demanded Kent fire her and muddy her reputation. And when Kent took a deep swig of whiskey and said, "And what if I don't, asshole?"—Maurice said if that was the case, then he just might have to put a bullet in Jennylee's thick, fucking skull.

While he doubted Maurice would actually turn violent, the episode was worrisome. Prudent thing was to call the police, of course. Maurice had mentioned homicide, after all, and Kent was in a position of knowledge and responsibility. But Maurice was too wimpy to shoot anybody, and cops would ask questions. Why hadn't he mentioned Jennylee's bad test-drive earlier? Wasn't it his job to protect his salespeople? Was he just sitting around his office drinking whiskey all day? Another angle was to go ahead with his initial plan and convince Donovan Crews to recommend Jennylee be let go. Definitely the simplest fix, but it didn't feel right. Not with her having a sick daughter and Maurice having brought his troubles upon himself.

"Well, what have we here?" the consultant said, pointing up ahead.

Kent slowed and peered into the darkness. Halfway around the next bend, a car was parked down a weedy path. "Reckon they broke down?"

"Going down is more like it," the consultant said.

But as they rolled closer, he noticed something else: a frame surrounding the parked vehicle's license plate—THOMPSON'S FORD, in bold red and silver. Closer still, the vehicle was clearly Kelsi's Impala, steamed windows and all.

"Stop the truck, dummy," Donovan Crews said. "Maybe we'll see some skin."

Kent chugged his beer, tossed the empty bottle to the floorboard, and stomped the gas. Tires barked and rubber peeled. He ground his teeth and squeezed the wheel as if to snap it in half. Strangely, though, no matter how hard he squeezed, he couldn't feel his hands. In fact, all of him was numb—all of him except for the rage deep in his gut. Dan Thompson was back there sweating up the beautiful leather seats he'd paid for. The man had defiled his daughter, taken a teenage mistress, and lacked the decency to even spring for a hotel room. And this had all happened right under Kent's nose. Probably started the day he'd called Thompson's and gotten Kelsi the goddamn job. *Step on into my office and let's talk about your duties, young lady...*

Kent wanted to puke. He felt a bolus of fried food and booze and regret coagulate inside of him, although from the neck down he swam in a milky, anesthetic gel. He struggled to both clear his head and ignore the consultant's incessant blabbering.

Dan Thompson.

Dan Thompson the cradle robber.

Dan Thompson the vile scum sucker who'd gone and broken every code known to man and fathers, who'd callously torn the Regent's license frame right off Kelsi's rear end and stuck his own vainglorious insignia in its place. The bastard even had the gall to take her parking on Paradise Lake Road, just like Maurice had tried with Jennylee.

THOMPSON'S FORD...

Kent groped for another beer, splitting the box's seams and blindly knocking bottles to the floorboard.

...THANKS YOU FOR YOUR BUSINESS.

"Did you see that Impala rocking?" Donovan Crews said. "Betcha some hot little babe's putting heel marks in the roof liner."

The Heineken foamed over in Kent's lap, wetting his crotch. The Silverado banged through a pothole. The suspension bucked and Donovan Crews bounced around the cab with a series of gleeful yee-haws.

"You fucker!" Kent shouted, spittle flying. "You dumb fucker!"

"No, *you* fuck her, Kent," Donovan Crews shouted. "After all, you brought her!"

More beer spilled. He couldn't feel the bottle. What was wrong with his hands?

DAN THOMPSON PERSONALLY THANKS *YOU*, KENT SEASONS...

The road narrowed like the barrel of a rabbit gun.

...FOR LETTING HIM BONE YOUR DAUGHTER.

Inexplicably, not a quarter mile downwind from the parked Impala, Kent Seasons's Silverado left the road. Donovan Crews shrieked and sprayed Heineken all over the dash. Branches scraped the doors. Kent's knees hit the steering column, the seatbelt cinched his chest, and his good foot jabbed for the vanished brake pedal. The consultant, having neglected to buckle-up, bounced around like a zero-G astronaut stuck in fast-forward. The truck snapped up and down, boom bang boom, sky dirt sky, and Kent's chin popped hard against his breastbone.

He tasted blood and white-knuckled the wheel as the maniac headlights lit a tree—a *big* tree—suddenly planted square in their path. The grill crunched and Kent's insides slalomed around his ribcage and the night woods flipped topsy-turvy.

The airbag had slugged him flush in the face, like an enormous gag-reel boxing glove, and chemical dust filled the cab, pale and swirling. His mouth throbbed, although the pain still didn't quite cut through the haze. He feared he'd urinated in his slacks but was buoyed by the fact of having spilled so much beer that nobody could tell the difference. Amidst such thoughts, things went gray and fuzzy. All was quiet and still except for the tinkle of broken glass, the click and hiss of the dying engine, and a faint groaning somewhere nearby.

Paul had left the gym early that night, knowing he still needed to slap together a set for his gig at the Buck. He figured he'd warm up the audience with covers until they might actually listen to an original or two—his *old* originals, that is. But the thought of strumming Tom Petty and Bob Seger tunes all night, of giving voice to what was, in effect, the cliché soundtrack of radio-sanitized lives, was a real downer.

The Y wasn't its usual sanctuary either, even though Team Regent's handily beat a team from a dealership in Marshall. The victory would've been a good warm-up for their rematch with Thompson's Ford during Saturday's championship game, except that Lloyd Rivera hadn't looked at Paul, spoken to Paul, or slapped five with Paul—let alone passed Paul the basketball—all night long. At first, Lloyd had pretended everything was fine, pretended he hadn't heard the talk of how he got his pants pulled down by Junior while Paul broke out the lube, but Tom Partlow's outburst had been loud and public. Not to mention Tom quit the team that same day, saying he no longer trusted his teammates.

The debacle left Paul reeling. He'd done a bad thing, or at the least he'd been strong-armed into doing a bad thing, which at his age was one and the same. He had to fix this, but how? Just giving Lloyd the commission wasn't enough, as that would do little to rebuild their trust or assuage Lloyd's wounded pride. Then again, apologies didn't pay the rent, whereas cash did.

On his way out, Annie smiled and asked if he was ready for his big show.

"Absolutely," he'd said. "Can't wait."

She lowered her voice so the retirees milling about wouldn't hear. "You are gonna look so fucking hot up on that stage."

"Easy now."

"I told my cousin you'd be great."

"Well, I hope I don't disappoint him."

"Are you kidding?"

"It's just been a while."

"Will you play that song you told me about? You know, the one about jeans and how screwed up the world is."

"Oh, yeah," Paul said. "501 Blues."

It wasn't that he was nervous to perform in front of Annie—or at least not especially so. Nor did he give a damn what her bar-managing cousin thought of his investment in live entertainment. No, lately Paul wondered if his plan to split for Nashville and become a professional songwriter was actually a tacit acknowledgment that he'd never be a paid performer, and if that was a greater loss than he'd dared admit. Because while he'd always enjoyed writing, hadn't he once dreamed of being onstage—of being known? In fact, wasn't the idea of performing live (like the illustrious Travis Bryson) how this whole romance with music got started in the first place?

It occurred to Paul then that he'd actually settled twice: car salesman instead of songwriter; songwriter instead of star. Motivation had waned in the past, but this felt different. He didn't want to play for the hicks at the Buck. Nobody would really listen anyway. They'd just pound Bud Light and shout at him to cover "American Pie." The pay was crap too. Hardly enough to buy the booze necessary to maintain his dignity.

Crossing the parking lot, exhaustion set in. His gauge was on E, and Citgo didn't sell the brand of fuel he needed. There'd been a slow leak ever since college. In all the places he'd traveled and all the jobs he'd suffered, something precious had been

seeping out—hope or patience, ambition or optimism—leaving
a spotty trail in his wake.

Languishing in such melancholy, and despite knowing he'd
hurt Annie (much like he'd known he was hurting Lloyd) Paul
skipped the gig in favor of driving aimlessly around the countryside and drinking beer. He looked at the parched cornfields
and thought long, dark thoughts. After all, only psychopaths
don't indulge a suicide fantasy every now and then. How easy
and peaceful it'd be: no more selling cars, no more failing to
write great songs, no more having to explain away his middling
life to judgmental dimwits, and no more guilt over neglecting to
floss his teeth. Or maybe he could disappear to some faraway
tropical isle—Tahiti came to mind—never to be heard from
again? Burn nut-brown in the equatorial sun, fish for his dinner,
strum a ukulele for the tourists.

But instead of all that, Paul drove the blacktop roads and
listened to Hayes Carll's *Flowers and Liquor,* an album he could
almost imagine having written himself. He didn't kill the entire
six-pack, though, because later a bunch of cops and an ambulance screamed past on the road out to Paradise Lake. For
a moment he'd felt sure they were coming for him—that the
authorities somehow knew he'd gone AWOL.

He dumped the remaining beer and set the cruise five under
the limit.

Kent Seasons emerged from a dream of floating in balmy salt-
water down in the sunny torpor of the Keys, where he used to
vacation with his father. What'd brought him back from this
comfy oblivion was the coppery taste of pennies.

He blinked his eyes open to a world gone oddly cockeyed:
grassy mud pasted to a spider-cracked windshield, trees standing left to right, seatbelt digging into his ribs. The Silverado
seemed to be lying on its passenger side, an orientation that
meant they must've had an accident, which in turn suggested
the groaning he heard was likely owed to Donovan Crews's
head being jammed up under the glove box. Kent turned a stiff

neck to see the soles of the consultant's loafers wiggling mere inches from his nose.

He gently pushed those loafers away.

Despite considerable pain—in his jaw, primarily, but in other places too—he felt curiously mellow. Was this shock? Or those damn pills Sharkey'd given him? In light of the present circumstances, it seemed distinctly possible those pills just may have been contraindicated, as the labels often read, for consumption with alcohol and the operation of heavy equipment, not excluding bourbon and Silverado pickup trucks. Or better yet, had he and the consultant actually been killed—were they soon to float away from the smoking crash, a pair of car salesmen on their way to stroke St. Peter at the pearly gates?

Whatever the case, trouble was coming. A man trapped in a totaled vehicle and bathed in Heineken (if not also his own piss) can safely assume what's barreling down the mountain isn't just six white horses.

"You hurt, Crews?"

"Fuck yes, I'm hurt, you cocksucker!"

Kent grinned at this, but his satisfaction was brief. Someone was tromping through the woods and shouting. A man's voice. Then it clicked, and Kent realized—horrified, mortified—that he was about to be rescued by none other than Dan Thompson himself. With this, his emasculation would finally be complete. There was quite simply nothing worse that could befall him, no humiliation any greater.

"Mr. Seasons…?" said the face mooning down through the shattered window.

At first, Kent feared head trauma. Brain hemorrhage, hallucination. But the details were too sharp: the lacquered hair, the sandpapery jaws and beady eyes. A Regent's polo, untucked and wrinkled.

"Sharkey?"

Erik Sharkey's head was on a swivel, as if he expected a SWAT team to burst from the woods at any moment. "Jesus, you okay?" He peered deeper into the cab. "Is that Mr. Crews down there?"

Then the tumblers finally fell, clanking, clunking, and it all made sense. Sharkey. Kelsi. THOMPSON'S FORD. Tears in the driveway and Linda keeping secrets. Nauseated, Kent turned his head aside and bathed Donovan Crews in pre-owned beer. He managed to grab a breath, but then his guts clenched and he puked again. Amidst the consultant's indignant howls, Kent basked in the dumb physical relief of the whiskey-sick.

Sharkey ran back toward the road, fanning the air like a man signaling a plane.

Donovan Crews, freshly bathed in a steaming morass of beer and bourbon and peanuts, extricated his head from under the dash and righted himself, cursing and whimpering. A cut above his eye gushed blood and he held his wrist like a lame paw.

As for Kent, he ran his tongue over his teeth and felt one move—front, top row. He put his fingers in his mouth and wiggled. A big shard, or maybe even the entire tooth, came loose. He tongued it down between his gum and lip like a plug of Beech-Nut.

"Listen up, Crews," he said, the words mushy around the impediment, "I'm gonna need you to recommend to ownership that we fire Erik Sharkey."

Kent started to laugh but laughing hurt his chest and also dislodged the broken tooth from its keeping place. To hell with it. He spat onto the consultant's shirtfront and watched the tooth topple down inside the breast pocket, like a bank shot with just the right english. "He shoots, he scores," Kent said, and pantomimed the best jumper a guy can pantomime while trapped in a flipped-over Silverado. But again it cost him pain.

Donovan Crews was too busy staunching the blood from his face to appreciate it anyway. After a while, the man's belly-moaning got Kent to wishing somebody sober would hurry up and come arrest them. Didn't Crews realize the importance of maintaining a dignified humor at times like these?

But then the chest pain came again—he hadn't moved this time—and it was fiery and deep. He couldn't seem to draw a full breath. A wave of dizziness washed over him.

While this could've owed to the booze and jostling, Kent suspected he wasn't so lucky. For years now, everyone had worried about his father's heart, while Kent was towing around his own bum ticker. It made perfect sense. After all, Jerry didn't keel over while eating a bowl of quinoa at ten a.m. during his retirement. No, it'd come after a long day on the lot, when the grinders and pea-brained salespeople and closefisted bankers finally got to him, when there wasn't enough beer or smokes or nine irons in the world to let off the steam trapped under his hood.

Regent's had tried to kill Jerry Seasons, and now it'd come for his son.

"I'm think I'm having a heart attack, Crews," Kent said, then added, "you dumb sonofabitch."

Donovan Crews was burbling blood into his hands—the pinkie ring looked like it'd been dipped in red paint. "Good," he finally managed. "I hope it hurts!"

Another jolt of pain and Kent grimaced and dug his fingers into his chest. Eyes clinched tight against the next burning wave, he swore at Donovan Crews with all the most vile words he knew, a cornucopia of cum stains and bloody douchebags and needle-dicked-motherfuckers and far, far worse—he yelled these obscenities as loudly as he could manage, considering his shortness of breath, because to die on a country lane with deviants like Erik Sharkey and Donovan Crews as witnesses, let alone with his defiled daughter helplessly left to watch, was a punishment unearned.

Kent Seasons harbored no illusions of having lived a perfect life. He'd sinned, erred, coveted, and fucked up. But God simply could not cut him this raw a deal. He wouldn't be dragged to the kill-box and closed on like this. Not here, not now. The pain came again, a viselike burning, and he swore more so than prayed that he wasn't done yet. To hell with this lousy write-up. He wouldn't sign the papers. He'd grind. No damn way he was gonna lie down and roll over and let fate take a pounder off him...

Step Five: Overcoming Objections

27

A battery of tests at Paris Community Hospital revealed that Kent's chest pain was not actually due to a life-threatening myocardial infarction, nor was it an attack of angina, and it wasn't even broken ribs, but just a nasty case of pyrosis, a common symptom of gastroesophageal reflux, more popularly known as heartburn.

"Thought my ticket was punched, doc. Truly, I did."

The emergency room physician, an underfed man in his forties who didn't even bother to hide his boredom, flipped through the chart and made a point of not answering.

"Getting riled up like that is humiliating. But you must see this stuff all the time."

Still the man ignored him.

"There I was thinking I was a goner, only to find out I put too many barbeque wings on top of too much beer."

The doctor finally glanced up, stethoscope swinging from his bony neck. "Your blood pressure is high."

"Heck, I could've told you that."

"Medication can help, but you need to watch your stress and reduce your alcohol consumption."

"Somehow, I don't think tonight's gonna make all that any easier."

The man shrugged and began to walk away.

"Say, doc? If you're ever in the market for a new or pre-owned vehicle"—Kent held out a business card—"just give me a call. I owe you one."

The physician brightened. "You're a car salesman?"

"Sales manager. I run the joint. And I know just the ride for a professional guy like you. Believe me—one good turn deserves another." And as the man slipped the card into his pocket, Kent said, "By the way, my foot's been killing me..."

By then, it was the early hours of Friday morning, and he'd

already had a less than pleasant talk with Linda, who'd been waiting outside the ER along with Kelsi even before they'd carted him out of the ambulance. Once it'd been established that he wasn't actually dying—although in definite need of some cosmetic dentistry—he was discharged and his night took a custodial turn. First, an ode to Lady Miranda. Then a taxpayer-financed lift to Edgar County jail, where Linda was content to let him stew.

But the drunk tank provided time to ponder the week's events, in particular those having to do with Mr. Erik Sharkey. Now it all fell into place. Sharkey, as Thompson's assistant sales manager, must've been sent to the Indianapolis auction where he'd met the same Ford man Kent bumped into. Being a pathological self-aggrandizer, Sharkey had claimed he *owned* Thompson's Ford, that he *was* Dan Thompson, and also—lastly—had bragged about seducing Kelsi.

Kent got back to Regent's around nine-thirty, after finally managing to get a lift via the county's lone taxi service. Prudence would've suggested he go home first, shower and scrub the ink off his fingers, brush his remaining teeth, and put on a clean shirt and slacks, but facing Linda again was even less appealing than marching into work on Friday morning looking like a Bosnian refugee.

"Hell's bells," Brad Howard said, having just hung his windbreaker on the coatrack. "You get mugged?" But Kent ignored him and made for Sharkey's (and Jennylee's) office, only to find it empty.

"Sharkey came in early," Brad said, "if that's who you're looking for."

"You're damn right that's who I'm looking for."

"He's got an up already. An appointment, I guess."

"You tell him to drop everything and get his butt into my office."

"Sure thing, but I do believe he's out test-driving Junior's yellow Avalanche."

"Whatever. I'm serving that fucker his walking papers."

Brad nodded, as if Kent had said he planned to inquire as

to which TV shows Sharkey had enjoyed the night before. This, Kent understood, was how people behaved when they're afraid you've lost your marbles. The calmness, the measured tones.

"Hate to ask," Brad said, "but how'd you lose that tooth?"

"Frozen Snickers bar," Kent said, and walked away.

Seen by a man fresh off a night in jail and branded with an aggravated DUI, the sales manager's office looked remarkably cozy. He unlocked his desk drawer, took out the bourbon bottle, and unscrewed the cap. But a few moments passed, then a few more, and still he hadn't taken a sip. Because besides the onslaught of legal battles and marital melees in his near future, he was also under physician's orders to abstain.

He'd told the ER doc how he'd awoken Monday with his toe all swollen. How the pain of this mysterious affliction worsened by the hour, how he could barely walk. Was it the booze? Had he whittled away his bones to porous little twigs? But the man had shrugged off his questions, performed a quick test, and diagnosed him with gout. Uric acid was apparently crystalizing in his joints, which led to inflammation and pain—pain commonly mistaken for a bone fracture. Listening to this, Kent imagined itty-bitty yellow spikes, like the jacks he'd played with as a kid, converging upon the crease of his big toe.

"Gout?" he'd said. "I thought only old fat people got gout?"

"Actually," the doctor said, "it's common in the middle-aged obese, as well."

"Touché," Kent said.

The doctor explained that gout was referred to as the disease of kings, because it could be triggered by too much rich food and alcohol—"such as the fried chicken wings and beer you mentioned earlier." He suggested they aspirate the joint and shoot it full of steroids, to see if the flare-up would resolve. Sure enough, Kent was feeling much better.

But while he had no desire to aggravate his condition—and remained a bit rattled by having flipped his Silverado and nearly killed himself and another man—it was remembering how the doctor looked at his toe that ultimately made Kent put the bottle down. Underlying the doctor's pompous sneer was the knowledge that his patient had suffered awful pain for a week, suffered it ignorantly and unnecessarily, like a common drunk. So Kent simply let the Jim Beam breathe. Just kept it there on the desk as a reminder of the amber-shaded glass through which he'd been viewing life as of late.

"Knock knock?"

He glanced up to see Brad Howard in the doorway. "Find Sharkey yet?"

"Little early for the rotgut, ain't it?"

"The hour's always later than you think."

Before Brad could reply, Junior nosed in, blustering and flapping his raggedy wings. He obviously saw the whiskey bottle, and then pretended not to have seen the whiskey bottle. "What in the golly-gee-willikers happened last night, Kent? Donovan Crews is laid up in his hotel room with the blinds drawn. Says he's got a fractured wrist, twelve stitches in his eyebrow, and a grade-two concussion."

"Grade two? That's nothing. He oughta be here teaching us how to shake hands."

Junior paused, having obviously noticed Kent's missing tooth, and then pretended not to have noticed the missing tooth. "What the heck's going on around here?"

"Come back later, Billy. We'll talk."

"Later? Jumping Jehoshaphat, Kent! You better explain just exactly what—"

"Go suck hair somewhere else, Junior. I mean it."

And Junior did. Just turned around and left.

"I'm gonna fill some sandbags and hunker down," Brad said. He glanced again at the whiskey. "Be cool, Kent. And holler if you need anything, okay?"

But what Kent Seasons needed Brad Howard could not provide, because—the gods of the car lot being as inscrutable as they were unscrupulous—Erik Sharkey managed to sell Junior's yellow Avalanche that very same morning.

Kent waited in his office for over an hour while Sharkey

romanced his up. Recalling how Sharkey howled and flexed his
muscles when the contest to sell the Avalanche was announced,
he felt ill. He'd have sworn he raised Kelsi better than that—
better than Erik Sharkey, at least.

Had Sharkey been foolish enough to venture anywhere near
the sales manager's office, Kent well might have added assault
and battery to his DUI, but after the demo Sharkey dragged
his dazzled buyer straight down the hall to Junior's office. No
one ever did this, but then Regent's of Paris had never seen a
salesman quite like Erik Sharkey. They emerged twenty minutes later, Junior beaming and patting Sharkey on the back. The
customer had rolled over and paid sticker, Junior's boneheaded
inventory was finally off the books—which meant Nautical Bill
would finally be off his case—and Erik Sharkey was now officially the golden goose.

On his way out to bid his buyer happy trails, Sharkey had
given Kent, who'd posted up in his office doorway, a most curious look. It took Kent a moment to recognize that look, but
sure enough, it'd been one of approval-seeking. So arose the
possibility that Erik Sharkey might be—hell, probably was—in
love with Kelsi, and in some insane leap of illogic likely viewed
selling the Avalanche as a first step toward his and Kent's recon-
ciliation. Sharkey no doubt realized a girl like Kelsi would never
fall in his lap again. That she was his last chance to bat out of
his league. His last chance, quite possibly, for happiness.

Sickened, Kent returned to his desk. Chin on his chest, he
stared at the bourbon bottle, which now rested like a patient
hound on the tiles at his feet. He still had to fire Sharkey, of
course. No way around that, save shooting him. But the yellow
Avalanche complicated things. How to justify canning their
strongest salesman? Yes, Sharkey had apparently impersonated
Dan Thompson at an industry event. And, yes, he'd seduced his
manager's daughter. But the guy could *sell*, and cash trumped
ethics every time.

Then Brad Howard rolled back into the office. "Just got off
the horn with Bill Sr."

"Sucks for you."

"How about I close the door, Kent? For some privacy."

He asked what was up, but Brad merely studied him, smoothing his chocolate-brown mustache. "You still got that Kentucky firewater handy?"

"Yeah, but I'm on the wagon."

"Since when?"

"Since this morning. Doctor's orders."

"That's bad timing," Brad said, "because after hearing what I got to say, you may wanna pour us both a stiff one."

28

D own the hall, Paul Stenger could've used a stiff drink of his own.

He sat hunched over his desk with his moleskin journal open to one of the few pages not filled with calorie counts and weight-lifting numbers. While he hadn't written lyrics at work in months, upon first starting at Regent's he'd often used downtime creatively. A good arrangement, this pondering of higher matters on the company dime. He was nurturing his creativity through the workaday doldrums while simultaneously pulling a fast one on capitalism. In his more ethereal moments, he'd almost fancied Regent's his patron.

And today, after all the fretting and procrastination and excuses, after all the worry about Nashville, he'd finally put pen to paper once more. The new song was inspired by a letter he'd found under his windshield wiper blade over lunch. He'd approached it slowly, warily, and removed the letter from its envelope as if anthrax might pour from the sharp folds.

Annie's voice breathed upward from the creamy YMCA stationery. He could almost hear her, as if she were right beside him, whispering sad nothings in his ear. The missive was short and to the point, but still he had to stop and collect himself to get through it. Nevertheless, in the letter's words hid the song he'd been waiting on all these months. Something along the lines of "Not Dark Yet"—although that song only came to mind due to its haunting refrain:

She wrote me a letter and she wrote it so kind
She put down in writin' what was in her mind

Annie had certainly done that, and the sentiments expressed weren't entirely unkind, but reading it was a kick in the nuts. So how better to honor this pain than by marching straight back into Regent's and rereading the letter over and over, while dreaming up a melody cheerless enough to complement its found lyrics?

Yet again, he slowly read through it, digesting each syllable:

Dear Ex-Almost-Boyfriend,

Thanks a million for making me write this stupid letter. And thanks for dodging my calls and making me sneak around and stick it on your stupid car (you need new wiper blades, by the way). I've been crying all morning. Everybody probably thinks I'm on the rag.

Okay, so usually breakup letters follow the Oreo cookie model. You know, sandwich the bad news between the good. If I was to write you that sort of letter, I guess I'd start by saying how great a guy you are, how much I've enjoyed our three lousy days together, how I know you'll make it big with your music, blah, blah, blah.

Then I'd dump your ass.

I'd close by saying how I hope we remain friends, how I'm sure we'll look back and think of each other fondly. Sorry, but I can't write you that sort of letter. Think of this as the opposite. As bad news sandwiching worse. When you didn't show up at the Buck last night, I was humiliated, but not because I vouched for you. Paul, I was humiliated FOR you. Because I realized you won't ever show up. It's always tomorrow, but I'm here now. Sorry, but I'm sick of waiting on guys like you to grow up.

I actually do think you're pretty great (look, I'm doing the Oreo thing after all) but I'm not so sure we're great for each other. I'm no psychiatrist, so I won't give you any advice. It'd be awfully bitchy to do that in a breakup letter anyway. That said, should you rethink the music thing? Stop using it as an excuse for always being so miserable. Stop pretending to love something you don't even apparently like well enough to do on a random Thursday night.

You're almost thirty, Paul.

—Annie

29

"My teeth or lack thereof," Kent Seasons said, "are none of your goddamn business."

He'd blown into Jennylee's office like a redheaded twister, plucked the phone from her hand, and punched the END button. She'd been busy prospecting—cold-calling, fishing—but mostly just killing time while awaiting a call from Maurice Currant. Before she could think better of it, she'd gone and asked about his missing tooth.

"Had an interesting chat with our friend Maurice yesterday," Kent said.

"He called you?"

Kent's eyes were unreadable. "You've certainly got his attention, Jennylee."

She'd figured Maurice might blab about her offer, but she'd also assumed Kent would just ignore it the same way he'd ignored Maurice's roadside sexual assault. It really was a curious situation though. In fact, upon waking that morning Jennylee could hardly believe she'd found the guts to follow through with her plan. Considering Kent Seasons had long ago written her off as a roll-over, he was probably just as surprised. But why did he look like he'd been in a car wreck?

"No offense, Kent, but you seem frazzled. Everything okay?"

"He says you're blackmailing him. Really twisting his berries."

"I made him a reasonable offer. In fact, I'm expecting his call any minute now."

"Wait. Maurice Currant has an appointment to call you—here?"

"I'm pretty sure I turned a tire kicker into a buyer," Jennylee said.

And had the ghost of a smile flitted across his face—had she actually said something Kent Seasons found *funny*? That missing tooth was ghastly though. Missing teeth are cute on little kids, but not on balding, red-nosed car lot managers.

"Jennylee, you really crapped in the casserole this time. I cannot have my salespeople threatening customers, now can I?"

Taken aback, she shook her head and insisted that Maurice Currant was certainly no customer. No, purchasing a vehicle was just about the last thing on his filthy mind.

"How's that daughter of yours, anyway? She had some tests done, right?"

This, too, set her off-kilter. Why was Kent asking about Chast if he'd only come to chew her out? Sure, he had a daughter of his own, so maybe he sympathized, but he was all business around the lot. And didn't he realize he reeked of booze?

She told him what the doctors had said: that Chast would probably be okay, so long as she got all her expensive treatments.

"Must be tough. Especially considering Regent's doesn't offer insurance."

She shrugged. "It's tougher than you can possibly know."

"Oh, you don't think I've struggled? You think I don't have worries?"

"I'm sure you do. But you asked, so I'm telling. I can't worry about anything right now except for my daughter's health. Frankly, nothing else matters."

"Not even selling cars?"

"And, yes," she said, "insurance would be nice."

"What about extorting money from local photographers—you've apparently got plenty of time to worry about that, huh?"

"That's between me and Maurice."

"Yeah, then why's he set to call you here at work?"

"I could step outside and call him on my cell, if that'd put your mind at ease."

"What would put my mind at ease," Kent said, the humor draining from his face, "is if you vacated the premises right now. Consider yourself fired, Morticia."

❧

"What in Sam Hill are you writing, anyway?"

Startled, Paul glanced up to find Kent Seasons leaning in his office doorway. He looked like hell, like he'd slept off a bender in the back seat of a Volkswagen Beetle.

"Nothing," he said, and stuffed the journal and Annie's letter in a drawer.

If he did well in Nashville, would he still be embarrassed about writing songs? Would validation—praise, money—cure his shame, or was it intrinsic to his inborn Midwestern distrust of anything not puritanical and levelheaded?

Kent sauntered in and dropped into a chair. No doubt about it: he was viciously hungover. The pores on his face were tiny taps leaking malty beads of yeast and rye.

"What's up, boss?"

"I ain't your boss anymore, superstar. At least not like before."

Kent Seasons was missing a front tooth. He looked like a deviant, a madman. Then the words registered—not his boss anymore?

"Aren't you gonna ask?" Kent peeled his lips back to better show the gaping hole.

"I hadn't noticed," Paul said.

Kent gave him the finger. "Those double-dealing douchebags Junior and Nautical Bill"—Paul glanced at the wide-open door—"have decided Regent's needs a managerial shakeup. Apparently, Donovan Crews suggested it over the phone this very morning."

"They let you go?"

"You think those greedy fuckers wanna pay severance? No, I have been demoted. Dee-mo-ted. They're trying to smoke me out. From now on, I am *co-assistant* sales manager. And wouldn't you know it, co-assistant sales managers take ups and work the phones, just like any other lot lizard."

"I'm sorry to hear that."

"Brad Howard is the new deputy around these parts, and

he'll be moving into the sales manager's office shortly. Guess who I'll be sharing his old office with."

Then it clicked: co-assistant sales manager. He was finally being promoted.

It wasn't really all that surprising, though, considering he'd been at the top of the sales board. Along with his education, his recent string of deals must've made him the obvious choice for management. Thinking about this, Paul's cheeks actually flushed. Not that he could accept the promotion. No, he had a dream to chase. Still, it felt good to know this lousy place needed him. It might even be fun to stay awhile and see how things shook out. What would his new salary be? And the insurance and benefits his mother was always carping about—might all that finally be coming his way too?

But these thoughts led to others, and a new wave of melancholy washed over him. He wouldn't be able to share this news with Annie. Tonight he would not go to her apartment, would not cook dinner with her, and would not sleep with her or awaken beside her. It dampened everything—even the brief pleasure he'd feel when he told ownership they could take their promotion and shove it.

"Sharing an office with you would be an honor, Kent. But lately I've realized I need to spend more time on my music. To be totally honest, after the Blowout Sale I'm planning to leave for Nashville."

Kent stared at him oddly. Then he guffawed and slapped the desk like some hideous, toothless donkey. "You? *You?* Promoted? Oh, that's rich. No, my finely feathered friend, you got a brand-new boss to answer to."

"What?"

"And his name is Mr. Erik Sharkey."

Any other day, this would've embarrassed the hell out of him. Instead, the news was almost soothing. Good to know things didn't change—the sun will rise in the east, April 15 is tax day, and hard work and good intentions will never go unrewarded at Regent's American Dream Motors.

"Jesus," Paul said. "They really bent you over. It doesn't seem fair."

"Fair's for kindergartners, pretty boy. If you haven't figured that out yet, then I probably do deserve to lose my job."

"You've always done right by me, Kent."

"Remember that speech I gave you back on Monday—the *Karate Kid*? That one always wets the peepers a little."

"It's a great speech."

"Thank you."

"So, what's your plan? What's the next move?"

"Funny you should ask. I've been pondering that all day and seeing how I'm still *a* manager here—if not *the* manager—I think I'll start with some housecleaning."

"Jennylee's being let go?" Paul lowered his voice and leaned across the desk. "Have you broken the news yet?"

But Kent aimed a finger at his face. "This news is all for you, muchacho."

"For me?"

"That *Karate Kid* speech was just smoke up your ass," Kent said. "You ain't the best I've ever seen. Not unless we're talking about the best at dicking off."

Paul fell back in his chair, stunned.

"You're fired, Wally Szczerbiak. Now pack up your pomade and hit the bricks."

ာ

"Fired?" Jennylee said.

"Correctomundo. You have just been fired. Fired as in terminated. Terminated as in shit-canned. Now saddle up and hit the trail, cowgirl."

She felt scalded by his words. Not that Kent had ever been on her side exactly, but she hadn't thought of him as cruel. Despite considerable evidence to the contrary, she'd always believed there was a genuine person in there somewhere—a man with feelings, with kindness in him. Looking at Kent Seasons now, though, at this familiar whiskey-bloated fucker who she still couldn't help but want to please, she felt like crying.

"But I didn't do anything wrong."

"What about abandoning a customer during a demo? That's a breach of the dealership's insurance policy. We've got licenses and permits at stake."

"What was I supposed to do—explain financing options while Maurice played with himself?"

Kent dug his palms into his eye sockets. "You were supposed to do your job."

"You didn't do a thing about it, Kent. How's that fair? How's that doing *your* job? You being the sales manager, knowing what that man did, and then blaming me…"

She wouldn't be able to hold back her tears much longer, but to cry in front of Kent would merely confirm he'd had her pegged all along. He was behaving strangely though. Just sat there, eyes closed, like a man steeling himself for a dreaded chore. What was the deal here? If he'd been forced to fire her, wouldn't he just blame ownership? Or at least not be so darn mean about it.

Then the phone rang, startling her.

Kent raised an eyebrow. "You always have been afraid of the phones," he said.

She lifted the receiver and recited the standard greeting, only to be met by Maurice Currant's voice, breathy and low. "Kent talk sense to you yet?"

"He's right here, actually. We were just discussing you, Mr. Currant."

"So I assume we can put this little problem of ours to bed?"

"No, I'm afraid we can't do that," Jennylee said. "Not yet, anyway."

Kent studied her from across the desk, just like back when he'd first trained her in phone sales technique. Observing, taking mental notes, seeing what she was made of.

"People who extort money go to jail," Maurice said. "They go to jail for a long time. And they don't see their kids except for an hour a month through a pane of glass."

But she'd already considered the likelihood of Maurice calling the law. No, his threats were as empty as his conscience.

"After talking with Kent," she said, "it appears I have nothing left to lose."

Hearing this, Kent leaned back and crossed his arms over his chest.

"What's that supposed to mean?" Maurice asked.

"It means you won't be getting any better deal."

"Now I don't know what Kent said, but you'd better smarten up before—"

"So take it or leave it."

Maurice screamed at her for an impressively long time, so long she eventually held out the phone so Kent could hear the wild cussing. Kent smiled and closed his eyes, as if Maurice's belligerence were the "Moonlight Sonata." Finally, Jennylee managed to get a few rational words out of him.

"So I'll be seeing you tomorrow morning, Mr. Currant," she said, and when Maurice commenced shouting again, she just talked right over him, "at eight a.m. sharp."

After hanging up, she felt a tremendous relief. But then she returned her attention to Kent, who—she suddenly recalled—had been in the middle of firing her.

"Eight a.m. sharp, huh?"

"Figured it was best to catch him early. You know how it is."

"You at all worried he might just shoot you rather than pay up? Because I feel obligated to inform you that he expressed something along those very lines."

"Does he own a weapon?"

"How the hell would I know?"

"Well, because you two are friends—"

"I am *not* friends with that gold-digging rapemeister, understand?"

Jennylee apologized and Kent rubbed the stubble on his chin. "So was he happy with the final offer?"

"He'll have to live with it," she said.

"Sounded to me like he's having second thoughts."

"No, sir. He rolled over and spread his cheeks."

With this, Kent Seasons took a deep breath and drummed his fists on his thighs, like he was absolutely dying to share something, but for whatever reason couldn't. "Seeing as how you've become a blackmail artist," he finally said, "I'd best warn you against trying any of that cornpone vigilantism on this dealership."

He'd spoken with an odd inflection, his voice rising at the end of the sentence. He was also dirty and disheveled and possessed of a weirdly mystic glow.

"Vigilantism?"

"Christ Almighty, Jennylee." He buried his head in his hands again, and all she could do was stare at his freckled bald spot. "Listen to me carefully. Regent's is firing you for abandoning a customer and being an all-around fuck-up. Now how does that make you feel?"

"Not particularly good."

"Let me guess—you don't think it's fair?"

"No, I don't."

"Why, because management failed to provide a safe working environment?"

"Well, I hadn't thought—"

"And then fired you without reasonable cause or any sort of process?"

She hadn't thought in those exact terms either. "Something like that, yeah."

Kent nodded. "And you'd best not think about filing for unemployment. No way you're gonna sit around the house and cash checks for watching *Judge Judy*."

"But you're firing me. I can't get unemployment if—"

"You're damn right, you can't. Not if you don't call the state and explain exactly how your job separation transpired, how your employment was terminated without reasonable cause, and beg for your goddamn grocery money. But if you *do* do all of that—which as an agent of this dealership I must advise you against, although it likely *is* within your rights—I suspect, considering the circumstances, that Regent's wouldn't even contest your claim, much as we'd like to. Believe you me."

Jennylee was too shocked to reply. And Kent Seasons wasn't done anyway.

"I'd also think twice before contacting an attorney who specializes in employment law," he said. "Wrongful termination? Hell, you're probably thinking lawsuit, aren't you? Claim you were discriminated against for being female. Sexism and all that. Maybe get a settlement to pay your daughter's medical bills. Probably even have some funds left over to become a funeral director, or whatever other bizarre shit you got up your sleeve."

"Kent, I just don't understand how—"

"The company, this dealership, Regent's of Paris, has officially decided you are toast."

"Toast?"

"Toast," he said. "Finito."

While Jennylee processed all this, Kent Seasons seemed content to sit across the desk and wait. Her head spun with new ideas. Lawsuits? Wrongful termination? Settlement money? She'd never thought of herself as the suing type, but maybe it was the humble people, those too scared to bark back, who kept the bullies and business owners of this world flush? But—and this much she *was* certain of—lawyers cost big money.

"I don't have the resources to hire a lawyer. You know that."

Kent laced his hands behind his head, paunch spilling over his belt, and sucked his split and scabby bottom lip. She was about to ask if he was feeling sick—he looked pasty and feverish—when he piped up again. "In cases like the one you're cooking up, lawyers don't get paid unless their clients win or settle. But you already knew that, huh?"

"I've never sued anybody in my life—"

"Well, you'd best not even think about suing Regent's," he said, "you fucking numbskull."

"Kent! Have you been drinking?"

He stood, smoothed his wrinkled slacks, and fixed her with an icy blue stare. "Funny you should ask."

Wally Szczerbiak? Was *that* his nickname?

Wally Szczerbiak had been a professional basketball player a few years back, but he wasn't really a star. All that Paul remembered about him was he looked like a wannabe *GQ* model. Copious hair gel, waxed eyebrows, winter tans. An insult lurked here. He'd always assumed Kent nicknamed him after a singer-songwriter. Kris Kristofferson, maybe. But a washed-up NBA player? That didn't even make sense. Why *wasn't* he named after a singer-songwriter?

Wait—had he just gotten fired?

"Look on the bright side," Kent said. "You could file for unemployment. String up a hammock and spend all day writing songs on Nautical Bill's doubloon."

The office was too warm; sweat dampened his armpits. "What grounds do you have? *Can* you even fire me, now that…?"

"Hell yes, I can, you cocky fucker. But I won't if you really want to stay on. Just thought I'd give you the opportunity." Kent wore a faraway little grin. What an endearing quality: this sense that, despite the rough talk, deep down Kent Seasons was rooting for you. "Seriously, though, if you had big brass balls like Morticia"—Kent jerked a thumb toward her office—"you could do anything you wanted. Believe me."

"What's she got to do with anything?"

Kent crossed one knee atop the other. "Saw you were supposed to open for Pete Townshend last night. Cold feet?"

So Annie and Kent had both witnessed his no-show.

"All the hours I've wasted in this place," Kent said, gazing wistfully around the brick walls and ceiling, "all the years." He drew a deep breath of the stale air. "Paul, if I could have that time back, I'd be like Scrooge on Christmas morning. A man reborn."

Booze had apparently softened Kent up (and probably knocked his tooth out) but Paul was glad to talk off the cuff. They'd spent so much time together over the last few years. A shame that they'd never spoken of anything more meaningful than credit scores and down payments. "Kent, can I ask you a personal question?"

"I'm on an honest streak. Shoot."

"Does selling cars ever make you feel, I don't know…undignified?"

"You'll have to define that one for me, college boy."

"Dignity. You know, self-esteem. Self-worth."

"No, Wally"—Kent Seasons tongued the hole in his smile—"define *feel*."

•

Step Six: Closing

30

Despite his rather unceremonious demotion, Kent Seasons showed up at Regent's bright and early that Saturday, as he still had a few pans in the fire.

First, sacking Jennylee Witt. He'd had to lay it on pretty thick, but it seemed she'd finally caught the drift. While he wasn't entirely sure Jennylee could win a wrongful termination suit, it'd make for fine theater regardless. And even if she opted not to sue, if she just went home and tended to her family, unemployment checks would match her measly salary and piddling commissions, so no harm there. Plus, if she *did* opt to sue, the resultant filings would almost certainly bring Maurice's lechery to public light, and Jerry Seasons might finally have to admit what a scumbag his old chum really was.

Would it look bad for the dealership, considering Kent waffled on that ugly incident? Sure it would. But Nautical Bill and Junior had already pulled his pants down, so fair's fair. No, firing Jennylee was ultimately a win-win, as firing Paul Stenger would've been, if only the guy had the good sense to recognize opportunity when it came knock, knock, knockin' on his office door.

But Kent had bigger worries than Paul and Jennylee.

After offloading Junior's yellow Avalanche, Erik Sharkey had claimed a headache and taken Friday afternoon off. But the pissant couldn't hide forever. Kent finally tracked him down under the awning out past the garage. Sharkey had just lit a fresh cig and his nicotine-stained fingers dented the paper as he raised it to his lips. Kent settled in beside him and mimicked his pose: one foot kicked back against the wall, shoulders hunched, eyes trained across the lot. Red, white, and blue streamers and balloons—last year's leftovers—decorated the rows of vehicles, while a new banner hung over the entrance, boldly welcom-

ing shoppers to the 2009 AMERICAN DREAM BLOWOUT
SALE!!!

"Sharkey, if you don't mind my asking, what's your exact
date of birth?"

"I'm a Pisces. You?"

Kent closed his eyes. "Your credentials were so impressive
that I never even bothered to have you fill out any paperwork,
let alone take photocopies of your driver's license. Figured we'd
get to all that later."

The sonofabitch just stood there, mulling over another set
of lies. Finally, he ashed the cigarette and leaked a wisp of
smoke from his mouth up into his nostrils. "Mr. Seasons, my
feelings for Kelsi are genuine."

"Before you commence kissing my ass, answer my question."

"I just turned thirty-six, sir. If that's what you're getting at."

"That is exactly what I'm getting at."

"I was truthful with you back then, Mr. Seasons. If you'd
asked my age—"

"Back then? Your interview was barely three days ago."

"I never lied to Kelsi either."

"No? But I'll bet you let her think you were a smidge younger."

"No, sir."

"Just while you got to know her, I mean. While you two were
building a rapport."

The brick was cool in the awning's shade. Power tools
shrieked in the garage. Kent squinted against the sunlight burning off the polished windshields. "See that Denali over there?"
He pointed out an old SUV that'd come in on trade. "It's just
like you. Showy and macho, a real attention-getter. But in the
long run a vehicle like that is bound to cost whoever depends
on it—to cost them bigtime."

"I love her. I love your daughter. Truly I do."

"You, Sharkey, are an example of what those of us in the car
game refer to as a *lemon*. You're a bad deal, Sharkey. A beater, a
dud…"

As Kent was going on like this, a dust-cloaked Ford Explorer pulled in. A woman climbed out and took to peering at stickers.

"Looks like I'm up," Sharkey said. Then he crushed out his smoke, smearing ash on the brick wall.

"Don't do that."

Sharkey apologized and brushed the bricks with the flat of his hand, but Kent snatched his arm before he could walk away. "We're not through here either."

Sharkey gazed longingly at his lost up, then tapped loose another cigarette at the exact moment Jethro burst from the showroom, high-striding in his cowboy boots. His down-home rap carried across the lot. *Golly gee whiz, ma'am. Sure is hot today, ain't it? A real butter-melter. Test-drive with the A/C blowing sure sounds nice, don't it? And have you heard about our Blowout Sale pricing specials?*

The day's gruesome humidity oiled Kent's ribs. He took a sip of warm air and reminded himself to stay loose, to focus his chi, to keep on seeing around the corner. He'd always been the coolest cucumber around, the unshakable one, the Zen master.

"I swear upon all that's holy and true," he finally said, "that I will rip your lying head off, Sharkey, and shit straight down your ugly, fucking throat, if you ever so much as glance at my daughter again, you scum-crusted jizz-stain."

A long moment passed before Sharkey replied. "With all due respect, Mr. Seasons, after this talk we had just now, I'm not sure us sharing an office is gonna work."

The words took a moment to sink in, just floated in the soupy air between them, and then the heinous absurdity of it all doubled Kent over. He dug his palms into his kneecaps, coughing, his diaphragm convulsing, rendered helpless by a weird laughter that shook him to the very core. He laughed despite his indignation, laughed until it hurt, until nothing but dry barks escaped his throat.

Once he'd finally caught his breath, he straightened up and made a go of expressing his deeper concerns: of course he didn't approve of Sharkey pursuing his daughter (and he sure as hell didn't appreciate the locker-room talk with the Ford rep), but beyond that were his worries for Kelsi's future. "You know she's been talking about skipping college. I don't suppose you feel any responsibility for that?"

"Mr. Seasons, I—"

"Have you tried talking sense to her? Because as a guy who so nobly proclaims his love, I'd think you'd try real hard to convince her not to screw up her life."

"What's the big whoop about college? Look at you and me, after all. We didn't waste four years with a bunch of bookworms and we're doing great."

Doing great? As Kent pondered this, a rusty Dodge Neon zipped past with a Domino's Pizza sign on the roof and two grand worth of rims on a ride hardly fit for auction. A racing spoiler was glued to the trunk, although the puny engine would barely tow a fat kid on a skateboard. An omen lurked here. Kent could feel it.

"Kelsi's just not sure she's the college type," Sharkey said. "Truthfully, she'd rather save money for a while. Just live life and have fun."

"And I suppose you've impressed upon her just how much fun it is on the lot?"

"I love my job."

"You love selling cars and you love a car guy's daughter—that's your story?"

"Yes, sir."

"Match made in heaven, eh?"

Sharkey was smart enough to finally shut up. In the silence to follow, Kent recalled barging into Dan Thompson's office, ready to choke the man with the silk tie knotted around his apparently decent neck. A shudder passed through him, a nauseating mixture of anger, regret, and feeling the fool. "So now I finally understand why Dan Thompson let his strongest salesman walk. Wait—hold on. He *fired* you, didn't he? After he caught wind of what you were up to with my little girl?"

"Dan wouldn't listen." Sharkey met Kent's eyes. "He acted like I'd committed some sorta crime."

Kent considered pointing out that Sharkey probably *had* committed a crime, depending on exactly when his dalliance with Kelsi began, but he couldn't bring himself to talk about it anymore. He felt ill and weak, like Sharkey's presence was his own personal Kryptonite.

"What were those pills you gave me, anyway?"

"Like I said, the dentist—"

"Dentist my ass. What were they?"

"Just some OxyContin."

"I fucking knew it. I sank down so deep into the seat of my truck that I needed a ladder just to reach the steering wheel."

"Mr. Seasons, if I'd known you were gonna drink on them—"

"We were drinking when you gave them to me!"

"They were just some leftovers. I don't push pills."

"Pharmaceutical-grade heroin just happened to be clinking around in your pocket?"

"They're for pain," Sharkey said. "People really do have pain."

Which was perhaps the only true thing Erik Sharkey had said all week. Able to stomach no more of this, Kent walked away. Pain—the guy didn't seem to realize how close to pain he'd come, messing with a teenage girl like that.

But before Kent had gone a dozen steps, a beater pulled in and a father-daughter tandem climbed out. Dad immediately started kicking tires on an '04 Honda Civic. Shopping for his little girl's first car, most likely. While it was no Chevrolet Impala, the Civic wasn't a bad choice, so long as dad could stomach his daughter going Asian.

Then Kent realized that Sharkey had missed his turn in the rotation, which meant—considering his recent demotion—that *he*, Kent Seasons, was next up.

Watching the father and daughter scrutinize the pre-owned Civic, Kent Seasons gave serious consideration to simply walking away from the only job he'd ever known—but he didn't. Maybe he hung in because the pair reminded him of buying Kelsi's first car, which in turn reminded him of both better days and his still-pressing financial obligations. Or perhaps he was morbidly curious to ride out the wreck of the last twenty-four hours. Whatever the case, Kent Seasons swallowed his pride and kicked off that year's Blowout Sale by taking his first up in well over a decade.

31

"**G**ood morning, Maurice," Jennylee said, once again on the stoop of Currant Family Photography. "And happy Crust Fest. I just love this time of year, don't you? Gloria must love it too, considering the festival's named after the family business."

She waited politely with her hands clasped at her waist, feeling clever for having reminded Maurice she knew about his wife's money, and for remembering to use both his and Gloria's names. The first time she'd met Maurice, she'd forgotten to ask his name and worried that might blow their deal. While they'd ended up striking an entirely different sort of deal, there truly was no sweeter sound than a person's very own name.

"Happy Crust Fest to you as well," Maurice said, "you scheming cunt."

"Have you not had your latte yet, Maurice?"

"Are you seriously planning to go through with this?"

"You bet I am."

"Come inside then," he said. "Last thing I need is my fellow business owners thinking I voluntarily consort with trailer trash."

The cheap insult set her mind at ease, and she followed him into the studio, no longer afraid he might simply decide to shoot her. Because she'd appraised Maurice correctly. He was a coward as well as a creep, and he probably would've handed over twice what she'd asked, rather than risk a crimp in his lifestyle. Today Maurice looked older and less cocksure, but he was still undeniably handsome. Awful to think how often he must've used those looks to take advantage of people. Add in wealth, and you had a real monster on your hands.

Then he pulled a roll of cash from his pocket and tossed it on the desk. "Take it and go."

She eased forward, cautious, ready to squeal bloody molester if Maurice so much as twitched. But he just stood there and watched her count his money. It was more than she'd ever seen, and enough to make a sizable dent in Chast's bills. But she wasn't done with Maurice quite yet. No, he'd be buying some more expensive camera equipment in a couple months, depending on how the meeting went with the lawyer she'd phoned.

After Kent Seasons fired her, she'd done exactly what he warned against—warned against with a funny look on his face—and hunted down an employment law attorney out of Champaign. The man had done his coursework locally, at the University of Illinois, and was familiar with the Paris area. He'd sounded interested too, based on her answers to his preliminary questions. And Kent was right: the lawyer worked for free until they received a settlement or judgment.

"Nice doing business with you, Maurice."

"Wait," he said.

"It's way too late for an apology now."

"What did Kent say? When you discussed our little imbroglio."

"Imbroglio?"

"Our entanglement," Maurice said. "Our snafu."

"He fired me, actually."

Maurice cocked his head. "He did? Kent fired you for fucking with me?"

"Something like that."

"It probably didn't help that you're dumb as a sow."

"Maybe not," Jennylee said, "but it's also possible he actually did me a favor. Because now I no longer have to be alone in cars with men like you."

And with that, Jennylee Witt pocketed Maurice's money and walked out the door.

32

As he watched Kent cross the pre-owned lot, Paul Stenger—who'd also been watching the father and daughter from inside the showroom—was distracted by Chadwick. "It's for the glory of the dealership, Billy," Chadwick was saying. "That's what we play for. For pride. For honor."

Just like the year before, Chadwick had to convince Junior it was in the dealership's best interest for Team Regent's to head downtown over lunch to play Thompson's Ford for the annual Crust Fest 3-on-3 championship.

"Hooey," Junior said. "Why should I excuse half my crew on our busiest day of the year?"

"We'll be back in an hour." Then Chadwick lowered his voice to a stage whisper. "And there ain't nobody here yet anyway."

"You guys had your chance to be basketball stars back in school."

"And what better word of mouth could the dealership get," Chadwick said, "than beating Thompson's Ford in front of the *whole* town?"

"You lost last year," Junior pointed out.

"By just one basket."

Now it was Junior's turn to stage-whisper. "In front of the *whole* town."

"We been practicing, Billy."

"What you guys need to practice are your scripts and walkarounds."

"Been practicing those too."

Junior buckled his nose, but finally relented. "Go get 'em, fellas." He awkwardly cuffed Chadwick's shoulder. "Show those Thompson's boys what we're made of."

Ultimately, Junior was more than happy to risk a salesman's

broken ankle if it might bring a few buyers to the lot, but between the rift with Lloyd and Annie's letter, Paul had been hoping they wouldn't play at all. He didn't feel ready for what was sure to be a heated and dirty game. Paul may have been Team Regent's ace, but he obviously wasn't much of a leader. Was that the elusive quality Kent Seasons had been trying to instill in him? *You've got natural leadership qualities, Paul,* Kent had said during one of his pep talks, *but people won't follow a soft-sale artist. You gotta seize this world by the throat...*

Maybe Kent's criticisms had more validity than he'd cared to admit?

Paul was thinking all this over and picking at the finger foods laid out for the Blowout Sale when Chadwick ambled up, snagged a cocktail weenie and a handful of potato chips, and then casually mentioned amidst meaty chews that Lloyd Rivera was out in the wash bay talking trash about a certain backstabbing gringo puta sonofabitch.

"He actually called me that?"

"You better go smooth things over."

"This is all Junior's fault."

Chadwick dunked a weenie in ranch dressing, but the little torpedo was so oily it repelled the ranch, leaving a reddish stain on the ivory surface. "You sure about that?"

"What good's an apology?" When Chadwick didn't respond, "I still haven't found a chance to talk to Tom either."

"You may as well skip that. Tom says he won't play with a dishonest teammate."

Dishonest? It hurt to think—no, to *realize*—the guys thought of him that way. Although didn't he secretly think of Chadwick and Kent as dishonest? Chadwick in a do-anything-for-a-buck sort of way, Kent in a more Machiavellian sense. For a true-blue salesman, being called dishonest was a badge of honor, as it implied you'd gotten over on somebody. But Paul didn't want to be a true-blue salesman. Junior had threatened to fire him should he make any further noise about the Caprice deal, but Junior could go choke on his chocolate milk.

"Time to make things right," Paul said.

He took the plate of onion rings and mini corn dogs he'd compiled and jammed them into Chadwick's hands, who cursed and fumbled to keep from dropping the whole mess. In the restroom, Paul cleansed the crumbs and fryer oil from his fingers. He was nervous. Apologizing had never come easy. He had a hard time seeing himself from anyone else's perspective, and therefore never really believed he was in the wrong.

Out in the garage, he found Lloyd sifting through a bin of castoff parts. He was streaked with axle grease to his elbows and the bandana around his head was dark with sweat. Crazy how hard the garage guys worked for so little pay. The situation was a lot like restaurants, where the waiters made twice as much as the cooks for a quarter the effort. This only made his role in the Caprice deal so much the worse.

"Can we talk, Lloyd?"

Lloyd tossed a broken CV joint, and Paul hopped backward, the hunk of metal nearly scuffing his shoe. "You got another good deal for me, Paulino?"

"I've been thinking about how things went down."

Lloyd still hadn't made eye contact. "I been thinking too."

"I know you've been hearing a lot of talk, but—"

"I been thinking," Lloyd said, "dat you need to come work at de turkey plant."

The turkey plant?

"That way, you maybe learn something."

"Lloyd—"

"You learn how it feel to work hard, how it feel to not have money come easy."

Paul kept his expression neutral. He couldn't just brush off Lloyd's words, naïve as they were. As if America really was a fair place for the honest and hardworking, as if social class and skin tone weren't ninety-nine percent of the rigged game. Here in Lloyd Rivera, this Horatio Alger character in garage blues laid bare the waxed and glittering dream the country exported—exported both abroad and into the souls of those already here—and it was one slick piece of salesmanship. Greeting, script, and close, all rolled into one shiny package.

"Lloyd, I know you work hard. That's why we have to straighten this out."

"No, you think I just another grease monkey."

"I don't think that."

"But you make very good worker for de turkey plant."

"You're actually suggesting I go kill turkeys for a living?"

"Si, Paulino. You already do."

"Lloyd, please just—"

"*Muerte*, Paulino." Now Lloyd made a blade of his thumb and dragged it across his neck from ear to ear. "You kill de turkeys dead."

At a loss, Paul dug into his wallet for a blank check. Who cares what Junior thought? If that dildo hassled him, so be it. Besides, after Annie's letter, Nashville was sounding less like a pipe dream and more like a good plan he'd been foolishly thinking of abandoning for a girl he barely knew and a job he couldn't stand.

"Been meaning to do this," he said. Trying for casual, he braced the check against a beam, clicked his pen, and made it out to Mr. Lloyd Rivera for $700, the exact amount of bonus he'd taken on the Caprice deal. "Apologies are cheap," Paul admitted, handing Lloyd the check. "But seven hundred bucks says I'm sorry."

Lloyd stopped digging through the bin and studied the check. His fingers smudged the pale green paper. He mumbled something in Spanish.

"Take it," Paul said. "Please."

"No."

"At least hold on to it. Think it over. That's almost two weeks' pay, right?"

"No, that your money. You *earn* it."

"Junior said he'd fire me, Lloyd. But I don't care."

"You and Junior love money," Lloyd said, and wagged the check in Paul's face. "You marry money."

All the service guys were watching now, faces betraying nothing. Fuck the service guys though. They were the cooks of a dealership—social misfits who hid in the back because they couldn't deal with people. For all Paul cared, Junior could bend over every last one of them. Still he resigned himself to taking back the check. He'd have to try again later, after Lloyd had some time to cool off and think of his family. But as Paul's fingers closed upon the now soiled check, Lloyd's free hand came around whip-fast across his left cheekbone. The slap echoed throughout the garage. Mechanics stopped even pretending to turn wrenches. Somebody whistled. Someone else said, "About damn time."

Lloyd cursed and ripped up the check and let the shreds flutter to the oil-stained concrete. He squared his shoulders and stared up into Paul's face, ready to fight. But as the numbness in his cheek gave way to needles, Paul's eyes watered hot and blurry, a reaction he'd believed vanished years ago, right around the time he'd made a wrong turn into Regent's. He began to say something, he wasn't sure what, but then just turned and walked away—and bumped directly into Chadwick, who'd been eavesdropping while finishing his plate of hors d'oeuvres.

On his way back to the showroom, Paul passed Tom Partlow's office. The big man stood in the doorway, stone-faced. Moments later, Paul hooked a sharp right into the empty sales manager's office. He closed the door and sat behind the desk. The photograph of Kent's wife and daughter were still there, and Kent's loopy scribbles covered the appointment calendar. Although Brad Howard had been named the new sales manager, for all appearances the office still belonged to Kent Seasons. And, sure enough, that bottle of Jim Beam still rested on the floor. Paul whizzed off the cap, tilted his head back, and took a gulp. Shivering and wet-eyed, he wiped the foul poison from his lips. Then he took another gulp and sank down deep into the abandoned captain's chair.

While Kent Seasons would've been tickled pink to know Paul Stenger was sitting in his old chair and drinking his whiskey, the Civic's back seat had him in considerable discomfort. The Japanese were a smaller people, of course, but they weren't *this*

small. And it wasn't like Honda's engineers were unaware that Americans tended to be big-boned, if not downright plump. Perhaps the tiny car appealed to those who bought based on what they *wished* were true, not necessarily what was true? Vehicle as totem of the idealized self. A new model so sparkling clean that, like youth, we know deep down it can't last, much as our dreams fade before our disbelieving eyes.

Puttering along, the daughter clung to the steering wheel like a life preserver, while her father peppered Kent with all the usual questions: What sorta mileage this rice-burner get? She come with a warranty? Who was the previous owner? And don't you try and tell me it was some little old lady…

Barely listening, Kent studied the girl's elfin profile. Hard to believe she was old enough to drive. In certain turns of light, she could've still been playing with dolls and bouncing on daddy's knee.

"I'd like to finance half of Theresa's vehicle," her father said. "Assuming you guys offer a decent interest rate."

"Thing is"—Kent brushed a small, scuttling cockroach from his thigh—"we're born and made to feel unique, like we're not just another nobody…"

He kept talking, yet his thoughts remained with the little roach. How long did such a creature have? Six months? A year? He'd heard houseflies lived only a couple of weeks, which struck him as magnificently sad.

"But then one day," Kent continued, "we find out the truth—that we really are just ordinary, no different than our parents, our neighbors, our friends, all of whom we'd secretly believed were somehow lesser than ourselves. But that feeling of specialness, even though we know it to be false, remains. It's a stubborn thing, maybe the most stubborn of things. And so instead of letting it fade away, we pass that feeling down to our kids. This is no gift though. No, we put that weight on the shoulders of our children because we *have* to. Because something's got to remain sacred amidst all the profane."

The father eyeballed him; Kent smiled and showed his missing tooth.

Beyond the windows, fields stretched away under a burning noon sun. Kent imagined the coming dusk, his unfamiliar sobriety, going home and attempting to explain to Linda all the messes he'd made. Sunbaked asphalt slipped under the Civic's tires with a low tender ache, and he closed his eyes and inhaled, diaphragm bowing from his spine. He paused for a beat and then let go, let the pressure ease up and out of him, ribs sinking, the bones heavy inside his flesh. Only then did he notice the odor: a smell like cinnamon and smoke and the changing seasons, and beneath that something musky. Honest sweat from a hard day's work. An occasional cigarette. No chain-smoking, nothing neurotic, just a solitary dot of fire come eventide. These were imprints of the vehicle's previous owner. Remnants of a stranger's very life, sunken into the upholstery.

"You feeling okay, buddy?" the father asked.

Stiff as a mannequin, Theresa made a sphincter-clinching left into oncoming traffic.

"The trouble with cars," Kent said, "is depreciation. Soon as they roll off the lot, the rusting begins, that slow wearing down on the road to the junkyard. Childhood isn't so different—hell, maybe parenthood too. In both cases, life makes sense at first and the world seems like a halfway decent place. Then one day there's no such thing as right and wrong anymore. Or at least nobody seems to mind very much."

"Theresa," her father said, "turn around up there. See that driveway?"

"You folks want this car, no problem. I'll even show you our invoice."

"Oh, I bet," the father said.

"Life's gonna come knocking any day now," Kent said, "and your daughter will be gone. Just memories and pictures on the mantel." He laid a hand on the father's shoulder. "But you'll still be here. You'll still need a reason to keep on keeping on."

The man smiled, but it was an ugly smile. "That so?"

"Trust me," Kent said, "I'm a car salesman."

Theresa performed a slow three-point-turn and killed the

engine. She ground the starter and then jerked backward half-way into the ditch.

"What's your game, buddy?" The man peered at him. "Been talking to slick dudes like you all over the county, but I can't say I've heard this rap before."

Kent Seasons did not care to be spoken to in that tone. He relaxed as best he could and ignored whatever else the man had to say. Fifty years on this planet, fifty years paid in full, had earned him the right not to be spoken to like that.

Back at the dealership, he led Theresa and her father into his new office.

"Folks, it's been my pleasure getting to know you both, but I think Erik's the man you should be dealing with."

"Why's that?" Theresa's father asked, clearly smelling a trap. "He know something about that Civic you don't?"

"Not necessarily," Kent said, "but he is our resident expert when it comes to the needs and wants of teenage girls."

Neither this entendre nor the testy conversation under the awning was any impediment to Sharkey smelling green in the water. A sickle-like grin split his jaws and his eyes flattened and turned dark as ingots. Yet, strangely enough, as Sharkey pumped Theresa's father's hand, the man looked truly comfortable for the first time.

"Take care of these nice people, Erik," Kent said. "They deserve your very best."

33

Driving across town to the Crust Fest, Paul felt dizzily certain the other vehicles were all about to crash into him. Traffic was heavier than usual, naturally, but these near-calamities were entirely in his own jittery head, and while he *knew* this was the case (and that Kent's bourbon probably hadn't helped matters) the sense of impending calamity, of gloom and doom, only intensified as he made a series of lefts to bypass the parade route.

But then he got lucky and found parking not far from the Crust Fest's main tent. He climbed out and popped the Camry's trunk.

The makeshift 3-on-3 court was ringed with spectators watching Team Thompson's warm-up. Dan Thompson worked the crowd in a pair of high-tops and baggy shorts, chatting with people and pressing the flesh. A faint cheer rose when Dunkenstein caught a pass from Seth for a slam that rattled the portable hoop. A moment later, Paul spotted Annie. Hair in a ponytail and sporting a YMCA T-shirt, she sat between a flip-the-numbers scoreboard and a donations box. She smiled and talked with passersby, doing her best to wrangle a few dollars in charity that'd otherwise go to carnival games and elephant ears made from deep-fried Good 'n' Crusty dough.

Chadwick and Lloyd were on their way. After the scene in the garage, Chadwick had apparently convinced Lloyd that since he'd shown everybody that Paul Stenger was his bitch, it was okay for Team Regent's to try and prove the same to Thompson's Ford. Reeling from Kent's sour mash, Paul had listened to Chadwick explain all this amidst the constant stream of cocktail weenies vanishing down his throat. Chadwick, he'd finally understood, was crazy. They were all probably crazy. Selling cars? Pulling people's pants down? *Pounders?*

For Chadwick's benefit, Paul had pretended to laugh the whole thing off. Like Lloyd's slapping him was actually playful—"You're not really friends with a guy," he'd said, "until he takes a swing at you." But ever since, he'd felt like he was riding one of those motorized walkways at the airport, zooming along a bit too quickly for comfort.

Just as Paul reached into his trunk, the sky darkened and a smell like wet stone churned on the wind. Scraps of carnival litter tumbled across the park and dust scoured the nearby vehicles. A block down he saw Chadwick's enormous truck pull in, Lloyd Rivera's miniature silhouette riding shotgun. Chadwick was already decked out in his sleeveless shirt and shorts, but Lloyd still wore his garage blues. He'd wait until the very last minute to strip them off, making a show of it, like always.

Paul returned his attention to the trunk, studying its contents, but then found himself caught in an out-of-body moment, as if observing some other Paul Stenger from afar, waiting to see what this version of himself would do, this weird doppelgänger whose heartbeat thumped so loudly in his ears. Finally, he removed what he needed and closed the trunk's lid. He began to walk, focusing on Annie as he weaved through the crowd spilling out of a nearby pavilion with paper plates sagging under mounds of fried catfish.

Once on the court, Seth noticed him. "Where are the other runners-up?" he asked, spinning a ball on his pointer finger.

Seth's nose was swollen and bruised. Paul had done that, hadn't he? He'd hit this guy, this other car salesman. Smashed a basketball into his face. Stranger still, he'd *planned* it. For months, he'd practiced the move, visualizing it, timing it, all the while knowing that eventually, when the moment was ripe, he'd wallop this other person in the nose with an inflated leather ball. He'd done this bizarre thing because he hated this other person—truly, deeply hated him.

"Forget your gym clothes?" Seth asked. He fanned the spinning ball with the flat of his hand. "And what's up with the guitar?"

Walking onto the court, Paul again briefly saw himself from outside, as Kent Seasons was always urging him to do. In this way, Paul realized that he intended, apparently, to sing a young woman a song he'd written. But he hadn't practiced this move, hadn't quite worked out the timing. He was struck by the weird *hereness* of the world. The smell of oily fish and strewn hay. The sun disappearing behind a cloud, as if suddenly rendered shy. Children shrieking and teenagers lurking and fat people everywhere—a million pounds of loose white flesh lumbering about, gobbling down whorled pink wands of cotton candy and jugs of icy soda pop.

Basketballs struck the concrete with metallic pings.

Despite being a musician, Paul had never been one for drama. Thoughts of losing Annie, though, of just letting her drift away, drove him to what would later seem (to both Paul and all who witnessed it) insane ends. Perhaps the stress of the previous week, while largely unacknowledged—combined with a brisk slap to the face and Kent's bourbon—had left him in a fragile state of mind. Or maybe he'd been building up to something like this, some grand gesture, ever since college. Regardless, he strummed for quite a while before anyone noticed. He was at a carnival, after all. People must've thought he was just another of the Crust Fest's many entertainments—which, in a sense, he was. But eventually the crowd horned in on him. Paul stood on a three-point line of carefully laid red tape, the guitar strapped over his shoulder, a pick in his sweaty fingers. Plucking chords, he realized this constituted the largest crowd he'd ever played for.

He sang the downbeat opening lyrics:

"It's always tomorrow, isn't it, baby?

But I'm here now, and I just can't wait..."

He watched Annie as he sang, strumming harder and projecting his voice as the song built to its hook. She sat frozen behind the scorer's desk, holding an envelope halfway down the slit in the donation box. She wore the same expression car buyers often did after being handed a pen and told to sign here, here, here, and here.

Off to his right, a basketball dropped to the court and bounced away.

But he focused on Annie, kept his gaze glued to her, determined not to let this moment spin out of control. Still, from the corner of his eye he couldn't help but notice Seth's face melting with laughter, like a Greek comedy mask under that oily gangster hairdo. Paul closed his eyes and focused on hitting the proper chords, and in his private darkness the little court felt as cavernous as Assembly Hall. The crowd fell silent now, a curious and almost reverential hush, and a breeze heavy with coming rain sucked his Regent's polo tight against his ribs.

With all the gravity he could muster, he sang:

"If I was to write you that sort of letter,
I'd tell you I know you're headed for better…"

Annie rounded the scorer's table and made a beeline toward him.

He exhaled as she drew near, his body relaxing. A part of him had feared she might get spooked and run, if only due to the very public nature of this gesture, but it'd been right to lay his soul bare like this. Sure, it might've seemed corny to the man he'd been, the conniving and sarcastic car salesman, but Annie had opened his heart. It'd taken almost losing her to realize it, but surely it wasn't too late. Not for them. And as he opened his arms to embrace her, he understood he'd been living so cynically for so long that he'd almost traded in Annie Turner for some fool's cocktail of pride, fear, and ego.

But she stopped a few feet shy. Her face was expressionless, her body stock still. She whispered, "What are you doing?"

"I wrote it for us."

She stepped closer.

"For me and you."

Then, before Paul could fully register his mistake, his many mistakes, Annie snatched his guitar and ripped it loose. Her eyes never left his as she backed slowly away, holding the instrument by its slender neck with both hands. The now-broken shoulder-strap fell to the concrete at the exact moment a solitary raindrop kissed Paul's cheek, right where Lloyd Rivera had slapped him.

He feared for a moment, based on how Annie stood with her feet spread wide and the guitar clutched like an ax, that she meant to bash it on the court. But then something came over her face, a change Paul couldn't quite interpret, and she stood up tall and held the guitar with just one hand. With her free hand, she pointed first at the guitar, then at someone or something over Paul's shoulder.

Then she held up her index finger and twirled it at the sky.

"Oop!" Annie Turner shouted, just before she heaved Paul's guitar over his head, in the direction of the portable hoop.

Standing there, still not having turned around, Paul heard a hollow bang, an off-key twang, and the sound of splintering wood. When he finally did turn and look, there was Dunkenstein, standing over a mangled kindling of frets and busted string. He'd caught yet another alley-oop pass, but this time, instead of dunking it through the basket, he'd merely slammed it straight down on the hard concrete.

The crowd roared, as much out of bewilderment as amusement. But Paul just stood there, knowing in his bones that this moment would haunt him. This wasn't a thing he'd eventually live down. Never would it come to seem funny. This was a soul-searing humiliation, a branding... He closed his eyes and focused on stilling his shaky legs. Then he felt a hand on his shoulder.

There was Lloyd Rivera, looking up at him. "Remember when I tell you, Paulino, that you no need worry about a woman's mean words?"

"Yes," Paul said. "I remember that."

"Well, maybe now it be time you start to worry."

"I'm really sorry about the Caprice deal, Lloyd."

The words had just spilled out, but Lloyd Rivera shook his head and explained he had no choice now but to make his payments—and also to key the shit out of Junior's car. "I probably have to key your car too, Paulino," he added.

Meanwhile, Team Thompson's fell about the court, consumed with joyous howls of laughter. Seth pantomimed playing a guitar while Dunkenstein covered his big, bony face in his huge hands and mock-wept. Then Seth—having switched roles—reenacted Annie's alley-oop pass while Dunkenstein knuckled his eyes and clasped his breast.

"Just so you know, Paul," Seth said, having finally caught his breath, "I was gonna kick your ass for that little cheap shot you gave me"—he pointed at his swollen nose—"but now I don't see much point in it."

Through it all, Dan Thompson had done his best to remain above the fray. The obviousness of his struggle not to laugh made it so much the worse.

"You always were a real prick, Seth," Chadwick said. He manned Paul's other shoulder now. "Even clear back in high school." As if to emphasize his point, Chadwick spun a basketball on his finger, much as Seth had done earlier. But Chadwick flubbed it and the ball bounced away. "Boys, I say screw this. Screw the championship game and screw the Blowout Sale. Paul, I do believe you owe Lloyd here about a thousand dollars' worth of cervezas. Figure you may as well buy me a couple too."

Paul barely listened though. He'd been watching Annie. She'd grabbed her things and fled in a hurry—fled in tears. People made way.

"The beautiful woman," Lloyd Rivera said, "she make a man loco."

34

Although it meant she and Chast would miss the opening day of Crust Fest, the coming storm made for a lovely sunset. Clouds rolled in low over the distant fields and something about the quality of light made the earth seem to glow from within. The air itself, hot and raw all spring long, smelled green and sweetly alive.

Jennylee enjoyed all this from her porch steps, sipping coffee rich with milk. She remembered that today was the basketball matchup all the guys got in such a tizzy over—the big showdown with Thompson's Ford—and then she remembered Alice Higgenbottom saying how much she loved basketball. She really should've invited Alice to head down and watch Team Regent's play, as it would've been an ideal chance to introduce her to Chastity. But by the looks of things, the game would get rained out anyway.

Sure enough, a flurry of fat drops soon pocked the aluminum steps, although Jennylee stayed dry under the retractable canopy. Inside, Chast was putting together a London Bridge puzzle, one she'd started by first organizing the edges. With that puzzle as with so much else, Chast had started the right way, the smart way, and soon enough she'd have the whole picture completed.

Earlier that afternoon, while driving back from her meeting with Maurice Currant, Jennylee hadn't felt relieved so much as utterly pooped. Yes, she'd gotten the money, but it'd cost her considerable stress. Lacking any better notion, she'd stashed the roll inside the Nissan's spare in the trunk. She'd have to explain it eventually though, somehow or another, as husbands got nosy when it came to wives and cash. But upon arriving home, Derrol had surprised her in a good way—he'd prepared Chast the special breakfast the dietician at St. John's recommended (egg whites, cottage cheese, and juice, but no fruit or toast) and he'd even tidied up the kitchen. Then, casually, as if it were no big deal, he claimed to have an interview lined up. He'd need the Nissan for a couple of hours. Where were the keys?

"An interview for what?"

"For a job, what else?"

"What *sort* of job?"

"Talking about it'll jinx me. Now can I please just have the keys?"

"I'm taking Chast downtown to the Crust Fest later. We'll need the car."

"Fine, but I gotta—"

"That means no bumming around with Randy Bauble afterward."

"Would you get off my back?"

"Good luck, Derrol," she said, as he snatched the keys from her hand.

After that, Jennylee sat at the kitchen table with her daughter. Chastity's hair was in pigtails, and by the rosiness of her lips and cheeks it appeared she'd gotten into Mommy's makeup again. Jennylee didn't mind though. She'd played with her own mother's makeup too—although Evelyn Sykes had punished her for it, scrubbing her face with a steaming hot rag and saying little girls who wore makeup looked like Jezebels. But Evelyn was nuts. Not certifiably nuts, but nuts in the way of people who spend all their life in Paris or some similarly forgotten place. The religion hadn't helped either. What sort of god demanded the punishment of children who put red wax on their lips? And why did her mother's god seem to share sexist prejudices with the likes of Maurice Currant?

Chast barely nibbled the food. "Daddy put salt on the eggs," she said, crinkling her powdered nose.

"Finish your plate, honey. Daddy tried his best."

Not until later, while she and Chastity were sacked out watching a movie, did Jennylee recall that Derrol had been wearing black jeans and muddy combat boots when he left. He hadn't worn his Metallica T-shirt, thankfully, but what sort of job let a prospective employee get away with dressing like a high school dropout from 1997?

Best not to worry though. Sure, Derrol had probably told a fib, but maybe she'd driven him to it. She really had been on his case lately, after all—not that he didn't deserve it. But henpecking was more Evelyn's style than her own. Thinking back, Jennylee realized that for all those years, Davis Sykes had endured Evelyn's nagging and put on a good face for her, his little girl, much like she now did for Chastity.

Jennylee kissed Chast atop the head, where she still smelled fresh as a quilt just out of the dryer. She was a good kid. If her parents had to fake it once in a while, maybe that was okay. And who knows, maybe Derrol really did have a job interview? One that didn't require dressing up, like construction or landscaping.

As afternoon faded into evening, however, Jennylee's texts received no response. In all likelihood, this meant Derrol had spent the day not job-interviewing, but beer-drinking and fishing, which was more than a little irritating. But just when Jennylee was about to head inside, the gold Nissan appeared, flashing like a nugget down Route 150.

But why in heavens was Derrol driving so fast?

She dumped the last of her coffee into the rocks as the Nissan zoomed around multiple vehicles, slaloming lane to lane, its engine screaming for mercy. Derrol was coming so fast and reckless that by the time Jennylee reached the yard, he'd already skidded clear across the driveway and fishtailed to a stop. She actually had to hop backwards to avoid the bumper. The Nissan stank of overheated rubber and burnt oil, and an ominous hissing came from under the hood.

"What are you thinking, Derrol? You know that car's been acting up."

Almost like it'd heard her, the engine sputtered and died. Derrol scuttled from the cab, his combat boots sinking into the muddy gravel.

"And here you are hot-rodding. What's the matter with you?"

He ran his fingers through his hair and an odd groan issued from deep in his throat. Rain streaked his grimy face and his eyes were flat and unfocused. She had to ask what was wrong three separate times before he finally answered.

"There's something in the trunk."

So he'd found the cash already. She considered drumming up a lie, saying it was severance from work, something like that. But she hated lying, especially to Derrol. He lied to *her* all the time, about piddling stuff that wasn't even worth the breath it took, let alone the trust it cost them, but she took their vows more seriously than that.

"I realize how that might've come as a shock," she said. He lit a shaky menthol and paced the driveway. "Don't worry about where it came from, okay? I can explain."

But Derrol just kept pacing, smoking, and muttering. Strange, his being so agitated. It wasn't *that* much money, after all. And she'd have thought Derrol the type, upon finding unexpected cash, to rejoice first, think second, and worry (if ever) dead last.

"So how'd your job interview go?"

"I didn't know what else to do," he said, still wearing that blank look.

"Derrol, are you okay?"

Then he keyed the trunk's lid. But he didn't let it pop open. He kept it closed, only cracking it the barest inch or two. He bent low and peeked inside, as if afraid a snake might jump out. Smoke from his menthol leaked up into his squinting and watery eyes.

Behind them, traffic streamed into town. More traffic than any other time of year. Paris folks loved the Crust Fest and weren't about to let a little rain keep them home.

"We'll use it for Chast's doctor bills," she said, circling the Nissan. "That's what it's for. Seriously, don't act so spooked—"

Then her antenna prickled, and she felt spooked herself. Derrol's eyes weren't just watery from his cigarette. No, he'd begun to cry. Then that crying turned into bawling—a rush from deep in his belly, tears pouring out as furiously as that day at age seven when he'd peed under their twin desks and shamed himself.

Jennylee came around the car and followed his wet eyes down to the trunk. "Derrol?" she said, and then curled her fingers under the lid, half-expecting that imagined snake to fang her hand. He resisted her opening it for a moment, actually laid his palms down flat, but she continued with the calming words until he finally stepped away.

The rain-pocked gold lid creaked open, inch by inch, and Jennylee stared down into the trunk. Then, after a moment of wildest confusion, she jumped backward and swore in Jesus's name. Randy Bauble lay inside. Randy Bauble, Jennylee's eyes continued to insist, was curled atop their spare tire—the same tire in which she'd stashed the money. Randy's face was puckered, eyes rolled back, skin bone-white and lips robin's-egg blue. His Boston Celtics jersey was muddy, and he was missing a sneaker. The sock lolled from his foot like a dirty gray tongue.

"Honey?" she said, her own tongue gone dry as ash.

"It was those propane tanks," Derrol said.

"Those tanks?"

"Randy claimed he'd doctored them up…"

"Derrol Witt, look at me." He did as told, if only long enough to make her wish he hadn't. "Now slow down and explain exactly what happened."

"He fucking *died*. Ain't that obvious enough?"

She spoke slowly, carefully, and kept from looking at Randy again by way of keeping whatever remained of her composure. In fact, the shock was the only thing holding Jennylee together—some instinctive reaction. But this calm was a window, a thin and brittle pane between herself and the world.

Derrol's menthol had burned down to the filter. He flung it fizzling into a puddle.

"Don't do that," she said.

"Jen?"

"I've asked you time and again to stop tossing cigarettes like that."

The yard was littered with butts, like a field of stubby white clover. For years she'd been asking her husband to dispose of his butts properly, but why she felt compelled to fight about it now was a mystery—although it was, undeniably and insistently, the problem at the forefront of her mind. Given the situation, this was surely inappropriate, but that didn't temper her pressing need to make him stop this bad habit, this thoughtless behavior, this tossing of dead cigarettes in his own, in *their* own, yard.

"I'm so sorry, Jen."

"Cigarette butts in the yard looks cheap."

"I swear I had no idea this could happen."

"It makes us look like trailer trash. Is that how you want people to think of us, Derrol," she said, her eyes still fixed on what lay in the Nissan's trunk, "as nothing but common white trash?"

Derrol wiped his eyes. "What was I supposed to do, just leave him there for his poor old mother to find?"

Then Jennylee shut the trunk's lid and began asking questions. The coming minutes were filled with angry and confusing talk, with long-simmering accusations that both of them felt suddenly free to voice. But the story, insofar as Jennylee could decipher it, was that Randy Bauble had been stealing anhydrous ammonia from the farm next door to his mother's place. Siphoning the chemical into those rusty propane tanks she'd first noticed back on Monday afternoon. Something had gone wrong though. Randy was screwing around with the outdoor tank, clowning and bragging how it was an ideal day to borrow a little anhydrous, considering everybody was down at the Crust Fest getting swindled by the carnies, when he took a fat dose square in the face.

"He just kept gulping and thrashing around," Derrol said, demonstrating how Randy had clawed at his throat, "like he was choking on his food."

A minute or two later, Randy Bauble lost his life.

"It happened so fast," Derrol said. "I had no idea it could… There just wasn't nothing I could do."

While Jennylee asked many questions, she didn't bother asking *why* they'd been stealing the ammonia. That much was clear: they were cooking drugs, or at least aiming to. Drugs fit. Randy's having gotten so skinny and jittery lately, and all Derrol's hush-hush calls and texting. Combine that with his frustrations over not finding work, over watching his truck get repoed and living off his wife, and it was almost surprising this or something like it hadn't happened sooner. Lots of folks around Paris had gotten mixed up with drugs in the last few years. The *Beacon-Herald* tended to bury the stories on page three, but the problem was right there in the plain sight, loitering around the cold-medicine aisle at Walmart and creeping around Rural King with shopping carts full of strange chemicals. There'd been arrests and busts, unexplained fires, and robberies turned senselessly violent.

After the shock lessened a bit, she went inside to check on their daughter. Chastity looked up from the puzzle and took off her earphones. She'd been listening to music on a garage sale Walkman Jennylee had given her, along with her old CD collection. Half those CDs were so scratched they wouldn't hardly play, but from Chast's reaction you'd have thought she'd been given a sack full of rubies.

"Is Daddy home?"

"You'll have to stay inside for a while, okay?"

Chastity looked out the screen door. "Daddy!" she said and hopped up.

Jennylee headed her off at the couch. "Sweetie," she said, massaging Chast's temples with her thumbs, "you have to let Mommy and Daddy talk outside by ourselves. It's grown-up stuff."

"But I want to go see—"

"Oh no, you don't," Jennylee said. "And you won't, you hear?"

Then she led Chast back to the table, helped her fit a couple of pieces into the London Bridge's dark underbelly, and clamped the headphones over her ears.

Outside again, she climbed into the Nissan. But upon turning the key, the engine wouldn't catch. Two clicks, buzz, and nothing. She cranked the ignition over and over, despite knowing it was useless, squeezing and jamming the key deeper into the ignition housing. Derrol watched her with stupefied eyes. Behind him the blinds parted in the kitchen window and Chast's pale face appeared, the bulky earphones making her skinny neck appear even skinnier.

Jennylee popped open the door and yelled at Derrol to get behind the car and push. Once he was ready, she shifted the transmission into neutral and steered while they inched forward. It took a long time to get the car rolling over the rough and soggy yard. Whenever they finally generated some momentum, the tires would sink into a depression or the ground would angle upward, and Derrol, his face oily and sallow in the rearview, would have to dig for footing all over again. Throughout, Chastity kept watching them from the window.

"Push, damn it!" Jennylee shouted, having now climbed out to push alongside and steer with one hand. It was difficult going, but by dusk they'd managed to get the Nissan out of sight behind the horse stall. This was slim comfort, though, as their dead car now had a dead body covered in stolen drug chemicals in its trunk—a body sprawled atop a roll of cash that'd be awfully hard to explain, considering the circumstances.

"Don't you do anything," she said to Derrol. "Don't call anyone. Don't text anyone. And don't you even think of going anywhere near my daughter."

"Well, what are you gonna do?"

"I don't know yet. I need a moment alone."

"Jen, I—"

"Here," she said, and took the cigarette from behind his ear and poked it between his lips. Then she reached into his front pocket, found his lighter, and fired up the smoke. He could've been a shell-shocked infantryman and she his nurse. "Now you just try to stay calm, okay?" She pressed the lighter into his hand. "I'll be right back."

"We can't never tell nobody," Derrol said, and grabbed her arm. "We gotta—"

She ripped her arm free and aimed a finger at his face. "Just so you know, me and Randy fooled around once. Back before you and me ever got together."

The menthol dipped and quivered between his lips.

"And you know what else? Randy couldn't get it up."

A plug of ash fell onto Derrol's shirt.

"He had a flopper, Derrol."

"A…flopper?"

"But here's the thing," she said, "if Randy *had* been able to, who knows how things would've turned out. Because I might've seen something in him. I might have even started going with him steady, and then you and me never would've happened. And if you and me never happened, Chast wouldn't have either."

Jennylee walked off toward the stable. Over her shoulder, she left Derrol with a parting thought. "And if Chast hadn't happened, then you better bet I wouldn't still be living here. And if I wasn't still living here, then you couldn't have shown up tonight with a corpse in the trunk of my car and ruined all of our lives."

Once alone in the stable, having spoken her piece, she actually felt a little better, although she was cognizant enough to see this relief for the dangerous illusion it was. Bugles watched her, eyes gentle beneath those long and delicate lashes. She touched his broad flank and then laid her body flat against him.

There, smelling that familiar bouquet of hay and manure, listening to the horse's deep breaths and feeling his ribcage sink and heave as his powerful warmth flowed into her, Jennylee closed her eyes and prayed. The urge hadn't come upon her like this in years. She prayed hard and earnest, as she'd done as a girl when Evelyn broke the news of her father's illness and said they had to fall to their knees and beg God's mercy. And while those prayers went unanswered, now Jennylee spoke to God again. She asked for guidance, for help in making the right decision. She told Him this was her time, her moment, that it had come strangely and all of the sudden, that she was lost and in need.

Thoughts came in the darkness. Childhood memories of her

father taking her out on the lake on a balmy day. How his shirt clung to his back as he rowed them across the bug-laced water, how the oars rubbed in the locks and little windblown waves slapped the boat's hull, the smell of moss and decay in the cattails along the bank. And she remembered her mother as a younger woman. How Evelyn carried herself more lightly, how she'd smelled different, sweeter, how even her voice seemed to belong to another person entirely, as if age made aliens of us. And then Derrol. First the two them as kids, then as blind teenage lovers, then as bewildered young adults bringing an infant home from the hospital.

These images ebbed and flowed and Jennylee made no attempt to control them. Instead, she listened. She waited and listened for a long time. But despite reminding herself to be patient, to be open to guidance in whatever form it might take, she finally began to strain, to push against the weight of her need and, ultimately, to wonder if she'd somehow brought the result—a resounding silence—upon herself. As if all her years of belief amounted to nothing. As if belief itself held no more substance than a dream.

This silence was too much to bear, and so she allowed herself a long-overdue heresy: faith was either true, or it wasn't. Either she was part of something unseen, or she was alone with what she could see and touch in the here and now. And besides herself, the only presence in the stall that evening was a clomping and fly-ridden horse.

Seconds ticked away. Minutes passed. But when Jennylee Witt finally opened her eyes, she found Bugles had craned his neck toward her. The horse blinked once, long and slow, as if to say, *Gird up now thy loins like a man; for I will demand of thee…*

35

When Kent Seasons finally got home that evening, his daughter's Impala sat in its accustomed spot in the driveway. Due to his Silverado's untimely death, he'd had to ask Brad Howard for a lift. They didn't talk much on the dark and rainy drive, but just let the silence hang, let their thoughts unfurl privately, and banked on each other possessing the manly fortitude to keep their respective traps shut.

"You can pull up there, behind Kelsi's car."

"That's a real nice car, Kent. A good first car."

Thunder grumbled and the rain thickened.

"I got a spare umbrella," Brad said, "that you could borrow."

Barra, he'd pronounced it. Brad Howard was a native son, Paris to the bone, and listening to him, Kent couldn't help but wonder if they'd missed out on a real friendship—if he and Brad had let the competitive nature of their jobs, of their very lives, keep them from bonding like men with such similar backgrounds rightly should've. Because what was life without friends? That said, how many men did Kent know who enjoyed true friendships? Here was something else time took away: a winnowing down from childhood's community to the island of family, and finally a lonesome old age.

"See that?" Kent said, and pointed at the Impala's bumper.

Through the falling rain and the headlights' reflected glare, the red and silver license frame was just visible: THOMPSON'S FORD.

"I wouldn't take it personal, Kent. She's just proud of her first job."

"That's exactly what Linda said."

"I didn't snipe you." Brad hadn't shifted into park, but just kept his foot planted on the brake. "Bill Sr. says you're a loose cannon, says he needs me to step up for the sake of the dealership."

"So this is all just charity on your part?"

"He more or less begged me. Swear to God."

Kent opened the door and climbed out. "We're car salesmen, partner."

"We're more than that though."

"Are we?"

"Me and you, we've always had an understanding."

"Yes, we have. And that understanding has proven true once again." Kent dug his knuckles into his sore lower back. "Like I've always said—Big Dog Eats."

Brad shook his head. "No hard feelings then?"

"None I can't live with."

"It's important to me you feel that way," Brad said. "Because I'm gonna need to lean on you. I want to learn your way of desking a deal. Your scripts and comebacks. That show you give grinders where you pretend to leave, looking all glum, but then whip around in the doorway with one last idea to get her done."

"My father taught me that one," Kent said.

Brad dropped the transmission into reverse. "So we're all good, you and me?"

"C'est la vie."

Kent clasped Brad's outstretched hand and shook.

"A. B. C.," Brad Howard said, grinning. "Another Brad Close."

"Blow me, dickhead," Kent said, and gently shut the passenger door.

Then Brad reversed into the cul-de-sac, beeped his horn, and sped off, tires cutting a looping S on the wet pavement. Alone now in his driveway, warm rain peppering his scalp, Kent took a moment to collect himself. Along the street, cicadas hissed in the sycamores like feedback from a busted speaker, and his neighbors' homes glowed like jack-o'-lanterns, windows printing neat yellow squares on inky lawns.

Inside his own house waited a wife with a lot of questions.

But he was glad Linda still cared enough to bust his balls. God knows he'd tried her patience. Being married to a woman like Linda was a good thing, and for too long he'd been ignoring the good things in his life, having allowed what he didn't have or feared he'd never get to sour what remained. He rocked on his heels, face lifted to the emptying sky. The clouds hung so low it seemed he might reach up into them and cleanse his hands.

He was as sober as he'd been at this hour in many months, and there was a distinct absence of flavors on his tongue—no sweet bourbon, no bitter beer, no cloying mint, and no aftertaste of what now seemed clearly his own private shame. Sobriety was simple, actually. All it'd taken was losing a tooth, losing his job, and discovering that his cherished daughter was rutting with the slimiest pig on the whole farm. That, and at least a smidgen of hope things might get better.

Then the loose change jingling in his trouser pocket gave him an idea. He squatted on his heels and used the edge of a dime to unscrew the Thompson's Ford license frame. Finished, he rose and studied it. A flimsy thing, just a strip of cheap plastic and nothing more. Again he glanced at his home and thought of his family, thought of what he must explain, what he must not allow himself to lie about any longer, the responsibilities he still had to honor. Kelsi was a young woman now, and young women had a right to their own mistakes. This he'd best accept, just like he'd best accept his father's decision to sell their stake in the dealership, as well as the fact that General Motors, a great American company he'd yoked himself to for the lion's share of his manhood, was for largely unfathomable reasons—delusions of empire, spiritual malaise, entropy—bound and determined to flush itself down the crapper.

But he'd learned a lot selling cars. He was a closer, after all. A shutter. The last pencil. And any good closer understands that once you've made an offer, it is imperative not to speak a word, no matter if you have to sit Buddha-still for hours. Once the truth has been voiced, silence must reign. Because he'd made his offerings a long time ago. Offered up all he ever would have and all he ever could be—first to his father, then to Linda, and finally to Kelsi. Now was the time to stand pat. To stay strong. No time to blink or bargain against himself.

C'est la vie? Not on his watch.

Kent Seasons cracked the license frame over his knee, then wrenched the plastic back and forth until it whitened and lost tensile strength and finally came apart in his hands. He tossed the pieces into the wet grass and headed up the walk, his wing-tips clicking the rain-slick pavers in time with a peppy tune whistling from his lips.

36

While Jennylee Witt had been feeling more capable as of late, she hadn't anticipated life testing her newfound resolve quite this quickly—let alone this sternly.

She crossed the night fields, dressed in a hooded slicker and gloves with the fingertips snipped off. Windblown rain stung her eyes and stormwater pooled atop the hard-baked clay, as if the parched land was sickened by drinking up too much too fast.

"Good boy, Bugles," she said, and tugged the bridle.

Bugles had always been skittish of standing water—not to mention thunder and lightning—and each booming strike shivered his flanks. Fearing he'd rear up and pitch over backward, she squeezed the saddle between her knees and pointed her booted toes in the stirrups, ready to bail. Then she reached back to check the bindings. Her knots were a little sloppy, but everything felt secure enough, at least for now.

She'd wrapped Randy in a nylon tarp and tied off the ends to keep the water out. After Derrol helped lug him atop the horse, she'd lashed him behind the cantle, running straps through the rigging dees and under Bugles's ribs. She'd done a careful job of it too, because if Randy came loose, she'd have to drag him. An unpleasant prospect at best.

A flash of lightning made bones of the distant tree line and Jennylee flattened in the saddle. A few beats later came the thunder, unfurling across the dark fields like a gigantic whip. Bugles hitched and thrashed his head, hooves skidding in the muck. The crops were stunted, at least, which made for easier riding. And the storm wasn't entirely bad luck. Nobody was driving the back roads, for one thing, especially not with the Crust Fest having lured everyone downtown. Plus, the rain made them harder to spot from the highway.

She rode on. But closer to town now, wetter, colder, her initial clarity of purpose drained away, and she felt keenly the madness of her predicament. This could land her in jail, most likely. Or at least she'd have a lot to explain, most of which approached the unexplainable. To keep from losing heart, she blocked out thoughts of police and prosecution, of social services workers and separation from Chastity. Because what other option was there? Let Derrol take the fall and watch Chast grow up without a father, just like she'd done? They couldn't even sink the Nissan (and Randy) to the bottom of Paradise Lake, as the lemon wouldn't run. And burying him was impossible: the ground behind the trailer was hard as brick, and even if they managed to chisel out a grave, it'd just fill up with rain and sludge (Jennylee imagined Chast coming upon her and Derrol digging the hole—*Mommy? Daddy? What's that?*). Besides, who could carry on with life knowing a body was hidden on their property?

No, this was her true test. She'd prayed hard and yet received no answer, or at least none other than that big horse standing right in front of her. Prayer, she'd finally decided, was the last recourse of the helpless. As for Randy Bauble, he wouldn't mind whatever became of him now, and while this wasn't the most dignified of endings, he hadn't valued his dignity much while still alive. Randy's mother was another story, and though Jennylee felt awful for the woman, Mrs. Bauble would just have to assume her boy got himself into some kind of fix and skipped town.

Rain sheeted from the black sky and peppered her slicker. Bugles lurched, buckling to starboard. She gripped the bridle and steered them westward, thinking that no matter how this night played out there was one person she couldn't help but do wrong. If all went as planned, this person wouldn't necessarily *know* she'd been wronged, but Jennylee would know, and this person's opinion meant the world.

Jennylee hugged Bugles's neck and inhaled his earthy scent, focusing on the rhythm of his muscular canter as the saddle rose and fell. Then, far across the fields, a big SUV hurtled out of the black, headed eastbound on 150 way too fast for conditions. Her breath hitched, but the vehicle barreled past her into the darkness and was gone.

After beers with his teammates, Paul returned to Regent's, but the storm had put a damper on the Blowout Sale. Bill Sr. was so disappointed he shipped out early for the Lotus Parlor, while Junior stayed well past the dinner hour, pacing the halls while wringing his bony hands and muttering how they'd shoot a better commercial next year, something truly neat-o.

As for Paul, he spent those hours watching the sky darken and traffic splash past. The Crust Fest disaster had left him numb—just an empty shell dressed in a twelve-dollar polo shirt. He closed his eyes and leaned his forehead against the cool showroom glass. His breath fogged the pane and the storm pulsed through. He determined to spend the remainder of Memorial Day weekend doing little else.

But then Annie Turner's old, primer-gray Saab sped onto the lot, headlights punching holes through the murk. Even after she'd parked, Paul didn't move. Finally, she crossed the lot and stood nose-to-nose with him through the glass. She waved, knocked, and finally banged with the flat of her hand. Due to the gathered darkness outside, his fluorescent reflection stood between them, luminously transparent. He stepped back and the fog from his breath faded, but Annie was still there, hair pasted to her neck. Her voice bled through the watery pane, demanding he stop sulking and come outside.

"I'm a ghost," he shouted, not caring if Junior heard.

"You're an idiot," Annie shouted back.

"No, I'm a *ghost!*"

"I'm getting soaked for nothing," Annie said, and walked away, her untied sneaker laces dragging through the puddles.

Paul grabbed a dealer plate and hustled outside, fast on her heels. He slapped it on the nearest vehicle, a midnight blue Chevy Suburban.

"You drive," he said, and tossed Annie the keys.

Thirty-one-inch radials gripped the sluiced road as the behemoth cut a wake through the washed and dripping darkness, past glowing burger joints and residential neighborhoods, past weedy lots and abandoned gas stations. Alone, they passed through one shimmering pool of yellow lamplight after another, the intersections deserted except for a smearing of shiny wet leaves, the only sounds the storm and their ratcheting wiper blades. Paul wanted to breach the silence, but what could he possibly say?

So, Annie, how about that song I wrote... Catchy, huh?

Annie accelerated into the barren countryside, rain drumming the roof as they hurtled along. Paul glanced at the fields north of the highway, and for one surreal moment, silhouetted by a spear of lightning, he thought he saw an alien shape in the distance. Something bear-like and Grendelish marauding through the stunted corn. But the Suburban's windows were nearly opaque with rain, and by the time he craned around for a second look, the shape, whatever it'd been—if it'd been anything at all—was gone.

Then Lady Gaga came on the radio—"Poker Face."

"Nice choice," Annie said, patting the Suburban's wheel. "Guys are always this way."

"What way is that?"

"Don't really want you until you dump them, then they're suddenly all about marriage and kids. Look at this thing, Paul. The Brady Bunch could fit in here."

"It was the first vehicle I saw."

"Sure, but why did you only happen to see it now?"

Paul decided not to answer that one.

"Seth begged me to take him back, you know? Down on his knees, crying and swearing he'd change his ways and stop fucking everything that moved."

"You dodged a bullet with that scumbag."

"Don't call him names. He loved me."

"Funny way of showing it."

"You think? I'd say he was pretty typical, actually."

Paul pointed out that Seth had cheated on her, that he'd passed her an infection, and had she noticed his greasy hairdo?

"He cheated because he was afraid. Just like you."

Annie was trying to bait him, but Paul's sore feelings only cemented his silence. He focused on the Suburban's powerful engine, how it hurtled along with hardly a whisper. In fact, Annie had pushed it up near eighty. Too fast for the wet road.

"So let's hear it," she said.

He kept his eyes trained ahead, uneasy with the speed and bad music. "Annie, look, I meant those lyrics. If you'd only—"

"Zip it." The speedometer ticked higher. "I've had all the sincerity I can take."

"Then what do you want?"

"I want your best sales pitch."

He pleaded with her: "What gives? You want a fifty-thousand-dollar SUV now? I realize it's over between us, I realize the song was a stupid idea, I realize..." Then she brushed away a strand of hair and glanced his way, which caused him to avert his own eyes. The radio was getting to him. It was a night for Leonard Cohen or Jeff Buckley, not Lady Gaga. He reached for the dial, but Annie slapped his hand away.

"Don't sell me an SUV," she said. "Sell me Paul Stenger."

Paul reclined his seat and sank into the leather. If Annie wanted to kill them both in a fiery wreck with corporate pop for a last ballad, so be it. He laced his fingers over his stomach. New-car smell rose from the seat, seductively rich and definitely poisonous. A person would be better off huffing glue.

"I'm not sure I'm the right model for you anymore," he finally said.

Lame words, sure. But what else could he say? His behavior at the Crust Fest had been absurd, a delirium of lovesickness. Ultimately, though, he was really just sick of himself.

"Remember how I said my boss nicknames everyone? Well, I finally found out what he nicknamed me."

Annie waited, expressionless. Finally, he told her.

"Wally who?"

"I've spent years assuming I was James Taylor. Garfunkel, Clapton, even Joan Baez or Janis Joplin. But, no. Apparently I'm Wally Szczerbiak."

"Nicknames are intimate." Annie toggled on the high beams and cranked up the radio. "But you won't let anybody in. People can feel that, Paul."

"Or maybe"—he had to shout over the music—"being a musician is just so farfetched that even a car salesman can't bring himself to make fun of me about it."

"At first," she shouted back, "I thought it'd be nice to date a thirty-year-old."

"I'm twenty-nine."

"Seth told me you said you were only twenty-eight."

A big whiff of new-car smell got him coughing. "I didn't realize you and Seth still talked."

"I thought a thirty-year-old guy would be more mature, more self-assured."

Paul glanced over the dash. A pickup ahead in their lane, red taillights pooling on the wet highway. Annie veered left and shot past it.

"Slow down!" he hollered. Jittery sweat leaked down his neck. He cupped his hands to his mouth: "And my birthday's not until July!"

"What?" She pointed at her ear and shook her head.

He lunged at the offending radio and snapped it off. But in his frustration, he used too much strength and broke the dial. He fingered it in counterclockwise circles, the delicate mechanisms inside stripped and ruined. At least it was finally quiet though.

"Slow down," he said. "Please."

"You blame your unhappiness on being a struggling musician, but do you even enjoy music? Really?"

"I love you, Annie."

With this, her knuckles whitened on the steering wheel. Then Paul remembered something Kent Seasons said on his very first day at Regent's: *The feel of the wheel seals the deal.* But car lot advice didn't always translate.

"You're a control freak," Annie said, "but only about what doesn't matter. Like that fruity little book you carry around to record your weightlifting heroics."

"I also use it for my songwriting—"

"But when it comes to what does matter, like us, or like the fact that you obviously hate your job, you're totally careless."

As Annie spoke, reflections of rainwater glimmered on her skin. Oncoming headlights lit the cab and her ink-black pupils spun like antique vinyl. In some private corner of his mind, Paul even then composed lyrics. As always, there were two Paul Stengers riding in the Suburban that night: Paul the artist, who lived in la-la land and heard magic tunes in his head; and beside him (or maybe atop him, smothering him) was Paul the car salesman, who—as Annie had rightly noted—hated selling cars almost as much as he'd come to hate his hitherto cherished loneliness.

Ten minutes later, Jennylee walked Bugles under the leafy oaks behind Higgenbottom's. There were no streetlights this far from town, which was a relief, but lights nonetheless burned in the windows of the scattered neighboring homes.

Jennylee tethered the shaking and agitated horse to a wrought-iron gate, kissed his cold nose, and began unstrapping her night's cargo. Rainwater had swollen the bindings and she had to use her phone for light before finally managing to loosen the knots. Now that she was soaked and alone and far past the point of turning back, part of her wished she'd just called the law. Let them ask their questions, cast their judgments, and arrest her husband. No doubt this would've been the course people could've ultimately sympathized with. In fact, this is probably what she *would* have done, had she slept on it. But the sight of an old classmate dead in the trunk of your car has a way of scattering a person's thoughts. She wasn't seeing around the corner anymore, not at all.

Holding the bindings in her hands, Jennylee had a look around. The land was dark and empty, so much so that she felt weirdly alone on the planet, alone with the rain and the night. She hauled Randy down feet first, intending to cradle him, but she was tired from the long ride and the tarp was slick. His head thumped the lawn so hard it bounced.

Thankfully, Higgenbottom's was as deserted as the fields. Not a light burning, not even on the porch. She dragged Randy through the gate and then, with a stab of guilt, used the key Alice had trusted her with on the back door. She propped it open, then dragged Randy down the steps and around the corner. He'd lost so much weight that the dragging was easy enough, but he was already stiffening up and this made maneuvering him awkward. She scooted backward into the embalming lab while wondering how best to clean the sloppy mud trail the tarp left behind.

She hustled back up the steps, checked on Bugles, and then closed the door behind her and went back downstairs again. She traced the wall blindly for the light switch until her bare fingertips located it, and a long and uncomfortable moment passed before the fluorescents finally winked on. The lab was neat and tidy and—except for the lumped and muddy thing on the floor—empty. She'd done it. She was actually here. But the worst of her night's chores still lay ahead.

Alice Higgenbottom claimed the Power-Tech 3K Smokeless brand cremator could reach two thousand degrees in a pinch. And a pinch this most certainly was.

"That's a nice thought, but I'm still in college, remember?"

"Nashville has colleges too."

Annie looked at him. "Nashville also has car dealerships, but so what?"

Speaking of, they were almost back to Regent's, Annie having cut a U-turn shortly after he'd professed his love. What he'd said about them moving together was impulsive, but he'd nevertheless felt a glimmer of hope. Now, however, the future they weren't going to share slide-showed through his mind: Annie cooking their first Thanksgiving meal, looking sweet and sexy in a little tank top and apron; him playing a gig, scanning the audience for the one person he knew would always be there; them waking together in tangled sheets with motes winking in the lazy Sunday light…

But he'd puked all over the table and blown the deal. Then he remembered yet another Kent Seasons-ism: *Without commitment, you got nothing.*

Back at Regent's, Annie hopped the curb onto the lot. Streamers lay soaked and flat along the rows, and balloons bobbed on last breaths of helium. Paul met her at the driver's-side door, and they faced each other in the rain, both a little cold now, both a little tired, their skins beaded and streaming just like the sleeping vehicles jacketed in sealant and cloaked in wax. Three stories above them loomed the dealership's sign, like an abandoned watchtower.

"Rumor has it Nashville's nice come fall."

"Fat chance," Annie said.

"So this is it?"

"I stopped at the mall on my way here," she said, "and bought you a new guitar. But, Paul, if you really want it"—she grabbed his belt and hauled him close—"it's time to start playing a different tune."

"Jennylee? Is that you, dear?"

She shut her eyes and went stock-still. The voice was unmistakable, prim and eloquent, and hearing it now meant that Alice Higgenbottom was standing in the doorway right behind her, looking at her wet clothing and the puddled water at her feet, and surely wondering why her new assistant was here at this late hour. Moments earlier, Jennylee thought she'd heard a noise from upstairs—a creaking hinge, a whisper of footsteps—but she'd written it off to guilty ears.

"And why is there a *horse* nibbling on our honeysuckle bushes? I accused our neighbor of senility when he phoned."

Our, she'd said.

"Ma'am"—Jennylee turned and faced her—"I'm awful sorry about all this."

And that's when Alice saw Randy Bauble. From where she stood, he was partially hidden, already loaded on the Power-Tech's lift. Jennylee had been fiddling with the instrument panel and trying to recall the proper sequence. Cautious now, never breaking eye contact, Alice approached. She stopped in the center of the room and studied Randy for some time. Then she studied Jennylee, paying careful attention to her hands.

"Are you a danger to me right now?"

"No, ma'am, of course not."

"Are you armed?"

"Alice, no."

"Look at me when you speak, Jennylee."

She did as told, but only after wiping away fresh tears. She'd gone and betrayed the only person besides her father who'd ever shown her any faith whatsoever. She'd proven herself untrustworthy, proven herself a sneak, proven herself the worst sort of criminal, and all to the most generous woman she'd ever met. The awfulness of these realizations caved her knees and she collapsed on the lift, her soaked rump mere inches from Randy's staring eyes. She buried her face in her hands and wept.

Finally, Alice—who still hadn't moved—asked the dead man's name.

"They were doing something with drugs, Alice. Him and my husband, they—"

"Shall I phone the authorities now, or would you prefer to finish explaining?"

In truth, Jennylee almost wished Alice would call the police. Seeing the expression on Alice's face (not to mention the expression on *Randy's* face) had finally allowed Jennylee to see her own actions clear of the haze of panic. All throughout this ordeal, she'd felt deep down the rightness of her ends, the sanctity of what she had to protect, but through Alice's eyes it came clear just how truly ghastly were the means.

"I'd have scoffed, Jennylee—*scoffed*—at the mere notion you would engage in such base illegalities, let alone risk my professional reputation, especially after the courtesy I've shown you.

Is this why you were so eager to intern in the first place—for a convenient way to dispose of corpses?"

But then Alice came closer and inspected Randy Bauble's face. She reached out and touched the skin of his neck and cheek. "Or perhaps not," she said. "This man appears to have died almost within the hour."

"You don't understand," Jennylee said. But Alice really did understand. She understood this was her reward for having trusted some trailer-trash woman who sold cars for a living to behave like an intelligent and civilized human being.

Using her thumbnail, Alice chipped a flake of dried mud from Randy's earlobe and crumbled the flake between her fingers. "My judgment," she said, "is apparently not as keen as I'd believed." Alice stared at her until it burned, until she wanted to climb onto the lift right alongside Randy and be done with it all. "I suppose I got carried away with notions of mentorship, if not even friendship. I was touched by your situation, by what I'd perhaps mistaken for bravery. My sympathies seem to have blinded me."

Then, if only to keep further tears at bay, Jennylee asked Alice to give her five minutes to explain herself, to tell her story, before she called the law.

"Five minutes," Alice said. "Very well."

So Jennylee blurted it all out: from how the test-drive with Maurice was worse than she'd let on ("He exposed himself?" Alice said) to her father's cancer and the miseries of growing up with only her Bible-beating mother, to how she'd planned to use Maurice's money for Chastity's medical bills ("Serves the cad right," Alice said), but how instead that money ended up under Randy Bauble in the broken-down Nissan, and so on to Randy's stealing the anhydrous ammonia and to her getting wrongfully terminated from Regent's, and finally her fears that Chastity would grow up with a daddy in the penitentiary if she didn't make this whole mess go away; how she'd prayed to God for guidance only to finally accept that God was make-believe, but more so how she'd realized it was up to her to do something, anything, whatever it took, to protect her daughter, even though now she realized everything was ruined and over, and her attempts to fix this horrible mess had—like everything she'd ever tried to do in her whole stupid life—only made a bad situation worse.

"Forgive me, ma'am," Jennylee said. "I'm feeling a little dizzy."

"It seems to me," Alice said, having quietly listened, "that when a woman finds herself on horseback on a dark and stormy night, disposing of a corpse on behalf of her drug-dealing husband, that perhaps the nuclear family *beau idéal* is beyond salvaging."

Jennylee wiped her nose. "I don't know if he's exactly a drug dealer—"

"Stop that, Jennylee. You *do* know. If you think back, if you parse emotion from memory, isn't it possible you've always known?"

"I'm so confused. I'm sorry."

"Ack, ack, ack." Alice raised a finger to her lips. "Answer me this simple question: Is your marriage worth saving?"

"Well, I—"

"After all of this—after tonight?"

"But I have to think of my little girl."

"My point exactly."

"So you're saying I should get a divorce?"

And then Alice Higgenbottom began to laugh, a sound Jennylee had never heard before. It was an odd laugh too— little burps of mirth popped from the woman's mouth and floated about the lab like soap bubbles. She rocked to and fro and her shoulders jiggled with each spurt, as if something huge and painful lay trapped deep inside her small body. "I'm no attorney," Alice finally said, pointing at Randy, "but if not this, then I fail to see how the phrase 'irreconcilable differences' holds any meaning at all."

"But Chast loves him so much."

"Which says much about her but less about him. And here we reach the crucial point, Jennylee. *You* know this husband of yours is a bad parent. In fact, you know him to be a felon. An active danger to you and your daughter. And as a responsible parent, you also know the importance of acting upon the truth."

Something hitched in Jennylee's chest. She recognized these thoughts as her own. But they were thoughts she'd discarded, discounted, the inner voice she'd never quite mustered the courage to trust. Alice always knew just what to say. Or maybe we can only see our biggest mistakes, the mistakes we love, through another's eyes?

"Furthermore," Alice said, "have you considered what all this means for me?"

"Again, I am so sorry."

"Because you work in this community, because you grew up here, you understand the nature of gossip. So surely you are aware a situation as salacious and grisly as this would tarnish the Higgenbottom name irreparably and would forever prohibit my doing business within three hundred miles of this zip code."

Rain sluiced down the windows and a heavy gust walloped the house.

"I wish I could take it all back, Alice."

"But you cannot take it back, can you?" Jennylee lowered her eyes. "And I rather like living and working here," Alice said, gesturing toward those same rain-streaked windows. "Paris is my home too."

There was simply nothing left to say. She'd gone and done the worst and most deceitful of things, and she'd done it to the best and most honest of women. She had to clinch her jaw to stop her teeth from rattling, but this only reminded her of how together they'd bolted shut Norvis Bell's jaw back on Wednesday.

"We find ourselves in quite the pickle here, Jennylee."

And then they both took a long, sober look at the pickle where it lay on the steel lift in its NBA replica jersey.

"I could take the body and go."

"Sling the deceased back atop your steed? Ride off into the night like a ghoul?"

"I got him here. I could get him away from here too."

"Only to make me an accomplice."

"I'd never tell a soul. Not a whisper, not even on my death-bed."

Alice pursed her lips. "I believe that, Jennylee. But *I* would still know."

For quite some time, the two women stood in the basement of that mortuary, lost in their private thoughts, looking in turn at each other and at the body of Randy Bauble. Alice asked a few questions about the logistics of navigating the flooded cornfields on horseback and seemed impressed by the answers. Outside, the storm beat and howled. For Jennylee, those moments counted the longest of her life. She was cold and jittery and her jeans were soaked. She understood her future hinged on what Alice decided, and she felt at peace with that. Whatever conclusion Alice reached was the course they would follow, even if it meant punishment and grief. Jennylee trusted Alice Higgenbottom completely, even though she'd made it such that Alice could never trust her again.

"Three hours from now," Alice finally said, glancing at her watch, "I will respond at the behest of a concerned neighbor who phoned with an implausible tale about a horse grazing in the backyard. While investigating this call, I shall find you here, Jennylee—I will come upon you for the *first* time tonight—and I will ask why you've entered the mortuary. Your answer to this question will determine our future course. If you are here alone, perhaps studying or merely tidying up, and if nothing seems amiss, then I will bid you goodnight after requesting you return your key to prevent future breaches of etiquette. If you are not alone, however—"

"I'll be alone, Alice."

"If you are *not* alone, I will do what is necessary to protect myself."

"Yes, ma'am."

"I've always thought I'd like to try horseback riding"—Alice floated toward the door, sensible shoes pressing the tiles—"but now I'm not so certain."

After the door clicked shut, Jennylee collected herself and faced the cremator. Calmer now, she recalled not only how to operate the lift, but how to fire the gas and set the temperature. A rumbling *whoosh* issued from the belly of the oven, and a soft orange light bloomed beyond the small window. Then Jennyl- ee recalled something Alice once said: That whatever we are, whatever is best in us, can't be burned. Or at least she hoped that's what Alice had meant.

As Randy Bauble slowly rose, she grasped his stiffened fin- gers and told him she was sorry he'd lost his life in such a shame- ful way. Then, for one odd moment Randy's hand wiggled and his eyes danced with the gas fire's Halloween glow—but this was no miracle. Just a tremor from the machine, and whatever light had once lived behind Randy's eyes was extinguished, like a candlewick pinched between licked fingertips.

Feeling a need for ceremony, Jennylee reached into her pock- et and dug out a pair of quarters. She closed Randy's eyelids and placed the coins atop them. It helped some, but still wasn't quite right. Then she went to the bank of drawers adjacent to the refrigerator. She located the first aid box Alice kept, clicked it open, and found the item she required.

Back with Randy, she peeled away the strips of sterile paper before centering the Band-Aid on his left cheekbone, the way he'd always worn it in life. Then she took a breath and gathered her thoughts, and these thoughts took on words, and those words became a sort of hymn. This was the last prayer she would ever say—a prayer meant only to be felt, and only by her. Then she smoothed the wrinkles from Randy Bauble's Celtics jersey and told him goodbye, told him she wished he'd found more peace on this earth. She told him that once upon a time she'd believed he had a good heart.

"But times are wont to change," Jennylee said, and cranked open the oven door.

Amidst that crackling dance of flame and shadow, she fold- ed the hands and wrists across the chest, having to press down hard through the gathering rigor. Immaculate light bathed them both—his flesh, her flesh, the walls and ceiling of the lovely old mortuary, the storm-lashed windowpanes like satin one mo- ment, like mirrors the next.

Step Seven: Follow-up

37

Just over a week later, on June 1, 2009, General Motors—a company which tilted the great wars of the twentieth century, inspired the Beach Boys, and produced a working moon rover—declared itself hopelessly broke and filed Chapter 11. Parcel to a government-guided restructuring, GM received over fifty billion in taxpayer dollars, which was enough to keep the lights on. Yet barely three months after that ill-fated Memorial Day, Regent's American Dream Motors of Paris, Illinois, closed her doors for good, having returned the unsold fleet and dumped the beaters and lemons for wholesale.

In the frosty lead-up to Christmas, Kent Seasons found himself at the Citgo just across the way, shivering and stomping his feet while fueling up a brand-new Ford F-150 in Dark Blue Pearl. As the meter spun and gasoline flowed in arterial spurts, Kent sipped coffee from a paper cup and studied the deserted building and icy lot. The showroom glass was cloudy gray. The furniture had been carted off, the garage machinery auctioned, telephones and fax machines boxed up for storage. Emptied of vehicles, of salesmen and customers and oomph, it was mere brick and mortar, glass and speckled tile, nothing more. Just a couple acres of cement where Kent had once plied his trade. Never mind he'd grown up there, played there as a boy and become a man there, learned who his father was there, and learned also the greater part of whatever he might come to know in this life. Never mind that the tall, bone-colored sign swaying in the December wind still showed the ghostly remnants of his own last name.

Never mind that he'd loved it.

He'd just finished some last-minute gift shopping and was pondering grabbing a burger somewhere when a familiar voice said, "Sharp truck, pal."

Kent turned to see Tom Partlow standing there bundled and

shivering, his breath frosting the thin air. "Dig the license plate frame," Kent said.

"Heard you were working for the enemy, but I couldn't hardly believe it."

"Can't be the enemy if it's the last man standing."

"You could always go sell Toyotas."

"I haven't stooped quite that low, Tom."

The big man smiled. "They cut you a deal, at least?"

"Invoice. Dan Thompson even knocked off the holdback and incentives."

"And maybe gave you some incentive to come work for him?" Tom shook his head. "I just can't picture you selling Fords. It's like when Michael Jordan came out of retirement to play for Washington. He just didn't look right without that Bulls uniform."

Then Tom filled him in on the latest. After Regent's closed, he'd found work with John Deere. Turns out managing the service department for farm implements wasn't so different than managing service for Chevrolets. Better in some respects, in fact.

"And there's no Junior to deal with," Tom said.

"Amen to that. Hey, you still go to the YMCA?"

Tom studied him for a moment. "Sure do, and so does Paul."

"No kidding? Figured he skipped town. Lit out for Nashville or wherever."

"He did, actually," Tom said, and then shared what he knew. After the Blowout Sale, Paul Stenger had gone down to Nashville and bounced around waiting tables and playing music. This lasted about twelve weeks. Then his girlfriend, who he'd been dating long-distance, gave him the inside track on a gig at none other than the Paris YMCA. Assistant Program Director. Salary, benefits, and forty easy-breezy hours a week.

"He seems happier," Tom said. "Less spacey, if you know what I mean?"

"He was the least committed car salesman I ever saw. Even when he was closing deals, he was someplace far, far away."

"From what I can gather, he spends most of his time shooting hoops with the gym rats and daydreaming about that pretty girlfriend of his."

"A guy could do a lot worse," Kent said.

The mentions of Michael Jordan and basketball had brought to mind Maurice Currant, who kept that framed print down in his smutty man-cave. But Kent had heard neither hide nor gloriously white hair from Maurice. According to Jerry Seasons, Maurice was working long hours at his photography studio, even picking up gigs out of town. Jerry was confused by his old pal's sudden work ethic—if he needed money, why not just dip into his wife's pie-crust fortune? But Kent had kept the answer to himself.

Then Tom asked about his family, about Kelsi. College? Or was she still greeting for Thompson's? So Kent related the roundabout way his daughter ended up at the U of I. Against his objections, she'd deferred enrollment and gone full-time at Thompson's. However, Kent had made it conditional upon his agreeing to close deals for Dan Thompson that he also be allowed to make his daughter's job a living hell. It'd taken him a mere three days to send Kelsi cussing and spitting down the right path.

"Her mother's got her all settled on campus. I think she'll be just fine."

"She still mad at you?"

"Oh yeah. But that too shall pass."

Tom Partlow was too polite to ask about Kelsi's relationship with Erik Sharkey, which everyone caught wind of in the fallout of Kent's wreck, but the situation had worked itself out. Once Sharkey was no longer forbidden fruit, Kelsi saw him for the nicotine-toothed huckster he truly was. She dumped him without much warning. There'd been one tense night where Sharkey showed up at the house drunk and bellowing out his best Marlon Brando imitation. Kent went outside and rubbed Sharkey's back and commiserated upon the incredible heartlessness of women. Then he'd poured Sharkey four ounces of whiskey from a bottle gathering dust above the fridge, cut it with cherry NyQuil—not quite OxyContin, but the best he could do—and then topped his own tumbler with iced tea. Sharkey passed out thirty minutes later, the tears still wet on his cheeks. Kent tucked him in behind the wheel of his car. "Just close your eyes and rest, little buddy," he'd said. Once Sharkey was snoring, Kent nestled the whiskey bottle against his ribs, slashed all four tires, and called the cops.

Overall, a fine evening.

"Hear anything out of Jennylee?" Tom asked. "Paul keeps asking about her."

"Actually I have. Couple weeks back she called me and we hit the Buck for lunch. She's been busy. Divorced that bum of a husband, sued the fins off Nautical Bill, and got hired at some equine veterinary clinic over in Terre Haute. Shovels manure all day, then studies online at night."

"No kidding?"

"She seems totally at peace."

"So she wasn't sore over you firing her?"

"Not at all. In fact, she claims I did her the second biggest favor of her life."

"Second? What was the first?"

Kent had to admit he wasn't sure. He'd asked Jennylee this very question, but she hadn't answered. Just smiled and shook her head.

"Paul says he still owes her an apology," Tom said. "Something about a Chevy Blazer."

Paul had sniped Jennylee on a Blazer, hadn't he? Right before the Blowout Sale, just before the wheels came off for good. Kent remembered the deal, but vaguely. Drinking days. Plus, his mindset had been all screwed up back then. Encouraging his salespeople to snipe each other hadn't seemed like what it actually was—unethical behavior, irresponsibility, meanness—but a fun and profitable diversion.

"He probably does owe her an apology. I know I already gave her mine." Tom nodded. "Strange, isn't it," Kent said, "how you look back on what you've done in this life and just can't believe it. I mean, you know you're guilty—you remember committing your crimes—but the guy in your memory seems like a completely different person."

The gas nozzle clicked and sent a tremor through the hose. The pump's readout showed a dollar amount that, according to the commercials on late night TV, would feed a starving Ethiopian child for three whole months.

"Work changes us," Tom said, "but I don't see how it could be any other way."

"I told Kelsi to be real careful what work she chooses, though I'm not sure that's a lesson a person can really hear. It's probably a thing you've got to live yourself."

"But then it's too late for the knowledge to do you any good."

"So you do what you can and tell your kids."

"Who also won't understand until it's too late."

"And so the best they can do is tell *their* kids, who won't understand either."

"'Round and 'round we go."

"Until we all fall down."

A semi rumbled past, tires fanning salted brown slush. In its wake hung a veil of smoky exhaust which faded, particle by sooty particle, in the frozen air. Beyond stood Regent's, abandoned.

"Paul loves to reminisce about how much he hated selling cars," Tom said. "But to hear him talk about it, you'd almost think he misses it."

Kent didn't find that particularly strange though. But he couldn't make a practical guy like Tom Partlow see the car business how he saw it, or maybe how he'd once seen it. The romance of waxed steel and fresh leather. The art of turning tire-kickers into buyers. The blood rush of the hunt. Instead, he found himself apologizing for not setting a better example, for just dangling Paul out there like bait.

"Him and Jennylee both," Kent said. "I let those kids down."

"Water under the bridge. You tried your best."

While Kent appreciated the sentiment, he'd actually wanted

a different response. Wanted Tom Partlow to tell him that he'd meant something—even if that something wasn't necessarily good—in his salespeople's lives. Otherwise, what had it all been for?

"So there've been rumors," Tom said, "as to why exactly Bill Sr. shut her down. Chadwick still hangs around the Y too. He claims it was all Donovan Crews's idea."

"That dude didn't call himself a consultant for nothing."

"Franchising?"

"Not sure about that," Kent said, "but they're definitely expanding the scope of operations. Or at least they were scheming along those lines before Jennylee and my dad sued their crooked asses to Timbuktu."

In closing the dealership, Bill Sr. claimed he could not in good conscience sell GM steel under the directive of a Euro-socialist pickpocket like President Obama. He felt awful for all his employees in sales and service, and for the community that'd always counted on Regent's to provide quality American-made cars and trucks, but this was a moral imperative. Not a month later, however, a quiet public notice appeared in the *Beacon-Herald* announcing the leasing of retail space and application for licensure to open a series of therapeutic massage parlors throughout Edgar County.

"Orchid Parlour, LLC," Kent said. "A British-sounding variation on the Lotus Parlor massage place out past the mall. That was the name those geniuses settled on."

"Nautical Bill and Junior were a lot of things," Tom said, "but creative wasn't one of them."

"Best I can figure, it was Donovan Crews's brainchild. Must've dreamed it up while convalescing on the company dime after that little wreck of ours. No doubt he required lots of Asian massage to get healthy enough to fly clear back to Dallas."

"A triumph of capitalism," Tom said.

"Think they offer financing?"

"How much does a guy need for a down payment on a deal like that, anyway?"

Kent smirked. "Nobody leaves the Orchid Parlour with buyer's remorse."

But Kent Seasons did feel remorse. After all, it's not easy to watch a business your father dedicated his life to be shanghaied like that. So he'd finally voiced his suspicions of cooked books and floating inventory. To his great relief, his father hadn't raged himself into another coronary. Instead, Jerry Seasons asked a few simple questions, nodded, and then dialed his attorney. Nothing was settled yet. The attorney believed they had a strong case for breach of fiduciary duty, but the complaints and answers and motions would drag on for years.

"Good seeing you, Kent," Tom said. They shook hands, squeezing hard through their gloves while taking each other's measure, like veterans having stumbled across each other years after the armistice. Then Kent waved goodbye as Tom Partlow climbed into his own truck and drove away.

After he'd racked the dripping gas nozzle, he dunked the wand in a half-frozen chemical tub and scrubbed and bladed the F-150's windshield, and then replaced the wand and climbed inside the cab, careful to first stomp the slush from his wingtips.

The seat was cool through his slacks and his pale breath clouded the glass. A faint assembly-line perfume lingered like a broken promise. After blowing into the court-mandated interlock device, he keyed the ignition and felt the engine kick. Then he removed his gloves and molded his hands to the wheel, letting the warmth of his flesh bleed into the serpentine rubber. The dashboard indicators assured him all was fine. Fluid pressures in check, electrical system sparking, the air outside a crisp nineteen degrees.

He dropped her into Drive and rolled forward, but the truck beeped madly, demanding he stop and buckle his seatbelt. He resented the machine's insistence at first, as it felt like an intrusion, but then he asked himself why he felt this way and could come up with no logical answer. So he reached across his chest and clipped plate to latch.

The big Ford instantly quieted, purring and ready.

Strapped in for the ride now, feeling about as safe as any

man can rightly feel come winter, Kent Seasons cast a final lingering glance at that hollow edifice of concrete and glass which lay forgotten across the highway, before he eased his foot off the brake and plunged headlong once more into the snowy river of traffic.

ACKNOWLEDGEMENTS

First, I'd like to thank my writing teachers for sharing with me the tools necessary to bring a long piece of fiction to life: Rus, Robin, Boz, and Craig. Thank you.

Also, the generous readers who gave their time and attention to this novel as it progressed: Evan, Dave, Melissa, Nick (go Blazers!), Muriel, and Madeline, and special thanks to Chris Schacht, whose insightful comments helped propel the story from rough draft to something with a heartbeat. Also, again, Rus Bradburd: you're the best—thanks.

Much gratitude as well to Jaynie Royal and Pam Van Dyk and all the other savvy and book-loving folks at Regal House.